Praise for
The Illumination

"*The Illumination* might invite comparisons to *The Da Vinci Code*. Some similar plot twists aside, this is a better story. More nuanced characters and vastly superior writing quality make for a breathlessly fun read." —*The Star-Ledger*

"The intrigue is high. The excitement is palpable. The story is priceless. Combining mysticism, history, and fanaticism, this is one thriller that's simply impossible to put down until you've reached the ending—breathless and so well satisfied. Tintori and Gregory are first-rate storytellers!"
—M.J. Rose, international bestselling author of
The Memorist and *The Reincarnationist*

"Jill Gregory and Karen Tintori return with another extraordinary thriller after their outstanding *The Book of Names*. Their new novel, *The Illumination*, skillfully weaves history, ancient art, dark legend, and religious fanaticism into a story of high-stakes terror and international intrigue. The excitement stays at a high pitch from the opening scene at the looted Iraqi National Museum to the final sensational twist. A page-turner extraordinaire." —*New York Times* bestselling author
Douglas Preston, co-author of
The Monster of Florence and *The Wheel of Darkness*

"Stirring and imaginative. A tense, intelligent, and surprising thrill. Drum-tight in execution, fueled by imagination, the plot is as sharp as a broken shard of glass. If you like your tales loaded with intrigue, treachery, and a wealth of secrets, you're going to love *The Illumination*." —*New York Times* bestselling author
Steve Berry, author of
The Charlemagne Pursuit and *The Templar Legacy*
MORE...

Praise for
The Book of Names

"WATCH OUT, DAN BROWN. Intelligent suspense. . .combines the Kabbalah, tarot, and the forces of good and evil into a tense murder mystery...*The Book of Names* self-assuredly fulfills the requirements of the religious thriller."

—*The Economist*

"Relentless and riveting, *The Book of Names* speeds you across continents and centuries in the ultimate seductive read. From fascinating characters to real-life legends, this debut ranks as unforgettable."

—Gayle Lynds, *New York Times* bestselling author of *The Last Spymaster*

"*The Book of Names* grabs you on page one and doesn't let you go. Weaving together the Kabbalah, the tarot, and the forces of good and evil, this chilling thriller has a self-assured voice and all the right elements to make for a nonstop, nail-biting read." —M. J. Rose, international bestselling author of *The Reincarnationist*

"Convincing characters and a rapidly moving plot combine to create an enjoyable religious thriller." —*Library Journal*

"Intricately plotted historical suspense . . . an intriguing synthesis of Jewish mysticism and modern murder mystery. A swift, intelligent thriller." —*Kirkus Reviews*

THE
ILLUMINATION

Jill Gregory

and

Karen Tintori

St. Martin's Paperbacks

This is a work of fiction. All of the characters, organizations, and events portrayed in this novel are either products of the author's imagination or are used fictitiously.

THE ILLUMINATION

Copyright © 2008 by Jill Gregory and Karen Tintori.
Excerpt from *The Book of Names* copyright © 2007 by Jill Gregory and Karen Tintori.

All rights reserved.

For information address St. Martin's Press, 175 Fifth Avenue, New York, NY 10010.

Library of Congress Catalog Card Number: 2008029878

ISBN: 978-0-312-36526-4

Printed in the United States of America

St. Martin's Press hardcover edition / January 2009
St. Martin's Paperbacks edition / December 2009

St. Martin's Paperbacks are published by St. Martin's Press, 175 Fifth Avenue, New York, NY 10010.

10 9 8 7 6 5 4 3 2 1

For my parents with love.
And for my wonderful husband and beautiful daughter,
Who bring such luminous light and love into my life.

J.G.

For the people who most light my life with love and
laughter—my husband, Lawrence; my children, Mitchel
and Leslie, and Steven. And especially for Seth Mindell,
a true life saver.

K.T.

ACKNOWLEDGMENTS

With appreciation and warmest thanks to the many people who were so generous with their knowledge and their time—Richard Rytman, former Special Agent with the FBI, and Greg Suhajda, former Special Agent with the FBI, both now at Veritas Global; Professor Paul M. Kintner Jr. at Cornell University; Seth Mindell, M.D., Marianne Willman, Charlotte Hughes, Hy Safran, and Liat Ayzencot at the Israel Antiquities Authority; Robert Woznicki and Alessandra Gesualdi in Rome; Frank Olivo, Christina Papakirk, Mary Knoll, Melissa Flashman, and Dr. William Lanford at Ion Beam Lab, University at Albany, State University of New York; Cindy Shaffran, Frank Viviano, and Benjamin Neumann at Exploration Systems Mission Directorate, NASA; Nancy L. Green, friend and historian; Michael Stone, Deede Auster, Yossi Benjamin, and Haiping Sun, Ph.D., at Electron Microbeam Analysis Laboratory, University of Michigan; Jay Knoll at Energy Conversion Devices; and Daniela Di Castro, director, *Museo Ebraico di Roma* (The Jewish Museum of Rome).

Special thanks to our insightful first readers, Rachel Greenberg and Steven Katz, who have once again noticed what we missed, and offered numerous brilliant suggestions.

We're also grateful for the support of the entire team at St. Martin's Press, especially our editor, Nichole Argyres, with whom it's always a pleasure to work, and to Matthew Shear, Kylah McNeill, Christina Harcar, and Kerry Nordling. Major thanks as well to our agents, Ellen Levine and Sally Wofford-Girand, for all of their support and creative input.

Light is sown for the righteous.

—Psalms 97:11

The light of the wicked is withheld.

—Job 38:15

PROLOGUE

Iraq National Museum
Baghdad
April 12, 2003

Ibrahim Baaj picked his way through the darkness.

All around him, irreplaceable history lay shattered. As U.S. troops advanced along the dusty streets of Baghdad, chaos and pandemonium ruled. And so did greed.

Ibrahim understood greed. He was driven by it. It was greed that called him here tonight as common looters stormed the great museum. Little did this rabble know that *his* greed surpassed even theirs. As did his daring.

He was betraying men so powerful, so far-reaching, that he himself marveled at the brazenness of his own audacity.

Ibrahim smiled to himself through the sweat dripping from beneath his mustache. This steamy stone building was home to 170,000 of Mesopotamia's oldest cultural treasures—some dating back to the cradle of civilization. Yet the crazed throng coursed through the galleries, shooting, grabbing, smashing, and plundering as if they were in a junk shop.

Very few were professionals as he was, searching with purpose and discrimination, carefully selecting the booty they would spirit away. Yet he suspected that amid this greedy throng there must be one or two agents who'd been sent by the United States or Israel, for both nations knew that this museum hid the greatest treasure of them all. The treasure he'd come for and intended to claim before the night was over.

Ibrahim gasped for air as he descended alone into the windowless, blackened bowels of the building and the oxygen-deprived chamber closed in around him. He paused to listen, blinking as beads of sweat stung his eyes. Despite the clamor above, he could discern no sounds down here besides his own ragged breaths. Trying to ignore the stale stench, he edged forward, prowling through the tomblike underworld of the museum's five basement storerooms. The narrow beam of his flashlight was nearly useless, barely illuminating the floor directly beneath his feet.

No matter. He'd had twelve years while Saddam's Republican Guard patrolled the compound—fearing another American strike—to memorize the crudely sketched layout that Aslam Hameed had given him. Twelve years to rehearse in his mind's eye, waiting for a night like this one, with Saddam in hiding, the Americans on the march, and the museum's courtyard gates smashed open. Now the moment was upon him.

He must seize it.

Nejeeb Zayadi knew the fifth storeroom as well as he knew his own wife's body. Lovingly, he'd cared for the treasure secreted within it, just as his family had for generations. They were a family of caretakers.

Only a few outside of his brood knew what lay nestled here within the lockers. The slim storage bins looked innocuous enough—like the metal lockers outside any school gymnasium. But these compartments that he tended, checking daily to make certain they were secure, held wealth beyond measure. Coins, gold, silver—and the Eye.

Even the director of the museum knew nothing of the Eye's presence. She didn't even possess keys for all of the locks in this vast museum. It was he, Nejeeb, who had slipped the treasure deep inside the back set of lockers in 1966, transferring it from the old museum alongside the Tigris, where his father had preceded him in watching over it.

Nejeeb's father had been a child when the vigil began. He'd told Nejeeb many times about how he was awakened by the voice of the stranger who had come to *his* father in the dead of night.

"Guard this until I return. I will make it well worth your trouble," the stranger had said in a voice that sounded to the sleepy boy like the wind howling across the sand.

As Nejeeb's father had peeked through the crack in the door, he'd watched his father shivering in his nightshirt, staring down at something in his palm, looking stunned.

"What is this?" Nejeeb's grandfather had asked.

"Something dangerous in the wrong hands. I am entrusting you with it because your family name is an honored one, recorded among those who served in the court of King Nebuchadnezzar. Your table will always have bread and your sons will always have honor if you keep this safe."

Nejeeb's grandfather was dead now. Nejeeb's father was dead, too, and Nejeeb himself was an old man. Soon *his* eldest son would step into the role of caretaker. *For how long?* Nejeeb wondered. Year after year, the money still came, but the strange man had never returned.

Nejeeb hoped that in his lifetime he would learn the truth about that which he guarded. If he could keep it safe through tonight . . .

A sudden sound in the darkness made Nejeeb jump. Footsteps. The creak of a drawer opening. *One of the looters has made his way to the treasure rooms. Someone who knows to search for the keys.*

Nejeeb's gnarled hand tightened momentarily on the key he kept pinned inside his shirt, then fell to his side as he groped for his gun. *But what good was a gun in the dark?* Swearing under his breath, his fingers latched onto his pushbroom—it would sweep in a wider arc.

Fear congealed in his bowels as he heard the footsteps coming closer. More drawers opening, closing. A quick gleam of light, a shadow—all he needed to pinpoint the intruder. The old man lunged, lashing out fiercely with his broom, but it sliced through dead air. He swung it again and this time it connected— but he found himself suddenly dragged with it, pitching forward, down. Hitting the ground, he choked on dust and fumbled in panic for the gun—but it was too late.

He felt the blade nick at his throat an instant before it slashed his Adam's apple in two.

Blood spurted across Ibrahim Baaj's beard as he dispassionately searched the old caretaker's body in the dark, hunting for a key ring. Nothing had jangled when he'd fallen.

Ibrahim's search was quick but thorough. His fingers froze on the single key pinned inside the old man's shirt.

One key. Interesting. It could be the one.

He switched on the flashlight for an instant, and located the lockers. Then, careful not to slip on the blood pooled around the old man's body, he moved toward the lockers, praying for a perfect fit.

There wasn't much time. He was surprised he hadn't already been forced to dispatch a competitor tonight, one armed with inside information as accurate as his own. But the air held only the smell of must and blood and death, no hint of the adrenaline sweat of another human.

Noiselessly, he slid the key into a dozen locks before a tumbler finally clicked home. His heart thrummed with excitement as he pried open the door.

His fingers found a worn leather pouch tucked behind boxes of metal coins, clay cylinders, and small pottery figurines, all of which he ignored. He tore at the drawstring. There was no time to study it now, but he beamed the light inside just long enough to glimpse the dull gleam of ancient gold and the gem-emblazoned eyes staring back at him, one from each side. He had it: The prize countless men around the world had been seeking for centuries was in his palm.

Through pitch darkness, Ibrahim retraced his steps. Barely breathing, he slipped through the mob of thieves like an eel through deep water, smuggling the treasure through the chaos and rubble, easily concealing it within the pocket of his coat.

Then he was racing through the shouts and the gunfire of the streets. Panting, he sank into his car and sped north until he came to a field far from the city, far from the gun battles raging through Baghdad.

Ignoring the thick curtain of unrelenting heat, Ibrahim hacked at the dirt until he'd dug three feet down. He paused only for a moment to wipe the sweat stinging his eyes and to gaze upon the treasure again before he buried it.

It was just as it had been described in the crumbling manuscript he'd been shown: the timeworn leather drawstring pouch, painted on each side with a black-rimmed eye of bright blue.

A shiver ran through him as he untied the pouch adorned with the ancient protective symbol, thinking of the riches its contents would bring him. Carefully, he found the golden chain nestled within, and he drew the egg-shaped pendant out.

The Eye. It was magnificent, like no other—a pendant of hammered gold inlaid on both sides with jewels depicting an eye. He turned it over to make sure—smiling as he saw the identical orb staring at him from the opposite side.

Greedily his fingers traced over the red and yellow gemstones forming the center of the Eye and around the borders of lapis lazuli lined thick as Cleopatra's kohl.

But Ibrahim dared not break apart the pendant to gaze upon the treasure locked inside.

His hands shaking slightly with urgency, he shoved it back inside the pouch and buried it, as war raged throughout his homeland. The treasure and its innate power had lain hidden for centuries here in Babylon. It would remain hidden a bit longer, until his price was met.

Ibrahim Baaj snuck back into the city by the same route he'd left it. Tomorrow, while the world learned how horribly its cultural history had been plundered, he would betray those who had hired him to seize it and would launch the bidding war for his prize.

But there was no tomorrow for Ibrahim. As he listened to the sounds of war exploding through his city, war came to him. A rapid burst of gunfire ripped through the windshield and blew his left eye through the back of his head.

1

Five years later
Baghdad

The sand was everywhere—in her throat, in her eyelashes, embedded beneath the screw-on cap of her Gatorade bottle. Dana Landau had always loved the beach, but after three months in Iraq she'd be more than happy to never again feel the grit of sand between her toes.

"A few more minutes and I'll have the rest of the footage," her cameraman, Rusty Sutherland, called out.

"Make it fast." Dana glanced warily around as he panned the wreckage yet again. She'd seen enough. And every minute they were out here, away from the fragile security of the Green Zone, they were in the devil's hands.

Her chest tight, Dana picked her way across the bomb-torn terrain in search of a patch of shade.

Another day, another car bombing, she thought grimly, turning her back on the convoy of military vehicles that had accompanied them, their driver, and their interpreter to this grisly scene. The strike had taken out two truckloads of newly trained Iraqi soldiers.

The network had allotted her ninety seconds to sum up today's chapter in this ongoing odyssey of death, which they'd edit down to a sound bite that could never reflect the enormity of the carnage.

Dana had busted her buns to snag this assignment. She'd

fought for it harder than she'd ever fought for anything, but she had to concede that when she left Iraq next month she wouldn't miss this danger-fraught nightmare—the thunder of bombs puncturing the night, the stench of burned flesh and rubber, the thin high wails of the children. She'd gladly trade the sandbags piled against the windowsills of the MSNBC villa, the razor wire surrounding it, and all the paranoia, grittiness, and uncertainty of life in a war zone for some humdrum assignment covering schoolteachers on strike.

But she'd keep that to herself. Her father had always cautioned her and her sister about shedding tears for answered prayers. This stint in Iraq was what she'd wanted, and it was establishing her as a prime-time contender right alongside all the big boys—the older anchors who'd cemented their careers covering battlefields and the world's hotspots.

But I won't miss it—and I damn well won't ever be able to forget it, she thought, gulping warm Gatorade as she leaned into the meager shade of a date palm. She'd miss Rusty, though. Having been in Baghdad a full month before Dana had arrived, her cameraman was leaving in the morning for two weeks R & R stateside.

"Done! Let's get outta here." Rusty slammed the trunk of the armored car. She knew he was already halfway home, envisioning his reunion with his wife and kids back in Connecticut.

After Baghdad, American suburbia would be paradise.

"Coming." She pushed herself away from the tree, eager to be on the move as quickly as possible. A quick cell call from an insurgent spotting them out here would be enough to bring a car bomb speeding this way with their names on it.

As she straightened, the Gatorade bottle cap slipped from her fingers. Swearing, she stooped to retrieve it from the hot sand and spotted something peeking out of the explosion-rocked earth a few feet away. A patch of weathered leather, half buried in the sand. Even from a distance she could see it was decorated with a painted eye.

Dana crouched and tugged it from the sand. Yep, it was most certainly an eye. A blue eye, rimmed in black, painted on a leather pouch half the size of a playing card. A blue eye was a familiar talisman, especially in this part of the world; it was used as protection against the evil eye.

Just like this one, she thought, touching the dainty silver charm shaped like a downturned open palm dangling at her throat. Her fingers brushed quickly along the seven small amethysts edging her *hamsa* amulet to find the turquoise cloisonné eye painted in its center and dotted with a single pearl—her mother's pearl. Natalie had sent this necklace to her as an olive branch right before she'd left for Iraq. The *hamsa* was a perfect going off to war gift from her sister, since if anyone knew about protective talismans and good luck mojo, it was Nat.

Her older sister had spent fifteen months honing her doctoral thesis on the history of ancient Mesopotamian protective amulets, charms, and talismans. Now she was a curator at New York's Devereaux Museum of the Ancient Near East, and though her specialty was Mesopotamia, she could rattle off just about anything you'd want to know about protective charms and customs around the world—and the incantations associated with them.

Not only everyday customs, like your typical knocking on wood or carrying a rabbit's foot or four-leaf clover for good luck, but esoterica like Arubans recoiling if a black butterfly entered their houses, fearing it portended death. And that ancient Greeks believed that owls flying over battlefields were a sign of imminent victory, while ancient Romans thought their cries foretold death or disaster. Owls were downright terrifying to the ancient Chinese, who named the summer solstice the Day of the Owl and believed children born on that day had a propensity for violence.

Dana had often teased Nat about her encyclopedic expertise, referring to her sister as "the doctor of superstitious voodoo."

But she hadn't teased Natalie about anything in a long time. They were barely back on speaking terms.

Hurrying toward the convoy, Dana flicked sand from the leather pouch and suddenly realized there was something inside it. She loosened the black drawstring and shook out a tarnished pendant on a gold chain. The egg-shaped pendant was decorated with blue, red, and yellow stones arrayed in the same distinctive "eye" image as on the pouch.

"Yo! Ms. Landau!" The handsome young army officer in charge of their convoy barked over the engines. "Time to move!"

Dana dropped the trinket back inside its pouch and broke into a run, stuffing her find into the pocket of her olive cargo pants. *Maybe some poor tourist's loss will be Natalie's gain,* she reflected as she ducked inside the armored car.

She didn't give the pouch or the pendant another thought until she reached into her pocket for lip gloss after dinner in the villa.

"Damn. I almost forgot." She tugged out the pouch and eyed Rusty Sutherland across the creaky dining table. "How'd you like to do me a little favor and deliver a fabulous treasure to my sister when you get home?"

"What do I look like, a pack mule?" Rusty wadded up his napkin and stuffed it into his plastic cup. At forty-two, he sported a Yul Brynner dome, which he achieved by ruthlessly shaving any straggling strands of the reddish-blond hair that had earned him his nickname. He was solidly built but quick on his feet, and he'd been nominated for the Pulitzer not once, but twice. Dana was certain the bags under his somber brown eyes had doubled since he'd stepped foot in Iraq.

When she dumped out the pendant and held it aloft, his brows lifted.

"Worth all of two bucks max, but Natalie might get a kick out of it. You're sure you don't mind?"

"No sweat. You never know—that thing could turn out to be the centerpiece of her next exhibit. We'll see if anyone can tell the difference between trash and treasure," he snorted.

"Natalie knows her stuff. She'll know exactly what this is. I'll stick a note inside tonight and give it to you in the morning. What time are you choppering out?"

He grimaced. "Four A.M. The hour of the revolving cameramen. Linc jumps off the plane at three—you won't like him nearly as much as you like me, by the way—and an hour later I get on. And get out." He shoved back his chair and stood up, stretching his arms over his bare head. "So I'm passing on the high-octane coffee tonight. If I don't hit the sack now, I may as well pull an all-nighter."

"See you in the morning, Rusty. Don't forget to knock on my door before you leave."

She lingered at the small table after he went up to his room, swallowing down an unexpected surge of homesickness. The green-tiled dining room was empty save for the skinny young Iraqi who worked in the kitchen and kept the place in some semblance of order for the network staffers bunking there. Tonight the villa felt more desolate than usual, despite the fragrance of the lush vegetation outside and the proximity of Saddam's former palaces.

Villa. The word conjured up images of wealth and splendor, palm trees and servants. But now this villa was anything but idyllic. Would this country ever again know any luxury—even the "luxury" of peace?

After the hotels had been bombed, MSNBC and other news agencies had been forced to rent headquarters in assorted villas or large private homes within the Green Zone. All of them were in various stages of disrepair, yet they were still safer bases of operations than the hotels, which were far more visible targets.

Not that any place was actually safe here.

She thought for a moment of countless dinners in New York, of relaxed people laughing in crowded restaurants, of the festive clink of flatware and glasses, and the short walks afterward to snag a taxi or jump on the subway. She flashed on all the Friday nights she'd met Natalie for dinner after work, and the Sunday mornings she'd jogged through Central Park, and suddenly Dana became nostalgic for grass damp with dew. And for her sister. There was so much she missed, especially the normal, simple freedoms of life lived without the fear of kidnappings and beheadings.

You wanted this, she reminded herself, scooping up the pendant from the table, jangling the chain in her hand. *And in only a few more weeks you'll be done—choppering out at four A.M. yourself. So suck it up and smile for the camera, baby.*

"Excuse me, Miss Landau . . ." Duoaud, the young Iraqi, leaned in to set a small cup of thick black coffee before her. "Is there anything else you need this evening?"

"I'm set for tonight, Duoaud." She glanced up at the thin young man with the movie-star eyelashes who hovered at her elbow. "I'm turning in for the night, too."

She angled the pendant back into its pouch as Duoaud gathered up the plates and napkins. As he worked, his gaze followed the glint of the chain as it slid into the hollow of waiting leather.

"A most beautiful amulet, Miss Landau. Almost as beautiful as you," he added with a flashing grin. "My girlfriend, she would enjoy wearing one like that. Did you buy it here in Baghdad?"

She scraped back her chair and turned toward the stairs. "Actually, it found me. G'night, Duoaud. Please tell Wasim the lamb was amazing this evening. The best I've ever tasted."

But Duoaud didn't tell Wasim a thing. As soon as Dana left the dining room, Duoaud raced through the kitchen and out the back door, tearing down back alleys stinking of garbage and dog piss, past tall and vacant hotels, past gas stations and trinket shops, until he stood at a stately home near the far outskirts of the Green Zone. At the door of Aslam Hameed, who was paying him to keep an eye on the Americans and to keep an ear out for whispers about the Eye of Dawn, he pummeled the thick wood with the side of his fist.

"It's true. It exists—it's here. *The Eye of Dawn.* I saw it with my own eyes. Tonight—at the villa."

The words poured out of him faster than the sweat sliding down his dark, razor-sharp cheekbones. The obsidian eyes of Aslam Hameed pinned him.

"Inside." The heavier man jerked Duoaud into the stone entryway of his comfortable home, quickly scanning the street in both directions before he stepped back inside his residence and slammed the door.

"Tell me everything. But first, tell me who has it."

Duoaud was still panting, yet exhilarated by the full attention of Aslam Hameed.

And when Hameed reports my discovery to Hasan Sabouri himself, insha'allah, *I, too, might be in line for an important position with the Guardians of the Khalifah.*

"A woman has it. She is a reporter. For an American television network—MSNBC. Her name is Dana Landau."

2

New York City

The cab lurched down the Avenue of the Americas like a fitful donkey and Natalie swayed against the backseat as if she were riding one. She was already late for her 4 P.M. meeting with Oscar Charles, chair of the Treasures of the Tombs fund-raising gala. And they only had an hour to finalize a wish list of major donors to underwrite the event. *Someday, when I'm on staff at a bigger museum, like the Met,* she thought wistfully, *fund-raising will be handled by its own department.* But the Devereaux was only a tenth the size of the Met, and its curators had to wear many hats.

She was frazzled and fatigued, despite the fact that she was doing exactly what she'd dreamed of doing ever since her grade-school field trip to the King Tut exhibit. That day, in the Sackler Wing of the Metropolitan Museum of Art—built to house the Temple of Dendur exhibit—she'd fallen in love with the mystery of the ancient world, its grandeur and glamour. It wasn't until years later, while in the field for hours on end digging beneath the broiling Jordanian sun, that she finally appreciated the amount of grit and grunt it had taken to unearth those ancient treasures from the bowels of the desert and get them into their neat, temperature-controlled glass-and-velvet display cases.

As the cab finally jolted against the curb at Seventy-fifth and

Third, she scrounged in her shoulder bag for a twenty-dollar bill, past her penlight, her cosmetics bag, her cell phone. She stopped short at the sight of her passport, still there amid the crumpled boarding pass and the tin of Altoids.

What is my problem? Tonight this is getting put away, she chided herself, tossing the twenty at the driver. With a cacophony of horns blaring behind her and the intense pulse of the city pounding in her blood, it seemed like forever, not merely a week, since she'd departed Florence, still heady with the thrill of opening her first exhibit abroad.

Her exhilaration when Dr. Geoffrey Ashton, president of the Pan-European Association of Antiquities Scholars, called her to the podium was only a memory now. After having conferred with so renowned an expert for more than a year while she planned and coordinated her first international traveling exhibition, it had been an incomparable adrenaline rush to hear him introduce her. Now those heady moments were behind her. The exhibit of ancient Greek Orthodox *tamata* crafted of clay, wood, and metal was on the road now. The little *tamata* are still used as church offerings, only today they are made of tin, silver, or gold, and embossed with specific body parts representing an ailment. As in days past, the faithful hang them near an icon as they light a candle and pray for healing for themselves or others, even for a sick animal.

Her exhibit of rare artifacts dating back to the Bronze Age was headed next to Sydney. And she was home, swamped to her shoulders in new work—cataloging several new acquisitions, catching up on a mountain of correspondence, planning this gala—all while racing against a looming deadline for her first article in *International Antiquities Journal.*

Someday she'd use that passport to get back to Florence on her own dime and explore the museums and architecture like a proper tourist, but right now she couldn't even think beyond the projects screaming for her attention, let alone remember to put away her passport.

Pushing through the door of Crush, Natalie spotted Oscar at once and waved. His mop of curly silver hair made him hard to miss in any crowd. An off-Broadway producer, Oscar Charles personified enthusiasm, and he had the connections to guarantee that they'd fill the gala venue to capacity. He was an ebullient man, a people magnet, and a stickler for perfection—and by now she knew he liked his Grey Goose dirty, with extra olives on the side.

She plunged through the jammed, dimly lit restaurant, then stopped short, her attention diverted by the sound of her sister's voice flowing from the television perched high in the corner of the bar.

Dana was reporting from the site of a roadside bomb attack in Iraq. It was a repeat of the broadcast Natalie had seen on this morning's news. Still, her head swiveled up to her younger sister's image, and she felt the same pang in her gut she'd felt on learning that Dana had snagged the Iraq assignment.

Get the hell out of there, baby, she thought, staring hard at Dana's small, serious face, trying to reconcile the whiny kid sister who wouldn't step outside in the rain without an umbrella to the petite, poised woman speaking calmly in the godforsaken desert without a flak jacket. *God, I miss you.*

". . . and in other Mid-East developments, Israeli police today fired tear gas to break up a demonstration by the right-wing Jewish extremist group Shomrei Kotel, which is protesting next week's historic summit in Jerusalem. Security is already tightening in preparation for the arrival of UN Secretary-General Gunther Ullmann, who brokered the deal between Hamas and—"

Suddenly, static filled the screen and the audio turned into an irritating rasp.

"This is the third time today it's gone out," the bartender griped.

"Someone forget to pay the cable bill?" a woman at the bar drawled, eliciting laughter.

By then the transmission had been restored, but Dana was gone. Her report was over.

Still, an eerie chill swept along Natalie's nape. Her shoulder-length dark hair, caught loosely in a barrette, seemed to crackle with an odd electricity. She knew what her childhood friend Kara's grandmother would have said. She'd have clucked that someone had just walked over Natalie's grave.

Natalie shook off the thought, and the chill with it. Dana was fine, no doubt sound asleep by now. And Oscar was standing there waiting, offering her the chair opposite his.

She relaxed her shoulders and leaned in to greet him with a two-cheeked European kiss, reminding herself that by the night of the gala, two months from now, she wouldn't have to worry about Dana being stationed in Iraq anymore.

Two months from now Dana would be done with this assignment and home, safe and sound.

3

Baghdad

Rusty Sutherland struggled to keep his eyes open. Waiting for his boarding call, he slouched against the airport wall with a copy of Greenspan's *The Age of Turbulence* tucked under one arm and his duffel at his feet. All around him U.S. military personnel waded with authority through the stream of journalists, diplomats, and wary travelers eager to exit the war zone.

Flights here were few and far between, and often canceled at a moment's notice. He felt too fuzzy-headed this morning to read, but he wouldn't be able to close his eyes and relax until he was on that plane and the boarding door had been bolted shut.

He could almost smell Elaine's hair as he stood half a world away from her. She had the softest brown hair, and it smelled like ginger. He was sure the kids had made a homecoming sign for him, as big as the one they'd drawn for his fortieth birthday, and he found himself grinning at the memory.

When his flight was announced he stooped down quickly to grab up his duffel, and the book tumbled to the floor. Grabbing it up, he tried to jam it inside the canvas bag already bulging with his cameras, lenses, journal, and an assortment of honey-eyed Arabic pastries to tide him over on the long flight. As he searched for a free corner to shove the book into, his watch caught the drawstring of the pouch Dana had given him, dragging it out and spilling its contents at his feet.

Rusty swore in exasperation. Clumsily, he extricated the pouch from his wrist. People were surging past him toward the boarding gate. Impatient just to get on the damned plane, he snatched up Dana's note and pendant, cramming them back into his carry-on. With loping strides, he hurried toward the gate.

Behind him the gray eyes of a tall fair-haired man narrowed like a falcon's on Rusty's retreating back, watching until he disappeared through the door. Then Elliott Warrick, U.S. Assistant Undersecretary of Defense, lifted his cell phone and punched in a series of numbers known only to a select few in the world.

Dana dozed fitfully in the armored car shuttling her and the new cameraman back from Kirkuk. The sun boring through the windshield all but negated the fan she'd positioned to blast chilled air straight at her face. The long dangerous drive out to the north and back—coupled with abandoning her bed at an ungodly hour to see Rusty off—had depleted the last of her energy.

She wouldn't have the stamina to shower, or even to think about dinner, let alone to sit upright long enough to eat it. Dana's thoughts were no longer centered on the Kurdish families she'd interviewed at length today, exploring the contrast between their present shaky circumstances and the horrors suffered at the hands of Saddam Hussein. All she could think about were cool cotton sheets and a long undisturbed sleep.

Her new cameraman, Linc Sanchez, made a beeline for the liquor cabinet the instant they got back to the villa, but she trudged toward the stairway in a stupor. Cresting the landing, she fairly staggered down the hall. As she opened her door, she heard a soft clink on the wood floor and glanced down to see that her *hamsa* necklace had fallen from around her neck. *The clasp must have come loose while I dozed in the car,* she thought, stooping wearily to retrieve it.

Clenching it in her hand, she stepped inside and pushed the door closed behind her—and only then did her dazed eyes focus on the chaos around her.

Drawers out of the dresser. Her clothes and underwear and

toiletries dumped across the floor. The bed stripped, cotton sheets lying like deflated white parachutes alongside the mattress. Pillowcases in shreds, feather stuffing layered everywhere.

Ohmygod, Dana whispered, fumbling for her cell phone. She heard a small creak—the sound of the bathroom cupboard closing.

Someone's still here. In the bathroom. Run!

She spun toward the door, adrenaline surging, her exhaustion evaporating. But as she seized the doorknob she felt strong hands grab her from behind and lift her into the air. In a split second, an unseen attacker had flung her across the room.

4

Paris

"The plan is progressing according to schedule. By the time our enemies realize what is happening, the final battle will be upon their heads."

Iranian businessman Farshid Sabouri's eyes glittered as he surveyed the three men in expensive suits gathered in the flat on the Avenue de la Bourdonnais overlooking the Eiffel Tower. On the streets below no one suspected that six stories above them four of the wealthiest, most powerful terrorists in the world were finalizing an unprecedented conflagration.

"*Insha'allah,* from the river to the sea, Islam will again prevail," Farshid added, as the other key leaders of the Guardians of the Khalifah listened raptly. "The invader in our midst will fall before the sword of Allah."

Siddiq Aziz, a clean-shaven man with manicured hands and diamond cuff links, leaned forward upon the low suede sofa. He was handsome enough to grace the pages of *GQ,* and his financial cunning exceeded his looks. "And Palestine will glory in the obliteration of the infidels," the Saudi banker murmured.

Stretched across the wall behind him, the golden-hued painting of Al-Haram al-Sharif, the Noble Sanctuary, caught the sunlight splashing through the window. Each of the men glanced involuntarily at the image of the sacred site.

The ancient stones of Jerusalem seemed to glisten with a

holy radiance that spilled from the golden sphere dominating the hilltop. The infidels called it the Dome of the Rock, but these men knew it as Qubbat as-Sakhrah. Each man in the apartment was acutely aware at that moment that with the sweetness of impending victory there would come a price.

The Noble Sanctuary, Islam's third holiest site, had towered over Jerusalem since the ninth khalif, 'Abd al-Malik ibn Marwan, oversaw its construction in A.D. 685. Byzantine craftsmen sent to ibn Marwan from Constantinople had built the octagonal shrine over the sacred Noble Rock. According to Islam, Allah had instructed Abraham to take his son, Ishmael, to the rock to sacrifice him, and from that same rock the prophet Muhammad had ascended through the center of the golden dome and on to heaven, accompanied by the angel Gabriel.

The Noble Sanctuary had withstood centuries of war and turmoil, even defilement by the Crusaders who conquered it. Augustinian priests had converted the Qubbat as-Sakhrah—the Dome of the Rock—into a church. Crusader King Baldwin I took the Al-Aqsa Mosque as his palace, and later the Knights Templar had used it as their headquarters, believing the ruins of King Solomon's Temple lay nearby.

But soon, the terrorists knew, the magnificent gold foil–covered pinnacle above the Noble Sanctuary would stand no more.

"In a very short time the world will once again call the city by its rightful name, Al-Quds. 'Jerusalem' will be no more," Sabouri reminded them, sensing the emotions running through the room.

The sacrifice would be steep, but temporary.

The bin Laden family, powerful construction magnates who held the exclusive rights to repair the holy sites of Mecca and Medina, would rebuild a perfect replica. But first, every edifice of the Noble Sanctuary compound—the Dome of the Rock, the Al-Aqsa Mosque, the Dome of the Chain, the Dome of the Prophet, the Dome of the Miraj, the Dome of al-Nahawiah, the Dome of the Hebronite, Minbar of Burhan al-Din, the Golden Gate, Musalla Marwan, Ancient Aqsa, and the Islamic Museum, totaling one sixth of the walled city called Jerusalem—would be gone in a cataclysm of fire and thunder.

And all of Islam would rise up in rage.

The bombing had been in the planning for two years—fueled by the continued defilement of Arab holy lands by the West. The presence of the infidels had grown increasingly unbearable to the Shi'ah. Even the Sunni majority in Saudi Arabia resented the U.S. audacity in forcing the boots of its military upon Saudi Arabian soil. Defiling the land where Islam's holiest shrines stood was bad enough, but America's two arrogant and criminal invasions of Iraq, and the proliferation of their heretical Western culture, further enraged the faithful. But their greatest source of fury was the continued illegal existence of Israel.

Now all of those outrages were about to be avenged by these men, the leaders of the Guardians of the Khalifah, dedicated to the return of the khalifate.

There had been no khalif since the Ottoman Empire fell in 1924, dissolving into the Republic of Turkey. The khalif—the earthly successor to Muhammad and the Islamic head of state—was also known as the Prince of the Believers, a man who would unite all of Islam and bring all Muslims under his rule. Restoring the khalifate was the Guardians of the Khalifate's ultimate goal.

"We must meet the deadline." Siddiq lit a cigarette and tossed his monogrammed lighter on the coffee table. "There are only six days left until the summit."

"We will meet this deadline, Siddiq." Farshid Sabouri smiled. "Forty cylinders of C-4 explosives are already in the tunnel, and the last of the detonators will be secured tonight. Do you forget that it is my brother, Hasan, who has planned the entire operation? He has given me his assurance that his team has everything at the ready. That in six days the flames will outshine the sun."

At the mention of Hasan's name, each of the men flinched, and Siddiq reflexively shielded his eyes. To cover the awkward moment, the Yemenite, Jalil Haddad, spoke up quickly. "And Hasan is sure the Israelis are none the wiser?"

"Even were they to discover anything amiss they wouldn't be able to stop us," Sabouri sneered. "They will never find the tunnel in time. Everything will be in place when the president of the United States and the Secretary-General of the United Nations ascend the platform. And the world will be watching as they stand with smug, stupid smiles to witness the signing of the peace accord they think they've brokered."

The honeyed pastries, bowls of fruit, and pots of once steaming dark tea sat untouched on the glass-tiled coffee table.

"And our Hamas brother, Mu'aayyad bin Khoury?" Wasif Al-Mehannadi, the Bahraini whose sister Fatima was married to Hasan, snorted. "The traitor who shook the hand of the Israeli prime minister and sold out his people?"

There was a ripple of laughter.

"That faithless cur and his followers will know nothing until he is engulfed by the flames." Sabouri frowned suddenly at the shrill interruption of his cell phone and reached into his pocket.

He recognized the number at once. Aslam Hameed. It was a call he had to take.

Hameed's words came rapid-fire. Sabouri's eyes brightened as he listened.

When he pocketed the phone and turned back to the group, excitement thrummed through the voice of a man known throughout the Arab world for his legendary calm when everyone around him succumbed to turmoil.

"Great good news."

The other leaders of the Guardians of the Khalifah tensed, watching him.

"The Eye of Dawn has returned. It is a sign from Allah, as the mullahs declare: *The Eye of Dawn shall be a beacon heralding the triumph of Islam.*"

As excited murmuring ran through the gathered men, Sabouri's eyes glistened with triumph. "Even now, my brothers, Aslam Hameed and his men are pursuing it. In six days' time, the Eye of Dawn will be the light of Islam."

5

Baghdad

Dana hit the windowsill headfirst. Red spots and dark pain pulsed in her eyes as she slid to the floor.

Get up. Get up.

But her limbs refused to respond to the urgent command that seemed to come from far away.

Somehow she pushed herself to a sitting position. It seemed to take forever, just as it seemed to take forever for the contents of her tote to clatter to the floor while she watched her attacker shake it.

He was huge, a human tank. Dressed in dark pants and a brown shirt, his head swathed in a darker brown *hijab*. Watching him paw through the jumble of her things, tossing aside tampons, her notebook, her maps, and her sunscreen, she fought back the urge to vomit. Her head was roaring now, throbbing like it never had before.

Dizzy with the pain, she forced herself to stare up, up, at the immense figure now moving toward her, towering over her, his face hidden.

She could see only his eyes. Liquid, seething, driven eyes the color of ink.

"Where is it?" he growled. "*The Eye of Dawn.*"

"I don't—know—What eye—?"

Agony ripped through her cheek as he backhanded her, the metal setting on his ring tearing her skin.

"Don't lie to me, *sharmuta*! I know you have it—so *where is it?*"

Tears streamed down Dana's bleeding face as she scooted back toward the window. *What . . . is he . . . talking about? He's in the wrong room. If I can . . . just get to . . . my phone. . . .*

"Mis . . . take," she gasped. "You've made a mistake. I . . . I don't have anything you want—"

He lunged toward her, and fear clogged the scream in her throat. His thick fingers closed around the *hamsa* necklace that had tumbled from her fingers and landed near her feet.

"Like this!" He shoved the *hamsa* charm in her face, showing her the eye emblazoned in its cloisonné center. "The Eye! You have one like this—I want it! Now!"

That pouch . . . the pendant, Dana thought in shock. *That piece of . . . junk I sent Natalie?* She tried to speak calmly, in the dulcet TV voice viewers had come to respect, but her words were a croak.

"It's gone. I . . . don't have it anymore—"

"Liar! *Sharmuta!*" He belted her again, cracking open her lower lip.

Dana's vision doubled. One of her teeth was lying against her tongue. She didn't have the strength to spit it out. She had to get up, away, but she was too dizzy even to stand.

She started to scream then, as loud as she could, screaming in terror, screaming for help.

Her voice reverberated through the room like the shrieks of a scalded cat.

Yusef's fists clenched. The only thing he wanted to hear out of her was where she'd hidden the Eye. It wasn't in this room, *that* he knew. Did she have an accomplice? She'd tell everything before he was done. Overwhelming pain was a great motivator. Soon she'd be begging for the chance to tell him where it was.

He lifted her easily, as though she was a hollow mannequin, and threw her across the room. But she was slender and he overestimated his strength against her slightness. Instead of landing on the bed, she slammed into the dresser, her head hitting the sharp edge with a crack.

Silence circled the room.

Yusef hurried toward her. She wasn't screaming. Wasn't moving. She was out cold.

Cold water will take care of that.

But as he rounded the bed, he could see the impossible angle of her chin, and the blood pouring from her ear.

She wasn't going to be waking up.

Fury and frustration surged through his chest. And so did a spurt of fear. *The anger of Aslam Hameed will be uncontrollable. But it will pale in comparison to the fury of Hasan Sabouri.*

He broke into a sweat thinking of the powerful Iranian with the ice blue eyes. The evil eyes. Hasan Sabouri had killed his own mother, and countless others, with just his glance. What would happen when he learned of this failure to secure the Eye of Dawn?

His stomach contracted. *I let my zeal get in the way. How could I have been so careless?*

Still clenching the dead woman's silver chain and its jeweled charm in his fist, Yusef fled the room as quietly as he'd entered it, leaving the tiny American journalist with her blood soaking the tangled strands of her blond hair.

6

The White House

Secretary of Defense Jackson Wright scowled as he barreled into the Oval Office. President Owen Garrett threw down his pen and rubbed the fatigue from his eyes.

The commander-in-chief's campaign-perfect mahogany hair was newly peppered with wiry gray that glinted in the sunlight from the windows behind him.

Only two and a half years in office, and already Garrett was looking a decade older than his forty-nine years. Presidents aged quickly in this twenty-first century, marked as it was by worldwide terrorism, sectarian war, Islamic jihadism, and the Damocles' sword of nuclear holocaust.

"Bin Khoury hasn't backed out of the agreement, has he?" Garrett asked without preliminaries. He had high hopes that this week's historic visit to Jerusalem for the signing of an accord between Hamas leaders and Israel would be the first legacy of many in his presidency.

But nothing of value came easy. Not only were Arab factions across the Islamic world staging violent protests, but the small Israeli right-wing extremist group, Shomrei Kotel—fixated on erecting the Third Temple—had now threatened to blow up the Dome of the Rock and clear the site for rebuilding.

"Actually, we've got another situation, sir." Wright's mouth twisted in the unconscious grimace that had been mercilessly caricatured by comic impressionists on *Saturday Night Live.*

"Warrick called in just before boarding his flight from Baghdad." The President's former law professor paused for a moment, knowing the impact his next words would have. "He has a bead on the whereabouts of Firefly."

Silence hung in the historic room. Even President Washington, gazing down from his portrait over the mantel, seemed to be holding his breath.

Garrett slowly steepled his hands before him on the desk. *Firefly.* He hadn't been briefed on Firefly until his second week in office, and the news of its existence had raised the hairs along his spine more than any other piece of classified data he'd been privy to since taking the oath.

"What sort of a bead?"

Without being asked, the Secretary of Defense drew up a chair and folded his bulky six-foot frame into it.

"One credible enough that I've activated the means to retrieve it."

The NSU, Garrett thought. Only a handful of people in the government knew about the top-secret unit, which had been created by his predecessor. The stealth unit, independent of the CIA was charged with ensuring the security of the United States—at any cost.

"Firefly is still in Iraq?" he asked. "It's been there all along?"

Wright nodded grimly. He could see the President's agile mind racing. Not much showed in Owen Garrett's controlled, intelligent face, but as one of his oldest friends and supporters, Wright recognized the subtle tightening of his broad knuckles and knew that the leader of the free world was experiencing the same surge of hope, fear, and trepidation as he.

"What are they doing to get possession of it?" Garrett demanded, his prominent slate-blue eyes scouring Wright's face. "Because you know damn well the Mossad is doing the same or better." He slammed his fist on the papers piled in front of him. "We thought we had a lock on it at the damned museum five years ago, before it managed to slip through our fingers. That cannot happen again."

"It won't, Mr. President. This time we're doing everything necessary."

Garrett leaned forward, a muscle twitching in his neck. "Like what?"

Wright winced, then pushed himself to his feet and met the chief executive's eyes.

"I hope you'll excuse me from answering that question, sir. It might be better if you don't know the details."

7

The Radiant Light of Heaven Church
Pensacola, Florida

On a normal Sunday morning, the Radiant Light of Heaven sanctuary vibrated with the energy of a thousand voices raised in praise. The Reverend Ken Mundy knew how to bring his flock surging to their feet. All eyes were fastened on his homely, heavily jowled face, supersized on the screen suspended from the vaulted ceiling. It was a face of sincerity, a face of passion, a face flush with the conviction that the End of Days was near.

It was the same face, the same message, seen on videos every Sunday in the five Radiant Light of Heaven churches scattered throughout Florida, Georgia, Texas, and Michigan. He'd managed to gain an impressive following, despite the fact that the media had branded his church a cult and Mundy himself misguided. The entire mainstream Christian world had disavowed him, his message, and his tactics.

And those narrow-minded fools would disavow my plan, as well, if they knew of it.

Fools. The majority of Christian leaders in the United States—across the world—were passive, misguided fools. They were content to wait, to merely build alliances with the Jews, to pray and prepare themselves for the End of Days. Not one of them had the vision or the courage to be proactive.

But he did. He had not only the vision but the resources. His was a small but mighty cadre of believers. Where mainstream evangelical preachers could reach millions on an average Sunday, he reached only a few thousand.

But he didn't need a massive following—not when he already had power, money, clout, and the courage to take action.

Waiting patiently at the podium, he looked out at the camera crew, makeup artist, and director preparing to videotape his weekly sermon, then back at his notes. Only those who knew him best—his wife, his attorney, and his closest ally, known to the inner sanctum as the Sentinel—would have recognized the exhilaration humming like harp strings through his soul.

On the surface was a gloss of composure and assurance as thick as the pancake makeup that had dried on his cheeks, but beneath the smooth equanimity there pulsed an energy that would light up this entire church compound if he could plug it into a socket.

Even as he stared intently into the rolling cameras, to meet the eyes of his unseen followers—even as the first words of his sermon resonated through the hall—Mundy wasn't present mentally. He was focused on a time in the not too distant future when all he'd worked for had been realized.

He was envisioning himself in the Holy Land, preaching from a different podium, preaching from the heart of Jerusalem.

Preaching from the Third Temple his followers would build.

A vision had told him that the Rapture was at hand—the ascension of the believers was near. The time of Tribulation foretold in the New Testament was coming—Jesus' return to face off against the Antichrist in the final battle between good and evil. *Armageddon.* Finally Jesus would reign over a world at peace for one thousand years, before delivering it to His Father.

And then all those who had called him a fringe lunatic, a cult leader, a deluded bigot would finally have to accept the truth. He was the only one who had known Armageddon was at hand.

"Ken"—the director's voice snapped him from his reverie—"give us the last three lines one more time. We had a little problem with camera two."

"Should I pick it up from 'And on that day, all of our work

and our prayers' . . . ?" Mundy asked, shifting his weight to his other hip.

"That'll do it. Another two hours to edit after that, and it'll be a wrap for this week."

The taping finished, Mundy headed toward the boardroom at the rear of the low-slung office building adjacent to the church. He greeted the church secretary with a smile and a wave as he yanked off his tie, then he shoved his passkey into an imposing mahogany door. It opened into a long hallway that was plush with sculpted carpeting that silenced his footfalls as he hurried to the soundproofed, private boardroom only a chosen few were permitted to enter. Only his inner sanctum, the Sons of Babylon, were privy to the plans and preparations that went on here.

The Sentinel was waiting for him, leaning back in a club chair, restlessly rustling the pages of the *Wall Street Journal.*

"Has anyone else seen the picture?" Mundy demanded, slinging his navy suit jacket across the leather chair.

"Not a soul." The Sentinel smiled as he snapped open his briefcase and pulled out a photograph.

Mundy's spirits soared.

The Sentinel never smiled.

Reaching for the glossy image, Mundy's stomach pumped with adrenaline. He stared at the 4×6–inch print and gaped at the famed golden talisman he'd only ever attempted to imagine, and felt the room slant. *Good God, it was real. It was beautiful. It was true.*

He couldn't wait to see the miracle hidden inside.

"Just as it was described in the Scroll of Daniel." The Sentinel leaned in closer, his sharp gaze fixed on the full-color image of the jeweled eye. "The Light is coming home."

"Not if we can't ensure its safe passage." Perspiration mottled the front of Mundy's shirt as a thousand fears raced through his head. He knew how crucial it was that the Light come to *him.* In the wrong hands . . . He shuddered to consider the consequences. "Where is it now?" he asked.

The Sentinel pushed himself to his feet. The stubble bristling across his jaw annoyed him. He took pride in his appearance, and he hadn't even shaved today. But there hadn't been time. Weariness clung to him like a wet suit, but he had no time for weariness either. If the prize dropped out of sight again, if they lost the trail, the ancient prophecy would never come to pass in his lifetime.

Without the Light's power and presence, the Sons of Babylon would fail to inaugurate the Rapture. And they were *this close* to raising the Third Temple and to filling it with the Light.

For it was foretold in the Scroll of Daniel that the Light would reappear on earth and shine forth from the Third Temple. And Mundy knew the Light was the key—the all-important precursor to the End of Days.

"It's being taken care of even as we speak," the Sentinel told Mundy, with a calm that belied his inner tension.

"Barnabas." Mundy never lifted his gaze from the photograph.

"And I'd like to alert Derrek that we might need him for backup." The Sentinel watched the reverend's brow furrow, and he headed off the coming argument with a raised hand. "Ken, this is too crucial to be left in the hands of one man. Even Barnabas."

Mundy traced the talisman in the photo. "I've no objection to alerting Derrek—but Barnabas needs no one's help."

For a moment they both pictured the fresh-faced young man full of ferocious faith. An anticipatory smile curled the corners of Ken Mundy's full, friendly lips. He could almost smell the fires of the final days.

He thought back to the first time he'd shown Barnabas the model of the future Third Temple. The seventeen-year-old youth leader's eyes had glowed, as if he'd just been anointed by the Holy Spirit itself. The boy had seen it clearly, seen it all: the unfolding of the Rapture, the ascension of all true believers, the beginning of the End Times.

Even then the boy understood the essential role the Third Temple would play in setting the stage for the greatest moment in history—Armageddon, the final battle between good and evil.

On the spot, Barnabas had handed over his pizza delivery tip money, pressing even the loose change into Mundy's palm with the promise to help raise the temple any way he could—even if it meant building it with his own two hands.

He'd been a skinny kid back then, fatherless since he was a toddler, but in the intervening years he had built himself up. He'd followed his basketball coach's weight-lifting regimen religiously, until his muscles had doubled, tripled, and quadrupled on his once slight frame.

Barnabas seemed to possess boundless energy, despite the drains of school, work, church, and caring for his mother, who'd battled cancer and died two weeks short of his college graduation.

Mundy saw himself in Barnabas's struggles. He'd survived childhood hardships of his own—the least of which was growing up without a father. So throughout the travails of Barnabas's youth, Mundy had continuously reassured him that God would provide.

Just as God had provided for Mundy. Now, in Barnabas, He had provided a tireless disciple whose commitment to the Church was as strong as his body.

"Barnabas could have his hands on the Light any time now," the Sentinel said.

Mundy didn't answer. He was transfixed by his own thoughts, by the excitement churning through his blood. Within a matter of days he, too, might be holding the Light in his hands, God's creative power at his fingertips. Mundy stared at his palms. He never would have imagined that one day he, a poor, humble boy from Tennessee, would hold the light of creation, wielding it in the name of the saved.

The discovery of the Scroll of Daniel among the ancient scrolls found at Qumran had provided a miraculous glimpse into the biblical past. Daniel, the prophet who served in Balshazzar's court and interpreted the king's dreams, had been privileged to see the Light. Experts were still deciphering parts of the Scroll, but had already uncovered Daniel's meticulous description of the unique Light created by the word of God at the dawn of time. Daniel had written that God's Light would reappear in the world when it was most needed, in the darkest of days. It would resurface to illuminate the path of the Messiah.

For Jesus.

And he, the Reverend Ken Mundy, founder of the Radiant Light of Heaven Church, creator of the secret Sons of Babylon, scorned by the mainstream Christian community, a man who walked a lonely path like his Savior had, would be the one to hold it aloft.

The Sentinel guessed at the thoughts simmering in Mundy's mind. How many hours had the two of them worked, planned, and prayed together for this moment? For a goal that none of Mundy's devoted congregants yet knew anything about—just as they remained in the dark about how much of their weekly offerings their pastor regularly diverted to fund this glorious mission.

Even the wives and children of the Sons of Babylon knew nothing about the task for which Mundy had handpicked these men—to raise the Third Temple in Jerusalem, to rebuild the Jews' holy edifice that was destroyed for the second time in the year A.D. 70. To deliver the predestined place where Jesus would unite the world in the one true faith.

"The Light is almost home." The Sentinel snapped his briefcase closed and met Mundy's hope-filled eyes. "Pray that no one else realizes it has surfaced."

Mundy tucked the photograph deep into the left breast pocket of his suit as they started together for the door. "I'll spend the rest of the night speaking to the Lord, asking him to guide Barnabas's hand."

8

New York

"I'm sorry, Mr. —" Lita Smith glanced again at the security badge clipped to Rusty Sutherland's shirt pocket and offered a rueful smile. "Mr. Sutherland. But Dr. Landau left for lunch not five minutes ago. You must have crossed paths at the elevator."

Rusty cocked his forearm to check his watch. He'd been on the go for more than sixteen hours and was falling off his feet. Not to mention the fact that he had a family waiting, a family he hadn't seen in months.

"Can I leave something for her, then? I just got back from Iraq, and I'm dropping off a gift from her sister."

The young assistant, who sported spiky red hair and rings on every finger, glanced down at the pouch he pushed across the reception desk. "Oh! From Dana?" A warmer smile. "I know Dr. Landau is counting the days until her sister gets back."

She stood up and reached for the pouch. "Sure, I'll put it right on her desk."

Rusty thanked her wearily and trudged back toward the elevator. The Simon and Garfunkel refrain, "Home . . . homeward bound . . ." circled in his head. His steps quickened as he crossed the lobby.

But as he stepped toward the curb to hail a cab he was nearly knocked sideways by a jogger plowing into him.

"Whoa, sorry. Are you alright? I guess I wasn't looking where I was going . . ."

Rusty blinked, trying to clear his head. He felt woozy suddenly, with a strange warmth rushing through his body, like he'd just tossed back half a dozen shots of tequila on an empty stomach. The husky kid who'd collided with him was staring at him in concern. He couldn't have been more than twenty-four or twenty-five, clean-cut, his brown eyes sincere and worried.

Rusty tried to speak and couldn't. He swayed, and the young man gripped his arms.

"Sir, are you alright? Let me put you in a cab." With that the brawny, blond-haired kid's arm shot up, his finger signaling toward the stream of oncoming traffic.

A haze filmed Rusty's eyes, but blinking didn't clear his vision. Why couldn't he speak? He felt himself being eased into a cab, but with a curious sense of detachment, as if he was watching from someplace outside of himself.

He was thirsty, and he was sweating.

I'm going to be sick.

He heard the young man give the cab driver an address, but he couldn't make out the street. Home. He wanted to go home. He had to get to the train station. He tried to tell the cabbie to take him to Grand Central Station, but all that came out was an unintelligible croak.

"He's in bad shape, man. But I'm his sponsor. I'll get him to his AA meeting."

What the hell is he talking about?

Rusty could see the door handle; he just couldn't reach it. His hand felt too heavy. His eyelids were heavy, too. He fought against the enveloping darkness but felt himself slipping deeper into its suffocating spell.

And then he couldn't breathe, couldn't move, couldn't hang on any longer. *Darkness.*

Lita surveyed the uneven stacks and piles that had accumulated across Natalie's desk while she was in Italy, and thought better of adding to the chaos. Instead, she slid open the center drawer where Natalie kept her appointment calendar and nestled the pouch up-front, where she couldn't miss it, between the yellow marking pens and the stash of peanut M&Ms.

She made a mental note to call Natalie and tell her she had a gift waiting from Dana.

But then the phones started ringing, and the printer jammed twice while she was trying to churn out thirty collated copies of the report Dennis wanted on his desk by 3:00 P.M., and she forgot all about the pouch she'd tucked inside Natalie's desk.

She didn't even remember it when Natalie said good night and sailed out at 4:30 for a meeting with a private collector before her weekly dinner with her friend Peggy.

Lita's memory wasn't jogged until the phone call came from Rusty Sutherland's wife.

9

Natalie couldn't decide which annoyed her more—Lita's forgetfulness in not informing her about the package until she was halfway through dessert or her carelessness in not asking Rusty Sutherland's wife for a phone number.

It was frustrating to think that she'd been at her desk nearly four hours unaware that a present from Dana was right inside the top middle drawer. Impatience and excitement chafed at her as she left her old grad school study buddy, Peggy Lim, at Serendipity 3, polishing off her after-dinner Yudufundu Fruit and Fudge, and grabbed a cab back to the museum five minutes after Lita called her.

Natalie's heels clattered up the stone steps, echoing loudly in the cloud-filtered moonlight. Reaching the wide double bronze doors, she fished her plastic security card out of her handbag.

Moments later she was exiting the elevator on the fourth floor and striding past the reception desk and the bank of lush floor plants towering nearly to the pressed-tin ceiling.

The museum feels different at night, she thought, catching a glimpse of her reflection as she swept past the window just beyond the reception desk and turned down the low-lit corridor leading to the offices. The building was hushed and sleepy now. By daylight there was a pulse of energy in the museum, a thrumming in the air as visitors and staff shared a breath of the ancient world.

The offices were all on the top floor. In the carpeted halls and galleries below, a wealth of culture glimmered beneath discreet spotlights. Golden bowls and jeweled goblets from third-century Sicily. Thirteenth-century flasks from Mameluke, Egypt. Persian candlesticks forged of bronze. Ancient Phoenician and Roman glass. A three-thousand-year-old mosaic from the Galilee in Israel. All were among the most prestigious centerpieces of the permanent exhibits, as were extensive examples of fine Islamic pottery, pre-Christian talismans, and Babylonian jewelry.

Natalie's footsteps hastened as she neared her office, thinking about Lita's description of the pouch Dana had sent. It was decorated with a *mati,* Lita had told her, using the Greek name for the amulet designed to ward off the evil eye.

She wondered if Rusty was home by now. According to Lita, his wife had sounded almost in tears when she called at five o'clock. Rusty had phoned her from JFK before noon, while waiting for his baggage, to say he only had to make one quick stop at the Devereaux to drop off a package for Natalie, and then he'd be on the train.

But he'd never called back to tell her which train to meet, and he wasn't answering his cell phone. His wife hadn't heard a word from him since midday.

He must be home by now, Natalie told herself, as she switched on her office light and hurried around the desk.

The pouch was exactly where Lita had said it would be. Natalie scooped it up, moved that her sister had reached out to her in this way. With practiced fingers she tested the texture of the cracked leather. Switching on the desk lamp, she peered at the hand-rendered image of the large bold eye with its blue iris and thick black outline. Her instant impression was that the pouch was old, worn with sand and time.

Where did Dana get this? she wondered, intrigued. The leather and the knots on the black drawstrings reminded her, in feel and in workmanship, of ancient Sumerian money pouches she'd studied from Lebanon.

She carefully loosened the fastenings. The brief note from Dana—*A tiny treasure from the Middle East*—brought a wry smile, but it faded as she spilled the "treasure" into her palm.

It was a pendant. Heavy. Striking. It gleamed up at her like a small golden egg, encrusted with jewels of lapis lazuli, carnelian, and jasper. *The classic eye, one of the most ancient symbols of protection.* Carried or worn by people across the earth nearly since the dawn of time, it was among the oldest, most pervasive talismans in the world.

For nearly five thousand years the image of the eye had been written about, drawn, carved, and displayed. If eyes truly were the windows of the soul, as stated by Lao-tzu, the ancient Chinese philosopher who had written the greatest treatise on Taoism, it was no wonder that humans had always feared the envious glance, the evil intention glinting from one pair of eyes to another.

From the beginning, Natalie knew well, people have always found a prolonged stare unnerving. That's why, throughout history, most cultures have replicated the open eye as a protective amulet—like the one in her hand—to reflect back the evil effects of a suspect gaze.

She'd always found it fascinating that people in the Middle East, since the days of early Sumeria, believed that light was generated in the heart and projected outward through the eyes, and that an evil heart cast an evil eye capable of harming whatever it looked upon.

It seemed that humans had always worried that a covetous undercurrent flowed beneath every glance of admiration. That one could cause intentional or inadvertent harm with the naked eye. In many languages and through many centuries, there was a single name for the feared glance—the evil eye.

The Italians called it *malocchio,* the Scots *droch shuil,* the Jews *ayin ha'ra.* In Spanish it was *mal de ojo,* in Polish *oko proroka,* in Farsi *bla band.* And the Greeks called it *matiasma.*

Even the Torah spoke of the evil eye. In the Book of Proverbs, King Solomon cautioned, "Eat not the bread of him that hath an evil eye." And St. Paul wrote in the New Testament, "Oh foolish Galatians, who has cast the evil eye upon you?"

The evil eye had intrigued the ancient Romans Cicero, Virgil, and Pliny, all of whom had commented on it in their writings. As did the first-century Greek historian Plutarch, who wrote that certain men's eyes could bring harm to infants and young animals whose bodies were still weak and vulnerable, but that these same gazes couldn't wield the same power over adults. Except for Thebans, of course. Plutarch was convinced that their eyes possessed the power to harm both infants and adults.

Natalie had spent years examining and cataloging hundreds of protective eyes from the ancient Middle East and Mediterranean basin. The eye amulets had come from Egypt, Mesopotamia, Greece, Africa, Italy, Turkey, Persia, Iraq, and Israel.

But she felt a special spark of excitement as she tilted the eye pendant from Dana beneath the lamp. Though she'd inspected countless amulets painted or engraved with the protective eye, she'd never come across one quite like this.

Like the others she'd studied, it was old and outlined as if with the greasy kohl commonly employed by men and women alike to protect the eyes of the wearer since before the days of Cleopatra.

But the eyes on this pouch and amulet were different. They were doubly encircled with thick blue borders of lapis lazuli. And the red stones forming the irises—carnelian, she guessed—were not set against the usual background of white, but against a sea of yellow. She wondered if the yellow stones were jaspers. All three of those gems had been used for adornment as far back as the Babylonian period.

Lost in thought, Natalie chewed her lip. There was a heft to the darkened gold setting—and she'd bet her fifth-century Etruscan amulet emblazoned with the head of Medusa that the setting *was* of real gold—that told her this pendant was crafted for someone of wealth and importance. From what she could deduce on first glance, this necklace was far from the trinket Dana's note had jokingly suggested.

Dana has no idea what this is, she thought, shaking her head. *But then, neither do I.*

And there wouldn't be time to properly investigate it, she realized with a disappointed sigh, not until she'd dug out from a backlog of work that could fill an Egyptian burial chamber. Still, it was an enticing mystery waiting to be solved. More important, it was an overture from her sister, an opening for a much-needed conversation.

A sliver of apprehension suddenly tingled through her. She hoped to God Dana hadn't bought this pendant on the black market, inadvertently paying next to nothing for an unrecognized treasure that had been looted in Iraq at the start of the war.

Tomorrow, she promised herself, she'd have to make time to check the latest list of antiquities still unaccounted for—and pray she wouldn't see this evil eye pendant staring back at her from her computer screen.

As she lifted the pendant by its chain to slip it back into the pouch, Natalie paused, once again struck by its heft. *But it isn't only the gold,* she realized with a start. *There's something inside.*

She reached for her magnifying glass and peered at the metal ring through which the chain was threaded, probing it to see if it doubled as a clasp. But it didn't—the pendant wouldn't open, and its surface appeared intact. She couldn't detect a seam anywhere in the gold.

Suddenly her concentration was broken by the sound of a drawer closing. *What was that?* It seemed to have come from down the hall.

A moment later, the sound came again.

Who else is up here after hours? Dennis? Did he leave his wedding ring in his desk again?

Her eyes narrowed at the thought of the Armani-obsessed associate curator whose office was a few doors down. Dennis Bellweather considered himself hot stuff, with his five published pieces in *Art News* magazine and his frequent lunch dates with a series of women half his age. *You'd think by now the little Lothario would be more adept at juggling his double life.*

Just then she heard a crash and she rushed around the desk.

"Den—" But the word died in her throat as a figure appeared in Dennis's doorway twenty feet away. And it wasn't Dennis.

It was a man, but one tall and twice Dennis's girth, with shoulders hewn from either sweat or steroids. He could have been a linebacker for the Giants, except he wasn't wearing a red-striped helmet or a royal blue uniform. He was wearing a black ski mask, black gloves, and baggy gray sweats.

After the first thump of fear slammed through her chest, logic spun out an answer. *Valerie finally hired a private detective to nail the scumbag.* As the thought flashed through her mind, the stranger started toward her with a lumbering gait.

"Quiet," he warned in a throaty baritone, lengthening his strides to close the gap between them.

"Security!" Natalie took a step backward, shouting at the top of her lungs.

He burst into a sprint, charging toward her. Heart hammering, she veered to the left, darting toward the reception desk and the alarm button on the underside of Lita's keyboard shelf. Private detective or no, he was moving like a man determined to shut her up.

She made it only three strides down the hallway before she heard him directly behind her. At that, her training kicked in, and she spun to face him.

He couldn't slow down fast enough, and his momentum was exactly what she'd counted on. Her arm shot out, the heel of her palm aimed toward his nose as she leaned her body into the slam. Reflexively, her other fist—the one clutching tight to the pendant—shot up to protect her face.

Ski Mask grunted at the impact, stunned by the sharp jolt of pain and the blood spurting from his nostrils. Through the eye slits in his mask, she could see the pain glaring from amber-flecked brown eyes. Without giving him an instant to recover, she drove her heel down hard on his instep.

The maneuvers bought her another second. She lunged for the reception area once again, but as she rushed toward the desk and the buzzer, her heel caught on the wheeled base of Lita's chair and she tumbled against the bookshelves lining the wall, her shoe flying in the opposite direction.

Then she felt his hands tangling in her hair. He was on her in a fury, dragging her backward as pain ripped from her hairline to her nape. The force of his grip brought tears.

"I'll take this, ma'am." His voice was thick with a mouthful of blood. A faint drawl tinged his words. He grabbed her hand in a fist the size of a gorilla's and began prying her fingers from the pendant.

In the instant it took her to realize what he was after, her fingers clamped tighter around the amulet and she fought back, ramming her free elbow backward and up toward his sternum.

"Security!" she screamed again, frantic. *"Zone 6!"*

His foot hooked around hers, brought her down hard. She hit the carpet like a roped calf. As he dropped down to straddle her and grabbed for the pendant once more, she pitched it past him—sending it deep into the leafy jungle of plants.

To her shock, he scrambled to his feet to lurch after it. On his hands and knees, he began groping among the porcelain pots cradling split-leaf philodendron and ficus. She clambered to her feet and saw the thin beam of his penlight probing the dirt, fronds, and carpet. The sound of voices and pounding footsteps filled the stairwell.

"Here!" she yelled. "Reception!"

The exit door burst open, and Ski Mask sprang up, tucked his head down, and made a beeline for the elevators, hitting the buttons repeatedly with the flat of his gloved palm. The center door slid noiselessly open, even as Natalie launched herself toward the plants.

Had he found the pendant? Had he taken it?

Then her breath whooshed out in relief as she caught its glint from the carpet behind the cycas palm. Her fingertips scrabbled for the hammered gold as the security guards surged past her and toward the elevator bank.

But they were too late. All they caught sight of were the doors closing on a huge ski-masked man—and Natalie rising from her knees amid the array of plants, trembling, wearing only one high-heeled red shoe.

10

Barnabas kept his steps to a measured pace as he walked toward Central Park, his hands stuffed in the pockets of his sweatshirt. Behind him sirens screamed, but he forced himself not to run, hoping it was too dark for anyone to notice the blood dried beneath his nostrils and speckled across the gray fleece fabric covering his chest.

In the dark, the spots could easily be mistaken for sweat. To passersby he was merely a jogger on the way home from his nightly run. No one looking his way would possibly guess how he'd gotten tonight's workout.

Blood and sirens pounded in his ears as he reached the park and ambled down a winding path. He skirted the Great Lawn at Turtle Pond, keeping his pace steady. Though outwardly calm, inside he was raging, and it was a struggle to keep his breathing even.

How could he have let himself fail? The Light had been a hand's breadth away, and he'd been driven off by a woman's slap and a bunch of rent-a-cops.

That green-eyed woman had surprised him. She was trim, no more than five feet six, but toned like a female who took her elliptical workout seriously. Still, he'd never expected her to fight back like that—she was much faster and stronger than he'd have guessed.

How would he tell Reverend Mundy that a woman had bested him?

Tears of frustration squeezed from the corners of his eyes. He'd had four chances today—four—but each time he'd been a beat off the mark. If only he'd been able to take it from the bald guy before he'd ducked into that cab at JFK. He'd followed fast enough in the next cab, but had gotten hung up at a traffic light, and by the time Barnabas had jumped out and run across the street, someone else was in the bald guy's cab and the target was entering the museum.

Even when he'd finally caught up with Mister Rusty Sutherland outside the museum and managed to inject him with two milligrams of Ativan without anyone being the wiser, he'd still failed. He'd dragged Sutherland up two flights of stairs in a condemned building in Alphabet City, and searched him thoroughly, but hadn't found the Light in his backpack or anywhere else.

Barnabas had been left with no other choice than to bind the man like Abraham had bound Isaac—rendering him a ducttaped sacrificial lamb ready for the altar of interrogation.

He'd had to wait nearly two hours for the Ativan to wear off, but he'd used the time to pray, certain that the Lord would aid him in getting the information he needed without having to resort to violence. But the Lord had different plans, and they were not for Barnabas to question.

Pain normally worked quickly on people, but Sutherland had proved stubborn. Barnabas realized the Lord was testing him in this task. Even after he'd snapped several of Sutherland's fingers like pencils, the bald man had refused to say what he'd done with the Light.

Barnabas had assured him that he didn't want to inflict any more pain. Everything would have been so much simpler if only Sutherland had complied. Though Barnabas had apologized over and over, he'd found it necessary to force the man into cooperation. The most he could get out of him, even as he held him by the feet over the abandoned elevator shaft, was that Sutherland had left the Light at the museum.

The museum. *That was my fourth failure. Why, Lord? Why didn't you see fit to bless my quest? Why are you testing me?*

Now everything was far more complicated. The police would be looking for him, and the woman still had the Light.

What is she telling the police about it? How much does she know?

Sweat soaked along his hairline as he began to pray again, praying now for guidance, for God to grant him the Light. His lips moved beneath the murky glimmer of the streetlights as he walked. He was heedless of the passersby and of the pain throbbing through the nerve endings in the center of his face.

The pain in his soul was far worse.

Suddenly the answer crept into his mind, like a whisper from above. *The Sentinel.* If anyone could find out the woman's identity, it was the Sentinel. He needed to call Reverend Mundy and ask for that help.

And admit his failure.

Barnabas's shoulders were bent by the time he entered his room in the Skyline Hotel two miles away.

His voice cracked as the reverend answered his cell phone. Reverend Mundy sounded so eager.

"Please don't be disappointed in me, sir. I failed you tonight—but I will do better, I give you my promise. We don't have to worry about the man anymore—but now the Light is in the hands of a woman."

Or in the hands of the police, he thought in panic, not daring to give voice to such a possibility.

"I need the Sentinel to find out who she is, sir. The woman who works in the museum." He rushed on, delaying the moment when he would hear the disappointment in the reverend's voice. "Tell me who she is, and then, in the name of the Savior, I'll find her. And the Light will be ours."

11

"Fill me in on something, Dr. Landau. Why were you here in the building after hours?"

Detective Marv Henderson inspected the tiny sloping scrawl across his notebook, then lifted his glance once more to Natalie's drained face. He sat stout as a beer keg in the seat across from her in the museum director's office, a no-nonsense man with bristly gray hair, nibbled-down fingernails, and an unwrapped cigar sticking out of his breast pocket.

Throughout the museum, every light blazed as police fanned out to search the galleries, storerooms, and corridors, assisted by staff members who'd been summoned to ascertain whether anything had been taken or damaged. Roberta Flaherty, the museum director, had rushed over from the theater still clutching her program.

"As I told Officer Garibaldi already, I came back to get something from my desk." Natalie slouched back in her chair wearily, Dana's pendant clenched between her hands in her lap.

The detective was once again studying his notes from behind his thick eyeglasses, his manner almost distracted. "And you were here how long before you heard the intruder?"

"Five minutes . . . ten. No more."

"And are you in the habit of returning to the museum after hours?" At that, his gaze locked on hers.

"Of course not." She bit back her annoyance. "It's my *habit* to go home at the end of the day."

"But not today?"

"No. I told you, just as I told Officer Garibaldi, I had dinner with a friend and then came back to get something from my desk."

"And what was that?" His pen was poised in midair. His eyes looked twice their size, magnified by the thickness of his lenses.

Slowly Natalie unclenched her hands and held out the pendant she'd retrieved from the tangle of plants.

"It's an evil eye amulet. I was planning to study it at home this evening."

Detective Henderson's brows slid together, colliding in the middle of his creased forehead. "Are you in the habit of taking museum property home with you in the evenings?"

"Absolutely not." Natalie felt a twinge of alarm. The amulet had nothing to do with the break-in. And the last thing she wanted was for the police to get sidetracked. "This isn't the museum's property. It's mine." She closed her hand around the pendant again and met his magnified eyes. "My personal property."

"You said the intruder tried to take it from you. And that he was wearing gloves. Which means the only prints on it would be yours, Dr. Landau?"

"Yes, that's right. He was wearing gloves. Black gloves. The thin cotton kind you'd wear for gardening."

He paused to scratch again at his notepad and Natalie waited uneasily. She suddenly felt too warm in her belted gray cashmere sweater. Detective Henderson's manner reminded her, uncomfortably, of her childhood neighbor, Mr. Petroskey, who spent every spring accusing her or Dana of picking his precious tulips.

"Is it valuable? Your amulet?"

The question jolted her, and her mind raced in a panic.

How was she to answer *that*? She had no idea yet whether it was valuable or not. And if she told him it might be, he'd ask her where she'd gotten it—and then what? She'd have to tell him that her sister, the famous newscaster, had sent it from

Iraq. Without knowing its provenance, the last thing she'd want
was to inadvertently get Dana in hot water or to embarrass her
network.

Natalie's thoughts flew ahead. What if Henderson followed
up—and it turned out the pendant *was* an antiquity and valuable? That Dana actually *had* unwittingly sent her something
looted from the Iraq museum?

Her throat went dry. Dana's career could go up in flames like
one of the car-bombed armored vehicles she reported about.

*I can't risk it. If there'd been some horrible mistake, it can
be taken care of quietly. Diplomatically. Not tossed in the lap
of an NYPD detective on a wild goose chase.*

"No, it's not valuable at all." The lie just sprang from her
lips. And then it was too late to take it back.

It's a very small lie, Natalie told herself. *If it even is a lie.* It
wasn't as if Henderson needed the truth about the amulet for
his investigation. She didn't even know what the truth *was* yet.

"It's just a trinket . . . a souvenir." Natalie's throat felt so
parched she was surprised her voice didn't creak.

"So why did you bother coming all the way back for it?" the
detective pressed.

She sat up straighter in her chair. "Because it's a gift. One
that has sentimental value for me. Believe me, Detective, I never
would have come back here tonight had I known there was going
to be a break-in."

"I heard you handled yourself pretty well," he said slowly.
"You described the intruder as a large man, approximately six
feet what?—six two, six four? One hundred eighty pounds?
And he attacked you. You don't look much the worse for wear."

"My Krav Maga training kicked in."

He twitched the cigar from his pocket and began chewing
on its tip, his disconcerting eyes never leaving her face. "And
just how did you come to be so proficient at an Israeli self-
defense technique employed by government agencies and police
forces?"

Natalie stole a furtive glance at her watch: 11:30 P.M. She'd
been sitting across from him for nearly two hours. Her head
ached, her wrist was already purpling, and she was emotionally

drained. All she wanted was to get home, strip off her work clothes, and climb into a hot bath with a glass of wine.

"I picked it up in Israel a few years ago," she answered tautly. "When I was working on some archaeological digs."

She wasn't about to tell him her life story. Or what had happened to Maren Svendborg in Israel, the horrific attack at Bet She'an that had robbed Natalie of her friend and impelled her to learn Krav Maga.

"Are we almost finished, Detective?"

"One more question, Dr. Landau."

Natalie braced herself.

"Are you by any chance related to the journalist Dana Landau? The one in Iraq? You look a bit like her."

"You're very observant, Detective. She's my sister."

"Brave lady." He tossed down his pencil and almost smiled. "I guess it runs in the family."

"Our parents died when Dana and I were teenagers. We had to be brave." She leaned forward. "May I go now, Detective? It's a long trip back to Brooklyn."

"Brooklyn, is it?" He scratched his head. "Just sit tight a minute, Dr. Landau. I'll get Officer Lopez to drive you home."

It was a half hour later that Natalie finally reached her Williamsburg apartment. Her legs felt like jelly. She smelled onions and cumin lingering in the hallway, probably from Juan and Peter's kitchen. Normally, Natalie loved the aromas wafting from their apartment, one night Thai, one night Moroccan, but tonight food was the furthest thing from her mind. Every muscle ached, her scalp throbbed, and she was mentally exhausted from the questioning by both the police and her superiors.

She grimaced, remembering the way Detective Henderson had studied her with those piercing eyes until she felt like confessing—even though she'd done nothing wrong.

Had he sensed she was holding something back? God, she hoped not. The only thing he hadn't asked her—yet—was to go to the precinct house and look through endless books of mug shots. She'd probably been spared that only because the intruder had worn a mask, and all she'd likely be able to identify was a pair of slitted brown eyes.

As far as anyone had been able to determine, the intruder hadn't targeted any of the exhibits. But he had knocked out and hog-tied a security guard. And there was evidence he'd searched two storage rooms. But oddly, nothing appeared to be missing.

Then what was he looking for in the offices? she wondered, as she fitted the first of her keys into its lock. Natalie stepped wearily inside and flicked on the light switch, awakening her tiny living room from sleep. *A private detective hired by Dennis's wife wouldn't have riffled through the storage rooms. And he wouldn't have attacked a security guard—or me.*

She kicked off her shoes, resisting the urge to throw herself down on the overstuffed chintz sofa and simply close her eyes until morning. Instead, she padded across the wood floor to the galley kitchen, and removed the open bottle of Riesling from her fridge.

Wineglass in hand, she made her way to the bathroom to toss bath salts into the claw-foot tub. As she turned the water on full blast and took her first sip of the Riesling, she thought she heard her phone ringing above the rush of water.

With a sigh she hurried back to the kitchen and checked the number on the incoming call. She didn't recognize it.

"Hello?" She took another grateful sip of the wine.

"Dr. Landau? This is Brandon Wedermeyer from MSNBC. I'm calling about your sister."

Natalie's heart froze. "Yes?" *Oh, God.* "Is Dana alright?" *Please, let her be all right.*

"I'm very sorry to be the one to tell you this, but I have some terrible news. I'm afraid your sister has died."

"Died . . ." Her voice trailed off. An icy chill stabbed through her stomach, and she suddenly felt weightless. "That's . . . impossible."

"I'm very sorry, Dr. Landau. Dana has been killed. Her body was discovered less than twenty minutes ago. I don't have all the details yet, but I wanted you to know before it leaked to the media."

Killed? Natalie's mind balked, refusing to absorb the words. She felt like she was going to throw up, and she pressed her midriff against the granite countertop.

"She can't be dead. I saw her on TV yesterday." She was babbling. But she couldn't stop. Just as she couldn't stop her knees from shaking. "There must be a mistake, tell me there's been a mistake."

"Dr. Landau, is there anyone there with you? Are you all right?"

"My sister can't be dead." Her voice broke then. "She's all I have left. Was it a car bomb? I didn't hear anything about a car bomb—"

"No, it wasn't a car bomb. It . . . she . . . I'm sorry, there's no easy way to say this, but it appears she was murdered. In her room at the villa. It happened sometime between her return last night from Kirkuk and early this morning. Her crew became concerned when she didn't meet up with them. The military is investigating—"

The wineglass slipped from her fingers and cracked into a thousand pieces on the floor.

12

A fierce March wind whipped through Salem Fields Cemetery as Natalie lifted the shovel and heaved the first mound of dirt onto her sister's casket. Hearing that dull thud, seeing the dirt scatter across the simple wooden casket, she fought back the sob that burned in her throat. The last time she'd done this, it had been a mellow autumn morning. She and Dana had been teenagers standing shoulder to shoulder, ceremoniously scooping the earth onto their parents' caskets.

The rabbi had told them back then that the *mitzvah* of helping to bury a loved one was the most unselfish good deed of all, because it was an act of kindness that could never be repaid.

But this was wrong. It was wrong that she should be burying Dana. Her sister should be on the air tonight, her hair tousled by the dry desert breeze, her voice crisp with authority. Instead, she was here in the ground beside their parents, and Natalie was watching in numb disbelief as friends and relatives stepped up, one at a time, to grasp the shovel and toss dirt into Dana's open grave.

Afterward, she stumbled toward the limousine, barely registering the murmurs of sympathy echoing around her. She was chilled and empty and had never felt so alone in her life. First her parents had died too young, and now Dana's life had been cut short, too.

Aunt Leonora took her arm as the crowd of mourners began to disperse. "Rosalie has everything set up at your apartment, dear. Your neighbors, that nice Peter and Juan, brought over some extra folding chairs."

Rosalie was Natalie's older cousin, Aunt Leonora's daughter. As kids, Rosalie, Natalie, and Dana had been inseparable. Of all her cousins, Rosalie was the most family-oriented, the one who knew how to make matzoh balls and brisket and noodle kugel, who hosted all the Passover seders and remembered everyone's anniversaries and birthdays.

"So many people," Natalie muttered. "I hope they'll all fit in my apartment—"

Her voice trailed off as she felt a tap on her arm and turned. She didn't recognize the tall lean man of about forty who stood beside her.

"Sorry to meet you under these circumstances, Natalie. I'm Jim D'Amato—I was a colleague of your sister's at MSNBC. I wanted to offer my condolences."

D'Amato. Natalie knew the name well. She'd never heard Dana, or anyone else from the network, call their bureau chief by his first name, and had always pictured him as graying and avuncular. Yet the hard-driving superior Dana had been desperate to impress was anything but. Standing beside her, the wind tousling his dark black hair, he looked vigorous and athletic, with the tough good looks and lean build of an Italian race-car driver.

"Dana had great respect for you. Thank you for coming."

"No thanks necessary."

But as his gaze locked with hers, she caught something in his intelligent pewter eyes—something beyond polite sympathy. Worry. Hesitation. She sensed he wanted to say something more.

Before she could wonder what that might be, she felt Aunt Leonora leaning in close. "We really should go to the car," the older woman whispered. "People will be waiting for us."

Natalie's stomach churned all the way back to the apartment. And while friends and family swirled around her, trying to get her to eat egg salad and fruit and coffee cake, to sit and rest, her mind was tumbling with a single question.

Why would anyone want to kill Dana?

Baghdad

Aslam Hameed stumbled up from his bed and down his wide marble staircase in a slowly lifting fog of sleep. His alarm at the insistent ringing of his doorbell grew as he made his way to the peephole. *Who could be rousing him at the ghastly hour of 4:00 A.M.? Who would dare . . . ?*

Terror swallowed him as he saw the glittering pair of eyes staring back at him. *Blue eyes. The eyes of Hasan Sabouri.*

Aslam's hand froze momentarily on the door handle. The towering Iranian was the last person he'd expected to see at his door tonight. He didn't want to open it, but he had to.

Hasan cut off the welcoming words Aslam was trying to muster and pushed past him into the foyer. Aslam Hameed shuddered as he caught the glint of the curved scimitar in the Iranian's right hand.

"You have failed me. You have cost me the Eye of Dawn."

Aslam Hameed's swarthy face paled at the depth of Sabouri's rage. "This man . . . Yusef . . . ," he stuttered. "He's one of my best. How was I to know . . . ?"

Hasan Sabouri's arm swung up, flicking the long blade against Hameed's throat.

Struggling not to cower in his own grand foyer, Hameed couldn't decide if he was more terrified of the scimitar painfully nicking his flesh or of Hasan's cursed blue eyes boring into his.

"Please. I will get it back. There is still time. . . ."

"You are mistaken. Your time is over." The blade burned deeper, and Hameed could feel the warmth of his own blood as it leaked down his neck. Still, he couldn't look away from the eyes.

"Please, I beg you. . . ."

The knife angled deeper.

Upstairs, his wife and children slept. As death began to suck the strength from his knees, he prayed silently to Allah that they wouldn't stir, wouldn't put themselves in the path of the blade. Or be doomed by the gaze of the man who possessed the evil eye.

He had no hope for himself.

One hour later, in a garbage-strewn alley on the outskirts of Baghdad, Yusef faced the same man. The same blade. The same eyes.

He proved not as stoic as his employer, Aslam Hameed. Yusef quaked as the Iranian glowered, impaling him with those strange accursed eyes.

Frantically, Yusef dug through his pockets and yanked out the dead woman's necklace. He thrust it toward Sabouri with trembling hands.

"This was the only thing the American reporter had. Believe me, in the name of Allah, may he be praised, I questioned her. I searched her room—truly, she had nothing, knew nothing. . . ."

"So you give me this?" Hasan Sabouri sneered, holding up the delicate amulet on its broken silver chain. With his other hand, he tapped Yusef's chest with the blood-caked scimitar. "The Hand of Fatima in place of the Eye of Dawn?"

"I will find it. I promise you." Yusef couldn't keep his eyes from flicking down toward the blade. "I will do whatever you ask—anything!" he begged. "Tell me what you want."

"What I want? I want you dead," Hasan whispered slowly in the stench of the alley.

Yusef's heart raced in his great chest. "Please. I am worth more to you alive than dead. I can help you find the Eye of Dawn. I will not sleep, I will not rest, until—"

The blade slashed downward into his right hand, nearly severing it with the first blow. Yusef's screams circled through the dank air of the alley. But only for a moment. As he bent to clasp his dangling hand, the Iranian plunged the scimitar into the back of Yusef's neck.

It took but three furious strokes to drown the screams, reducing them to gurgles.

13

Natalie had no idea how she made it through the first night of shivah, the initial period of mourning. The day had seemed interminable. And by the time the *ma'ariv,* the evening prayer service, concluded, and people began to ebb away like shadows of which she was only vaguely aware, her head was throbbing. There had been so many people, so many stories about Dana. Dana as a cautious tow-headed child, as her high school's klutziest cheerleader, as a surprisingly mature journalist gutsy enough to shout her reports above the thunder of bombs exploding around her.

But no one else knew Dana the way Natalie did. As the kid sister who'd giggled uncontrollably when their *zayde* had hidden the *afikomen* in the toilet tank one year at the Passover seder. The sister who'd covered for Natalie when she got drunk at a friend's high school party. The sister who'd clung to her in numb shock after the sudden death of their parents.

And the sister who'd known for months that Natalie's fiancé had cheated on her, but had kept it from her until Natalie had been struck in the face with the truth herself, when she'd rushed home early from an anthropology conference. She'd sailed in, ready to jump Adam's bones, only to find him in their tiny aqua-tiled shower stall slowly lathering the ditzy single mom who lived downstairs.

Dana had known. She'd seen them together having dinner, snuggling. But Adam had sworn to her it didn't mean anything—it would never happen again. And Dana had kept his secret—leaving me in the dark.

Natalie remembered too well the rage and humiliation that had consumed her when Dana confessed to keeping silent. Natalie had felt more betrayed by Dana than by Adam. Now, twisting a cocktail napkin ever tighter in her grip, she wished she could erase the harsh words she'd hurled at her sister and swallow back the unchecked anger that had led to their estrangement. *God, if only I could take back those months that stretched without a word between us and fill them with everything we'll never get the chance to say.*

"Natalie—Natalie?"

She jerked herself from her reverie. Jim D'Amato had taken the seat beside her on the sofa. His expression was apologetic. In the kitchen a few feet away, she could hear Aunt Leonora washing the platters that had held sliced tomatoes, onion, tuna salad, and bagels. She was surprised to discover everyone else had gone.

"Sorry, I missed what you said. I was just thinking about Dana . . ." She shook her head and attempted a smile. "Of course I was, what else would I be thinking about?"

"Dana was one of the good ones." He offered a half smile. "And I don't mean just professionally, but personally, too. She had the open heart of a child and the courage of a Marine. Everyone who ever knew her will miss her."

"Thank you." Natalie met his gaze, expecting him to say good night, but he remained seated. Once again she sensed that there was something else he wanted to say.

"You know something about her killer, don't you?" she guessed suddenly. "Have they caught him?"

"Not that I know of, Natalie—not yet." Tension lined his forehead. Though he was dressed comfortably, in a black sweater and a sport coat, the tautness along his square jawline told her he was on edge.

"I'm not here representing the network," he told her. "I've been on sick leave for a couple of months now." He placed his hands on his knees. "Did you know that Dana went to Baghdad in my place?"

Natalie stared at him blankly. "What do you mean?"

"That Iraq assignment was mine originally . . . until I screwed up."

"I don't understand."

"I've been dealing with a personal problem." He shook his head. "Residual effects of the metal bits I still carry around thanks to a suicide bomber during my tenure as Jerusalem bureau chief. It's left me battling an addiction to painkillers."

Natalie shook her head. "I'd heard that Dana was vying with several other reporters for the chance to go to Iraq, but I didn't know you were the network's first choice. So . . ." She swallowed. "You're saying Dana wouldn't have been in Iraq if . . ."

"If I hadn't gotten my hands on more Vicodin—and relapsed. I had seniority." He looked away briefly. When he turned back, his expression was neutral, though he was fiddling with the plain gold wedding band on his finger. "At any rate, that's not the reason I stayed behind to talk to you."

Natalie stood up. "I'm sorry. I really need to get some sleep." What she really needed was time to absorb what he was saying. *If he hadn't screwed up, Dana might still be alive?* She felt chilled. Sick. As she started to walk away, he reached out for her arm. "Wait, Natalie. Please."

Urgency lurked in D'Amato's eyes as he rose to face her. "I'm here because I cared about Dana, and her cameraman, Rusty Sutherland. I'm worried, because Rusty is still missing."

His words caught her by surprise. *Missing?* "I knew he was late in getting home the other day. But I didn't realize . . ." She'd forgotten all about Rusty once she got the call about Dana.

D'Amato nodded. In the flickering light of the red memorial candle burning beside them, his eyes were unreadable. "I know . . . you have a million other things running through your mind. This is a horrific time for you, and I'm sorry to bring this up right now . . . but Rusty's still unaccounted for. His wife filed a missing persons report yesterday. And my reporter's gut wants to know if his disappearance is in any way tied to what happened to Dana."

"Think about it," he continued, as her eyes widened. "They were both in Iraq, working together closely, living in the same small villa. What are the odds of Dana being murdered and Rusty going missing at virtually the same time?"

Natalie shook her head, dazed. "Are you implying that Rusty's disappearance and Dana's murder are connected?"

He grimaced. "I'm just exploring the possibility. Did you notice anything unusual, anything off, in your recent communications with Dana? Was there anything she said—or didn't say?"

Natalie fought a fresh wave of tears. "I haven't *had* many recent communications with Dana. Our last real conversation was over a year ago."

D'Amato stood quietly, waiting. If he felt surprise he hid it behind those inscrutable gray eyes.

"We had a falling out," she said quietly, tears welling. "She kept something from me. I felt betrayed . . . and I lost it. Then Dana lost it, too. We were both so angry." She shook her head miserably. "And now . . ."

It took all of her effort to hold back the sobs that threatened to roll from her. D'Amato looked away as she fought to regain control.

Her last contact with Dana had actually been the note accompanying the pendant that Rusty had delivered to the museum. It was the second time that Dana had reached out to her since Natalie had sent her the *hamsa,* both for protection and as a peace offering. Dana had called to thank her, and though their conversation had been brief and stilted, it had been a start, a small move toward reconciliation.

Then the pendant and Dana's note had buoyed Natalie's hope that Dana was ready to forgive her, that in their next conversation they could both put their anger behind them.

"Now I'll never have the chance to talk to her again." Natalie's voice was barely audible.

D'Amato cleared his throat. "That has to make your loss even rougher. I didn't know. I'm sorry."

She drew a breath and pressed her hands to her temples. "I just can't concentrate right now. I don't have answers for you. You'll have to excuse me . . ."

"Of course." He stepped back, looking disappointed. "I'm sorry to have upset you." He dug into his breast pocket, pulled out a business card, and handed it to her. "Please call me if you think of anything. Maybe Dana spoke to your aunt, or another relative. In a few days, when things start to settle down, someone might remember something."

Without glancing at the card, Natalie nodded, then slid it under the candy tray on the coffee table. She heard D'Amato say a quiet good night to Aunt Leonora and take his leave.

But after her aunt had kissed her good-bye, and Natalie had changed into her softest jeans and a white T-shirt, she couldn't stop thinking about what D'Amato had said about Rusty.

Where could Rusty be?

She'd missed seeing him at the museum by a matter of minutes. If she'd been there, would he have told her something that might help her make sense of this nightmare? Something that might help her understand why her sister was dead?

Suddenly the silence in her apartment was unbearable. She stared at the borrowed metal folding chairs stacked against the wall, waiting to be set out again tomorrow for *mincha,* the late afternoon prayer service. Friends and family would return for the next four days to talk and pray and comfort her.

But as she watched the memorial candle glimmer in its tall red glass, Natalie was not comforted. She sat slumped on her sofa, barefoot, red-eyed, and remembering the awful moment when she'd first viewed Dana's body at the funeral home.

Through her tears she'd noticed that the silver necklace she'd sent her sister for protection was missing. On hearing Dana was going to Iraq, Natalie had taken apart their mother's cocktail ring and used the amethysts and pearl to design the special *hamsa* for her. It was an olive branch—one Dana had accepted.

Dana had told Aunt Leonora that she'd wear it, even to bed, until she returned. And she must have. Natalie had spotted it glistening at her throat during her reports.

But the funeral director had told Natalie he hadn't seen it.

So where was the necklace? Had Dana lost it? Had it been stolen?

If she'd had it on when she was attacked, Natalie wondered bleakly, *would it have protected her?*

She was suddenly possessed by an overwhelming need to have that *hamsa* back. Perhaps, she thought, it was packed away with Dana's things, still en route from Iraq.

Closing her eyes, she could almost hear D'Amato's words replaying in her head. *"They were working closely together. What are the odds of Dana being murdered and Rusty going missing at virtually the same time?"*

Were Dana's murder and Rusty's disappearance a coincidence—or a connection?

Possibilities spun through her brain. Had the two of them uncovered something over there, stumbled onto something that someone didn't want known? Had they been on the verge of breaking a major story?

But if that were the case, Rusty wouldn't have left for home. He'd have delayed his R & R and stayed to finish up whatever they were working on.

She opened her eyes and drew her knees up under her. Rusty *had* come home, though. He'd landed back in the States, called his wife, and told her he had only one quick stop to make on his way home.

And that stop was the museum.

To bring me the pendant.

Her heart turned over.

She jumped up, hurried to her handbag on the desk, and retrieved the pouch that had lain inside it since the night of the attack at the Devereaux. She'd found it too painful to look at since receiving the news of Dana's death.

Now, staring at the sparkling jeweled eye, she began to wonder if this pendant was the connection D'Amato was looking for.

After a moment she set the necklace on the coffee table, scooped up D'Amato's card from beneath the candy tray, and reached for her phone.

"You could be right, D'Amato. There may be a connection. Can you come back to my apartment right now?"

14

JFK Airport

Hasan Sabouri hid his impatience to get through customs. He was eager to retrieve what he'd come for and get out of the United States. But he was practiced at being polite. Businesslike. Harmless.

He was traveling under one of his assumed identities, of course, since his was a name most likely on every terrorist watch list in the world. It amused him that people in America met his eyes. It was a curious sensation. At home most feared to gaze at him—and even more, they feared that his gaze would fall on them.

In the Middle East many people knew what he'd done to his mother. The curse he was born with had first shown itself when he was barely ten months old. He'd been hungry and crying. His mother was busy, and she hadn't come quickly enough. His older brother, Farshid, had witnessed what happened next. When their mother had finally lifted him from the rug, Hasan's blue eyes had blazed at her with fury. A moment later she staggered to her knees, thrusting him into his brother's arms at the last moment as she toppled to the floor.

The doctor had said it was her heart. But everyone in the village had known it was the evil eye. *His* evil eye.

From ancient times his people had believed that those born with blue eyes possessed a curse and could inflict harm on others, willingly or without intention. The death of his mother following his baleful stare had been the first indication that he possessed this power. Many more deaths and injuries had followed.

People had whispered about it, whispered about *him,* all his life. And the stories had spread, all of them true. Everyone he loved—his uncle, his best friend, his bride, Fatima, everyone except, thus far, his brother Farshid—had been stricken in some way by his glance. Ill luck, ill health, ill fortune had befallen those in his path, so men avoided his gaze and shielded their eyes, even at the mention of his name, while women gasped in fear when he passed them on the street.

He was a victim of his own evil eye as well. With his life becoming one of increasing isolation, his heart had grown cold toward those who shunned him, and guarded toward those he loved.

Still, he relished the power his eyes held over his enemies. He almost smiled remembering how terrified Aslam Hameed and his inept assassin Yusef had been when he'd tracked them down in Iraq. They'd both been so paralyzed with fear of his gaze that he'd barely needed to drive in the knife before their cowards' hearts gave out.

Their bungling had cost the Guardians of the Khalifah too great a prize—neither had deserved the honor of a martyr's death. So they had died in terror and disgrace for killing the American journalist before she divulged the location of the Eye of Dawn. All that was left of her was the tiny silver and cloisonné Hand of Fatima she'd worn at her throat. It was in his pocket now, a lucky pearl at its center. Thinking of the Bahraini legend his wife had told him—that pearls had the power to help find lost objects—Hasan prayed that this minor trophy would lead him to the real treasure.

It was now his mission to personally hunt down and claim the Eye of Dawn for Allah. How fitting that one afflicted with the evil eye should now be the one destined to capture the most legendary amulet of them all—the evil eye pendant that concealed and protected the Eye of Dawn.

The curse he was born with held a strange kind of power,

one he had grown to relish. Yet, here in this accursed country, no one recognized it. Any dark-skinned Arab with blue eyes could walk among these unbelievers and not a one of them flinched or averted their gaze.

Fools.

The customs agent looked him in the eye, handed back his passport, and waved him through. Carrying his overnight bag easily, his tall, well-honed body sheathed in a dark European-cut suit, Hasan made his way to the taxi line.

There were only three days left. He needed to be in Jerusalem before that deadline to check the bombs in place beneath Al-Haram al-Sharif and witness the culmination of the Guardians' plan to destroy it, which would trigger all-out war with Israel. He needed to be in Jerusalem to watch the hoisting of the Palestinian flag above the Noble Sanctuary—*or what was left of it after the explosion.*

Then he would join in the triumphant march through Jerusalem's bloody streets as the Guardians of the Khalifah reclaimed the sacred city of Al Quds for Allah.

Hasan smiled coldly as he slid into the taxi that had sidled up against the curb, picturing the khalifate restored, with the earthly successor to Muhammad once again in place to oversee religious and civil matters throughout the Islamic realm. The glory of Islam would flourish once more, aided by the power contained within the Eye of Dawn.

The West's conventional and nuclear armaments would pale beside the new breed of weapons the Guardians would craft through harnessing the Eye. Soon Islam would dominate the globe, subjugating leaders from the Pope to the U.S. President.

"*Ahlan wa sahlan.*" ("You are welcome, among friends.") The Arab taxi driver, a member of the Guardians' New York cell, smiled, but refrained from looking directly at Hasan in the rearview mirror.

"*Ahlan biik, Khalil.*" ("Welcome to you.") Hasan replied.

"Where are we going first, my esteemed brother?" The driver flicked on the turn signal and merged effortlessly into traffic.

Hasan leaned his shoulders back against the seat, visualizing the Eye of Dawn, remembering that the overeager young Duoaud had told him that the woman reporter had a sister in New York. That her cameraman had flown to that city the morning after Duoaud had seen her showing him the Eye of Dawn.

"Brooklyn," he said. "Take me to the Williamsburg address of the woman my brother told your men to watch. It's time we made the acquaintance of Dr. Natalie Landau."

15

D'Amato frowned at the amulet Natalie placed in his palm. It had been an hour since she'd called, and he'd driven straight back to her apartment. She'd been filling him in on what little she knew about the pendant Rusty had brought her from Dana— from Iraq.

"What is there about this necklace that could be valuable enough to kill for?" he asked. "Its history?"

"Possibly. I'm convinced it's ancient, which makes it valuable to historians and collectors. How valuable I can't even guess without studying it further." Natalie pushed away thoughts of her sister having held the necklace just days ago. She leaned back against the sofa, staring at the ceiling, trying to quell her tears.

"Maybe this should wait a few days . . ."

"No. I want to deal with this now. This passed from Dana's hands to Rusty's. Now she's dead and he's disappeared. If it's because of this pendant, I owe it to Dana to find out." She sat up, staring at D'Amato.

"The other night, when I first looked it over, I had the impression there could be something hidden inside."

D'Amato shifted it from hand to hand. "It does have quite a bit of heft to it." He studied it more closely. "I don't see any way to open it."

"I know. And there's no obvious seam of solder, either, which would seem to indicate there's nothing inside."

"So how can we find out for certain? X-rays? Do you have some kind of equipment at the museum?"

Natalie shook her head. "Not the kind of equipment we'd need. The only way I can think of to peek inside is with the help of archaeometry."

"Archaeometry?"

She focused her gaze on him, forcing herself deliberately to set aside her grief, to use her brain and her training to help make sense of what had happened to Dana. "Archaeometry is where science meets archaeology," she said quietly.

She pushed herself to her feet and crossed the room to the coffee table. D'Amato watched as she tugged a thick volume from the pile of books stacked on its bottom ledge. Her smooth dark hair swung across her face as she bent over the pages, momentarily hiding the sorrow he'd seen burning in her eyes.

"Just to warn you, science isn't my strong suit," he told her, setting the amulet on the coffee table beside an antique bronze tray crudely embossed with elephants. She was a collector of small objects, he noticed. Mostly Middle Eastern items. There were more elephants—of varied sizes and composition—marching single file along the tall, narrow table flanking the back of her sofa. Every one of them had a raised trunk, signifying good luck, he knew, in the same way as the glasses stored mouth up in his grandmother's cupboard.

The two-tiered shelf on her living room wall was brimming with an assortment of small objects, all made of what looked to him like ancient, iridescent Roman glass. He'd seen plenty of it in Israeli gift shops. Among the items, he noted, was a chipped cruet, a shallow bowl that in its day might have held salt or spices, a cracked flask that might once have contained olive oil or perfume—each cast from the opaque glass and shimmering in varied shades of pale blue and sea-foam green.

On the long wall behind the desk she'd strung an assortment of unusual necklaces—some thick with dangling silver coins, others aflame with brightly colored beads threaded onto thin gold hoops. One with tightly coiled golden wires reminded him of the elaborate jewelry he'd once seen adorning a Yemenite bride back when he was in Jerusalem as bureau chief for MSNBC.

The bright, exotic items were an interesting contrast to the overstuffed shabby chic sofa and the floral, chintz-covered, over sized chair she'd positioned across from the coffee table. And to the bookcase filled with an eclectic collage of reading material. Graphic novels butted up against archaeology texts, collections of Norse mythology, a half dozen Stephen King novels, folktales from around the world, and the complete Jane Austen. Natalie Landau appeared to have a foot in each world—the ancient and the modern—and the ability to move between them with the same assurance with which she was searching the pages of her book.

"Think of archaeometry as the equivalent of MRI, CT, and PET scan—but for rocks and gems," she told him, finally looking up. He could see her pushing through her fatigue and grief, focused now on her area of expertise. "I gather you've heard of carbon dating?" She didn't wait for him to reply. "Since every living organism emits carbon-14, scientists are able to date that organism by measuring how long it has been emitting carbon."

"So this leather . . . ?" He plucked up the pouch. "It's possible to pinpoint how long ago this animal skin was tanned?"

"Definitely, except we'd have to destroy a portion of it in the process." She broke off, waiting as he probed inside the pouch with a finger.

"A few grains of sand in here . . . ," he muttered.

Natalie turned back to the book, quickly flipping through the pages once more. "But carbon dating is just one example— the most commonly known—of numerous scientific tests we can apply to archaeological finds . . ."

"Take a look at this," D'Amato interrupted.

She tore her attention from the book to look at him. He had turned the pouch inside out and was peering at something along the bottom seam.

Why didn't I think to turn it inside out?

Intrigued, she set the book aside and moved closer for a better look at the suede interior.

"It looks like an inscription." He was squinting at two tiny ows of script.

"Let me see. It could be an ancient stamp . . . or a rademark . . ." Natalie felt a surge of energy.

"Looks sort of like Hebrew."

"Hmmm . . . could be." Natalie leaned in, trying to discern he tiny characters. "Or it could be Aramaic. The two sets of characters are very similar. Actually, the Hebrew alphabet developed from Aramaic. So if this *is* Aramaic . . ."

Without finishing her sentence, Natalie jumped up and hurried to a kitchen drawer. She returned with a magnifying glass.

"And if it is Aramaic—then what?" D'Amato prodded.

"Then this pouch, at least, could prove to be very old."

"How old?"

She raised a slim eyebrow. "Let's just say Aramaic was the language Jesus spoke. And it was the primary language used to write the Jewish Talmud."

"You're talking to a lapsed Catholic." He grimaced. "If the nuns taught us anything about the Talmud, I probably had *Penthouse* hidden inside my comparative religions book that day. But it's a compendium of Jewish laws, right?"

She plucked the pouch from him, thinking back to some of her undergraduate course work. "That's a fair summary. I'd describe it as an encyclopedia of Jewish civil and religious law, along with ethical teachings," she answered. "It expounds on the Torah, recounting the sages' debates and commentaries on its meaning. It's actually many volumes, written by hundreds of Jewish sages over the course of four hundred years."

"And the time frame . . . ?"

She met his gaze steadily. "Two thousand years ago."

He digested that a moment. "So, roughly the same time period as Jesus."

"Give or take. The sages began compiling the Talmud after the destruction of the Second Temple in Jerusalem in A.D. 70. Up until then, all of the Jewish laws and traditions were passed down orally. But once the Romans destroyed the Second Temple—taking most of the Jews off to Rome as slaves—the sages decided it was high time they committed all of the oral teachings to writing."

"To preserve them . . . ," D'Amato mused.

"Exactly. For future generations. Particularly because the Jewish people was so scattered by then. Rome wasn't the first captivity. Many Jews were carried off to Babylon when the First Temple was destroyed six hundred years earlier—and a good portion of them decided to stay on, even after the Persians eventually freed them. And, of course, there were some Jews who had never left Judea."

She bent over the pouch with the magnifying glass. "So it was imperative to put the laws in writing so that the Jews who were now separated from one another would remain on the same page . . . so to speak. . . ."

Her voice trailed off. She peered intently at the faded lettering swimming beneath the powerful prism. The brief handwritten inscription seemed to begin with the Hebrew letter *tzadi*, the alphabet's *ts* sound. Still, Natalie knew from her archaeological work in Israel how similar some Aramaic letters were to Hebrew. This character could be from either alphabet.

"Can you tell? Is it Aramaic?"

"No, damn it." She bit her lip. "Not without consulting someone proficient in both languages."

"Can you at least read what it says?"

"I only recognize a few letters on this first line. This one looks like a *resh*—that's the *R* of the Hebrew alphabet. But it could be either an Aramaic *R* or *Y*, because those characters are written similarly. The others here are too faded for me to make out."

"Faded—you mean with age?"

"Or from the elements. But look." Natalie's voice hitched with excitement. "Part of the second line is darker and easier to read. I can make out a *shin*—and the word ends in a *resh*, like the one on the line above it, but the rest . . ." She shook her head in frustration.

Suddenly she glanced up, eyeing him with new respect. "What made you think to look inside? I was so caught up in the pendant, I didn't really focus on the pouch. The outside of it

idn't strike me as unusual, other than that it was painted to
imic the pendant. It's so simply constructed—just a basic
ircle of leather with a drawstring to close it—I didn't pay any
ttention to the inside."

"I'm a journalist." He shrugged. "It's my job to pay atten-
ion. To look at things from all sides. We like to turn things on
heir heads, and inside out. But go back a minute to what you
vere saying about testing the gemstones in the pendant. What
vere you planning to show me in that book?"

Natalie set down the pouch, reached for the book, and forced
herself to change gears. "I was starting to tell you that in the
ast we had to chip off a fragment of a gemstone if we wanted
o check its authenticity. We'd need a piece of it to test its chem-
cal properties in order to determine with certainty what it was.
But now, with the help of powder X-ray diffraction analysis and
aman spectroscopy, we're able to define exactly what a sample
s—and so much more. We can not only pinpoint the identity
nd age of a gem, but we can zero in on its place of origin—
ometimes even the mine it came from—and all without dis-
mounting it, or doing it any damage."

"In other words, you've got ways of peeking inside this
hing without sawing it open. How do you do that? Laser scan-
ers?"

Natalie skimmed to a section halfway into the book before
holding out the page for his perusal. "Here's how. Check out
hese photos."

D'Amato took the book from her and studied the page. He'd
changed from the sport coat and sweater he'd worn earlier into
traight-legged jeans, a khaki shirt, and a light beige windbreaker. Natalie noticed the laserlike concentration with which
he scrutinized the series of photos taken from various angles.
They were close-ups of a primitive statue studded with tiny red
gems.

"This artifact was found five years ago in a cave in Iran."
She ran her finger below the lines of text. "The gemstones on it
were dated and analyzed using ion beam techniques—particle-
nduced X-ray emission, or PIXE for short. PIXE determined
hey were definitely rubies and contained inclusions found only

in certain regions in the Middle East. Archaeometry pinpointed the age and the provenance, proving this statue indeed came from ancient Mesopotamia. And—it was all done without removing a single stone or submitting the statue to the damaging effects of chemical analysis."

"Pretty impressive." He picked up the pendant. "So where do we go to analyze this?"

Where indeed . . . ?

Natalie hesitated, chewing on her lip. *How about to the police?* she thought. Part of her wanted to call Detective Henderson back and simply hand the pendant over, but that meant facing ramifications from the police and her employers for having lied to him. She might even lose her job because she'd tried to protect her sister.

"There's an Ion Beam lab at UAlbany, but I'm not sure that's the next step," she said reluctantly. "If Dana was *killed* and Rusty is *missing* on account of this pendant, maybe we should go to the police instead. Although that might prove problematic. . . ."

She explained how she'd dodged Henderson's questions about the amulet, allowing the detective to conclude that Ski Mask hadn't been after it. "Because at the time, I never suspected he'd broken in because of the pendant. It's only now that I'm starting to wonder if that was his purpose all along. If he knew that Rusty had brought it to the museum . . ."

"Forget about the police." D'Amato snapped the book shut with a thud. His eyes darkened with purpose, like a hunting dog's after picking up a scent. "If this pendant is linked to an international murder, and to an interstate missing persons alert, and if it *is* an antiquity taken from Iraq, then the scope of any investigation will go way beyond the NYPD. I've got a better idea."

She stared at him, uneasy, waiting.

"We call a contact of mine at the FBI."

He began scrolling through the list of contacts in his cell phone. He paused and glanced at her, tacitly waiting for her assent.

The FBI. Natalie felt numb. She looked at the pendant and

the pouch with its tiny inscription, seeing them through bleary eyes.

Dana died for this? Why? How? I need to know.

"Go ahead," she heard herself say in a voice that sounded like a wan imitation of her own. "Call the FBI."

16

FBI Special Agent Luther Tyrelle sat across from Natalie at the coffee shop, sipping his second cardboard cup of chai tea and studying her with a tiger's caramel-colored eyes. He was a muscular black man with a receding hairline and a neck roughly the circumference of a gallon-size milk jug.

In between sips he scribbled notes on the pages of a small, bound, government-issue notebook as Natalie outlined how she'd come to receive the pendant and her assessment of its possible value. D'Amato sat silently between them at the small round café table, barely touching his extra-large decaf, black, three sugars.

When Natalie fell silent, D'Amato inched his chair closer to the table. "My gut says there's a connection between Dana's contact with this pendant and her murder in Iraq, and with Rusty Sutherland's disappearance after he handed it off at the Devereaux." He pushed the pendant from the center of the table to Tyrelle. "Not to mention that on the same day, presto, we have someone breaking into the Devereaux—and it turns out the only thing the thief hones in on is this."

"An amulet designed to ward off the evil eye," Tyrelle mused, lifting it by the chain. "You wouldn't believe how many of these eyes I saw in Turkey last year. They've got blue-eye beads hanging everywhere." The FBI agent shook his head and set the necklace carefully down on the table. "Even their national airline has huge eyes painted on the tails of their jets. It's wild." He leaned forward.

"They're so leery of the evil eye that some villagers actually defaced ancient cave murals there—scratched the eyes right off the damn faces. They destroyed irreplaceable ancient art just to stop those eyes from staring out at them from the cave walls and maybe putting a hex on them."

"In Cappadocia." Natalie nodded. "I've been there. But the evil eye isn't a big deal only in Turkey, Agent Tyrelle. It's a powerful superstition in a substantial portion of the world. The belief that the evil eye has the power to inflict harm, and the use of amulets like this pendant and those beads you saw to ward it off, dates back even to biblical times.

"It's the reason people began painting their eyes back in ancient Egypt. It wasn't because Cleopatra thought it was glamorous. The Egyptians believed the curse from the evil eye entered the body through either the eyes or the mouth, so both men and women outlined their eyes with kohl for protection as a way of mirroring back the image of the eye. It's why Egyptian women tinted their lips—to prevent evil from entering through their mouths. Fear of the evil eye permeates the entire Middle East and the Mediterranean, and on into Africa and Western Europe."

"I've got news for you," Tyrelle said. "It reaches into South Carolina, too. I've seen plenty of pale turquoise window shutters down there outside of Charleston, where my grandmother and aunties live. They all paint their shutters blue, convinced that that color has the power to ward off evil spirits. I suppose that's the same sort of thing."

"Well, blue's the key color when it comes to the evil eye," Natalie said. "In the Arabic world people with blue eyes are often suspected of possessing the evil eye, probably one reason amulets to deflect the eye are predominantly blue as well. Sort of like fighting fire with fire."

D'Amato lifted his coffee cup. "Well, we Italians use red to protect us. You should see how many red-ribboned horseshoes my grandmother has hanging in her house in Long Island."

"Jews use red for protection, too," Natalie said. "There's a long tradition of tying red ribbons on their babies' cribs to protect the infants from the evil eye."

"Like the red kabbalah strings people wear on their wrists," Tyrelle commented.

There was a pause as the FBI agent drained the last of his tea. "We're getting offtrack here. Let's go back to this pendant. Just how valuable do you think it might be, Dr. Landau?"

"I don't have enough data yet to give you a figure, Agent Tyrelle. All I know is, it's not the trinket my sister thought it was."

"I think it's valuable enough that someone killed Dana because of it," D'Amato interjected, "and then tailed Sutherland all the way from Iraq to get their hands on it."

Tyrelle shook his head. "Slow down, D'Amato. You're making some pretty big leaps here." He leaned back in his chair. "First of all, we don't know that Sutherland has met with foul play. Maybe he's just gone AWOL. Maybe his disappearance has nothing to do with Dr. Landau's sister. On the other hand, maybe it does—but not because they both came in contact with this pendant. Could be the two of them made some enemies in the course of their work, or uncovered some dirt on somebody who didn't want it exposed—"

"Then explain why the thief in the Devereaux museum was interested in only one thing," D'Amato countered. "Getting this away from Natalie."

Tyrelle threw down his pen. "You've got speculation, D'Amato, that's all you've got. Not one shred of evidence. So I'm not clear what you're looking for from me."

"Just be a sounding board, Luther. Off-the-record."

"Go on."

Natalie and D'Amato exchanged glances. "Natalie has some legal concerns about this pendant," D'Amato told him.

"How so?" Tyrelle's brows drew together in a frown as Natalie hunched forward.

"I'm worried that it might be an antiquity that shouldn't have left Iraq. That's only a guess," she added quickly. "I have no idea how this necklace came into my sister's hands. Since her death, I haven't had a chance to check it against my museum's database of missing antiquities, but if it does show up there, I'd appreciate your assistance in giving it back."

The FBI agent exhaled and folded his arms. "So you're unofficially telling me this might be stolen property."

D'Amato shrugged. "More or less."

Frowning, Tyrelle answered him in a voice that was as smooth as honey-laced hot whiskey. "Then I've unofficially heard you." He turned to Natalie. "But the instant this turns up on either your database or ours, Dr. Landau, we're on the record."

Natalie breathed out a sigh of relief. "Thank you, Agent Tyrelle."

D'Amato tapped on Tyrelle's small notebook. "Getting back to my theory, Luther—what if I'm right?"

"Like I said, no evidence, D'Amato. But for argument's sake, say the pendant is the common link. Then I'd say whoever's after it has some pretty powerful resources and won't give up until they get it."

Tyrelle squinted at the dark gold pendant, then looked at Natalie sitting silently, twisting her small paper napkin between her fingers.

"One thing I can do—order the manifests for the flights out of Baghdad on the day Sutherland left, then check the passenger list. See if someone on it sets off any alarm bells. And until we can rule out whether this pendant is a missing antiquity, I'll keep it secured at headquarters."

He was already extending a hand toward the pouch and necklace, but Natalie shook her head and scooped them up.

"I'd rather you didn't. It's my final gift from my sister. Until we know whether or not it's stolen, I want to hang onto it."

"You can take all the pictures you want, Luther," D'Amato interjected, as the FBI agent frowned.

"Your cell phone takes pictures, doesn't it?" D'Amato pressed dryly.

Tyrelle shot him a dark look. "Government issue. Of course it does. But on the chance your theory is right, D'Amato, I seriously recommend that Dr. Landau, for her own safety, turn this over to the bureau just until . . ."

"No." Natalie had to make him understand. She pushed back her chair and stood up, clutching the golden pendant even more tightly between her fingers. "Not yet. Not until we know something definitive. This is what I do, Agent Tyrelle," she said quietly. "I have colleagues who can test and appraise the amulet, and I'd like to be in on the process. Please, until you can verify that this belongs to someone else, I'd like to keep it."

"I have to tell you, I'm not sure you're making the right decision," the FBI agent countered.

"It's her call, Luther." D'Amato came to his feet and shrugged into his windbreaker. "So, you planning to get a few shots of this thing before we take off, or are you going to commit it to memory?"

Tyrelle snorted, and snapped six close-ups of the pendant from as many angles, plus three of the pouch and its inscription, then e-mailed them from his cell back to his computer at 26 Federal Plaza.

"Sit tight until noon," he advised Natalie as she slipped on her black leather jacket. "I should have the manifest by then. I'll get back to you."

Tyrelle left the coffeehouse first, his strides long and purposeful. He seemed oblivious of the light rain that had begun to spatter the pavement. Natalie paused at the door, and her eyes met D'Amato's troubled ones.

"I'm not sure what to wish for here. Aside from wishing my life had a 'restore' command, like the one on my computer. I'd love to wipe out everything that's gone wrong in the past two days, and go forward with Dana still alive. I feel like I'm living in a nightmare."

"Yeah, know that feeling." He pushed open the door, his expression shuttered.

They'd snagged a parking space near an art gallery down the street. As they retraced their steps through the rain-misted night, Natalie noticed D'Amato's gaze sweeping the street. He glanced from the all-night drugstore to the parked cars gleaming beneath the streetlights, skimming the low-lit doorways, then lingering on a woman walking toward them holding an oversized umbrella. He looked tense. Shivering in the damp air,

Natalie wondered just where D'Amato's nightmares came from. Maybe the pain he suffered, the urge to pop a pill to escape it.

Despite his friendship with Dana, Natalie knew very little about him. But Jim D'Amato struck her as a man more given to questions than answers, and for all those he'd asked her, dozens of questions—about her work, about Dana, about the pendant— he'd shared next to nothing about himself. *Which is fine,* Natalie thought, *because my brain is on overload as it is.*

She needed to sleep. They'd done all they could for tonight. Tomorrow might bring answers.

But it won't bring Dana back, she thought with a stab of pain, as she slid into the passenger seat of D'Amato's Accord.

17

Barnabas searched her bedroom first.

He worked his way methodically through the oblong room, starting with the frosted-glass jewelry box on her dresser, then sweeping the pale beam of his flashlight into the narrow painted drawers of her antiqued wooden nightstand. But all he found there was a Star of David necklace and a half dozen other pieces of good jewelry, a miniflashlight, a leather-bound address book, and an opened roll of quarters tucked beneath a package of gummy bears. Grimacing, he flattened himself on the wood floor and flicked his flashlight on again to peer under her bed. *Zip. Not even dust bunnies.*

The sudden peal of a door buzzer startled him so thoroughly that he jerked up, banging his forehead on the bed frame. He froze, clicking off the flashlight, his heart pounding.

It's only someone ringing her doorbell. Wait it out. They'll go away.

Barnabas wondered who was out there, then told himself it didn't matter. Only the Light mattered. And it had to be either here or with her.

So he waited, motionless, on the floor, in the dark. The buzzer rang a second time, then fell silent. He strained to listen, expecting the sounds of an elevator, but none came.

Once he was certain five minutes had passed, Barnabas resumed his search, heading now for the tall dresser—avoiding the windows and using his flashlight sparingly, so that no one looking in could detect so much as a shadow flitting through the rooms.

Then he turned his attention to the bedroom closet, the tiny medicine cabinet in the bathroom, the toilet tank. He searched her desk and beneath the sofa cushions, guided only by the pale light of the candle she'd left flickering in the tall red glass, then he checked the kitchen cupboards, and even the freezer and crisper drawers in her refrigerator.

Frustration grated through him. *She must have taken it with her.* He'd wait. She'd come back eventually.

The end of a matter is better than its beginning; likewise, patience is better than pride.

The verse from Ecclesiastes ran through his mind like a mantra, calming him as he made his way through the dark apartment and sat himself down on the sofa to wait.

Across the street, in a late-model green Ford, two government agents assigned to the National Security Unit were hunkered down, also waiting in the dark for Natalie Landau to return.

She hadn't answered the buzzer, but they knew what she looked like and what they needed to get from her.

18

"That was a good move, calling the FBI," Natalie acknowledged, as D'Amato pulled away from the curb. "I almost feel like we accomplished something."

"It helps to have friends in high places." His gaze was locked on the rearview mirror.

"Speaking of which, I've decided to drive up to Albany tomorrow and see what the Ion Beam lab there can tell me about this pendant."

"Want some company?"

She shook her head. "Thanks, but the truth is, I could use some time alone. There'll be enough company tomorrow night during shivah. I just need to roll down the window, keep the radio turned off, and let the breeze clear my head so I can think."

He didn't answer. He was still fixated on the rearview mirror, but his face had tightened and there were grim lines now around his mouth.

"What's wrong?"

"I'm pretty sure we're being followed."

She twisted in her seat, trying to see behind them, but D'Amato's voice stopped her in midturn.

"Don't do that. We don't want them to know we're onto them—yet. Get Tyrelle on the phone."

She punched the numbers he gave her, her heart racing. As she tried to hand her cell to him, he shook his head.

"You talk. I'll lose them."

Natalie held her breath, waiting for Tyrelle to pick up. After two rings a voice said hello. But it didn't sound like honey-laced whiskey. It sounded like sandpaper. Sandpaper with a Middle Eastern accent, she thought, quickly checking the display to see if she'd called the right number. "Special Agent Tyrelle?" she asked uneasily.

At that moment she was thrown against the center console as D'Amato took a sharp left and the Accord rocketed toward a red light. "I think there's a second car on our butt," D'Amato muttered. "Could be the '06 Lincoln that was parked by the drugstore."

He punched the accelerator and they shot through the inter-section like a missile, nearly colliding with the back end of a yellow Hummer.

"If you're looking for the FBI buffoon, you're too late," the scratchy voice taunted in her ear. "He's as dead as you will be if you don't do precisely as I tell you."

Oh, my God. "Who is this?" She could hear herself yelling into the phone over the dissonant chorus of blaring car horns assaulting them. "What did you do to Tyrelle?"

D'Amato was going seventy. The streets whizzed past, a diz-zying blur of neon and car lights as Natalie clung to the phone, trying to push down her terror.

"Shit. There *are* two of them—where's Tyrelle?" D'Amato narrowly missed the suddenly opened door of a taxi. "What's happening?"

"He says Tyrelle's dead," she whispered.

"It's true. Do I have your attention now?"

Sucking in a breath, Natalie hit speakerphone so D'Amato could hear.

"Don't think you can outrun us. Pull over now and we might still resolve this without anyone else getting hurt."

"I don't believe you." Natalie braced her boots against the floor as, tires squealing, D'Amato whipped right, then left, weaving through traffic like Steve McQueen on amphetamines.

She was overwhelmed with sudden rage. "You killed Tyrelle—did you kill my sister, too?"

"Stop the car now and turn over the Eye or you and your foolhardy companion will wish you had died in traffic."

Natalie spun toward the back window and peered into the headlights of the dark sedan swiftly maneuvering to keep right behind them.

We still might die—any second now, she thought, as D'Amato cursed, cutting the wheel sharply to the left to avoid T-boning a Pepsi truck.

"You're not getting this eye," she shouted. "Not unless you tell me who killed my sister."

"And you're not going to see morning unless you hand over the Eye. My associates are about to overtake you. Don't make us angrier with you than we already are."

"Tell him to go fuck himself." D'Amato sounded amazingly calm, though the tension that corded along his neck suggested otherwise.

Then he lowered his voice to an urgent whisper. "Natalie, you need to call Tyrelle's partner, tell him he's down. Now."

But she couldn't hang up, not yet. "Did you kill my sister?"

She heard what sounded like a low chuckle. "I would not have been so foolish as to have killed her before I made her tell me what I wanted to know. But you should know this," the man said with satisfaction. "I am at this moment holding a souvenir of your sister's death. A lovely necklace—the Hand of Fatima. Do you know it?"

Natalie went cold. *He has Dana's hamsa.*

D'Amato's right hand shot out, grabbed the phone from her, and snapped it shut. In the next instant he was slamming on the brakes, then shooting around the Explorer he'd nearly rear-ended.

"Why did you do that?" Natalie yelled. "I needed him to answer me!"

"You need to call Sean Watson. *Now.*"

"You need to stop shouting at me," she shot back. "Try giving me his phone number." She gripped the door as the Accord skidded around a corner on two squealing wheels.

At that moment, a pedestrian wearing a reflective jogging suit stepped into the street.

"Look out!" Natalie screamed. Her face was ashen in the glow of the console lights as D'Amato twisted the wheel and the car miraculously skimmed around the man, frozen in place.

Breathing hard, D'Amato rattled off the phone number and Natalie punched buttons with icy fingers.

"Yes?" The curt male voice left no doubt her call was interrupting something far more important.

"Special Agent Watson?"

"You've got him. Who—?"

"Watson!" D'Amato yelled before she could answer. "It's D'Amato. Luther's down. Maybe dead. Someone's got his phone. He and his pals are climbing up my butt—one's a black sedan, and I couldn't get a good look at the other one, but it's big—probably an '06 Lincoln, dark blue or black. You need to find Luther—"

"Where the hell are you, D'Amato?" the FBI agent barked.

"Grand and Humboldt, headed for the Long Island Expressway." Suddenly, the Lincoln zoomed forward and around the back of their car, sideswiping the Accord's back quarter panel. *"Damn it!"*

The impact knocked the phone from Natalie's hand.

"It's a Lincoln alright. The bastards just hit me," D'Amato yelled.

"Oh, my God," Natalie gasped. "One of them's got a gun."

"Get down!" D'Amato barked. "Now!"

Unlocking her seatbelt, she slid to the floor and fumbled desperately in the darkness for her phone. Her heart was slamming so hard against her breastbone she thought her ribs would fracture.

"Hang on," D'Amato told her over the blare of more horns as he floored the pedal. "I'm going to lose them."

"That's what you said before. Damn it. I can't find the phone." Natalie groped desperately across the floor, panic trembling through her fingers.

"I think it slid under my feet. I might have disconnected . . ."

She reached toward the pedals and cracked her head on

the console just as the phone jangled, startling her as it lit up inches away.

She scooped it from behind his left heel and huddled beneath the glove compartment, pressing it to her ear.

"You are both dead." The same Middle Eastern voice, a dark, menacing voice that scraped along her nape like the spines of a cactus. "We are taking aim now at your tires. You have thirty seconds to pull over and give us the Eye of Dawn."

19

Hasan Sabouri crouched in the back of the Lincoln, sizzling with controlled fury. The Americans weren't stopping. "Shoot them!"

Khalil was at the wheel, his foot keeping the accelerator pedal near the floorboard. He had exchanged his daytime taxi for the Lincoln after collecting Hasan from the airport. His nephew Marwan rather literally occupied the shotgun seat—his window down, his Glock pointed at the Accord's right rear tire.

"Now, Marwan!" Hasan urged.

The boy fired off a round, but missed the tire, his bullet ricocheting off the right rear bumper instead.

"Keep firing!" Hasan ordered, but it was too late. Accompanied by the blare of angry horns, the Accord sliced across two lanes straight into oncoming traffic and leaped onto the curb.

"What's wrong with you, Marwan?" Hasan bellowed, slamming his fist against the young man's headrest. "Did they teach you nothing in the camps? Go after them, Khalil."

Khalil obeyed, plunging across the oncoming traffic without hesitation. He checked the rearview mirror and saw that Ra'if, at the wheel of the black Cadillac, was following his lead. He'd accidentally caught a glimpse of Hasan's face in the rearview mirror and trembled, not at the cars and trucks scattering before their wayward vehicles, but at the rage sparking from the Iranian's strange marble-blue eyes.

Was Hasan cursing him and his nephew and all their descendants—should the boy live long enough, *insha'allah*? Marwan had only hesitated an instant, no doubt trying to get off the best shot he could, not from any lack of resolve. He was as committed to the reestablishment of the khalifate as Hasan himself was, of that he had no doubts. The khalifs were the true leaders of Islam. Hadn't the boy been trained from infancy just for this service?

Like other women committed to their cause, Khalil's own sister, Lama, had been flown to the city of Detroit in her seventh month of pregnancy to wait out her son's birth, ensuring that her boy would be born an American citizen, with all their inherent rights and privileges.

Including the right to an American passport.

But little Marwan had not remained long in the predominantly Arab suburb of Dearborn. He was not meant to grow up in the land of the infidels alongside other children of his faith. When he was but two months old, his mother had taken him home to Bahrain. And when he was four years old, she'd proudly kissed him good-bye and sent him to the camps to be trained as a warrior for Islam.

Tonight was his first opportunity to prove himself, Khalil knew, and it was of such importance, with Hasan Sabouri himself directing him, who could blame the boy for a slight case of nerves?

"Give me the gun," Hasan commanded from the backseat, his eyes fixed intently on the Accord now roaring off the curb. He yelled into his cell phone, ordering Amir, the marksman in the Cadillac with Ra'if, to take out the tires, then yanked away the Glock Marwan was handing him.

As Khalil gave chase to the Americans, Hasan angled the powerful weapon out the window and squeezed off two shots, but in the next instant a deafening explosion rocked the Lincoln, enveloping it in a reeking mass of smoke and shredded rubber. Amir's bullet had gone wild, striking their Lincoln's rear tire, turning it into seared shreds and sending the Lincoln spinning out of control.

It slammed into an oncoming Lexus, reeled sideways, and swiped against the Cadillac Ra'if was vainly trying to steer out of its path.

His efforts proved futile. As Ra'if corrected his steering to recover from the collision, he swung instead into the path of a Dodge Caravan, which hit him broadside, rolling his vehicle. He never saw the Explorer barreling toward him. It crushed the Cadillac like an empty soda can, killing its occupants instantly.

Khalil fared only slightly better in the fishtailing Lincoln. He was alive but badly burned by the gunpowder used to activate the airbag. Dimly he could hear Marwan groaning from the seat beside him, and then Hasan banging the bashed-in rear door, struggling to escape the car and screaming that they'd let the Eye of Dawn get away.

Natalie fought for breath as she crawled back onto her seat and watched the carnage behind them recede.

"Well, I . . . guess you lost them," she said shakily, refastening her seatbelt. "I doubt if anyone in that Cadillac could have survived."

"Better them than us." D'Amato had now blended into traffic, decelerating to keep pace with the law-abiding drivers around him. "What was that business about a souvenir?"

She explained quickly about the *hamsa*, then suddenly broke off. "He has to be an Arab, D'Amato. I just realized he called Dana's necklace by its Muslim name, 'the Hand of Fatima.'"

"Right. Named for Muhammad's daughter. I've seen those little hand-shaped necklaces all over the Middle East."

"Yes, to a Jew, it's a *hamsa*. That's Hebrew for five, like the digits on a hand," Natalie explained. "Some people call it the Hand of Miriam, after the sister of Moses and Aaron."

"Same symbol, different names."

"But still a form of protection against the evil eye." Natalie's tone was quiet now. "But the pendant," she said slowly. "He called that something, too—when he warned me that they were going to shoot. He called it 'the Eye of Dawn.' At least that's what it sounded like. Does that mean anything to you?"

"Not a thing," he grunted. "But I guess it's a start." He was still checking all the mirrors, his eyes shifting constantly. "You know this means there's no going back to your apartment. Whoever these guys are, I'm sure they're not working alone. And chances are they followed us to the coffee shop from your place. Some of them went after Luther, in case you'd handed off the pendant to him, and the rest . . . well, you know the rest."

Natalie wondered how he could sound so calm, so logical. Her heart was still racing, and she felt as though she'd just run straight into an electrified fence.

"Shouldn't we talk to the police? Luther's dead—and if the men who chased us had been better marksmen—or you less of a kamikaze driver—we'd be, too."

"Like I told Luther tonight, it's your call. If you want to stick around and answer questions for a few hours, file a police report, and look at mug shots, say the word. Or we could go back and officially involve the bureau."

"No, they'll want the pendant, too, and I'm not handing it over to anyone. It's all I have left of Dana." Her voice cracked. "If she died because of this, I need to know why. What about this is worth her life—and Luther's? Not to mention mine and yours. At the very least, I need to find out what I've got here. Eye of Dawn. I don't know what that means, but I doubt the police can figure that out any quicker than I can."

D'Amato started to speak, but she interrupted him. "I know someone who can help me identify this—my mentor, Dr. Ashton. I need to go see him. He's currently a visiting professor at the British School of Rome, and he's the world's foremost expert on ancient glyptic art. He can probably not only date the jewels on the pendant but pin down which mine in the Middle East produced the lapis lazuli."

"They have the facilities to test it at this school in Rome?"

"He wouldn't be able to carry on his research there if they didn't. Can you take me to the airport?" she asked. "I need to get on the next flight to Rome."

D'Amato glanced over at her. "It's too dangerous to go back to your apartment for your passport—"

"I don't need to—it's in my bag. Probably the first time in my life procrastination's worked in my favor," she muttered. "Just drop me off at JFK."

"I'll do you one better. I'll go with you. I've got a stake in this now, too." He stopped for a red light and waited for her to protest. It didn't take long.

"That doesn't mean you have to go to Rome with me." Natalie folded her arms. "Once Dr. Ashton analyzes the pendant, I'll call you—"

"You don't know me very well yet, Natalie. Once I find myself in the line of fire, I tend to take it personally. I'd like to meet with Dr. Ashton, too." D'Amato hit the gas. "Our immediate problem is finding a transatlantic flight before morning. We'll probably have to hole up somewhere safe until dawn."

Natalie turned in her seat to look at him. "And what will Mrs. D'Amato have to say about that?"

Still staring straight ahead into the damp night, D'Amato cruised through the next intersection. "Not a thing. There is no Mrs. D'Amato. Not for the past five years."

Natalie's brows lifted. "So why the wedding ring? To remind you to pay your alimony?" Then a horrible thought struck her—perhaps he was a widower. "Sorry, that was a bit too personal."

"Not a problem. You're right. I'm divorced." A short silence. Natalie sensed the tension in him, the hesitation to say more. She waited.

"My wife and I never got past losing our only child," he said.

She drew in a breath. "How horrible. I'm sorry for being so flip."

"You couldn't have had any idea." D'Amato blared the horn at a taxi straddling two lanes. "Tony had just turned seven," he told her quietly. "After he died, we couldn't find any way to console each other. We couldn't even have a normal conversation. We just sort of fell apart."

"I'm sorry," Natalie said again. She watched the windshield wipers in silence, unable to think of anything else to say. She knew something about things falling apart. Her relationship with her own sister . . .

"You asked about the wedding band." He lifted his left hand from the steering wheel. "It was my dad's. Tony was named for him."

Natalie nodded in the darkness. "So it's a connection to both of them."

"Yeah, something like that."

He was driving faster now. Maybe a little too fast on the slick streets, but she resisted the urge to tell him to slow down.

"What about *your* passport?" she asked at length. "I don't suppose it's tucked in your purse, as well?"

He managed a grin. "I'm hoping we can slip into my place and get it before any of our new friends ID me. Some of them are a little tied up in traffic right now, and hopefully whoever got to Luther hasn't had time to find my condo yet."

Luther, Natalie thought, seeing again the caramel-colored eyes brimming with spark and intelligence. *Dana, Rusty, now Luther.*

"Was Agent Tyrelle married?" she asked. "Don't you want to be there for the funeral, for his family?"

"It's not safe for either one of us to be where we're expected to be right now. Besides, grief can be postponed. Justice can't."

D'Amato had to circle the block twice to find a parking spot near his Park Slope condo, but at last he pulled into a space three brownstones away. "It won't take long to grab my passport and a change of clothes, but I don't think it's a good idea for you to wait out here alone."

Peering out into the dark night, Natalie wasn't tempted to argue with him. She climbed out of his car and into a puddle, surprised that her legs could still hold her upright and that she was able to hurry alongside him as steadily as if she hadn't been a moving target tonight. She couldn't stop glancing at every shadow. Suddenly, the words the man on the phone taunted her with sprang into her mind.

I would not have been so foolish as to have killed her before

*I made her tell me what I wanted to know. I am holding a sou-
venir of your sister's death.*

Revulsion and anger filled her. *That bastard knows who
killed Dana.*

She clutched her shoulder bag tightly against her as she
trudged up the stairs ahead of D'Amato. Each time a step
creaked or a voice rang from another unit—or a noise rose from
the street—she stiffened.

D'Amato's second-floor condominium was spare and orderly, its furnishings quietly masculine and streamlined. There
was a sheen to the dark cherry hardwood floors, unbroken by
any rugs, that made her wonder if he ever had visitors. He had
a taupe leather recliner and matching sofa, set around a low,
polished granite coffee table. She almost laughed at the straight,
tight row of electronic remote controls on top of it—more re-
motes than she'd ever seen.

The off-white walls were punctuated with an occasional ab-
stract print framed in heavy wood, and his chrome-and-glass
desk was as orderly as a dentist's tray. Not a single loose piece
of paper was visible beside the laptop.

At one end of the living room bookcases stood crammed
with hardcover volumes and periodicals. At the other a wide-
screen plasma TV was centered over the hearth of a modern
stone fireplace. Everything was disciplined and a little cold. The
place did not look lived-in.

After he disappeared into the bedroom to pack his duffel
bag, Natalie steeled herself and phoned her aunt to cancel the
shivah, telling her aunt Leonora that she had to leave town for
an emergency. Gritting her teeth at her aunt's cry of disbelief,
she reiterated, not untruthfully, that it couldn't be helped.

As she disconnected she could hear the sound of drawers
opening, closing in D'Amato's bedroom. She pulled out her cell
phone and dialed the airlines.

D'Amato stepped into his walk-in closet and closed the door.
Quickly, he entered the combination on the keypad, and his wall
safe whirred open. He removed five one-hundred-dollar bills

from the bank envelope and tucked them into his wallet, then selected four passports from the seven rubber-banded together. He put the one in his own name in his pocket and stowed the other three at the bottom of his duffel.

Then he looked at the Walther. No way to get it past airline security.

He'd just have to pick up another in Rome.

"You're right about the flights. There's nothing to Rome until 7:30 in the morning," Natalie told him as he emerged from the bedroom. "And then we'll need to race like hell to make our connection from London. I booked two seats."

"I'll pay you back." D'Amato grabbed two bottles of Perrier and a chunk of provolone from his nearly bare refrigerator shelves and stuffed them into his duffel. As Natalie started toward the door, he punched his cell phone voice mail.

Hearing his footsteps stop, she turned. His face had changed, gone ashen. Then she watched it flush with anger.

He pressed replay and grimly held the phone out to her.

Natalie listened to the words of a dead man. Luther had called as his assassins were closing in on him.

"Middle Eastern males, two . . . five feet nine, five feet ten . . . wiry builds." He sounded like he was running. She heard a shot. It sounded like it was at close range, as though Luther had fired. Then a burst of gunfire, a grunt, rapid voices shouting in Arabic, and then silence.

"Let's get out of here." D'Amato took back the phone and shoved it into the pocket of his windbreaker. "They've got my cell number. If they've already triangulated it, they could be here any second."

He ran to the door, keys in hand. She raced after him down the stairs, wondering when she'd begin finding answers rather than questions.

20

Jerusalem

The honeyed glow of sunrise shimmered over the Judean hills as Menny Goldstein slipped out the back door of the Yoffi Café, muttering under his breath as he took his first cigarette break of the day. Yesterday Eli, his brother-in-law and owner of the restaurant where Menny worked the early morning shift as prep chef and cook, had pronounced the restaurant "smoke-free."

He thinks declaring his restaurant "green" will save our lungs? Menny inhaled and erupted in a fit of coughing. It had been two days since the police had lobbed tear gas at the Shomrei Kotel contingent demonstrating against the Temple Mount summit, and his throat still seared. He'd been front and center at the protest, decrying the government's idiocy in permitting the United States and the Palestinians to use Israel's holiest site as a staging ground for a mock peace agreement. The Shomrei Kotel knew the peace would never hold, because they knew the Palestinian leaders didn't really want peace. They wanted Jerusalem—in its entirety—and soon, at the summit, the Israeli government would start handing the ancient city over to them, piece by piece.

Menny was grinding his cigarette underfoot when a tall young man with a short-cropped beard loped around the corner and headed toward him.

"The next meeting is tonight after *ma'ariv*." His friend, Shmuel, wasted no time in getting down to business. Menny sighed and pulled another cigarette from his pack.

"So we pray, and then we talk," Menny complained. "Tell me, what is Shomrei Kotel prepared to *do*? I'm done with lettering protest signs, Shmuel. The summit is only days away, and our holiest site will be used as a backdrop for our nation's suicide—beginning with the amputation of our heart—Jerusalem. What is wrong with our supposed leaders? Don't they see that?"

Shmuel put a hand on the shorter man's shoulder. "Listen to me, Menny, tonight's meeting isn't about the summit. There is something even more important that Shomrei Kotel must address."

Menny threw up his hands, oblivious of the cigarette ash tumbling toward the ground. "What could be more important than our national survival?" he demanded.

"It's all connected, Menny." Shmuel's smile was slight and secretive. "Come to the meeting and see."

Brooklyn, New York

Watching the clock in their green Ford tick toward dawn, NSU agents Foster and Biondi knew that capturing Firefly might be the most important mission of their careers. Prior to being recruited for this secret and elite branch of the Department of Defense, both had served their country with distinction—Foster in Special Forces and Biondi in the CIA.

By nature they preferred action to waiting, but were disciplined enough to know that both were equally valuable in the field. However, by the time the sun had peeked over the Brooklyn Bridge, Foster and Biondi were more than ready to get their hands on the search warrant for Dr. Landau's apartment. The woman was still MIA, and the only person they'd seen come or go from her building was a tall, muscular male in dark sweats who'd left the building and jogged down the street at 5:30 A.M.

A black Impala finally sidled alongside their green sedan,

and the driver lowered his window to hand off the search warrant to Agent Biondi. Biondi took one last gulp of his now-cold coffee as the Impala took off. He set the empty cup back in the cup holder. He needed to take a leak, but he could do that once they were inside.

"Let's do it," Foster said.

Almost simultaneously, they opened their doors.

They never saw the bomb hurtling toward them.

The explosion lifted the Ford into the air. The fireball engulfed Agents Foster and Biondi even as the roar of the inferno blew out the windows of the neighboring buildings.

Hasan Sabouri's skin burned from the heat as he sprinted past the carnage. He had only moments to get inside Landau's apartment before the street was filled with sirens and emergency vehicles. But he wasn't afraid.

If she returned here tonight, she was his.

And so was the Eye of Dawn.

The flight departed for London at 7:25, five minutes early. Still, as the jet lifted from the runway, Natalie fought back frustration at the long hours stretching ahead, hours in which she could only wonder what Dr. Ashton would uncover.

She'd slept fitfully at the Starburst Motel near the airport, wearing the jeans and white T-shirt she'd worn to meet Luther, and was grateful that the desk clerk had provided her with a toothbrush and enough toothpaste in foil packets to last her the day.

Yet, brushing her teeth, showering, going through the motions of a morning routine hadn't restored normalcy. Nothing could feel normal when someone was trying to kill her—and D'Amato. She wouldn't be safe until she found out who wanted them dead—and why.

Why was the pendant a magnet for evil? It was supposed to deflect harm, not attract it. But all it seemed to attract was death. Natalie didn't want to be its next victim.

Sandwiched between a compact older woman reading a paperback and a lanky college student with shaggy sand-colored hair and an iPod, Natalie felt safer than she had since Jim D'Amato had first broached his theory at her apartment.

Leaning forward, she glanced across her row at D'Amato in the opposite aisle seat. He met her gaze and nodded, then went back to his newspaper and his coffee.

She wondered if he ever slept. He'd been lying awake atop the cheap quilt on the second bed in the motel room when she dozed off for a few hours, and he'd been awake when she stumbled up at 4:30 this morning to shower.

She leaned back and closed her eyes, trying to get comfortable in the cramped economy seat, but the small of her back throbbed against the seat cushion designed for a man's spine.

No doubt by the time they finally made it through passport control and rented a car, Geoffrey Ashton would just be getting his second wind. The man was notoriously nocturnal, famous for haunting the sidewalk cafés until the wee hours of the morning. And when his companions staggered home to bed, he more often than not would head back, whistling, to his laboratory and work through the night, savoring the solitude and the quiet of a nearly deserted building.

She anticipated that he'd be more than happy to give the pendant priority over whatever else he might be testing in the Ion Beam lab. There was nothing Ashton relished more than a challenge. And she had one for him.

Natalie knew that if she could only drift off to sleep, the flight would go by faster. But she couldn't relax. She kept thinking about the man with the Middle Eastern accent who'd taunted her last night. About the cars chasing them relentlessly, about the gunshots.

About the Eye of Dawn.

21

The woman in the window seat fidgeted, craning her head to scan the inky horizon visible beyond the wing of the plane. As it shuddered on its descent into Rome, she crossed herself rapidly, once, twice, three times, muttering a prayer and giving a small shrug of apology to Natalie.

The woman squeezed her eyes shut as the aircraft jiggled again. "Oh, Madonna mia!"

As the plane leveled off, she opened them again and spotted what she'd been searching for amid the twinkling lights below. "San Pietro! San Pietro!" she cried, beaming at Natalie and gesturing out the window, where Natalie could see the outline of the cathedral's grand dome overlooking Bernini's perfectly symmetrical colonnade and the eternal city that stretched beyond.

"*Grazie di Dio,*" the woman exclaimed, clutching the filigree cross at her throat along with the small golden horn she'd strung beside it to protect her from the evil eye.

Natalie smiled wanly at her, shifting wearily in her seat. She could see that the woman was convinced her cross and her *cornu* charm had brought her safely home. Italians were one of the few Mediterranean people who didn't employ eyes to deflect a malevolent stare, preferring a horn amulet to protect them: a single bull's horn, if worn around the neck—a double one if formed by the fingers. She'd seen the gesture more than once—the two middle fingers pressed against the palm by the thumb, leaving the index and baby fingers extended to mimic a bull's horns, then jabbed in the direction of the perceived evil to push it away.

This woman wouldn't be the least bit impressed with the supposedly protective powers of the pendant in my shoulder bag, Natalie decided. She herself wasn't the least bit sure Dana's "treasure" *was* protecting her. It seemed instead to be drawing danger to her. The only thing she knew with total certainty right now was that every muscle in her legs and arms ached from the cramped flight. As the wheels touched down with a dull thump, she fought the urge to spring immediately from her seat and stretch.

"Why don't I call Dr. Ashton while you arrange for the rental car?" Natalie suggested to D'Amato ten minutes later, as they hurried past the throng congregated at a Terminal B baggage carousel.

"You shouldn't use your cell phone here. We'll need to buy new ones in the morning."

"Why? I switched my phone to international for my trip a few weeks ago—"

"It can be traced, Natalie. By anyone who has your phone number," he said, lowering his voice. "And by now, it's possible quite a few people have learned it and are on the look-out for us. I'm sure Sean Watson has the FBI eager to hear our story. It won't take long before they know we've left the country. They'll alert Interpol. And don't forget about our Middle Eastern friends from last night. Plus, we still know nothing about that bozo who went after you in the museum—if he's working with them or for someone else."

"Wonderful." Natalie kept in step with him as they hurried toward passport control.

By the time they exited the terminal's glass doors and headed out into the cool night air, she felt her adrenaline pumping again.

"So how do you propose I warn Dr. Ashton we're about to burst in on him in the middle of the night?"

"Theoretically, it takes three minutes to track a cell phone in use. It's risky, but if you can keep the call under that, you can give him a heads-up. Otherwise you're broadcasting the where-abouts of your cell phone to everyone who wants to know where you've gone."

Washington, D.C.

Elliott Warrick followed the petite gray-haired barracuda Jackson Wright employed as his secretary into the Secretary of Defense's walnut-paneled office.

"Eight minutes. Not a second more." She glared at him and checked her watch even before he could shake hands with Wright. "He's leaving for the NATO meeting in Oslo in ten minutes. I'll be back to escort you out in six."

"I thought you said eight."

"You've just used up two of them."

Warrick gave her the curtest of nods as he extended his hand to Jackson Wright. Justine Matthews annoyed the hell out of Warrick. She'd been with Wright since his days in the Senate, and she thought she owned him. Rumor had it that her propri-etary hold on him extended even to his wife, whose calls were screened just like everyone else's.

"Mr. Secretary, you've received the latest update."

Wright shoved the photos of Firefly across his desk. "And I've seen the pictures. What I want to know is, what the hell happened to it after Agent Tyrelle took these photos? And how is that MSNBC reporter's murder connected to all this?"

"We're still analyzing the data, trying to pinpoint the con-nection between Dana Landau's murder, Tyrelle's murder, the bomb that killed the two NSU agents—and another murder. Right before I came up here we got word that Rusty Sutherland, Landau's cameraman, has turned up dead in an abandoned building in New York. I believe every one of these is linked to Firefly—and to Dana Landau's sister, Dr. Natalie Landau."

"Explain." Wright's scowl took up most of his face.

"At nearly the same time we lost the NSU agents waiting to

serve Natalie Landau with a search warrant," Warrick continued, "we now believe she and MSNBC's Jim D'Amato were meeting with FBI Special Agent Luther Tyrelle. Tyrelle took these photos at that meeting and e-mailed them to his computer just before he was killed. Shortly after that meeting, Tyrelle's partner, Sean Watson, got a call from D'Amato and the woman with him, alerting him that Tyrelle was down and that they were being pursued by two vehicles in the area of Grand and Humboldt."

Wright shifted impatiently in his chair. "The three Middle Eastern males who died in that chase—and the one still in ICU—have you ID'd them yet?"

"Only one with certainty. Khalil Hadi, the driver of one of the two vehicles. He's been on our radar because of his link to the Guardians of the Khalifah. The survivor in ICU is a twenty-two-year-old American citizen, Marwan Younis. Born here but raised in Bahrain. He was one of the shooters."

"So. Word about Firefly traveled instantly." Wright drummed his fingers on his desk. The Guardians of the Khalifah were the most unpredictable of the new wave of terrorist groups spawned in Al Qaeda's wake. They were young, educated, and ruthlessly determined to restore the khalifate to Islam in their lifetimes, and to impose Sharia law throughout the world.

"That Khalifah gang got a hell of a lot closer to Firefly than we did," Warrick admitted.

"You realize what those Islamofascists will do with it if they get their hands on Firefly?"

Wright glared at Warrick, daring him to even try framing an answer. Warrick did not respond. He knew an internal battle was coming within Islam itself. Some factions wanted the new khalifah elected, others insisted he must emerge from the dynastic lineage. Regardless, the next man in line as Muhammad's successor would impose the most hard-line form of Islam on Muslims throughout the world, ruling like a Muslim "pope." There'd no longer be even a minuscule separation between mosque and state in the Arab nations, and non-Muslims throughout the world would become targets of forced conversions or death. Sanctions be damned—with Firefly in the possession of the Guardians of the Khalifah, they'd soon be producing a terrifying new breed of supernuclear weapon.

"If Firefly wasn't found in the wreckage," Wright continued grimly, "and wasn't found on Tyrelle, who has it now—the Landau woman?"

Elliott Warrick straightened his shoulders. "That's the assumption we're working on, especially since she's vanished, too. So has D'Amato. We're trying to determine if they've been taken out or if they're lying low. Either way, we'll find them. I'm personally checking the manifests of every flight out of New York and New Jersey. We're also following up on the report of a witness who saw a man of Middle Eastern descent bolting from one of the wrecked cars."

"We'd damn well better pray *that* guy doesn't have it. Firefly in the wrong hands makes our worries regarding their nuclear capabilities about as significant as a hangnail." Wright's face was nearly as red as his tie. "Keep me informed—" He broke off as Justine Matthews gave the door one sharp rap before pushing it open.

"Sir. Your car is here." She glowered at Warrick. "Good day, Mr. Undersecretary."

Warrick ignored her, turning to meet Wright's eyes directly. "The Landau woman is key. I'll make sure we find her."

The Defense secretary came around the desk and hefted his attaché case from the side chair. "Just make sure you find Firefly. Before anyone else does. And next time, don't sit on your hands waiting for warrants."

22

Rome

A half moon sailed high in the smoggy Rome sky as most of the city's inhabitants nestled beneath down covers. The daily roar of Vespas had dimmed, there were few pedestrians on the darkened streets, and most of the traffic lights flashed only amber.

The Renault Clio took the small hill on Bruno Buozzi easily, as D'Amato scanned the street looking for the landmark Geoffrey Ashton had given them.

"I see it." Natalie pointed. "The flower stall. He said we wouldn't be able to miss it, even at night. Turn there."

The British School at Rome sat at the northeastern tip of the Villa Borghese, one of the most magnificent parks in the city. The Accademia gleamed like a buffed pearl in the moonlight, perched at the crest of a wide, majestic staircase. Most of the tall, opaque windows were dark, as were the surrounding grounds.

Natalie caught the scent of springtime as they made their way in the chill, hushed night, past tall cypresses and rustling olive trees, to the private rear door Ashton had described to her. Their footsteps squishing into the spongy, damp grass was the only sound. Even in the faint wash of moonlight, the building's striking facade was impressive.

A heavy wood door swung open as they made their approach, and Geoffrey Ashton peered out at them. He was a distinguished-looking man in his early sixties, with wispy gray hair and sideburns and exceptionally long arms and legs. His chiseled features might have seemed aristocratic and intimidating if not for the impish amusement that gleamed from his intelligent, deep-set eyes. Natalie recognized the scent of his citrusy aftershave as she clasped his outstretched hand.

"What an unexpected treat." Ashton drew her through the doorway. "Delight doesn't begin to describe my pleasure at seeing you again so soon, my dear Natalie."

"You're very kind, Dr. Ashton, to see us at such short notice."

"Well, any time such a lovely colleague jets across the pond to ask my help, I'm intrigued." He shook D'Amato's hand as Natalie made introductions, then gestured toward the hallway at the end of the entry corridor. "Please, come in out of the night, and you'll tell me what this is all about."

Natalie caught sight of a passing security guard, who paused at the other end of the corridor. She lowered her voice. "May we talk privately, Dr. Ashton?"

"Didn't I tell you in Florence," he chided, "you really must call me Geoffrey now."

With a flourish, he led them to the end of the corridor, past the guard, who nodded respectfully, then down the hall to a spacious office that had every light ablaze, highlighting the intricate pattern of a twelfth-century Persian rug. The last to enter, D'Amato shut the door.

The impish amusement in Ashton's eyes dimmed as he studied Natalie's pallid face and the weary way she lowered herself into the olive green damask chair opposite his desk.

His expression grew grave as she told him of her sister's murder and of the unusual pendant Dana had sent her, and, finally, of the terrifying violence she'd just fled.

"Good God. You'd best let me see what we have here."

As she took the pouch from her bag and handed it to him, Ashton unsteepled his long bony hands and clasped the pouch, then positioned it on his desk. He studied both sides of the old painted leather in silence before finally drawing out the gold chain and pendant. Natalie watched his eyebrows swoop together in surprise. "What indeed . . ." His voice trailed away.

"We're hoping you can tell us." D'Amato had ignored the

third chair and stood leaning against the door. "We need your help appraising its value, estimating its age—and also your most educated guess where it came from."

"The man who tried to kill us called it 'the Eye of Dawn,'" Natalie said. "Does that mean anything to you?"

"'Eye of Dawn'?" Ashton shrugged one shoulder, still scrutinizing the pendant. "I can't say I've ever heard that term before. No, testing these gems won't be a problem—but I must say they look authentic to my naked eye. What's your assessment, Natalie?"

"I agree. They're genuine. And I'm fairly certain the pendant is gold—but it's heavier than one might expect from its size, which makes me suspect there's something concealed inside."

"Well, if it *is* gold, there's no way we'd be able to determine what's inside without carving it open. You can't see through gold. Not even with the Ion Beam machines. The beams won't penetrate gold."

Natalie couldn't hide her disappointment. "But will you at least be able to test the age of the stones and determine if the pendant's an antiquity or a more recent piece?"

"Of course, but based on the cut of this lapis and the technique with which the gold was hammered, my educated guess is that this is a very old piece, and almost certainly originated in the Middle East. I'd even wager a pint that it's Babylonian."

She leaned forward eagerly. "I thought the same thing, since carnelian, jasper, and lapis were a typical combination in Babylonian jewelry and amulets. On the other hand, it could turn out to be a copy."

"Well, we'll find out soon enough." Ashton scratched his ear. "The Babylonians were indeed fond of lapis. Imported great quantities of it from mines in Afghanistan—and not only for their jewels and amulets, mind you. Did you know, Mr. D'Amato, that the kings of Ur prized lapis for sharpening their swords, believing that the lapis made the weapons invulnerable?"

"Maybe some of that invulnerability rubbed off on us," D'Amato answered ruefully. "Since we managed to make it this far." He moved forward, resting his broad fingertips on the desk. "Let me point you to something else we found, Geoffrey. Look again at the pouch—this time turn it inside out."

Ashton obeyed, blinking as he leaned in closer to better examine the writing on the suede side of the leather.

"It does appear to be Aramaic," he announced. "Which would make me correct about a link to Babylon."

"What does it say?" Natalie inched her chair forward to study it as well. "Can you translate it, Geoffrey?"

"Doubtful. I might recognize a few letters, but I'm not conversant in the language." The room was silent as he studied the characters for another long moment. Outside, the Italian night was creeping toward daybreak. Soon, Natalie knew, the cafés would be crammed with impatient patrons vying for the attention of clerks doling out the customers' prepaid pastries and espressos. A sense of unreality floated over her in those few brief seconds while Geoffrey bent over the pouch. Was it only yesterday morning she'd buried her sister?

"This first line . . . I believe it might say Balshazzar." The surprise in Geoffrey's voice drew her back to his lamp-lit office in the Accademia Britannica. "Good Lord, could this possibly be from the court of Nebuchadnezzar's grandson Balshazzar?" he mused. Then he shook his head and frowned. "No, sorry, I jumped the gun. My knowledge of Aramaic is pitiful, as you know," he murmured. "I was close, but the letters seem to spell something else. Not Balshazzar. It looks like . . . Belteshazzar."

"Is that a name, a place—what?" D'Amato glanced from Natalie to Ashton.

"Definitely a name," Ashton responded. "I can see now that it's been pressed into this leather with a seal. If you look closely, you'll notice that some of the edges appear slightly blurred, as if the engraving surface was overinked before it was applied."

Natalie turned to D'Amato to elaborate. "Cylindrical seals made of carved stone were Mesopotamia's equivalent of signet rings. Each small seal was uniquely carved with figures, animals, objects, sometimes characters. People wore their seals like jewelry—on a chain around their necks—readily accessible to roll over wet clay when they needed to impress their signature."

"Mainly for legal purposes—on a proof of receipt, or to sign property transactions in ink." Geoffrey looked up from the pouch. "The seals were also commonly used for marking clay tablets and building blocks."

"The Iraq National Museum lost numerous collections of invaluable ancient seals during the looting in 2003," Natalie added.

"Mesopotamia. Babylonia." D'Amato weighed the two interchangeable names with his hands. "The bottom line is, we're talking about modern-day Iraq here. And that's exactly where your sister got the pendant."

Ashton returned the pouch to Natalie. "I'm afraid I can't make out the second set of letters except for a *tzadi* and a *resh*. The ink is too faded."

"*Tzadi* and *resh*—that's all I was able to pick out, too."

"We'll need some enhancements to decipher the rest—perhaps infrared will do it," Ashton mused. "But I'm thinking that second line of characters was hand-written, since their edges seem quite precise. You'll need an expert in Aramaic, really, to verify what it says."

Natalie was buoyed by a surge of hope. "The ion-beam testing, Geoffrey—can it all be done tonight? Can we get started now?"

"How long until we get definitive results?" D'Amato added.

Ashton smiled indulgently at him. "Oh, we can analyze this fairly quickly. Believe it or not, we have chaps dropping by here regularly with family heirlooms, hoping they've uncovered a treasure. They're always relieved to discover they don't have to entrust their finds to our care for any extended period. Of course, more often than not, they're mistaken about the nature and value of their 'treasure,' but in this case"—he held the pendant up to the light—"I'm convinced you've brought me something very special. These two items are unlike anything I've ever encountered before."

"Please." Natalie stood up and turned toward the door. "Let's get started."

They followed Ashton to the Ion Beam laboratory in the basement of the building. It was a large, brightly lit room with an epoxy-coated floor that had been polished until it shone like glass. The lab was filled with microscopes and complicated equipment attached to myriad cables, meters, and computer screens.

Shivering a bit despite her leather jacket, Natalie perched on a stool beside a huge cylindrical contraption that resembled an elongated CT scan machine, and watched the pendant slide inside its white-enameled tunnel.

"Sorry about the chill," Ashton said. "The lab needs to be kept at a cool temperature. We never turn the instruments off, and they generate a lot of heat."

In the fifteen minutes since he'd closed the lab's white metal door behind them, Ashton had already photographed and measured the pendant, carefully counting each of the gemstones and measuring their sizes. He had filled a long page of a leather notebook with his notations, and a number of descriptions written in his tight script radiated out from the rough sketch he'd drawn of the pendant.

"It will take about three, perhaps four hours to complete all the tests," he told them. "Then I should be able to give you some answers."

Gate 53
Detroit Metropolitan Airport

Barnabas's cell phone rang as he swallowed the final chunk of his Cinnabon dinner, his huge frame jammed into one of the uncomfortable bucket seats bolted in tight rows throughout the boarding area. Juggling a tall Starbucks cup and the pastry's sticky waxed paper, he glanced at the phone's screen.

The Sentinel.

Hurriedly, he licked the melted icing and cinnamon from his thumb and fingers and flipped the phone open with his chin. Beside him, a woman was rocking a thumb-sucking toddler on her lap while passing out triangles of pita bread to two small boys who'd been playing tag and tripping over his size-thirteen feet for the past half hour.

"Yes, I'm here at the gate, sir," he told the Sentinel. "And we're still on time. I'll be boarding in the next ten minutes."

"I have additional information for you. I've just deposited another thousand dollars into your account. And I now have names for the seventeen other passengers booked on the LaGuardia-London-Rome flights Natalie Landau took. Eight women, nine men—and Jim D'Amato's name is among them. Still, it's possible they've split up, and she may have passed the Light to him. That's only a guess, but we need to consider the possibility."

"Is Derrek going after D'Amato then?"

"I'll decide once I get a bead on D'Amato's location. Right now, just concentrate on Landau. Call me as soon as you touch down in Rome. I may have discovered her hotel by then."

"Is the reverend upset with me?" Barnabas closed his eyes, bracing himself for the answer.

"His faith in you remains unshaken. Mine, however," the Sentinel said coolly, "is beginning to waver. I expect results within twelve hours of your arrival."

The connection went dead.

Barnabas swallowed past the lump in his throat. He'd never tasted failure before. His strength and his faith had always propelled him to victory, but the Landau woman was becoming a thorn in his side—a painful one.

But the Savior had endured an entire crown of thorns, he reminded himself. Certainly, he could manage *one*.

By now the Light was in Rome, and he was only a half day behind it. His plane would touch down in the Eternal City early tomorrow morning. He'd sleep during the flight, and with God's help, he'd find the Landau woman—and the Light—before another sun could set on Rome. Before the Sentinel lost faith.

He didn't notice the dark-haired man sitting in the bucket seat two rows behind him. He didn't feel the hot blue eyes burning into the back of his head. Nor had he noticed the same man lounging near the Cinnabon stand.

But the man had seen him.

Hasan Sabouri had seen him come out of the airport restroom a half hour earlier and wondered where he'd seen the towering blond American before. And then, as Hasan took his seat at Gate 53, waiting for the flight to Rome, he noticed the brawny young man again—waiting for the same flight and realized he was the same man who'd sauntered out of Natalie Landau's Brooklyn apartment building last night, shortly before Hasan blew up the green sedan parked opposite it.

So, he thought, eyeing the pink-cheeked American with a facade of disinterest, *it is no accident that we are both headed for the same destination. Just as it is no accident that Allah has blessed me with this knowledge.*

Siddiq Aziz fortunately had returned to Rome from the council meeting in Paris by the time Hasan learned Natalie Landau was en route there. Hasan would have to count on Siddiq to track her until he himself touched down on Italian soil.

My path is clear. My enemies have been put within my sights. And soon, the Eye of Dawn will fall into my hands.

23

Accademia Britannica

When Geoffrey Ashton looked up from the computer screen and the trace element spectrum he'd generated, he peered first at Natalie, then at D'Amato.

"I can tell you with absolute certainty that the lapis used on this pendant contains the same types of pyrite inclusions found in lapis mined in ancient Afghanistan."

Natalie caught her breath. She wasn't sure if the buzzing in her ears was due to the continuous whir of the machinery or the impact of Ashton's fingerprinting findings.

"And," he said, his aristocratic face breaking into a broad smile, "the carnelian and jasper are also consistent with specimens known to have come from early Babylonia."

"And the evil eye belief was prevalent in ancient Babylonia, isn't that right?" D'Amato asked.

"Very much so." Natalie's mind was whirling. "Mesopotamia is one of the earliest places where the concept's been documented. The very oldest references to the evil eye appear in cuneiform—and not only the Babylonians, but the Assyrians and Sumerians feared the evil eye as well."

She and D'Amato leaned over Ashton's shoulders as he printed comparisons and pointed out areas of similarity between the gems on the pendant and the previously authenticated ancient samples.

"Somehow, Natalie, your sister seems to have gotten her hands on a piece dating back to the cradle of civilization. It's absolutely astonishing. This pendant could well be three thousand years old."

"Pin this down for me, Geoffrey." D'Amato raked a hand through his dark hair. "Would its age alone make it worth killing for? What's the value of something this rare? Millions?"

"Historically, it's invaluable. Any museum or collector would dearly love to possess something this exceptional."

"And there are plenty of unscrupulous private collectors who'd stab their firstborn through the heart to snag something far less remarkable," Natalie said grimly. "If this was stolen from one of them . . ." Her voice trailed off.

Ashton raised a finger. "Let's go back to what you suggested earlier, Natalie. That there might be something even more to this piece than meets the eye, you should forgive the pun." He moved to a simple balance scale and placed the pendant on a sheet of white paper.

"One more test. A simple one, which may tell us if your theory about something sealed within the pendant holds any water."

D'Amato paced the gleaming floor as Ashton weighed the pendant and punched some data into his computer.

"We know enough about the makeup of gold used in Babylonian times to calculate approximately how much the gold used in this piece should weigh. We know the standard thickness in jewelry back then, the types of impurities they contain, and so forth. Taking all that into consideration, along with the aggregate weight of these gems . . ."

The professor looked up and met Natalie's eyes. She'd been watching him in silence, her arms folded tightly across her stomach. "This piece weighs in fifty percent heavier than one would expect," he said triumphantly.

"So there *is* something inside." Natalie exhaled, feeling a surge of excitement as her suspicions were vindicated. "But what?"

"All I can say with certainty is that whatever's locked in here must have been sealed inside when the pendant was crafted nearly three thousand years ago."

D'Amato gave a low whistle. "You're sure about that?"

"Oh, I'm quite positive. Even the solder is consistent with the type jewelers used in ancient Mesopotamia. Look here."

Ashton traced the tip of a pencil around the pendant as if following an imaginary seam. "The solder line is barely visible, and well polished. This was clearly fashioned in two pieces—like the twin halves of a walnut—and then joined together."

"I don't suppose there's a chance you'd be willing to cut it open." D'Amato spoke without much optimism.

Natalie looked horrified. "Are you crazy? We uncover and preserve the past; we study ancient objects with a minimal amount of tampering." She shook her head at him. "Tell me, would you take a chisel to the Rosetta Stone?"

"Do you want to find out why your sister was killed?"

She was struck for a moment by the glint of steel in his eyes as he studied her evenly.

"There has to be another way," Natalie insisted. "One that doesn't include mutilating history."

"Fine. So tell me where we go from here." D'Amato rubbed his shoulder. "It'll be dawn in a couple of hours and we need a plan of action."

Natalie spoke without hesitation. "Whoever placed something inside this pendant chose an eye symbol to protect it. That indicates that what's in here was important. Whoever concealed it used the most powerful symbol of his time, a symbol that instilled fear and awe in his contemporaries. A symbol Mesopotamians would be terrified of breaching."

"So the eye symbol alone would scare off thieves, grave robbers, and such," D'Amato mused.

"Absolutely." Natalie was emphatic. "The ancient peoples of the Middle East believed eyes were windows to the heart. That whatever someone felt in their heart was projected through their eyes onto everything they looked at—people, property, children, animals, crops. They were convinced that eyes projected light from the heart—be it good light or bad light—to bless or curse the object of one's gaze."

"I get it. The old hairy eyeball." D'Amato folded his arms across his chest. "So even without knowing the pendant's contents, they wouldn't take a chance on unleashing an evil curse."

"Exactly." Ashton began collecting the printouts. "Even though the odds were fifty-fifty, they'd fear the worst."

D'Amato shoved his hands into his pockets. "What was so precious three thousand years ago—and yet small enough to fit inside that pendant?"

"That's the bazillion-dollar question." Natalie worried her lip between her teeth. "The inscription inside the pouch might be our best clue." She turned to her mentor. "Do you know anyone here in Rome who's an expert in Aramaic or ancient Semitic languages?"

"Offhand . . ." Ashton shook his head. ". . . I'm afraid I don't. I could make some inquiries in the morning. Perhaps someone in the Vatican Museums could be of help."

Natalie hesitated. "Without going to the Vatican—might there be anyone here in the Accademia who could read this tomorrow?"

"It's possible, but I'm beginning to think your next course of action should be consulting the authorities. It seems to me it's time to let them sort this out."

Dead silence met his words.

He gestured for her to have a seat. "We've just ascertained that this is a priceless antiquity, regardless of what's inside," he told her calmly, as she lowered herself onto a stool. "Now we have an obligation to go through the proper channels, follow the accustomed procedures, and return this to its rightful owner, if possible."

"I realize that, Geoffrey, but this is more complicated than the discovery of a priceless object in the field."

"Precisely my point. People are trying to kill you, Natalie! Both of you," he added, nodding toward D'Amato. "I think you're much safer turning it over to law enforcement. Here's what I suggest. Permit me to call Colonel Lorenzo of the Vigilanza—the Vatican police—to transport it there for further study at their Museum of Pagan Antiquities—"

"No, Geoffrey." She jumped off the stool and moved toward him, wondering how to make him understand how torn she was. She knew too well her professional obligations. But she also understood what D'Amato had told her in the car. This was personal now. "The men who killed my sister will come after me whether I turn this over or not."

"But, my dear, if you don't have it—"

"The FBI agent didn't have it, and they killed him anyway," D'Amato interjected, walking over to stand beside Natalie.

"Besides, Geoffrey, if I do turn this over to the Vatican, we might never learn its secrets. You know the tremendous hoard of antiquities in their possession. Who's to say they won't keep this pendant also—studying it themselves while hiding it away indefinitely? Perhaps forever."

Ashton frowned. He seemed to be clinging to his patience. Natalie had seen him nearly lose his temper in Florence when one of the museum directors had contradicted him on a minor point during the press conference preceding the opening. His serene composure had cracked for an instant before he'd pulled himself back from the brink of an outburst, and he seemed to be exercising a similar restraint now.

"Very well, then, Natalie." Ashton's tone held a chill she hadn't heard before. "Is there someone you *would* permit me to call? The National Museum of Oriental Art, perhaps? They have an extensive collection of Middle Eastern artifacts—"

"I'm not ready to turn it over to anyone, Geoffrey. Regardless of professional obligations." She drew herself up straighter, forcing herself to meet the disapproval in his eyes. "I have an even more important obligation—to my sister. Dana died because of this pendant, and I owe it to her—and to myself—to find out why."

D'Amato strode over to the scale and scooped up the pendant. He slid it into its pouch, then handed it to Natalie.

"Appreciate your time, Professor. Especially on such short notice." He headed toward the door.

"You're leaving?" Ashton stared as Natalie tucked the pouch into her shoulder bag, gathered up her copies of their findings, and followed D'Amato toward the door of the lab.

"It's after four in the morning, Geoffrey," she said over her shoulder. "We should let you get some sleep."

He took a quick step forward, his face flushing. "I've upset you."

"No." She turned and managed a wan smile. "I truly appreciate everything you've done tonight. But if you'll just forget we dropped in on you in the middle of the night, that would be the biggest favor of all."

"Well . . . of course, my dear." He spread his hands in a gesture of resignation, but his tone was stiff. "If you feel that strongly about it."

He led the way back upstairs, past his office, where the lights still blazed, and into the corridor where they'd first entered. There was no sign of the roving night guard, and, for a moment, all three stood at the exit in an uncomfortable silence.

"What will you do now?" Ashton asked at last, studying his protégé with unreadable eyes.

"We'll figure it out." Natalie leaned forward and kissed him somberly on both cheeks. "Don't worry. I'll be in touch."

He shook the solid hand D'Amato extended, then watched as the two made their way down the pathway to the parking lot. Slowly, he retraced his steps to the lab, gathered up all of his drawings, measurements, and notes, and carried them back to his office.

He slid them into a hanging file folder and slipped it onto the rungs in his credenza drawer, and then sat back, replaying the events of this strange night. Natalie's truculence had taken him by surprise. He could not approve of her insistence on deviating from protocol. Especially since she'd come to him for help and advice. By morning, perhaps, she'd be thinking more clearly. He could only hope he'd gotten through to her.

Picking up his pen, he twiddled it thoughtfully before scratching out a note and centering it on his desk.

Ring up Colonel Lorenzo—mezzogiorno.

Noon. It was the maximum his conscience would allow. He told himself it was for Natalie's own good. She had until noon to reconsider her ill-chosen path.

Washington, D.C.

Owen Garrett was sitting at his desk, wearing his coat and a frown of concentration as his secretary ushered Jeff Wexler into the Oval Office. The President didn't look up from the notes he was scribbling. Wexler shifted uncomfortably, unsure whether to hang back near the door or to approach the desk. He decided to stay put, his arm tight around a leather portfolio bulging with hard copies of data the president had requested.

It was unusual for the President of the United States to summon NASA's administrator to the White House, and Wexler and his staff had been given less than three hours to prepare the presentation. No administrator in recent memory had been asked to brief the President personally, although such meetings had been common in the Kennedy White House. Even more unusual than this summons was the subject matter about to be addressed: photovoltaic energy conversion—the direct conversion of light to electricity. Used to power everything from calculators to power grids, PV technology had been in ongoing development worldwide since the 1950s.

The U.S. space program's initial use of solar power was on its fourth artificial satellite, Vanguard I, in 1958. While NASA had advanced the technology during the space missions of the sixties and seventies, and today used photovoltaic energy on the International Space Station and the Hubble telescope, developing PV as a renewable energy source was chiefly the domain of the Department of Energy, whose Solar America Initiative aimed to provide the United States with readily available, cost-competitive, and efficient solar power by 2015.

That's going to be a challenge, Wexler thought, stifling the urge to clear his throat. Though advances in PV technology had been accelerating globally in the past decade, PV conversion still had its limitations. In space, PV could only power spacecraft traveling no greater distance from the sun than Mars. On Earth, solar cells or panels could only capture and convert the sun's rays during daylight hours, and the output of that energy could differ based on the composition and size of those solar cells or panels.

There was a lot of work yet to do, and Germany, Japan, Australia, the EU, and dozens of other countries were all racing to produce the most efficient and productive PV installations.

Wexler started at a sudden rap on the door behind him and turned as Dan Roderick, the tall, square-shouldered Secretary of Energy, stepped into the room. With a nod of greeting, Wexler held out his hand, and the older man shook it with a crushing grip.

"Take a seat, both of you." The President spoke at last, capping his pen and finally looking up. "Gentlemen, I have plans for our great nation, and for the two of you. NASA and DOE personnel are going to be spending a lot of time together in the next few months and working very closely on a matter of vital importance. Everyone involved will need top security clearance."

Both men straightened.

"What would you say if I told you that quite soon we expect to acquire a source of unlimited and incredibly powerful energy?" Garrett continued. "I'm talking about a source of energy purportedly seventy times more intense than sunlight."

He leaned back in his chair and watched their expressions change from interest to incredulity, then hit them with Firefly's most significant attribute. "And," he continued, "unlike the sun, this source of energy is totally accessible, twenty-four/seven."

Roderick braced his hands on the arms of his chair. "With all due respect, Mr. President, today isn't April first," he said with an uneasy laugh.

Owen Garrett looked over at the silent NASA chief. "And you, Mr. Wexler? Do you think this is an April Fool's joke, too?"

"No sir, but, frankly, I'd be mighty skeptical such an entity exists. Forgive me, but I'm fairly familiar with most bodies in our solar system, and I can't think of a single one with those characteristics."

"Well, think again," Garrett said. "I want your best minds working on this in tandem with NASA and DOE, sharing all research and information. Your people need to develop techniques to harness this energy source, both for exploration beyond the limits of Mars and for ending our dependence on all fossil fuels. Project Firefly supersedes the Solar America initiative's target date of 2015—I'm charging you with meeting our PV energy goals within the next eight months."

"Sir, we haven't even perfected the conversion of sunlight to electricity." Wexler hefted his briefcase, bulging with files. "And none of the materials we've used to convert solar rays thus far has proved ideal—"

"—either used singly, or in tandem," Roderick finished. "Mr. President, we have no idea how this power source you're talking about will react with currently available conversion materials. We'll need time—certainly more than eight months—"

"You damn well ought to be able to do it in six." There was an uncharacteristic rumble of annoyance in Garrett's voice as he leaned forward and clasped his hands together on his desk.

Stunned, Wexler groped for words, as Dan Roderick sucked in his breath.

Garrett looks as sane as ever, Wexler thought. *Solid, smart, sanguine. But he's talking fairy tales.*

"No, gentlemen, I'm not crazy." The President glared at them. "The United States is about to acquire a remnant of the same primordial light that created the entire universe. A tiny piece of the Big Bang. The whole world is after Firefly, and we're about to make it ours." Garrett rose from his chair, and both men also stood up.

"So the 2015 initiative—" Roderick began, his ruddy cheeks flushed brighter than usual.

"Irrelevant," Garrett snapped. "This project is top priority. You two are in charge of putting Firefly to work powering our PV arrays and grids. In the very near future, we won't need a drop of Middle Eastern oil—and we'll be equipped to explore galaxies so distant, Hubble can't even detect them yet."

Wexler found his voice. "Funding—"

Garrett held up a hand. "Whatever you need. Show them a PV power grid that can light up the entire country, and I guar-

antee Congress will hand you a blank check." Garrett's smile
was slow and deliberate. "Gentlemen, the United States of
America is about to write an entirely new Declaration of Inde-
pendence."

24

Rome

"Next step?" D'Amato asked, as he shifted the rental car into reverse and backed the Renault out of the parking space.

"I'll never be able to put one foot in front of the other if I don't get a few hours sleep—in a bed," Natalie said wearily. "But after that we should pay a visit to the Great Synagogue of Rome. The minute Ashton mentioned the Vatican Museums, I remembered—there's a small religious museum filled with rare antiquities and treasures right inside the synagogue."

"I didn't know that. I've seen the building down by the Tiber, but I've never been inside."

"It's a hidden gem. I spent a morning there about eight years ago when I stopped here in Rome. I treated myself—I needed a break after an especially grueling salvage excavation in Israel."

"Didn't know there was any other kind," he snorted. "I honestly don't know how you guys do it day in and day out. I've interviewed archaeologists in the field, and after only a few hours out there, I was ready to drop from the heat and the sun."

"It wasn't the elements that made it tough," Natalie replied quietly. "You protect yourself by drinking water and wearing hats and sunblock. But sometimes," she added grimly, "you can't anticipate everything that might happen." She was staring straight ahead, as if she was seeing something beyond the darkened city. "I made a friend there, a good one. And . . . she was killed."

As a journalist he knew that sometimes silence was the best way to elicit answers. Most people were uncomfortable with the sounds of silence.

"Her name was Maren Svendborg," Natalie said at last. "We were part of an international team sifting through some Byzantine ruins in the southern part of the city. Maren got there early one morning and . . ." Natalie's voice was so low D'Amato had to strain to hear. "She surprised a looter who'd unearthed a clay jug of seventh-century gold coins. Some of us were coming up the back road and saw him knife her. I watched her fall. She was dead before we reached her."

"I'm sorry," D'Amato said with a quick glance at her. "I know what it's like to see a colleague killed on the job. One of our news producers was killed in the suicide bombing that nailed me. I hope they caught the bastard who killed your friend."

"They did—within an hour. Not that it helped Maren—or her poor family in Denmark. The day after I returned to New York, I began training in Krav Maga. I couldn't stop thinking that if Maren had only known how to defend herself, she might be alive today." She was quiet for a moment. "Now I'll be thinking the same thing about Dana."

"Dana knew how to take care of herself," D'Amato said gently. "She wasn't a big person physically, but she could outthink, outargue, outsmart most anybody. She just ran into a situation none of us have a handle on yet." He slowed and turned right onto a road bumpy with cobblestones. "Have you kept it up? The Krav Maga?"

"Not regularly enough," she answered ruefully. "But a lot of it has become instinctive. Like roller skating, I guess. I just hope I don't need to use it again any time."

She shifted in her seat. "Getting back to what I started to say about the synagogue and the museum. It's possible someone there can help us with the Aramaic. Or at least direct us to someone else who can."

"I like it." D'Amato nodded in the darkness. "The synagogue's across the river from Trastevere. Let's find a place to crash near there."

As he merged into the light flow of traffic threading along the narrow warren of streets, Natalie noticed that D'Amato was checking the mirrors again. Warily she watched the headlights behind them in her side-view mirror. But the few other vehicles on the road either passed them or turned off onto other narrow cobbled streets, where cafés and shops sat dark and shuttered until dawn. Natalie's shoulders ached with accumulating tension. Her eyes burned with unshed tears and lack of sleep. The strain of the past thirty-six hours was taking its toll.

Crossing the courtyard of the Hotel Marcello di Mellini a half hour later, she was only dimly aware of its uneven cobbles, the ivy-covered old red bricks, the hotel's yellow mansard roof. Or of the three-story tenements hovering protectively around the ancient building.

"This place used to be a monastery," D'Amato told her, as they stepped inside the narrow lobby. "I've stayed here several times. It's nothing fancy, but it has real beds, and we'll be away from the crowds. I don't think anyone will track us here—at least not for the next few hours."

He wasn't kidding about the "nothing fancy." The lobby was short and narrow, leading only to a utilitarian elevator. Its only charm was its open medieval brickwork and beamed ceilings. Two slim antique wood tables holding baskets of oranges hugged the wall opposite the chest-high reception counter.

This lobby had no place for guests to congregate, and at this hour it was completely deserted. The only sign of life was the clerk on duty, a sleepy young man with a short Vandyke beard encircling his mouth and chin and not a whisper of hair on his pate. Contained in a claustrophobic work area the size of a narrow bedroom closet, he barely had to shift his stance to reach the numbered cubbies crammed with room keys. *Ergonomic, these Italians,* Natalie thought.

"I need your passport, Natalie." D'Amato already had his out. He reached for hers and then passed both sets of ID to the clerk.

"I noi documenti," D'Amato said in a beautifully accented

Italian. "On our honeymoon." He grinned at the half-awake young man. "She didn't have time to change her passport."

"Grazie, signore, signora." The clerk said something else that she didn't understand, just as she didn't understand why D'Amato had said they were on their honeymoon. But he seemed to comprehend Italian well as he handed over a credit card, and then accepted a single huge brass key with a heavy knob at its end.

It was a dozen steps to the minuscule cage that served as the elevator. *Good thing we're traveling light,* Natalie thought, squeezing beside D'Amato in a space not much bigger than a phone booth. Even a pair of suitcases wouldn't have fit inside its walls.

"Honeymoon?" Her brows lifted after the doors shut. "So that's our cover?"

"Partly. It also helps avoid any complications in sharing a room—and I think we need to stay together for safety's sake. But some of these Italian hotels still restrict unmarried couples from sharing a room, so . . ."

"In this day and age?" She shook her head as the doors clanked open two floors up, and she squeezed past him into the narrow corridor. "You've got to be kidding."

Their room was not much bigger than the elevator and was white-tiled and immaculately clean.

"You want the window or the door?" D'Amato asked, and she glanced at the two double beds with the two-drawer oak nightstand between them.

"Door." She tossed her shoulder bag onto the neatly turned-down floral coverlet and sank down on the edge of the bed.

"I was hoping you'd say that." D'Amato dropped his duffel near the window with a smile. "Anyone comes through that door, Krav Maga them."

"Don't think I couldn't," Natalie shot back, but she found herself smiling, too. "You don't snore, do you, D'Amato?"

"You can tell me in the morning," he said, taking off his shoes, easing onto the bed.

"If we're still alive in the morning." She hugged her arms around herself as D'Amato propped his arms behind his head.

"Thanks, by the way." She looked over at him with a small smile. " I'm actually glad you insisted on coming with me."

He yawned as she headed toward the bathroom. "You'd better reserve judgment until I pass the snore test."

By the time Natalie threw back her coverlet, and with the last of her energy slipped between the pressed sheets, D'Amato was watching CNN.

"Couldn't hurt to touch base with the outside world. Just for a few minutes. Do you mind?"

"Go for it," she mumbled. Her eyes were already closed. The broadcast was a vague, slightly irritating blur of white noise. From far away she heard something about the flooding in Sri Lanka. The upcoming summit in Jerusalem. The latest weather delay for the space shuttle. This was the longest "minute" she'd ever endured, Natalie thought foggily.

Suddenly she heard D'Amato curse, and he turned up the volume, sending the newscaster's voice blaring through the room.

". . . but New York authorities have ruled out terrorism in the car bombing that rocked the quiet Williamsburg section of Brooklyn last night . . ."

Eyes flying open, she heaved herself up on her elbows to squint at the screen.

". . . leaving two dead and seven injured. Unable to answer questions, the survivors remain under guard in intensive care at Woodhull Hospital. And in Sydney—"

"Was that . . . my building?" Natalie sat fully upright, all vestiges of sleep driven away by the shock of that burned-out car on the screen.

"It sure looked like it, didn't it?" D'Amato's face was grim. "We'll check it out in the morning, once we pick up the world phones. I'll make some calls—hopefully there's a few people at MSNBC still speaking to me."

Her heart still thumping, Natalie slumped back onto the pillow and folded an arm across her eyes. "They were after me. . . ."

"Someone knows a lot more about your pendant than we do." D'Amato clicked off the television, and Natalie heard him turn over.

Natalie closed her eyes, but found no refuge in sleep. She punched her pillow and tried to doze off again, but she couldn't shake the feeling that tomorrow things would only get worse.

Pensacola, Florida

Ken Mundy clicked off the phone, smiling as he set it down on the long oak table in his empty boardroom. He was pleased that his banker in Panama had recognized his voice instantly, though it wasn't surprising. Over the past month Mundy had been speaking with him on a nearly weekly basis, transferring up to a million dollars at a time into the secret bank account only he and the Shomrei Kotel could access.

No mean accomplishment for a kid whose only Christmas presents were delivered by the Salvation Army, he thought. His listless mother had received barely enough food stamps to keep bread and milk in the refrigerator and a few cans of beans and alphabet soup in the cupboard. There'd never been money for toys or books, although she'd always seemed to scare up enough spare change for a pack of cigarettes.

Sadness swept through him, not for himself, but for his mother. He'd forgiven her long ago, though she'd never forgiven him. From the earliest time he could remember he'd wondered why his mother almost never looked at him, not even when he threw his arms around her knees, crying because he'd hurt himself while playing outside.

It wasn't until he was fourteen that it hit him like a sucker punch why she didn't have even a single picture of his father. Why his last name was the same as hers and her parents. That day, he and Travis Wilson had come to blows in gym class. "Y'ain't nothin' but a common bastard," Travis had taunted, as he danced around Mundy, throwing punches while the other kids laughed.

A bastard, he'd thought, as he landed a solid right to bloody Travis's lip just before the gym teacher shoved himself between them. *Mamma lied. My parents were never married.*

The idea shocked and shamed him, but the truth had been even uglier than that.

"Oh, you're a bastard, all right." His mother's pinched face had flamed red when he'd explained to her why he'd come home with a detention note from the principal. "You really want the truth? Do you? Your father was some pervert who grabbed me on my way home from school and left me bleeding in a field," she'd bit out, years of hatred for her attacker finally spewing across their tiny, grease-streaked kitchen. "I never seen him before, and I never seen the son-of-a-bitch again, unless I look at *you*."

After that day Ken Mundy hadn't spent much time at home. He couldn't bear to burden his mother with having to look at him. He hung out at his friends' houses till bedtime, shared their families' simple meals and everyday conversations. He always kept a smile stretched across his face, belying how lost and worthless he felt inside—until he found his Savior.

Jesus had become his true parent, the one who loved him without reservation. And he had become a worthy son. Jesus had taught him how to hold his head up, how to become a man—and not just any man, but a leader. A visionary. That vision, a gift from the Lord, was guiding him still. Guiding him to the Light, guiding him to build the third and final Temple.

The funds he was transferring from the Sons of Babylon's offshore account in Panama to the Shomrei Kotel would soon purchase the precious cedar and stone needed to begin construction. He could only imagine all the souls he would save once that glorious edifice soared into the sky above Jerusalem, the Light glowing above its altar.

The Sentinel had been invaluable in teaching him the ins and outs of dummy foundations and corporations. The intricacies of offshore banking had become ridiculously complicated after 9/11. In an attempt to identify funds tied to terrorism, governments across the globe had agreed to cooperate, to assist each other in following money trails. Then the EU Savings Tax Directive of 2005 had limited the privacy of offshore bank accounts even further.

Switzerland and the Cayman Islands were no longer the safe havens they had once been, but with the Sentinel's guidance and personal introduction to a well-placed Panamanian attorney, Mundy had managed to transfer his church's substantial assets from Switzerland to Panama—one of the few remaining places that took no interest in its foreign depositors' finances.

Mundy reached into his breast pocket and pulled out the invitation that would allow him entry to the upcoming summit. He traced his fingers across the raised lettering on the cream-colored paper.

The Temple Mount. He, Ken Mundy, bastard son of a rapist, had come far indeed. Soon he would witness history from a front-row seat alongside heads of state and world leaders.

Even better: Once the Light was in his hands and the Temple was rebuilt, he himself would usher in the final chapter of the history of the world.

25

The next thing Natalie knew, a church bell was pealing and pale daylight was slanting behind the drapes. She pushed herself up and peered at the bedside clock: 5:00 A.M.

Her skin felt clammy and gritty, and her mouth tasted like cotton. She remembered that she hadn't even brushed her teeth last night. Now she couldn't stand the film on them. Stumbling out of bed, she pulled her newly acquired toothbrush from her shoulder bag and crept toward the bathroom. Her foil packets of toothpaste were long gone, but D'Amato must have some Crest in his toiletry bag.

She glanced over at him, still asleep, hunched on his side beneath the twisted covers, dark stubble across his jawline.

For an old hotel, it had a decent shower. The warm water pulsed over her in calming waves. But Natalie didn't feel calm. She was impatient to get moving.

She stepped out, towel-dried her hair, and dressed quickly in the clothes she'd been wearing for two days. Then she reached for D'Amato's toiletry bag, which was hanging on the back of the door. She peered past the straight-edged razor and spotted the tube of Crest alongside a travel-sized can of shaving cream. She also spotted something else. Something that made her heart stand still.

A packet of passports. Rubber-banded together, tucked to

the side, jacketed in navy blue, maroon, and dark green. She pulled them out, slipped off the rubber band, and flipped them open, one after the other. D'Amato's face stared up from each one, but each one showed a different name.

Giorgio Antonelli.

Clifford Black.

Dmitri Cassavetes.

She blinked through the steam of the bathroom, trying to make sense of the documents in her hand.

Why is D'Amato traveling with false IDs? What the hell is he up to?

She pushed her damp hair from her eyes and tried to think. Confused, she restacked the passports in the same order and slid the rubber band back into place. All she knew right now was that she wasn't ready to let on that she'd discovered these.

She squeezed a tiny blob of toothpaste onto her toothbrush, then stuffed everything back in his bag exactly as she'd found it and hung it back on the door.

Uneasily, she scrubbed her teeth, then swallowed the toothpaste so he wouldn't hear her spit it out if he was awake, wouldn't wonder if she'd borrowed it from his bag.

Get hold of yourself. Act normally. All you have to do right now is get back into bed and pretend to sleep. You don't want to call his bluff now—when you don't know what he's up to. Just play along for the next few hours.

She heard a rustling sound, and her hand froze on the doorknob.

He's awake.

She took a couple of breaths and opened the door. She eased out, expecting to find him waiting for the bathroom, but D'Amato was still across the room in his bed, exactly as she'd left him. Natalie exhaled a small breath and slipped back to her bed, then reached an arm down silently to the floor, checking inside her shoulder bag. The pendant was still there in its pouch.

She slid beneath the covers, and it seemed an eternity until she heard the bedsprings shift beneath D'Amato's weight. She feigned sleep and waited to see what he'd do.

She heard him pad across the polished wood floor and pause

beside her bed and somehow controlled the urge to open her eyes, the same way she controlled her breathing to convince him she was still lost in sleep.

When the bathroom door clicked shut behind him, she opened her eyes. It took him only fifteen minutes to shave, shower, and dress. Again she feigned sleep, not ready to talk to him, not ready to pretend she didn't know he was keeping something from her.

She rehearsed what she'd say, how she'd behave once he woke her. But he didn't wake her. The next thing she heard was the door to their room clicking closed behind him.

He was gone.

Natalie waited thirty seconds, then threw off her covers, sprang out of bed, and looked around. D'Amato's backpack was gone. So was his toiletry bag.

She grabbed her shoulder bag and raced for the stairs.

Barnabas lumbered toward the Basilica of Saint Peter, scanning a guidebook to Rome. Until the Sentinel gave him more information, he'd scope out the crowds of tourists converging on the Vatican and pray he got lucky. It seemed to him there would be no better place for Landau to hide the Light than in the impenetrable Vatican City.

Until he heard otherwise, he would follow the Sentinel's instructions and keep trolling the most traveled streets and ruins, until the Lord granted him the knowledge of where she and her companion were. Or until the Sentinel finally figured it out. In either case, he was ready.

Sooner or later he would spot her—and the washed-up journalist helping her.

His second meeting with Landau would be far more productive than his first.

26

D'Amato briefly used his cell phone in the hotel lobby. The call lasted far less than the three-minute window needed for anyone to trace it. He stepped outside and hailed a cab, then gave the driver an address near the Piazza Navona.

With any luck he'd be back before Natalie even noticed he was gone.

Peter Driscoll sat reading a newspaper just inside the door of the small café where they'd arranged to meet. His long legs were tucked beneath the table so as not to trip any of the customers flowing to and from the register. He appeared to be following the text intently, but D'Amato knew better.

Driscoll had packed on a few pounds since the last time they'd met, D'Amato noticed. But with his height, he could handle it. His longish sandy hair was now flecked with gray, and he sported a short goatee, but D'Amato had no difficulty recognizing him. His face was still ordinary enough that he could have been anybody—and any age from thirty-five to fifty, any national origin from Australian to American to Swedish. He wasn't memorable, which made him well suited for what he did.

Driscoll had bought them both a brioche and a cappuccino, but waited until he spotted D'Amato before he rose to join the throng at the counter and claim them from the harried clerk.

They took seats outside at a small, cloth-covered table offering a view of the most famous fountain in the piazza, Bernini's Fontana dei Quattro Fiumi—the Four Rivers. Pigeons waddled everywhere, pecking and flapping through the large square, but few people were out this early to feed them. The crowds would swarm the square later—now there were only the usual pensioners sunning themselves on stone benches, and passersby rushing, intent on reaching their favorite café for a hasty breakfast before work.

Through the window of the *farmacia* across the street, Natalie watched the two men talking across the table. Catching a cab had been easier than she'd expected as she'd watched D'Amato's taxi speed away from the hotel. But following him had been an unsettling experience, especially since she knew how observant he was. She'd been worried he'd spot her taxi and had let her driver continue on for another block, once D'Amato alighted, so she could double back on foot.

Now she studied him. He'd altered his appearance: a baseball cap, visor pulled low; aviator glasses that seemed to change the shape of his face.

She wished she could hear what they were saying over their coffees and pastries, but she didn't dare try to move any closer. She knew he'd be watching his surroundings. What she didn't know was who was with him and what was on their agenda.

"*Scusi.*" An elderly woman in a fashionable black dress reached past her to pluck a tube of insect-bite ointment from a glass shelf.

Natalie glanced her way for a moment, and when she looked back toward the café, D'Amato and his companion were walking away together.

Swearing under her breath, she edged out of the *farmacia* and craned her neck as they turned a corner. She hurried forward, keeping close to the fronts of the buildings.

She trailed them for three blocks, hanging back, busying herself with shop windows and an aimless demeanor. After an additional block they entered what looked to her like an old brick apartment building. *Now what do I do?*

Five minutes later he exited the building alone and headed

back the way they'd just come. Anger and curiosity propelled her after him. She crossed the street a dozen yards back, then quickened her pace as he disappeared around a corner.

Impatience was gnawing through Hasan Sabouri like a drill bit through a vault. His phone was already pressed against his ear as his plane taxied toward the gate at Fiumicino.

"Tell me how things stand."

"Our friends are in Trastevere. Guests of the Hotel Marcello di Montagna. They went straight to the British School in Rome from the airport last night."

"And?" Hasan's eyes narrowed in concentration, as all around him people began unbuckling their seatbelts and the plane came to a stop.

"They stayed inside for more than two hours, enough time for me to secure the tracker under their rental car."

Hasan unbuckled his own seatbelt, ignoring the passengers getting to their feet around him.

"And today?"

"The car is still parked near the hotel. I'm only a block away."

"How do you know they have not left on foot?"

Silence.

Hasan felt anger coil through him, and he suppressed his urge to shout into the phone. How was it he'd had to end up relying on this fool? But for the next hour or two, Siddiq Aziz was all he had. Almost everyone else was already in Jerusalem. Fortunately, backup from Naples was en route.

His lips twisted with contempt as he pictured Aziz with his international finance degree, his diamond cuff lnks and buffed nails. Aziz had spent too much time in the West—he had never been a foot soldier. He was a decent marksman, but he didn't like to get his hands dirty. He preferred sitting in his marble office and moving money around. And yet, this was the man now keeping tabs on the Eye of Dawn. Aziz, who thought he was so cunning, but who knew nothing of the streets or alleyways, and even less of dipping one's hands in the warmth of an enemy's blood.

"Listen to me carefully," Hasan bit out. "Get yourself to the front of that hotel and wait for me. Who is picking me up?"

"Jalil. He's already at the airport."

"If you see them leave the hotel, call me immediately. Follow them and do not lose them. Do you understand?"

"Of course." Aziz sounded resentful, but there was a hint of cockiness in his voice. "I'll take care of it."

"Above all," Hasan added, his voice thick with warning, "be discreet. Remember what is at stake. I will be there shortly."

Aziz slipped on his sunglasses as he watched the hotel doorway. Perhaps it had been a mistake to watch the car and not the entrance to the hotel.

Siddiq Aziz didn't like admitting making a mistake, not even to himself.

He only hoped his assessment had been right—that the Americans were still inside and that the Eye of Dawn was there with them.

Uneasy, he stepped off the curb and headed toward the lobby, an idea playing in his head. He would approach the clerk and bribe him into sharing the Americans' room number. By the time Hasan arrived, he would already have reclaimed the Eye of Dawn.

His SIG Sauer P226 was chambered and ready—and he had the element of surprise on his side. It would be even better if they were still sleeping. . . .

Wouldn't that take the sneer from Hasan's voice?

He thinks his contribution is greater than anyone else's. Without my expertise at moving large sums of money undetected, we could never have funded this project so quickly. I have more brains and ideas in my head than Hasan Sabouri and his brother Farshid both. I should be the one who claims the Eye of Dawn for the khalifate—and hand it to Hasan when he arrives. Let's see how he speaks to me then.

For a moment the daydream propelled him toward the desk, imagining the respect and admiration in Hasan's all-seeing blue eyes. And then he stopped short and remembered the nature of the man who had just arrived in Rome.

Hasan Sabouri was not only proud, but quick tempered. Aziz had seen him strike a man who was slow to reply to his question. Above all, Sabouri possessed the evil eye and did not hesitate to cast his wicked glance. He had killed many with his eye alone, even his own mother.

If something goes wrong with this plan, or if Hasan is offended by it, Hasan will not hesitate to kill me, too.

Aziz glanced around the minuscule lobby, at the high-beamed ceiling and single faded mural, and reconsidered. He strolled to one of the side tables and helped himself to an orange.

Then Aziz returned the female desk clerk's friendly *buon giorno* and ambled back outside and across the cobbled street to wait.

27

Natalie quickened her gait. D'Amato had slipped into a narrow, dim alleyway. The sun slanted and slivered between the buildings. A Vespa zipped past her, ruffling her hair. Up ahead, D'Amato turned right into an adjacent alley.

She skimmed around the same corner a moment later and shrieked as she crashed into his chest.

"What do you think you're doing?" he demanded.

"You're asking *me* questions? I'm the one trying to find out what *you're* up to!"

"I should've left you a note." His tone was calmer, but his eyes were unreadable. "I went out for some breakfast."

"You had company." Her eyes challenged him in the alley. "You didn't mention you had a friend in Rome. You also neglected to mention that you're a man of many identities. So who are you today, D'Amato? Or is it Cassavetes? Or maybe Antonelli?"

He frowned at her. "This isn't the place for this."

"You picked the place. I want to know what's going on."

"Not here, Natalie. It's not safe. It's not smart. Let's head to the synagogue. I'll explain everything later."

"No way." She shoved him away as he tried to take her arm. His matter-of-fact tone was infuriating her. There was so much she didn't know, couldn't figure out, and here he stood, stonewalling her about the one thing he *could* explain. "I want answers *now*," she demanded. "I'm not budging another step until you level with me."

A footfall sounded behind them, and they spun to face the noise.

A young man had entered their alley, a cell phone to his ear, and was heading toward them with a bouncy step.

D'Amato tensed. *Lanky, maybe twenty-three, twenty-four. Close-cropped dark hair, olive complexion. Jeans, sneakers—laces untied. Not a professional.*

Just the same, D'Amato's left hand slipped into his pants pocket as the stranger neared. It remained there until the kid had sauntered around the corner, lost in his cell phone conversation.

"Natalie. Just listen to me. Let's go back to the hotel, get you a cup of coffee. And then we'll talk. It's not secure here." He glanced purposefully at her shoulder bag. "You know that as well as I do."

She hesitated, her feet still planted firmly on the smooth bricks beneath them. But she knew he was right about two things: It wasn't safe here and they damn well needed to talk.

Around the corner the olive-skinned young man waited to see where the pair in the alley went next. As they headed toward him, he quickened his pace and skimmed into the shadows of a leather-goods shop, waiting until they'd passed.

Then he knelt and quickly tied his sneakers.

28

The reception clerk set down the stack of fluffy white towels she was sending up to room 3D and stared uneasily at the two men across the counter.

"The Americans. We're looking for the Americans, you idiot! What room are they in?" As the woman shook her head and reached for the phone, Hasan Sabouri leaned across the slim reception counter and backhanded her. She gasped, recoiling in shock, and dropped the phone. One hand went to her swollen belly as tears of pain sprang from her eyes.

In panic, she glanced frantically toward the elevator, praying someone would come down. But the lobby was deserted. Most of the guests had already gone out, their heavy knobbed room keys dropped on the reception counter for her to shelve in their cubbies behind her.

"*Per favore, signore.* Please," she gasped, blinking to clear the tears. Then she froze. The blue-eyed man had slid a gun from beneath his suit jacket. A gun with something stuck on the end of its barrel.

The young woman paled. She grabbed the registration book from its shelf below the counter and shoved it at him. "Look for yourself. I don't know these *Americani.* You find."

The well-dressed man, the one wearing diamond cuff links

and dark sunglasses, yanked the book from the counter and scoured it. His finger paused at room 2C.

Landau—Brooklyn, New York. D'Amato—New York City.

Siddiq Aziz grinned with satisfaction. The clerk who'd checked them in had neatly copied the information from their passports. "It's right here. Room 2C."

"Take the stairs," Hasan ordered, his gun still trained on the petrified woman. "I'll follow in the elevator."

Aziz loped toward the staircase. Hasan leaped over the registration counter, scattering the stack of towels to the floor. "Face down. On the ground."

The young woman backed up in the tiny space, her liquid black eyes fixated on the gun.

"Now!" The ferocity of his tone sent her crashing to her knees.

"Per favore, signore . . . il bambino . . ."

"Now! Face down!"

Quivering, she obeyed him.

The silencer swallowed the explosions as he put two bullets in her head.

There was no time to clean her blood from his shoes. He grabbed the room key from cubby 2C and sprinted for the elevator. Aziz was waiting for him outside the Americans' room, only slightly breathless.

But when Hasan twisted the key and shoved open the door, they found themselves staring into an empty room, barren but for the twin beds, rumpled and unmade. No personal belongings in sight. Seething with disappointment, Hasan checked the bathroom. The floor mat was damp and the tub still speckled with water droplets.

"You worthless idiot!" He spun on Aziz, his arctic blue eyes sparking with wrath. "Watching the car and not the door!"

"Patience, Hasan—we can wait for them. The car is still here. They will come back."

"Might come back!" Hasan spat. "The police might be here first." He glanced down at his shoes with a cold smile. "I'll have to leave them a message."

29

D'Amato held the hotel door open as Natalie gulped at a double espresso from her cardboard cup. As usual, the lobby was deserted. There wasn't even anyone manning the reception counter. Several room keys left by guests who'd gone out for the morning were scattered across it, theirs among them.

He palmed the heavy key with a frown. Not unusual for these small, understaffed, family-run hotels, but not ideal security either.

Neither spoke as they rode up in the elevator. Natalie had braced herself against the wall, away from him. Her face was tight with anger.

As the elevator jolted to a stop, D'Amato grimaced involuntarily. The pain he'd been trying to ignore all morning suddenly screamed through his left side: damned poisoned shrapnel, courtesy of the terrorists intent on reclaiming Jerusalem, who'd embedded it by design where no surgeon's knife could scrape it out. One minute he'd been scooping hummus onto pita bread and the next the café where he lunched most days had exploded into chaos, rubble, and body parts.

Sometimes the pain waited, dormant, merely a constant nagging ache. Other times it flared, searing without warning. On a scale of one to ten, right now it was soaring past seven. In days past at this point he'd be scrambling for a couple of Lortabs.

"What's wrong?" Frowning, Natalie followed him out of the elevator. "You're pale and drenched with sweat. Are you okay?"

"Never better." He glanced at his watch. Eight fifteen. Forty-five minutes until the Great Synagogue opened its fortified doors.

"When are you going to tell me who that man was?" Natalie prodded as he shoved the key into the tumbler.

"He's just a guy who happens to deal in cell phones." His voice was low as he pushed the door wide and glanced inside. He preceded her into the room, automatically scanning it. "He—"

D'Amato froze, and she nearly collided into his rigid back.

Smeared in red along the wall was a crudely drawn eye, staring out at them. In its center, like a bull's-eye, shone a bloody pupil the size of a basketball—pierced by a knife.

A scream froze in her throat. Seconds ticked past as thick silence sucked the air from the room.

"Let's go!" Suddenly, somehow, there was a gun in D'Amato's hand. With the other hand, he shoved her out the door.

Barnabas stopped abruptly in his tracks. He was opposite the Coliseum when it hit him.

Wrong pew.

Streams of people flowed around him as he remembered that the Landau woman was a Jew. He'd seen that Star of David in her jewelry case. How could he have forgotten?

He flipped through the pages of his tour guide. She would head to a synagogue. There was only one of any note listed. It had a museum. Right up her alley.

He memorized the address, folded the guide, and stuck it back in his hip pocket. In two quick strides he beat an elderly couple to a cab disgorging a trio of chattering college girls at the corner. And a moment later he was on his way to the Great Synagogue of Rome.

30

"Where did you get that gun?" Natalie demanded as they raced down the ancient stone stairs.

"Where do you think?" D'Amato shoved the Glock back into his windbreaker pocket as they reached the lobby. Not that anyone would have noticed he had it—the lobby was still deserted.

"And it's a good thing I got it this morning, since it looks like we'll need it. This way."

She followed him into a corridor off the lobby that she hadn't noticed before. "Are we getting the car?"

"No. Sure as they've found us, they've got a tracker on it. Put this on." He yanked off his baseball cap and shoved it at her. "Backward."

"I was beginning to hope we were safe here," she muttered, sweeping her long dark hair under the elastic band, her heart racing. She lengthened her strides to keep up with his. "How could someone have found us already?"

"A better question is, how do we keep them from finding us again. Especially if that pendant you've got is as special as a lot of people seem to think." As they ran, D'Amato reached into his left jacket pocket, yanked out a cell phone, and thrust it at her. "World phone. Untraceable. I've already programmed my number into yours and vice versa."

"My, you *were* busy this morning."

"It helps to have friends—and people who trust me."

"So the man you met—"

"Let's do this later, Natalie, okay? We need to concentrate on one thing at a time."

She chose not to reply. She was still furious with him, but she knew he was right. The danger had found them, and she and D'Amato needed to work together—at least for now. Whatever he was up to with those fake IDs, she couldn't believe he meant her any harm. She noticed the tension that seemed to vibrate through his entire body. He seemed different somehow. The efficient, thoughtful reporter seemed colder, more brusque than she'd seen him. He guided her through a side door that led to the back of the courtyard, where elaborate cement planters with ferns cascading from them appeared to seal off the small yard. But he pulled her between the greenery and through a black wrought-iron gate, ivy rustling as they swept past. Natalie doubted she'd ever have spotted the gate on her own.

The alleyway they entered was narrow and winding, a mere ribbon of cold, cobbled stone threading between buildings just tall enough to block the sun. Brightly colored laundry blew gently overhead, pinned on the web of clotheslines stretching between opposite apartment building windows. Running to keep up with him, she wondered when and how he'd discovered this way out—and if she'd live long enough to ask him all the questions percolating through her head.

Moments later they emerged into the watery March sunshine bathing Via dei Salumi, two blocks south of the hotel's entrance.

"We'll need to backtrack some now," D'Amato told her, slipping on sunglasses. "But once we hit Piazza in Piscinula, it's only a short walk to the bridge. We'll be able to spot the synagogue's dome from there. It's the only squared, aluminum one in all of Rome."

Piscinula, Natalie knew, had been Trastevere's port until it was destroyed to make way for the current embankments.

The streets here near the old Jewish Ghetto were narrow and twisting. Hurrying through the congested heart of Trastevere, she found herself confused by the complicated maze of tight winding lanes lined with medieval buildings, restaurants, and shops. Without a map, without D'Amato, she'd have easily gotten lost trying to find her way. On her previous visit to the synagogue, she'd taken a cab from the Coliseum.

She glanced repeatedly over her shoulder as they charged past lesser piazzas scattered around the main piazza, past waiters already at work setting out starched linens and arranging plates, glasses, and flatware, even though *il pranzo*, lunchtime, wouldn't start until well after noon.

"The bridge—this way." He slowed his pace now that they were out in the open and slipped an arm around her waist. "Pretend we're tourists," he told her under his breath, as he bought them each a cup of coffee from a street vendor. "A normal couple on a walking tour of the medieval quarter."

It was all she could do to paste on a carefree expression. As he made a show of pointing out the landmarks they passed, she responded mechanically, feeling none of the relaxed enjoyment of a tourist—let alone a lovey-dovey honeymooner. In fact, she barely heard D'Amato's voice and had to force herself to feign interest when all she could picture was that bloody eye on the wall. *With that knife plunged into its center.*

Her pulse quickened as they left the heart of the Jewish Ghetto at last and stepped onto the Ponte Cestio, the bridge leading to the island in the bend of the Tiber. Isola Tiberina—Tiber Island—was in turn connected to the opposite side of the river by the Ponte Fabricio, the oldest bridge in all of Rome, built in 62 B.C.

A wave of relief nearly buckled her knees as she saw the synagogue at last. Tall, imposing, and yet graceful, it stood at the corner of Lungotevere dei Cenci and via Portico d'Ottavia, opposite Julius Caesar's curved, ancient Theater of Marcellus—which had by now been morphed into an apartment building.

She fixed her gaze on the Great Synagogue of Rome. Built in 1904, after the emancipation of Italian Jews following Italy's unification, its style was an eclectic mix of Roman, Greek, and Assyro-Babylonian.

Il Tempio Maggiore di Roma. Guarded. Impregnable. *Safe.*

"How many men do we have covering the airport?" Hasan stared out the car window, scouring the faces on the streets as Jalil circled back yet again through the intricate maze of the Jewish Ghetto.

"Double that number," the Iranian barked into his phone, his face red with anger. "They must not get out of Rome."

He'd sent Aziz to the Termini, the central train station, ahead of the cell members converging on Rome. Those men were stationed now throughout the teeming terminal, roving between the trains and the ticket office.

But just as he had found no luck here in Trastevere, his brothers in the Termini were coming up empty-handed as well. He clamped the Hand of Fatima charm that had belonged to Landau's sister in his fist, its metal edges pressing into his flesh.

He needed the Eye of Dawn by tomorrow. The President of the United States was already en route to Tel Aviv. The triumph of the khalifate was imminent.

The Eye of Dawn would assure their victory. Wasn't it written by the mullahs? *The khalifate will rule once more, uniting all of Islam, and then the world, when the Eye of Dawn shines forth from Al-Haram al-Sharif.*

The Eye of Dawn, Allah's beacon, was right here in Rome. And he would soon have it.

Armed Rome police were first stationed at the Great Synagogue of Rome following the 1982 Palestinian attack, and they continued to patrol the street to this day—twenty-four/seven. Natalie began to breathe easier only when she spotted them along the building's perimeter.

Israeli security manned the revolving glass front door, allowing entry to only one visitor at a time.

"Hold on. I'll need to stash the Glock if I want to get through that door," D'Amato said into her ear. He held out his hand for her paper cup. "Finished with your coffee?"

Nonchalantly, he strode toward a trash receptacle ten steps away, and Natalie watched as he pushed both of their cups into the bin, his thick wrists disappearing deep inside. She hadn't seen the gun in his hand, but she knew he'd hidden it. *Since when did they teach this stuff in journalism school?*

He loped back, looking far more relaxed than she was feeling. "You first," he told her quietly, as they passed one of the palms that flanked the synagogue.

"You'll need to wear this." Natalie handed him back his baseball cap. "Men need to have their heads covered in the synagogue—a sign of respect."

A dark-skinned, fine-featured Israeli guard at the door studied her passport. He was an Ethiopian Jew, a descendant of those rescued from religious persecution, war, and famine in their native country and brought to safety in Israel between the late seventies and the early nineties.

"Step inside," he instructed in Hebrew-accented English, as he returned her passport and reached for the one D'Amato offered along with his press credentials. The muscular soldier was all business as he studied both sides of the Israeli press pass D'Amato still carried from his days as Jerusalem bureau chief.

The guard's large, round eyes gazed long and hard into D'Amato's, as if trying to discern his thoughts. Natalie found herself holding her breath until at last he nodded and waved D'Amato through.

Natalie felt relieved to be inside. Rome held danger for them, but their enemies couldn't touch them here.

They moved toward the ticket counter, where a sophisticated fortyish woman collected their €7.50 admission fee. She had cherry-red hair and a beauty mark near her upper lip. Oversized gold hoop earrings swung on her ears and a long gold necklace grazed the swell of her ample breasts. Her name tag said she was Giovanna Trentini.

"Is the museum director available?" Natalie asked her quickly. "I'm a curator from New York, here on a professional basis. I have some archaeological questions I hope he or she can help me answer."

"*Uno momento, signora.*" With an eye-crinkling smile, the woman flicked a switch on her walkie-talkie and spoke in rapid Italian before turning back to Natalie.

"If you'll have a seat in the sanctuary, Dr. Sonnino will be up in a few moments. She is more than happy to speak with you."

Natalie led D'Amato into the large, vaulted sanctuary, knowing it would hold its own among the countless gilded Italian churches and cathedrals D'Amato must have seen in his day.

They walked through pale prisms of light that poured from the stained-glass windows—most of it tinged in shades of yellows and blues. The light spilled to the floor and across the rows of wooden pews like a liquid kaleidoscope. The ceiling was painted with stars, and beautiful Moorish designs adorned the walls in rainbow hues from the floor to the ceiling. There were only a handful of tourists wandering through at this hour.

"What's up there, the women's seating?" D'Amato asked, glancing upward past the soaring columns that supported the galleries cloistered behind a wrought-iron balcony that wrapped north, south, and west.

"Yes," she said tightly. "The style is similar to the Sephardic."

She walked away from him, toward the plaques that listed the names of Italian Jewish victims of both world wars. She wasn't in the mood for small talk.

He followed her to the plaques. "Look, I know you're upset. You think I'm a liar and God knows what else. But I'm on your side—you have to believe that."

"Not good enough, D'Amato." Her gaze was fixed stoically on the plaques. "If you don't level with me right now, I'll walk out of here alone. I don't need help from someone who's not going to be up-front with me." Then she faced him, challenge in her eyes. "Why all the passports? What are you hiding?"

"If I tell you, I'm supposed to kill you."

"Get in line." Despite his facetious tone, she'd heard an undercurrent of truth that made her very nervous.

He lowered his voice. "Natalie, I'm exactly who I say I am." He looked away. Conflicted. "And something more."

She waited.

"During my stint in Jerusalem I was approached by our government. They told me I was in a position to help—as a journalist I had my eyes and ears on the ground. Exactly what they needed. So they trained me."

"The CIA?" Suddenly it was starting to make sense. "That guy you met this morning . . ."

"A Rome asset."

"He didn't only give you the phones; he gave you the gun."

"Unofficially. It was a personal favor. I'm not on active status anymore. They relieved me of duty when I first went into rehab."

"So what's the real reason you're helping me?" Natalie kept her voice level. "To get back in the CIA's good graces?"

His eyes narrowed. "I told you, Natalie, this has become personal. I'm not interested in impressing the CIA. I'm doing this because the two of us were shot at. I'm doing it for Dana. And for Rusty. And because I can."

Before she could think how to respond she noticed a tall, slim woman striding purposefully toward them.

Elena Sonnino was an elegant woman of about fifty. Her long brown hair, shot with a few strands of silver, was caught in a loose chignon at the nape of her neck, in a style that was effortlessly classic.

"*Buon giorno,*" she said, extending her hand.

Natalie introduced herself and D'Amato, and thanked her for seeing them on such short notice. Then she opened her bag and withdrew the photocopies of the infrared enhancements Dr. Ashton had made.

"I believe this is Aramaic, but I'm having difficulty deciphering it. Some of the characters are only partially visible. I realized that most of your collection is Italian, but I'm hoping you might direct me to someone who could shed some light on this."

Dr. Sonnino glanced at the enhancements. "*Mi dispiace.* I'm so sorry, but I, myself, can't read Aramaic."

"Are there any Aramaic parchment fragments here we could use for comparison purposes?" D'Amato asked quickly.

"I'm afraid not. Our collection here focuses on Italian Jewish art—tapestries, Torah mantles, silver ritual objects. For example, menorahs, havdalah sets, and kiddush cups," she explained. "We have many unique examples of Jewish culture as it evolved here in Rome since we were brought into captivity by Titus. But unfortunately, I don't believe we have a single fragment written in Aramaic." She handed the enhancements back to Natalie.

"Our rabbi may be able to help you, however," Sonnino added thoughtfully.

"Is he here? Could we show this to him?"

The museum director lifted a tanned arm and checked her watch. "Rabbi Calo is finishing up with the small study group he meets with twice a week. You're welcome to wait in his office, and I'll send him in to see you as soon as he's done."

"That would be wonderful," Natalie said.

Sonnino left them seated in small wooden chairs in the rabbi's study, where countless dusty volumes in cracked leather bindings gave off a faint musty odor reminiscent of old school buildings that have been closed up all summer. Opposite a small oak desk littered with papers hung a magnificent tapestry in shades of plums and golds, pumpkins and greens. It was a vibrant wedding scene depicting a bridal couple facing each other beneath their chuppah, surrounded by smiling relatives in fifteenth-century finery.

D'Amato contemplated the rich nuptial scene. "How about you? Ever been married?"

"Engaged. It was a close call."

He turned toward her with a raised eyebrow.

"Trust issues." She threw him a pointed glance. Then the creak of footsteps sounded from the wooden stairs, and they both stood as a small, wiry man with ebony hair came bounding into the room.

"Rabbi Calo?" Natalie had expected someone older.

"*Si, si.* Israel Benjamin Calo. Sit, sit, and welcome to Rome."

Barnabas alighted from the cab and studied the armed soldier at the synagogue's entrance. He was scrutinizing a woman's documents as she waited to enter.

He walked past the building, then around it, casually checking for exits and side doors. Then he returned to the front, strolling at a leisurely pace, the tour guide tucked under his arm. He leaned against a palm tree ten yards east of the entrance, pretending to study the guide.

But he had a clear view of the front door in his peripheral vision. They wouldn't get in or out without him knowing.

31

Ralph Gallagher had smelled death in the lobby of the Marcello di Montagna even as the policeman barring the door waved him through. It was a familiar metallic smell, one that never failed to trigger a spasm of nausea.

He suppressed the bile rising in his throat as Inspector Franco Rossini strode toward him. Rossini's fleshy face was morose beneath the heavy shadow of facial hair no amount of shaving could ever fully eliminate.

"Animals, my friend," the police inspector muttered, swiping a handkerchief across his brow. "They shot the poor desk clerk through the back of the head. A double tap. She was only twenty-three, and was four months pregnant."

"What about the Americans?" Gallagher had no time for niceties. He and the NSU team who'd been scouring Rome for Natalie Landau and Jim D'Amato had finally caught a break, but it had come too late. All night they'd been combing the city for Landau and D'Amato while the pair had been at this hotel. And now they weren't.

Someone, however, had discovered they were staying here and had left them a message written in blood. Gallagher needed to see that message.

Rossini had called him at the embassy as a courtesy, since

the room that had been violated belonged to two Americans. In addition, the Rome police department was interested in any information the embassy could share about who these Americans were and why this attack had transpired.

"The Americans are gone. No sign of them." Rossini turned to shout a directive at the gloved policeman gathering room keys from the reception counter into a plastic zippered bag.

"They haven't checked out"—he shrugged—"they haven't returned."

"And their room key?" Gallagher shifted his weight.

"We found it on the floor of their room. No doubt they saw the knife in the wall and fled."

Or they've been taken hostage, Gallagher thought, a slight headache beginning to pound over his brows.

The inspector was studying him closely. "Perhaps you have some idea, Senore Gallagher, why someone would attack the Americans' room in such a fashion and find it necessary to kill the clerk of this hotel?"

"None whatsoever, I'm afraid." Gallagher's face was a mask of neutrality.

To Rossini, Gallagher was nothing more than what his cover claimed he was—the attaché to the American ambassador in Rome. The Italian policeman hadn't a clue that Gallagher was NSU or that the missing Americans were being hunted by numerous interested parties.

Gallagher wasn't about to share with him the information that Interpol, the CIA, the FBI, and the Guardians of the Khalifah were among those bent on wresting Firefly from Natalie Landau—no matter what it took. It was imperative that Gallagher get to her—*to it*—first.

The sooner he scoped out the scene, the sooner he'd be able to redirect the rest of his team in hunting down Landau and D'Amato.

And Firefly.

Their room in this hotel gave him the starting point he'd been lacking. Now he had a trail to follow. A trail that wasn't nearly as cold as the desk clerk, lying with what was left of her face covered in the ambulance outside, about to be conveyed to the morgue.

"Show me the room, Franco. I want to see this drawing you told me about on the phone."

32

Rabbi Calo gestured Natalie and D'Amato back into their chairs and tossed a packet of study sheets onto his desk. He pumped D'Amato's arm with zest and Natalie's with similar enthusiasm.

He had a dazzling smile, a dimple in his chin, and deep-set, dark, puppy dog eyes that twinkled with friendliness behind wire-rimmed glasses. "How can I help you, my friends? Elena tells me you have some Aramaic writings?" He beckoned with his fingers, inviting them to give it over.

Natalie complied. "Any help you can give us, Rabbi, would be tremendously appreciated. We first need to confirm that this *is* Aramaic, and second, we need to know what it says."

His dark eyes first darted over the enhancements, then lifted to Natalie's face. "This isn't Hebrew, that much I can tell you. So we could deduce it is Aramaic, but I'm not nearly knowledgeable enough to read or translate it."

He was regarding them with a puzzled expression. "May I ask why you want to know about this—in what context did you find these words? Elena mentioned that you work at a museum—"

"Yes. The Devereaux Museum in New York. Rabbi, it's extremely important that I find out what they mean. Is there someone else who might know?" She leaned forward in her chair, her face betraying her desperation.

"Well, then. My good friend Father Caserta is a biblical scholar and quite renowned. The Babylonian Talmud happens to be one of his passions. It's written predominantly in Aramaic, as you might know. So I'm quite certain your question would pique his interest."

D'Amato surged to his feet. "Can you help us arrange it? And how quickly can we see Father Caserta?"

"Let's find out." With a smile, Rabbi Calo lifted the phone.

A few moments later the rabbi was leading them from the building.

D'Amato drifted away as Natalie engaged Calo in conversation. He loped over to the trash receptacle holding a wad of crumpled paper he'd taken from his pocket. Natalie knew he was retrieving the gun, and she didn't turn her head, even as he hurried to catch up with them.

If she'd turned, she might have recognized the burly young man in jeans and a gray hooded sweatshirt ambling after them on the other side of the street.

Bingo. Elation surged through Barnabas as he watched the Landau woman and the reporter hurry from the synagogue with a shorter man.

When the journalist hovered a moment at a trash bin, Barnabas frowned, watching closely. As the man rejoined the others, and they began walking east beneath the thin morning sun, Barnabas continued on behind them, keeping his anticipation in check.

The Light was right here in Rome. And he was following it.

33

"Well, now. How I wish all the questions people posed to me in my work were so simple." Father Giuseppe Caserta spread his thickly veined hands with delight. He was a tall, spare man in a short-sleeved black shirt and slacks, surprisingly casual in contrast to the ancient, gilded sanctuary where he preached. About sixty, he might once have been blond and as handsome as a film star. Now his hair was thinning, paler than straw, and he wore it longish, curling up at the nape. His face was angular and sallow. And kind.

The four of them were packed into the cramped back office of the tiny, ornate Santa Rosalia Church, which was tucked into the corner of a tree-canopied street. Rabbi Calo had explained to them on the way that the twelfth-century edifice had been built atop the ruins of one of the earliest Christian churches in Rome.

Since they'd left the synagogue, all of Natalie's tension had returned. She felt vulnerable once more—there were no armed guards patrolling the streets as they walked. And there was no security here at this quiet, out-of-the-way church where they'd found Father Caserta awaiting them in his cluttered office, which they'd reached through a short corridor that ran behind the marble altar.

"You're correct," the priest continued in his low, sonorous voice, "about these first two words. They are certainly Aramaic. *Belteshazzar* is a name—"

"Belteshazzar? Really?" Rabbi Calo interrupted excitedly, tilting his head to the side. "That's a Babylonian name, I believe. The one King Nebuchadnezzar's grandson, Balshazzar, bestowed on Daniel, the prophet who interpreted his dreams."

"Daniel?" Natalie's brows lifted. "The biblical Daniel in the lion's den?"

"*Ezzato!* Exactly." Pleased, the priest nodded at her.

"And what's the second word, Father?" Natalie was nearly out of her chair now. "Is that one a name as well?"

"No, no." Father Caserta was staring hard at the enhancements. "The second word . . . ," he said slowly, glancing at Calo, "is *tzohar.*"

The rabbi suddenly gripped the arms of his chair.

"*Tzohar* is a Hebrew word," the rabbi said before Natalie could ask. "It means 'brilliance, light, shining.'"

"Exactly. But here it is written in Aramaic characters," Caserta said.

"*Tzohar,*" Natalie repeated, puzzlement on her face.

"It's a word used only once in the Torah—in the Old Testament," the rabbi explained. "You'll find it in Genesis—in the flood story. God tells Noah to hang the *tzohar* in the ark."

D'Amato glanced between the two clerics. "What does that mean, 'hang the *tzohar* in the ark'? How do you hang something ephemeral, like 'brilliance,' in an ark?"

"A very astute question." Calo rubbed his palms along the top of his thighs, beginning to warm to his subject. "There are many legends about the *tzohar,* and I'll be happy to share them with you. But I would like to understand something also." He turned to Natalie, his dark eyes magnified behind his eyeglasses.

"Could you tell us more about this puzzle you've brought us? How did you find these two Aramaic words? Were they written together—as you show us here—or did you come across them separately?"

"They're very much together, Rabbi. I'll show you."

As she removed the pouch from her shoulder bag, Natalie slipped the pendant into her palm and closed her fingers around it. Then she carefully turned the leather covering inside out.

"My sister sent me a necklace from Iraq recently, right before she died."

"I'm so very sorry," the rabbi murmured. Father Caserta regarded her with sympathy from his kindly eyes.

Natalie nodded in acknowledgment. "We've been trying to determine the origins of the necklace. It was Mr. D'Amato who thought to look inside its pouch. Do you see this faint lettering? That's what we had enhanced in order to read it."

Rabbi Calo looked startled as he stared at the actual lettering on the ancient leather. Father Caserta's eyebrows spiked upward to form sandy arrows. Neither cleric spoke for several seconds.

The priest peered at the ink impressed on the soft leather. "This is quite ancient, isn't it?" he murmured.

"No wonder you brought it to our museum." Rabbi Calo spoke quietly, his gaze also glued to the letters. "And the Aramaic only confirms how far back it goes . . ." His voice trailed off.

"Right." D'Amato's keen gaze noted the two clergymen's stunned expressions. "We've scientifically determined it's roughly three thousand years old."

An odd expression flickered in Calo's deep-set eyes. "Daniel the prophet lived three thousand years ago."

Natalie noticed a faint tremble beginning in the rabbi's fingers. "By the shores of Babylon . . . ," he murmured.

By the shores of Babylon we wept . . . when we remembered Zion. The ancient words of exile from Psalms echoed in Natalie's head—lamentations for Jerusalem and the destroyed First Temple, written thousands of years ago by the Jews who'd been led to Babylon in captivity by Nebuchadnezzar. Natalie's heart began to race.

"Are you suggesting this could have belonged to Belteshazzar? To *Daniel*?"

Natalie had handled many ancient objects in her career, including many Jewish artifacts in Israel, but never had she held an object possibly linked to a biblical figure. Could this evil eye pouch truly have been connected to the prophet Daniel?

D'Amato had gone motionless beside her. For once even he couldn't seem to formulate a question.

"It is . . . possible," Rabbi Calo said dazedly.

"Your sister," the priest interjected, his eyes suddenly sharp. "You said she was in Iraq—ancient Babylon. The location certainly fits."

"But . . . what about *tzohar*?" Natalie asked.

Calo considered his words carefully. "Most people haven't heard of the *tzohar*, but it is one of the most fascinating of our Talmudic legends."

"Fascinating in what way? Could you be a little more specific?" D'Amato prodded. "We're talking about Daniel, the *tzohar*, and Noah's ark. How are they all connected?"

Natalie leaned forward. "The ark supposedly ended up on Mount Ararat, if I remember correctly."

"That wasn't part of ancient Babylon last time I checked my road atlas," D'Amato pointed out.

"Exactly." Natalie nodded. "And you could hardly call Daniel and Noah contemporaries." Puzzled, she glanced at the rabbi, but he still seemed to be collecting his thoughts. He stared at the pouch as he sank into his chair once more and gestured for them to do the same.

"Giuseppe, can we offer our guests a glass of wine or a coffee? This might take us a while." His expression was excited now. "The only place for us to begin, you see, is at the beginning."

Sir Geoffrey Ashton decided he couldn't wait for noon. He'd been grappling with his conscience all night, unable to settle into his work. And he hadn't heard from Natalie—not once, the entire morning. He'd hoped his words would have resonated with her. She was a highly disciplined professional who had always sought out and respected his counsel. Until now.

Ashton had been a model of professional ethics for the past forty years, and he couldn't bring himself to violate those ethics now—not even for a favored protégé. Natalie was obviously not thinking clearly. She was putting herself and the pendant at great risk. He couldn't let her do that.

At precisely 11:30 A.M., he picked up the phone and dialed the office of the Vatican police.

34

"'In the beginning,' as you no doubt know, God created the heaven and the earth." Father Caserta glanced curiously at Natalie's closed palm. "'Now the earth was unformed and void, and darkness was upon the face of the deep; and the spirit of God hovered over the face of the waters. And God said: "Let there be light—"'"

"And there was light," D'Amato finished for him, barely containing his impatience. He scraped a hand through his dark hair. "And if we're going all the way to *that* beginning, this is going to be a long story, isn't it, Father?"

"Not at all. This is a story about that first light of creation—a little bit of that light, anyways. Signore D'Amato, when most people think of Genesis and the story of creation, they assume that the first light mentioned in the passage I just recited was the light of the sun. But they are wrong."

"I'm not following," D'Amato said. He took a sip of the hot coffee the priest had brewed. "I don't remember much from my days in Catholic school, but I do remember that God said let there be light, and He saw that the light was good, He divided the light from darkness, and called the light day and the darkness night, and, bingo, the first day."

"You remember your catechism well, Signore D'Amato. But skip ahead with me to the *fourth* day. The day on which God made the two great lights, the sun to rule the day and the moon and stars to rule the night, and then set them in the firmaments. So *these* lights—the sun, the moon, and the stars—were not created until the *fourth day,* and are inherently different from that primordial light with which God spoke the world into existence on the *first* day."

"So, day one." Natalie stood up and paced to the desk. "God says, 'Let there be light,' and the world comes into existence. A sort of Big Bang moment, full of primordial light, but there's still no sun, no moon, no stars."

Calo nodded. "The primordial light from this dawn of creation was so intense it could be seen from one end of the world to the other. Our sages say it shone with seventy times the brilliance of the sun, that no living thing could look directly at it. This light was dazzling, splendorous, powerful. And it illuminated the Garden of Eden day and night with its magnificent, utterly pure light." He paused briefly to let them absorb his words. "And it did so until the day Adam and Eve were expelled."

"And then what?" D'Amato leaned forward.

"The legends say that God removed this primordial light from the world thirty-six hours after Adam and Eve sinned. That in His disappointment in them He concealed it—all but a trace, that is. Adam and Eve were bereft when the primordial light was taken from them." Calo spread his hands in an unconscious gesture, one he probably used in all of his sermons. "You see, my friends, of all the losses Adam and Eve suffered because of their sin, the loss of the primordial light was the most devastating to them. More than the Garden, more than the peace or the joy of their life in Paradise itself, Adam and Eve yearned for that unique, exquisite light. Craved it with intensity and longing. So God took pity on them. He took a fragment of that first light, encased it in a crystal, and gave it to Adam and Eve to carry with them out into the world. It would shine day and night to comfort them, and at the same time to remind them of all they'd lost. And that crystal, that divine jewel containing the tiniest bit of God's primordial light—that jewel is the *tzohar.*"

Natalie could feel the blood draining from her face. The rabbi's words suddenly seemed to be coming to her from far away.

"The jewel," Natalie asked shakily, her hands squeezed tight around the egg-shaped pendant in her hand. "Do the legends say what became of it?"

"There are numerous stories that have been passed down, both in legend and in folktale. I've already told you the only one that's written in the Torah—the Old Testament—about the *tzohar* illuminating the interior of the ark. The ancient rabbis explained that Noah had been given the *tzohar* by his father, after Adam passed it down through the generations."

Father Caserta spoke up. "Millions of readers the world over are also familiar with this brilliant light of creation encased in a jewel. You're familiar with the famous trilogy of J.R.R. Tolkien—*The Lord of the Rings*?" He strode to the bookcase packed with volumes at the far wall, plucked a hardcover from the shelves, and blew the dust off its top edge.

"Tolkien introduces it in *The Silmarillion*—the book that preceded *The Hobbit*, which in turn preceded *The Fellowship of the Ring, The Two Towers,* and *The Return of the King*. I was captivated when, as a young man, I first read the tales of Middle Earth. Not until years later did I become aware of the novels' parallels with the legends surrounding the *tzohar*. I am convinced that Tolkien based a part of his masterpiece on the legends of the *tzohar*."

"That's intriguing." D'Amato's brow furrowed. "I wouldn't have taken Tolkien for a Talmudic scholar."

"In a way, he was." The priest nodded. "He was a devout Roman Catholic who was fascinated by biblical and cultural myths and legends. He studied them extensively—he must have come across the legend of the *tzohar* in his readings. There are simply too many similarities between his work and the Jewish legends. Are either of you familiar with *The Lord of the Rings*?"

"I've read them all—but long ago," Natalie replied instantly. D'Amato shook his head no, as did the rabbi.

"I'm probably the only person alive who hasn't even seen the movies," D'Amato added, placing his fingertips on the desk.

"Well, then, think about this." Father Caserta set the book down on the exact center of his desk. "In *The Silmarillion*, Tolkien wrote about a light created before the sun. A primordial light which filled the earth and which later—after sin entered the world—was concealed within three gems. Does that sound familiar?"

"In our Jewish legend, there was only one gem," Rabbi Calo murmured, a gleam in his eyes. "Yet the concept is the same."

"Exactly. Both legends center around the same uniquely powerful light. Tolkien called his three crystal jewels the Silmarills."

D'Amato sat silently as Natalie nodded. "That's a pretty strong parallel," she allowed.

"Ah, but there are more," the priest assured her. "And they are striking enough that I don't see how they could be considered coincidental."

He hefted the silver coffee pot and refilled all of their cups. "In both legends the jewel-encased primordial light is lost. Noah's falls from the ark, while two of the three Silmarills similarly disappear—one swallowed by the sea, one swallowed by lava. The third Silmarill, however, is set in the sky as a brilliant star. Tolkien's star of Earendil. If you remember," he said to Natalie, "its light was reflected in Galadriel's mirror."

She nodded, gazing intently into the cup he'd just refilled. "Galadriel gave Frodo a fragment of it in a vial," she recalled.

"Correct." The priest strode back to the bookcase, found another book among his collection, and flipped through the pages.

"Ah, here it is. Galadriel's speech to Frodo when she gave him her gift."

He began to read.

"In this vial, is caught the light of Earendil's star. It will shine still brighter when night is upon you. May it be a light to you in dark places, when all other lights go out."

"Just as Adam and Eve had the *tzohar* with them—a light in dark places." Natalie's tone was quiet, contemplative, as she tightened her fingers around the pendant in her palm.

"Let's back up a minute." D'Amato held up a hand. "Explain

that bit about the *tzohar* falling out of the Ark after the Flood. Was that the last time anyone saw it?"

"Not at all." Father Caserta shook his head. "Jewish sages say that when it fell overboard, it drifted deep into an underwater cave. And there it lay until the floodwaters receded and the cave was no longer below sea level."

"And then?" Natalie lifted her cup to her lips.

"And then . . ." the priest said with a smile. "There is another Talmudic legend."

The Ethiopian guard stared at the two photographs proffered by the Vatican *gendarme*. "These two people are not here."

"Have you seen them?" The *gendarme* glanced at the Rome synagogue's security camera, then again, sharply, at the guard.

The guard shrugged. "They were here and they left," he said neutrally.

"We must speak to Rabbi Calo." The *gendarme* drew himself up, as if he could grow taller than his five-feet-nine-inch height. "We have reason to believe the woman is carrying something of great interest to us. It is urgent that we meet with Rabbi Calo at once."

35

"The next legend about the *tzohar* recounts what happened after it fell overboard from Noah's Ark," Father Caserta continued, glancing from Natalie's intent face to D'Amato's contemplative one.

"In the very cave where the *tzohar* washed up after it fell into the sea, Abraham, father of the Jewish people, was born. He found the sparkling gem as a child, and it became his treasured plaything, which he wore around his neck. Abraham passed it down to his son, Isaac, who in turn gave it to his son, Jacob, and Jacob gave it to his favorite child, Joseph. While some Jewish legends say it had great powers of healing, we don't hear that the *tzohar* also possessed the powers of divination until the days of Abraham's great-grandson Joseph, who like his ancestor, wore it around his neck."

The priest continued. "When Joseph's brothers took his coat and threw him into the well, none of them realized they'd left him with something far more valuable than that coat. Joseph had no idea either, until the jewel around his neck began to glow in the darkness of the well, frightening away the snakes and vermin. It's said that Joseph used it in Egypt to interpret the Pharaoh's dreams, and that Moses reclaimed it from Joseph's burial tomb and placed it in the Ark of the Covenant."

"And this is all in the Talmud?" There was amazement in

Natalie's voice. "I hadn't realized there was so much I didn't know about my religion."

"Well, we all have our areas of expertise, Ms. Landau. Mine is the Babylonian Talmud, on which I based my doctoral thesis. But I can assure you that you do know something about the *tzohar*. If you've been to synagogue, you are already familiar with a reminder of this special light."

His eyes crinkled at her puzzled expression.

"It hangs above the *bimah*—the altar—in every Jewish sanctuary," he informed her with a smile. "In every synagogue in the world."

"And not only there—it also hangs before the tabernacle on the altar of every Catholic Church," Rabbi Calo pointed out. He inclined his head, amused by her puzzled expression. "Now do you know what we're referring to?"

"The Eternal Light." It was D'Amato who answered. "Apparently we Catholics borrowed the concept from you."

Natalie leaned back in her chair, letting the answer wash over her. *The* ner tamid—*the eternal light*. The lamp in the sanctuary that was never allowed to go out, or to be switched off. The lamp that burned continuously, remained illuminated day and night, as a reminder of God's eternal presence.

Rabbi Calo's enthusiasm thrummed through his next words. "The *tzohar* is the original *ner tamid*, the eternal light shining from the dawn of time."

From the dawn of time. The words echoed in Natalie's brain. *Dawn of time. Eye of Dawn.* She started, the pendant suddenly heavy in her palm and the rabbi's words fading to a dull hum. The man who'd tried to kill them, who had Dana's silver *hamsa*. He had demanded she hand over the Eye of Dawn.

". . . and the lights burning on our *bimah*s and altars"— Rabbi Calo's voice penetrated her thoughts once more—"are all a remembrance of the *tzohar*, which was hung above the Ark of the Covenant after the First Temple was built in Jerusalem. The *tzohar* and the ark were ensconced in the Holy of Holies—the most sacred area of the Temple, which only the High Priest could enter. The crystal God gave first to Adam and Eve shone there until the sixth century B.C., when Nebuchadnezzar's army destroyed the Temple, carrying off all of its treasures, along with Jerusalem's captured Jews."

"To Babylon." Natalie spoke softly. "The treasures were carried off to Babylon. Has anyone seen the *tzohar* since then?"

"The Babylonians saw it." Caserta returned the Tolkien books to the shelf and came back to lean against his desk. "At least, those who gained entrance to Nebuchadnezzar's palace did since the king hung it there to remind everyone he'd conquered the Temple."

"But when his grandson was conquered by the Persians three thousand years ago," Rabbi Calo put in, "the *tzohar* disappeared again. And it hasn't been seen since. Only written about."

"Written about where?" Natalie's heart was thudding so hard she could barely get the words out.

The rabbi's eyes brightened, as if she'd arrived at the crux of the matter. "In a little-known Dead Sea scroll, Ms. Landau. One found badly damaged in Qumran. It's taken researchers years to piece some of it together and to uncover the writing. The words have been obscured in animal skins blackened by time. Perhaps you're familiar with it."

"Which scroll?" she asked. "I've seen several of them at the Dome of the Book in Jerusalem."

The priest smiled gently at her and leaned forward. "It isn't on display there. This scroll is still being studied, bit by bit, and few of its contents have been made public."

D'Amato squinted questioningly.

"This scroll was written by one of the last people in Babylon to see the *tzohar*," Father Caserta murmured. "By a man very close to King Balshazzar. So close that the king gave him a Chaldean name. Belteshazzar. But in the Bible he's called—"

"Daniel," Natalie finished for him, her eyes widening and the pendant seeming to tingle in her palm.

"Correct again." Rabbi Calo nodded. "The *tzohar* is described at length in the long-lost Scroll of Daniel."

36

Shock reverberated through Natalie. She'd handled countless ancient artifacts, categorized them, arranged them—but always as an observer of history. Now history, in all its wonder and mystery, had fallen into her lap. Filled with a dawning sense of awe, she stared down at the pouch, at its two Aramaic words— *Belteshazzar—tzohar*. Then her gaze shifted in disbelief to her fingers, concealing the ancient pendant encrusted with the protective eyes.

Something is enclosed inside it. Something from the dawn of time.

Slowly, still trying to grasp the magnitude of what she was learning, she extended her hand toward the Italian clerics. She unfolded her fingers, now marked by the impression of the jewel that had been pressed tightly against her flesh. She held the pendant out like an offering.

"This necklace was inside that pouch. It's the one my sister sent me from Iraq," she said through dry lips. "I know for certain that, like the pouch, it's three thousand years old—and that it has something sealed inside."

Hasan, Siddiq, and Jalil approached the church on foot. Three more Guardians, from the Rome cell, were on their way, but Hasan doubted their assistance would be needed.

He made a harsh gesture toward Jalil, and the lithe young driver nodded and crept toward the small patch of graveyard behind the spired building, his Walther P99 in hand.

Hasan drew his Beretta, a .40 caliber, chambered and ready to fire. And he would, the moment he claimed the Eye of Dawn from the Landau woman. He'd be back in Al Quds with the Eye tonight.

He noted with approval that Siddiq already had his weapon pressed against the side of his Italian suit as together they advanced on the small stone church.

Father Caserta jumped up from the desk, tumbling his chair behind him. He reached toward the pendant, but his hand froze in midair. Rabbi Calo hadn't moved, but his gaze was trained in fascination on the jewel-encrusted eye.

"Have you opened it?" He blinked rapidly behind his glasses.

"We can't. Not without damaging it," D'Amato replied.

"I have no idea how my sister got it." Natalie spoke quickly in the hush of the room. "But she was murdered right after she sent it to me. She was beaten to death. And from the moment I received it, people have been trying to get it away from *me*."

"The man who delivered it to Natalie was also murdered," D'Amato said grimly. "We've been chased and shot at, and someone just left a threatening message scrawled across the wall of our hotel room."

The rabbi snatched off his glasses and rubbed his eyes. "The light of the *tzohar* is a bit of the primordial light of creation." His voice was almost a whisper. "It has the power of healing, the power of divination. It was a part of that radiant light in the Garden of Eden—a light so bright it outshone the sun seventy times over. Just a bit of that light, encased in a crystal, had the power to illuminate the entire ark when the world was thrown into darkness." Calo took a deep breath. "The *tzohar* contains within it a spark of the very force of creation. It would possess a power men can only dream of. A power that, if harnessed, could do great good—or great harm."

"Basically, you're telling us that the *tzohar* is a trapped particle of pure creative energy." D'Amato's forehead furrowed in concentration.

Calo nodded. "And just imagine what one could generate with that kind of energy."

"It could make oil obsolete as our chief source of energy." Caserta's face lit with excitement. "It could be a God-given source of limitless clean fuel. Or," he added grimly, "humans could subvert it to manufacture horrific weapons."

"I shudder to contemplate the kind of destruction something so powerful could unleash." The rabbi looked stricken. "In the wrong hands . . ." His voice trailed away.

"If the *tzohar is* inside this pendant," Natalie said slowly, "I haven't seen any evidence of its power yet. Still . . . if others in the world believe it's as powerful as you've described, then I can understand why every nation, every power in the world would want it."

Reflexively, she clamped the pendant in her fist again. Was it her imagination, or was there really a tingling running from her fingertips all the way to her wrists, her arms, her shoulder blades?

"What does Daniel's scroll say about the *tzohar*?" she asked.

But before anyone could answer, the rabbi's cell phone interrupted. He spoke into it briefly, frowning with concern.

He tucked it back into his pocket with a sigh. "One of our guards. He says the Vatican police are at the museum." He looked at Natalie and D'Amato. "They're inquiring about the two of you."

Natalie stiffened, her gaze swinging to D'Amato. *Sir Geoffrey called them.* The same thought flowed instantaneously between them. Then it was forgotten as a slight scraping sound from the sanctuary reached her ears.

Apparently everyone heard it—they all turned toward the door.

"Somebody's out there," D'Amato whispered. He crept toward the door, signaling Natalie to draw the curtains across the lone window facing onto the graveyard.

"It could be a parishioner," Rabbi Calo murmured.

The scraping sound came again. Softer. Someone was working very hard not to be heard on the smooth stones.

"Is there a back way out?" D'Amato's voice was a breath.

"Not exactly." Father Caserta was staring in shock at the Glock that had suddenly materialized in D'Amato's right hand. "There's a door off the robing room, but that's on the other side of the altar. There's one other exit." He hesitated. "But it hasn't been used in years."

"Where is it?" Natalie whispered, as she plunged the pendant back into the pouch and stuffed both once again into her shoulder bag.

"It's beneath the altar. It's actually a trapdoor that leads down to an underground passage," the cleric said softly. "A leftover from the original church. The early Christians used it to escape the Romans back in the day. There's a circular tile that swivels aside—"

"How do we open it, Giuseppe?" Calo breathed. D'Amato was listening intently at the door. Natalie glanced frantically around the room, the words of her Krav Maga instructor ringing in her head. *Use whatever is at hand as a weapon.*

Then, in the blink of an eye, D'Amato was gone. The office door clicked closed behind him. She grabbed an embossed silver letter opener from the priest's desk and edged toward the door—freezing an instant later as gunfire roared off the high hollow ceiling of the sanctuary.

Then all hell broke loose. More gunfire thundered—and suddenly the glass window behind them shattered. A man dove through the splintered opening into the center of the room. He was young, dressed all in black, and he had a gun.

He lunged straight for Natalie. She struck out instinctively with the letter opener, aiming for his eyes, but he ducked just in time and escaped with only a shallow slash across his left cheekbone. She had a quick impression of dark malevolent eyes before he swung the gun up level with her heart.

"Give me the Eye of Dawn!"

"Didn't your mother ever teach you to knock?" Natalie's heart was pounding. She knew she had to distract him, to get out of his line of fire. As another burst of shots exploded from the sanctuary, she used his momentary distraction to take a step to the side.

At the same instant, Father Caserta dove low, hitting the gunman in the back of the knees and knocking him off balance. His shot went wide and ricocheted, pinging off the stone wall and slamming into the desk. Both Caserta and the gunman tumbled to the floor.

The attacker was younger and more nimble and was the first to scramble to his feet. But before the assailant could straighten, Rabbi Calo lunged for the gun. To Natalie's horror, the intruder swung the weapon up into Calo's chin, connecting with a sickening crack. Blood spurted from between the rabbi's lips as he toppled sideways against the bookcase.

Panting, the man wheeled again toward Natalie, but she attacked before he could take aim. With all of her strength, she drove the letter opener into his throat. This time she made more than a surface cut.

He let out a gurgled scream. As he struggled to pull the blade from his bloody throat, Natalie grabbed for the gun, wrenching his wrist at a forty-five-degree angle and wresting the gun away by its butt.

Good, pull the letter opener out, you bastard. You'll bleed to death all the faster. But her hands shook as she leveled the gun at his forehead. She couldn't allow herself to think that she'd inflicted a mortal wound.

"Give me the *hamsa* you took from my sister."

He was pressing his hands against his gushing throat. "That . . . Hasan's . . . trophy." He was having trouble getting the words out, but his baleful stare was one of pure malice. He seemed unaware of the amount of blood drenching his black shirt. "You . . . will . . . never. . . ."

Natalie jerked her head toward the sanctuary. "Hasan," she bit out. "Is he out there?"

He staggered to his knees, defiance blazing in his eyes. "The khalifate . . . will return," he gasped. "Hasan . . . will . . . succeed. Al Quds . . ." He fought for air. ". . . will be ours. And . . . the Eye . . . of Dawn . . . *Allah-hu akbar* . . . Allah . . . is great!"

Behind him a trembling Father Caserta was helping Calo to his feet. The rabbi's face was pale, his shirt smeared with blood. "Don't worry, I'll be alright," he gasped. He spit a tooth from his mouth. "Right now," he said shakily, "D'Amato needs our help."

The gunshots had halted. *There's either a standoff or everyone out there is dead,* Natalie thought. She pushed away the thought.

But even as she turned toward the door, the gunman collapsed, sprawling across the broken glass. Natalie pivoted and hurried toward him. Her stomach churned as she nearly slid on his blood.

"Check to see if he has other weapons," the priest cautioned.

Taking a deep breath, she felt for a pulse. Found none. She was afraid she was going to be sick. She'd never killed anyone before, let alone touched a dead body.

She closed her eyes for a moment, then opened them. She couldn't fall apart. She forced herself to focus. Gingerly, she patted the man's pockets, then remembered something else from her Krav Maga training—and yanked up the hems of his pants. Sure enough, there was a knife concealed in a leather holster lashed to his right calf.

She slid it across the polished wooden floor toward the priest.

"You might need this if we're going to get out of here, Father. Where does that underground passageway lead?"

37

D'Amato was crouched behind a statue of the Virgin Mary. He was hiding in one of the two front alcoves carved into the stone walls. He was a third of the way down the sanctuary, on the same side as the door to Caserta's office, pinned down by the gunmen.

He knew there were two of them out there. No more—unless there were others stationed outside. And unless he was mistaken, he'd wounded at least one of them. He'd heard a stifled cry after the first round of shots. They were hiding now like he was, concealed in an alcove on the opposite wall—not the alcove directly across from him—the one nearer the back of the church.

D'Amato was worried about the crash and the gunshot he'd heard in the priest's office. Thirty feet away, he could see the door—it was closed, exactly as he'd left it.

His throat was dry. He prayed Natalie was still alive and that she still had the pendant.

There was no way he could get from the alcove to that door without stepping into the line of fire. He couldn't get to the trapdoor beneath the main altar either. A beam of sunlight colored by the stained-glass windows slanted directly across the path he'd have to take.

The only other light in the gloom of the church was the

flicker of the votive candles lined up before the saints in each of the four alcoves.

He stared hard at the door to the priest's office, willing it to open. Slowly, stealthily, it did. His gaze swung to the alcove where his assailants were crouched.

He wondered if they'd noticed it, too.

He could see Natalie, Caserta, and Calo from the corner of his eye. They were sprinting low toward the main altar. Seizing an unlit votive cup, candle and all, D'Amato lobbed it across the pews like a baseball. It crashed not three feet short of the alcove from where the last shots had been fired.

Gunfire roared toward the splintering glass, and he dove from his alcove, flattening himself against the cold slate floor. He fired furiously at the alcove catty-corner from him, covering Natalie and the clergymen as they scurried and ducked beneath the altar.

Then a man's voice rang out.

"Natalie Landau!"

It boomed through the cold vaulted space. D'Amato recognized it at once. The voice on his cell phone in New York, the voice that had demanded the Eye of Dawn.

"I'm not a greedy man," the voice called out. It was an arrogant voice, thickly accented. An Iranian accent, D'Amato thought, as he began crawling noiselessly along the sides of the pews, inching his way toward the main altar.

"I offer you a trade, Natalie Landau," the man continued. "An eye for an eye. Your sister's necklace for the Eye of Dawn. If you come forward now and bring it to me, I'll even let you and your friends leave this place alive."

Silence met his words.

D'Amato crabbed on, hidden by the shadows and the low pews. The altar was only a dozen feet away. He heard the soft scrape of stone on stone coming from behind it. They were opening the trapdoor leading to the passageway.

"You couldn't shoot your mother if she was standing right in front of you!" D'Amato called. His words drew gunfire, but he was already rolling, propelling himself another ten feet closer to his goal as the bullets began to fly.

He heard footsteps crossing the church, hard shoes running on slate, and then, surprisingly, more shots, this time coming from behind the altar. *Which one of them got hold of a gun?*

Crouched behind the front pew, he spotted two men in silhouette slinking down the aisle on the other side of the church. Despite the shots Natalie, Calo, or Caserta had fired to slow them, they were still making for the altar.

The man in the rear was limping—wounded—just as he'd thought. D'Amato took aim and counted, noting how many seconds it took for the injured man to appear in the gaps between the pews. An instant before he knew his target would be in position, he fired. The bullet pierced the man's spine, and he went down like a puppet whose strings had been slashed.

One down. One to go. D'Amato had no idea if he'd shot the ringleader with the Iranian accent or a sidekick.

Suddenly, more shots rang out from behind the altar. As D'Amato saw the surviving gunman dive for the floor, he scrabbled across the remaining distance to the altar, up the three marble steps, and rolled behind it. Natalie, Calo, and Caserta knelt in the shadows, staring at him, white-faced.

Calo was injured. His mouth was swollen and caked with blood, but Natalie and Caserta looked okay. The priest had a Walther in his hand, and looked like he knew exactly what to do with it.

With relief he spotted the gap in the marble floor, only two steps to the right of where Caserta would stand to celebrate Mass. The large, circular trapdoor had been rotated away, revealing an opening just large enough for one person at a time to slip down into the dark recess.

"I'll wait and try to get this guy, you start—"

"We're all going down together," Natalie whispered frantically, but before she could finish the sentence, more men burst through the doors of the church, shouting in Arabic.

A hail of bullets rained into the altar.

"Natalie, you go first," the priest implored. "You have the *tzohar.*"

Natalie slung her shoulder bag across her chest, and Rabbi

Calo steadied her as she slid her legs into the narrow opening, scrabbling for a toehold.

"The ladder is to your right. It's rusted, but it's strong," Caserta whispered, as D'Amato leaned around the altar to fire off another round.

"Get them! They have no escape," the Iranian bellowed at the newcomers. "The woman has the Eye of Dawn!"

Natalie's head disappeared below the floor as D'Amato fired again, trying to pinpoint the shooters' locations, alert for any sounds of approach.

"Can I lock this thing behind me?" he asked Caserta as the priest swung himself through the trapdoor after the rabbi.

"You'll find the lock as soon as you slide it back in place. Hurry," the priest urged.

And then he, too, dropped from sight, and the only sounds D'Amato could hear were the soft scrapes of leather soles against the ancient metal rungs and the insistent pumping of blood in his ears.

He fired off a hailstorm at the three men charging toward him, emptying his chamber. And then he dove toward the opening, swung himself down, and heaved the heavy tile back into place above him.

Darkness swallowed him, black and thick as tar. From below, he heard an intake of breath, and the footfalls ceased.

Suffocating on the pungent, acidic smells of centuries-old mold and decay, he flailed his fingers against slime and cobwebs and cold marble in search of the latch. He couldn't even see his hand as he groped desperately, blindly.

Where the hell is it?

38

Natalie fumbled with the zipper on her shoulder bag, one hand still clinging to the ladder, the darkness smothering her like an Egyptian burial cloak. Her nostrils stung from the stench of dead air—an odor she knew well from countless digs. Breathing shallowly, she groped through her bag for her penlight.

"Hold on, I've got a light in here somewhere," she called softly upward.

A moment later her hand closed on the miniflashlight, and she yanked it out. A slender beam of light pierced the blackness.

"Let there be light," Rabbi Calo's voice chirped out, several feet above her.

She swung the beam toward her feet and saw she was nearly at the bottom. The ladder ran perpendicular to a shallow ghostly staircase carved from the subterranean stone but its steps were crumbling and impassable now.

"Not much farther," she called up. "How are you managing, Rabbi?"

"Don't worry about me." His words floated down to her. "It's only a tooth. A tooth can be replaced."

D'Amato's voice came from somewhere above the rabbi's. It was as grim and solid as the walls. "Where does this passageway end up? In the catacombs?"

"No, not at all. Contrary to what many believe, the early Christians never did hide in the catacombs." Father Caserta's voice wheezed as it echoed off the dank walls. "They wouldn't have built an escape tunnel straight to where the Romans knew they buried their dead."

"And they couldn't have lived long in the catacombs even if they'd tried to hide there," Natalie added, keeping her tone low, although she estimated she'd descended at least twenty feet and could no longer be heard by anyone still in the church. "The air was too toxic from the decaying bodies."

Suddenly her foot touched solid ground, and she called up, "I've hit bottom." Stepping clear of the ladder, she shone her penlight in an arc.

She found herself at the entrance to a small passageway, no more than three feet wide, its roof no higher than eight feet. Just ahead, the tunnel branched off in two directions. Uncertain, she waited for Father Caserta to lead the way.

She swiveled the light back up to shed pale illumination on the rusted ladder. Rabbi Calo had just reached the bottom rung; Father Caserta was only a dozen steps above him. Their movements were slow and cautious, their faces drawn.

She shivered in the damp of the tunnel and groped in her bag for the pendant, trying to accept the enormity of what she'd learned just before the attack.

The legends of the *tzohar,* the light of creation. She knew she was carrying an ancient pendant, but it was too big a leap to conclude that this was the legendary biblical gem. *A tiny treasure from the Middle East,* which had crossed the ocean to come into her possession.

What I think doesn't matter, she thought. *If others are convinced this pendant is truly the* tzohar, *it's no wonder they're willing to kill me to get it.*

D'Amato was the last to jump free of the ladder. He glanced around, dusting his palms off on his pants.

"So where exactly did the early Christians hide?" he asked, scanning the dank, claustrophobic space.

"They hid here. And in other similar subterranean chambers," Caserta explained. "It wasn't until A.D. 380 that Christianity became the state religion. Before then, if the followers of Jesus wanted to avoid being thrown to the lions as a sporting event in the Coliseum, they often had to escape underground."

"And our way back to daylight is . . . ?" D'Amato queried.

"May I?" Father Caserta held out his hand for Natalie's penlight and headed for the passageway on the left. "The one on the right is blocked off about a hundred meters ahead. This one will take us out into the ruins of an eleventh-century abbey."

"How far?" Natalie asked, trailing close behind him in the narrow corridor.

"A little more than three kilometers," the priest told her over his shoulder.

"About two miles," D'Amato translated.

"Those men back there—you've met them before?" Rabbi Calo asked her. He was trudging slowly, his injury taking its toll. One hand cradled his damaged jaw.

"They were involved in my sister's murder. And they came after us in New York."

"You'll remain in grave danger as long as you're carrying the *tzohar*," Calo cautioned. "What do you plan to do with it?"

"I think the best way to find out what this pendant really holds is to take it to Israel. If you're right, Rabbi, that's where it was stolen from in the first place. And if you're not . . ." She exhaled. "The Israel Antiquities Authority in Jerusalem is among the best in the world at studying ancient Middle Eastern artifacts."

Calo nodded approvingly. "Yes, take it to Israel. That's where some say it shone long before the world existed," he said. "For another of our legends recounts that the *tzohar* shone from the place that would become Jerusalem even *before* God spoke the world into existence."

"So the legends are contradictory," D'Amato said from the rear. "How do you know what to believe?"

"As with everything else in this life, that is something each person must decide for him- or herself," the rabbi said in the darkness, his voice labored. "But I believe your decision is the right one, Ms. Landau. The *tzohar* must return to its home. Jerusalem. The Israel Antiquities Authority will know best how to study and safeguard it."

On that, she agreed with him completely. The IAA had been established in the early nineties to collect, study, and preserve Israel's cultural and archaeological treasures. Its headquarters was in the Rockefeller Museum just outside the Old City.

Now all she had to do was get it there.

A short distance later the tunnel narrowed, its roofline slanting to less than six feet, forcing D'Amato, like Caserta in the lead, to duck his head as he walked. He tried his cell phone. There was no signal underground, not that he'd really expected one.

"When we get to the abbey, Father, take the rabbi to the hospital."

"And you and Ms. Landau? How will you get away?" the priest murmured in the darkness.

"We're working on it."

More like we're making it up as we go along, Natalie thought.

"I have an idea," Rabbi Calo offered. "You can use my car." His hand was already in his pants pocket, withdrawing a set of keys. "It's a red Fiat with a dent in the passenger door—it's parked in the lane behind the *gelateria* two blocks north of the synagogue. Drive to Florence. I have a cousin there who'll bring it back to me."

"Best plan I've heard all day." D'Amato pocketed the keys. "The trick is going to be getting back to your car without an entourage of bullets."

39

There had been only one cab in the vicinity when the four of them emerged at last from the tunnel and stumbled through the crumbling abbey and out into the sun. Both Calo and Caserta had insisted D'Amato and Natalie take it. Neither spoke as the cabbie circled back toward the Great Synagogue of Rome.

"Drop me off here," D'Amato ordered suddenly, wrenching Natalie from her thoughts. They weren't anywhere close to the *gelateria* yet. As she turned to him in surprise, he leaned over and spoke tightly in her ear.

"We just passed two NSU agents—I recognized one of them. He's former CIA. We worked together briefly in Jerusalem." D'Amato scrubbed a hand through his hair. "I don't know the agent with him, but they always work in pairs, and they have to be looking for us. They're only two blocks away from the synagogue—that's no coincidence. They must have tracked us there."

"NSU?" she whispered back.

"National Security Unit. It's a top-secret terror-fighting agency—Homeland Security's version of the CIA."

"They're after us, too?" Her heart sank.

"Not if I can help it. I'm going to draw them off." He thrust the keys into her palm. "You get the car, pick me up on the Via del Corso near the Spanish Steps. Know where they are?"

She nodded, bracing herself.

"There's a Benetton on the corner. Keep circling until I find you. Can you drive a stick?"

"It's what I learned on. D'Amato . . ." Her voice trailed off as the cab slid into the curb and he shoved his door open. He glanced back at her, waiting.

"Be careful."

His eyes were unreadable.

She sucked in her breath as he sprang from the car and loped off, back in the direction they'd just come from.

"It's up a few more blocks," she told the driver, her fingers clamped around the car keys. "The *gelateria*." She suddenly felt like she'd never see D'Amato again.

As the cab stopped to let her out, she scanned the clusters of people sitting outside the ice cream shop. They all looked like natives or casual tourists. Laughing. Dipping spoons into brightly colored *gelato,* enjoying the welcome sun and the spring day. Her own stomach rumbled with hunger as she pushed some bills at the driver and bolted from the cab, sprinting toward the rear of the building, car keys at the ready.

But even as she zeroed in on the rabbi's Fiat ahead, a man moved quickly into her peripheral view.

Her head snapped to the side to look at him. Then her breath caught.

She'd seen him before. The last time he'd been wearing a baggy gray sweatsuit. Today his tall, muscular body was encased in jeans and a hoodie. But there was no mistaking the powerful physique. The way he moved. It was Ski Mask.

The thug from the museum.

He spotted her at the same instant. A smile broke across his wide face, and he started forward.

She ran for the car, darting down the middle of the street, pressing the remote key frantically. He was ten paces away—she could still make it. But as she flung the door wide and threw herself onto the warm leather, he came on with a burst of speed that propelled him over the hood of the car in a split second.

She couldn't close the door in time, let alone lock it. He

reached in, seized her arm, and yanked her out, shoulder bag and all. She was pinned between him and the car, staring up into those amber-flecked brown eyes.

"Give it over, and I won't have to hurt you."

His voice was hushed, almost fervent. In it she heard the same soft trace of a drawl she'd heard in the museum.

How did he find me?

"Is it in your bag?" he demanded. "Or your pocket? Give me the Light now. I don't want any accidents, like I had with your sister's buddy, Sutherland."

"Rusty!" Natalie choked out. *He must have followed Rusty to the Devereaux . . . waited for him to come out. . . .* Horror swallowed her. *He came back to the museum looking for the pendant when he didn't find it on Rusty.*

"No one's here to help you this time. So do us both a favor— just give me the Light."

"What do you want with it?" She braced her feet against the ground, trying to clear the fear from her head. "Who are you?"

"That's not important. The Light is the only thing that matters. That's why it's resurfaced now—it's nearly time."

"Nearly time for what?" *Keep him talking,* Natalie thought. *And get ready. He's just a kid. A big, strong kid.*

But a big, strong, *dangerous* kid. His irises grew unexpectedly dark. He was studying her with a flicker of contempt. "You wouldn't understand. You're not a believer."

"I believe lots of things. I believe stealing is wrong. And that murder is evil."

That was a mistake. She realized it as soon as she said it. His face darkened, and he moved so quickly she never even had time to duck. He backhanded her, his knuckles cracking against her cheek, sending blinding pain through her ears. The sunlight dimmed.

His breath was hot on her face. "I'm a servant of the Lord. I do what is necessary to serve Him, and one cannot sin in the service of the Lord."

For a moment she couldn't see her surroundings, and she fought to keep her feet. Dizzily, she shifted the car keys in her hand, careful not to let them jingle. Through the haze of nausea and pain she worked them until they protruded between her fingers.

"The Sentinel has given me my mission. The Light must shine from the Third Temple. Its radiance will usher in the Rapture."

The Sentinel? The Rapture?

He's delusional. A loose cannon.

But someone powerful's giving him his orders. A loose cannon wouldn't have the resources to have tracked Rusty—or to find me in Rome.

Natalie struggled to speak through the pain eddying through her head. "Just let go of me and—"

He thumped her head against the car.

"I can wait," he said softly. "It won't take long. In the end I'll simply take the Light away from you."

D'Amato dodged through the warren of narrow streets, bearing north, working his way toward the Piazzi di Spagna—and the Spanish Steps.

He'd lost the NSU guys in the Piazza della Rotonda after ducking into the Palazzo Doria Pamphilj. He knew the vast stone museum well. With its four picture galleries off the court-yard, its Mirror Gallery, private apartment, chapel, and the Via della Gatta wing, they'd waste a good couple of hours hunting for him before they caught on. He pictured them dashing up and down all those stairways, through the numerous salons. Maybe they'd soak up a little culture while they were chasing his shadow. He'd be on the Via del Corso looking for Natalie before they realized he'd given them the slip—as slyly as the cat the Via della Gatta was named for.

He strode past the Colonna dell'Immacolata with barely a glance at its statue of the Virgin Mary. Suddenly, a young woman holding a baby shoved a map in his face, pointing, asking directions. D'Amato wasn't about to fall for this thieves' trick, common among the Gypsies who plagued Rome's tourists. He pushed her away and shouldered his way through the swarm of handsome, dark-haired, dark-eyed Gypsies intent on distracting him, one hand protecting the pocket in which he carried his passport and wallet.

But he didn't make it as far as the next piazza before he felt the unmistakable pressure of a gun digging into the small of his back.

A small car screeched to a halt two feet away.

"Get in."

The voice behind him was a terse whisper. The accent eluded him as the man jammed the gun harder against his spine.

Another man appeared from the street, dark and swarthy, swinging open the car door and allowing his jacket to fall open just enough for D'Amato to see that he, too, was armed. The gun at his back drove him forward, leaving D'Amato no choice but to duck his head as he was shoved inside the car.

40

The lane was still deserted.

Natalie could hear faint strains of laughter carrying on the breeze from the *gelateria*. She could taste the metallic tang of blood in her mouth—she'd bitten a gouge inside her cheek when he'd slugged her.

"Don't make this worse than it has to be. I know you've got it in your purse." The young thug's eyes bored into her. "Women keep everything in their purse. So hand it over, and I won't have to hit you again."

She sighed in resignation and let her shoulders slump as she balanced herself evenly on both feet. Then she reached with her free hand to grasp the purse strap, lifting it slowly over her head. As his gaze followed the arc of the shoulder bag across her body, she punched out desperately with her other hand, stabbing the protruding keys into his nose with all the force she could muster. He bellowed in pain and shock, doubling to his knees as blood gushed from his nostrils. Natalie kicked him straight in the face, and he tumbled backward, his nose now a crushed mass of blood and cartilage.

But before she could duck into the car, he kicked upward, leading with his heel, hitting her full in the side. Natalie would have gasped in pain as she slammed against the Fiat's door, but there wasn't a breath of air left in her burning lungs. Then he was up again, towering over her. Howling. Furious.

Struggling to draw breath, Natalie flung one arm across her face to stave off his blow. *Focus.* But how could she focus when she couldn't breathe . . .

Ignoring the crushing pain in her side, she took one step toward him to get clear of the car and pivoted toward him in a blur of motion. The next instant her entire weight slammed into a roundhouse kick. Her kneecap torqued through his midsection and up into his rib cage with shattering force.

He went down like a wounded bull, and she heard the dull thwack of his head hitting the pavement. As he lay on the ground, contorted with pain, he reached under his hooded sweatshirt into the waistband of his jeans, and yanked free a knife. It looked like a steak knife, probably stolen from a café.

For an instant, a vision of Maren being stabbed burst through Natalie's mind and then she was in motion, stomping on his wrist, forcing him to release his hold on the knife. She kicked the blade away, only to have his free hand clamp around her ankle and pull it out from under her.

She fell hard, toppling half across him, and grunted as his heavy body rolled and knocked her beneath him. Her shoulder bag slid away, several feet across the pavement. Desperately, she jammed the flat of her palm up and into his bloodied nose and heard a sickening crack. He bellowed in pain and his hands reflexively went up to protect his face. It was the opening she needed. She hooked her left leg around his right leg, giving herself leverage to thrust her left hip and roll his weight off of her. As the back of his head smacked on the pavement, she sprang from the ground and kicked at his head. She kept kicking until blood began to pour from his ear, trickling to the street in a sticky, ruby-colored stream. His hands never left his nose. He looked like he was in shock. Yet his lips were still moving.

Natalie spotted a billfold hanging halfway out of his sweatshirt pocket. Cringing, she snatched it out. As she backed away quickly, she thought she heard him whisper.

"The . . . Light . . ."

Then something soft and black was draped across her face. It was pulled tight and knotted at the back of her head. She struggled, striking out with a rear defensive kick, but she never made contact with her attacker. She felt herself lifted, clamped by four impossibly strong hands. The billfold was ripped from her grasp.

They captured her swiftly, and she was helpless, submerged in darkness. *Where's the* tzohar? she thought frantically.

The next thing she knew she was being hustled onto hard leather seats. She felt someone squeeze in beside her in the tight space. Car doors slammed as a powerful engine roared to life, even as her fingers tore at the knotted ends of the hood.

41

Air Force One

The President cradled the phone between his chin and his shoulder, swiveling in his overstuffed leather chair as the plane cruised at thirty-seven thousand feet.

"What kind of chatter?" he asked Jackson Wright. "Same stuff we've been screening for the past month—or something new?"

"Nothing out of the ordinary for this part of the world, Mr. President." The Secretary of Defense's voice boomed loud and clear from Oslo. "We're still getting intel about the Shomrei Kotel, independent of what the Israelis are sharing with us. Their right-wingers are still protesting, still threatening to blow up the Temple Mount—but no one believes that they have the ability to make good on their promises. Various Al Qaeda groups are making the usual noises."

Garrett closed his eyes. *Nothing out of the ordinary.*

He'd worked too hard for this—his dream of peace in the Middle East. His legacy. He wasn't about to let any fanatical thugs steal it from him and from the world.

"So we're on course. Let's keep it that way."

"Believe me, Mr. President, no amount of abstruse chatter is going to destroy a profound opportunity. Israel wants this treaty as much as we do. The Mossad is all over this summit like hummus on pita."

The words were reassuring, yet Garrett knew that in the Middle East, in an instant, anything could change. *In Oslo, Yitzhak Rabin thought he was brokering a peace, too . . .*

Suddenly the sun was glaring too brightly in his eyes, distracting him. Garrett snapped the plastic shade closed, shuttering the window beside him.

"Keep me updated, Jackson. Now give me the status of Firefly."

He heard a sigh on the other end. "The NSU has tracked the Landau woman to Rome. Firefly, however, is still in flight. We expect to have them both before you land in Israel."

"Capture it already, damn it." Scowling, Garrett ended the call. He wouldn't rest easy until the signatures were indelibly scrawled on the peace treaty and Firefly was secured. His plans for Firefly would supersede even his legacy of bringing peace to the Middle East.

He glanced at his watch. In just fifteen minutes he'd have to put on his most optimistic face and head back to the rear of the plane, where the press corps would pump him for comments on the momentous upcoming event. He refused to dwell on any possibility that the historic meeting on the Temple Mount could evaporate like the smoke trailing behind his jet.

42

"Give that back to me."

Natalie had escaped the blindness of the hood just in time to see the olive-eyed young man next to her pull the evil eye pouch from her purse. Ignoring her demand, he spilled the pendant into his palm and stared at the jeweled eyes winking up at him.

"I have it." He spoke in Hebrew to the two men in the front seat. "It's protected by the eye, just as the scroll says." His voice was tinged with awe. "I'm holding the *tzohar*."

Swift as a hawk, Natalie plucked the pendant from his grasp, her fingers closing on it like talons. "Not anymore you're not." Instinctively, she replied in Hebrew. He was an Israeli, that much she was certain.

She was shaking all over. She'd just killed a man. And been kidnapped in broad daylight. Her face throbbed with pain, but it was nothing compared to the agony arcing across her stomach from the museum thug's kick. Despite all that, she wasn't about to let anyone take the *tzohar* from her. Especially not this guy . . . *there's something about him . . .*

And then it hit her. She looked down at his feet. *Sneakers. Tied now.*

"You followed us into the alley," she accused, willing herself to appear strong. "Who are you?" She didn't wait for him to answer. "Just where do you think you're taking me?"

"To safety." The driver spoke over his shoulder.

His front-seat passenger turned, revealing a round, friendly face with dark stubble across his jawline. "*Kol b'seder.*" You're okay. "We had to grab you like that to get you off the street. There was no time to explain."

The man beside her cocked an eyebrow. "Do you know how many people are looking for you? You're much better off with us. And so is the *tzohar.*"

"You're Israelis—are you Mossad?"

"What do you think?" The round-faced man in the passenger seat tore his gaze from the pendant to smile at her, revealing dimples and perfect white teeth. "For now, let's just say I'm Rafi," he continued. "Our driver here is Lior, and the joker seated beside you is the infamous Yuvi, our resident ladies' man. Me . . ." He shrugged. "I have to work on my pickup technique—somehow the hood doesn't endear me to the ladies."

I'm sure kidnapping them doesn't either, Natalie thought, adrenaline still coursing through her. "I'm supposed to be meeting someone near the Spanish Steps." Her voice sounded steadier than she felt. "He's waiting for me. You have to take me there."

"Don't worry about Mr. D'Amato." Yuvi shrugged. "He's already en route to the same place we are. With a similar escort."

Somehow Natalie couldn't quite picture D'Amato with a black hood over his head. "Where are we going?"

"Where else?" The driver, Lior, who looked to be in his late forties, spoke up, his voice deep and lazy. "We're taking the *tzohar* back where it belongs. We won't allow one of our people's treasures to be stolen again."

Natalie sank back against the seat. She'd come to the same conclusion herself—that the Israeli government had dispatched these men to reclaim whatever was inside the pendant. All in all, she was almost relieved to have this particular escort. But she wasn't particularly overjoyed about having the decisions taken out of her hands.

"Let's get this straight. If anyone's going to deliver this pendant to the Israel Antiquities Authority, that would be me." Her voice was quiet now, resolute.

When they said nothing, she leaned forward. "Agreed?"

Rafi hesitated. Then Lior nodded and shifted his gaze from the road just long enough to glance down at the pendant before Natalie returned it to its pouch. "The IAA is already aware of your experience with ancient artifacts," Lior told her. "You won't be unwelcome."

"Sit back and relax. You won't even need your passport," Yuvi assured her as she drew a shuddering breath. "We have a private jet standing by. No one looking for you in Rome will be the wiser that you and your friend D'Amato are no longer here."

43

D'Amato stared at Natalie's bruised face as the wings of the private plane angled after takeoff. He ignored the two Israelis sitting across from him—his kidnappers—the red-haired Doron and the squat, balding Nuri, who was now sporting a broken nose. D'Amato had gotten in one quick punch when he'd spotted the length of steel pipe Nuri had shoved into his back, simulating a gun. He'd paid for it with a jab to the ribs that still kept him from sitting up straight, but then he'd always thought good posture was overrated. A good pain pill, on the other hand . . .

But he wasn't about to take a single step down that road again. He'd deal with the pain.

What bothered him most was that Natalie looked ten times worse than he felt. The ice pack the cabin attendant had given her had done little to lessen the swelling across her cheek. An ugly bruise was already purpling beneath her left eye.

"Who did that to you? These guys?" His eyes hard, he nodded across the aisle to where Yuvi, Rafi, and Lior were hunched around a laptop and sipping from mugs of steaming tea. He'd recognized Yuvi from the alley the moment he walked onto the plane and was ticked off that he'd dismissed an operative as "harmless."

Natalie shook her head. "It was the guy from the museum,"

she said in a low tone. "He attacked me just as I reached the car. He told me to hand over the 'Light.' That he was on a mission for some guy he called the Sentinel."

"And he did that to your face?"

She grimaced. "When I wouldn't give him the pendant, he stopped asking nicely."

D'Amato banged his fist on the tray table in front of him. "How did he find you here? And who sent him?"

The last question was directed more to the Israelis than to Natalie. He'd answered enough of their questions during the drive to the private airfield at the Fiumicino Airport; now he wanted some answers from them.

But it was Natalie who replied.

"They think they know." She tilted her head toward the Mossad agents studying the computer screen. "The thug's name is Barnabas Lewis, by the way. I managed to grab his billfold, but Lior took it away from me while I was being dragged to the car. In addition to a driver's license, he found some hotel receipts—"

"Charged to Reverend Kenneth Mundy," Lior interrupted in his lazy voice, without looking away from the screen. "Shabak has quite a file on the good reverend. He seems to think the *tzohar* can help him instigate the Rapture."

Shabak was the internal security service of Israel. Its equivalent of the FBI.

"Mundy heads up some fringe group out of Florida under the cover of the Radiant Light of Heaven Church," Lior continued. "His name is on the U.S. guest list for the peace summit." He regarded the other Israelis with a frown. "Though no one from the U.S. State Department seems to know how it got there."

The agents seated across from Natalie and D'Amato exchanged glances. D'Amato picked up on the subtle shift in their postures.

Then Yuvi unbuckled his seatbelt and stood, balancing easily despite the slight tremble of the plane. "The Office has been aware of Mundy for some time," he told Natalie and D'Amato. His close-cropped dark hair seemed to glisten in the overhead lights. "He has a secret core following—unknown to his congregation. They call themselves the Sons of Babylon. They've been socking away money in Panama to rebuild the Temple."

"His Sons of Babylon are loosely linked with Shomrei Kotel, the Israeli extremist group intent on the same goal," Lior added dryly, rubbing the back of his neck. "Mundy's so confident of his plans, he's even got the blueprints ready."

"Just how big a following does he have?" Natalie lifted her cup of tea and took a sip, her mind racing.

"A small one. It's no megachurch by any stretch of the imagination. Which is a good thing." Doron looked grim. "This guy is very off the mainstream, condemned by the entire evangelical community."

"And why is that?" D'Amato asked.

Wearily, Doron ran a hand through his red hair. "Because he thinks he has the power to do what only God can. Namely, bring forth the Messiah."

"Barnabas told me that's what the Light was for," Natalie murmured. "Mundy needed it to usher in the Rapture."

D'Amato's brows lifted.

Lior held up a hand. "Don't dismiss him. He's an extremely charismatic guy, and we know how dangerous *that* can be. At the end of the day, he's managed to attract hefty financial backing from a number of wealthy people."

"What happened to Barnabas?" D'Amato was still bothered by the bruises on Natalie's face. "He get away again?"

"He's dead." She was staring into her empty mug. "I killed him."

"She sure did." Yuvi's olive eyes glinted with admiration. "Lucky for us we got there in time to preview your proficiency in Krav Maga—or one of us might have ended up in a bloody puddle, too."

D'Amato saw the slight tremble run through Natalie.

"You had no choice, Natalie," he said quietly. "You had to save your own life."

"Not to mention the *tzohar*," Rafi chimed in, finally looking up from the computer.

Natalie felt all of their gazes on her. She sensed their sympathy and pushed back the tears that threatened to turn into convulsive sobs. Tears for the two lives she'd taken. Tears for the sister she'd lost. Tears for the insane pattern of running and hiding that had become her life.

"I want to know some things, too." Her voice sounded unsteady. She cleared her throat, started again. "I want to know about the man responsible for my sister's murder. The man who's been trying to kill me and D'Amato to get his hands on the *tzohar*."

"His name is Hasan Sabouri." Rafi's eyes darkened. "We've had him and his followers in our sights, but our priority in Rome was to get the *tzohar* and you to safety."

"How does he know about the pendant?" Natalie asked.

Doron, seated opposite, looked grim. His voice came from so deep in his chest, he sounded hoarse. "We're not the only ones who've read the Scroll of Daniel, or who know about the unfathomable power of the *tzohar*. Ever since Daniel's writings were first deciphered, people like Mundy and Sabouri have been hunting for it—scouring museums and flea markets and raiding private collections to find the distinctive jeweled pendant Daniel the prophet protected with eyes to ward off evil."

"Sabouri's group calls itself the Guardians of the Khalifah," Rafi told her. "Their ultimate goal is Islamic domination of the world by returning the khalifate to power. They've managed to pull together the most cohesive terror network in the Middle East, younger, stronger, more sophisticated than Al Qaeda."

"They're the masters of unlikely alliances," Lior added, leaning back in his seat. "They've attracted support and trained fighters from nearly every Arabic country. From Yemen to Azerbaijan, from Lebanon to Iran—"

"Yeah, I know exactly who they are." A muscle had tensed in D'Amato's jaw. "The Guardians of the Khalifah funded at least a half dozen suicide bombings inside Israel in the nineties, before the wall went up. And bragged about it. I'm left with some permanent souvenirs thanks to them."

Natalie drew in her breath. As Doron and Lior studied him with a new interest, he pointed to his right hip and leg. "Nail shards. Makes walking through airport metal detectors a real treat every time."

"Which attack?" Doron asked.

"The Number 27 bus."

Rafi looked away. For a moment no one spoke. The only sound was the usual faint whir of white noise in the cabin.

"Tell me more about Daniel's scroll," Natalie said, breaking the silence. "Have any of you read it?"

"I have," Nuri said.

She leaned forward eagerly. "What else does it say?"

At precisely the time Air Force One landed at the Ben Gurion Airport in Tel Aviv, the Reverend Kenneth Mundy and his wife, Gwen, boarded their overnight flight in Miami.

And Hasan Sabouri, proffering his forged Saudi passport, breezed through airport security in Rome and settled into his first-class seat on the Lufthansa airliner bound for the Middle East.

He was ready to see the last of Rome. Siddiq was dead, as well as two others. The backup team had arrived at the church too late to be of any use—by then the Eye of Dawn was gone. Again. There'd been no time to search for the secret passageway beneath the altar, no time to remove the dead before the sirens were blaring, shrieking closer.

The Eye will be mine regardless, he told himself, shaking open his linen napkin. *It is only a matter of time. The Eye is the reason I was born with these cursed blue eyes. It is my destiny.*

For now, his reunion with Fatima awaited. And so did the events of tomorrow. In one more day the bombs would rip beneath Al-Haram al-Sharif, obliterating the Dome of the Rock—and every other edifice within the Noble Sanctuary, including the Western Wall.

In one more day, the enemies of Allah who had engineered this peace treaty would be dead, vaporized: the President of the United States; the Israeli prime minister; the secretary-general of the U.N., and the most abhorrent enemy of all, Mu'aayyad bin Khoury—that cowardly Hamas traitor who would dare to trade the sacred khalifate for the West's abominable democracy.

Tomorrow the streets of Jerusalem would run with blood, and all of the carnage would be laid at the feet of the Shomrei Kotel.

Tomorrow—he smiled, as the flight attendant set a chilled goblet of tomato juice on the starched linen cloth before him—*would be a most momentous day.*

44

"How much do you remember of Daniel's story from the Torah?" Nuri asked Natalie, as the plane stuttered through a bump of turbulence. His voice was thick and nasal, thanks to the broken cartilage. He glanced darkly at the man who'd given it to him, as everyone refastened their seatbelts. "Perhaps you know this from the Old Testament."

"Daniel in the lion's den." D'Amato shrugged.

"That's one of his experiences," Nuri conceded. "Daniel also interpreted the king of Babylon's dreams. Some say with the help of the *tzohar*. But the more pertinent tale involves the final night of the reign of Nebuchadnezzar's grandson, Balshazzar. Of course," he added, "Balshazzar had no idea his reign—or his very life—was about to end. He threw a great feast—there was dancing, carousing, merriment. The goblets of gold and silver which his grandfather had stolen years before from the Temple were overflowing with wine. Then, abruptly, poof!" He flung both hands into the air. "The laughter died; the assembled nobles went silent. Strange words had begun to glow across the wall. It was as if an occult hand had drawn them there."

"Must've been some pretty strong wine." D'Amato adjusted his seat back as the plane continued to bounce.

Nuri ignored the comment. "These are the words that appeared on the plaster: *Mene. Mene. Tekel. Uparsin.* Everyone was stunned. Afraid. No one could make any sense of them. Balshazzar summoned his chief adviser and his soothsayers, but even they couldn't translate the words on the wall."

Lior took up the tale, stretching his legs into the aisleway. "So he screamed for Daniel, the man his grandfather had made the master of the magicians, enchanters, Chaldeans, and soothsayers."

"And Daniel told him what they meant," Natalie murmured.

"That he did." Nuri took back his story. "He told the king and his assembled guests that '*mene*,' which appeared twice, was Aramaic for 'number,' and that the days of Balshazzar's kingdom had been numbered by God, and He had brought that kingdom to an end."

"That must have put a damper on the festivities."

D'Amato was in rare form. Natalie shot him a scowl.

"Believe me, it only gets worse." Lior was interrupting again, obviously enjoying the story.

"Next, Daniel told them that the following word, '*tekel*,' meant 'to weigh,' and announced that the king had been weighed in the balances and found wanting."

"Now that took balls," D'Amato acknowledged.

"Ignore him." Natalie looked at Nuri. "I want to hear about the scroll."

"I'm getting there. Next came the final word, '*peres*,' which in Aramaic means 'divided.' Daniel told Balshazzar that his kingdom was now divided, given over to the Medes and the Persians. And on those words, horses' hooves suddenly thundered from the five courtyards surrounding the palace. There was pandemonium as everyone realized that King Cyrus the Great of Persia had breached the city walls. Within minutes, he'd stormed the palace—and Balshazzar lay dead."

"And that's where the Torah leaves off—and Daniel's scroll comes in." Rafi regarded Nuri over his mug of tea. "May I?"

Nuri shrugged, his short neck disappearing into his shoulders.

"According to the scroll, Daniel knew Balshazzar's downfall was coming," Rafi went on. "And he'd prepared for it. For years he'd watched the *tzohar* hanging in that palace in Babylon. And for years he'd longed to return it to Jerusalem, where it could hang once more in a rebuilt Temple. In the scroll, he wrote, he'd secretly commissioned a jeweler to craft an orb of gold. He described it as covered on both sides with protective eyes made of lapis lazuli, carnelian, and jasper. He hoped that this powerful symbol would help protect the last remnant of the Light of Creation after he'd hidden it inside."

Yuvi stood up and stretched, then headed toward the lavatory.

"Bring back some more ice for Natalie's bruise," Lior called after him.

D'Amato was regarding Rafi thoughtfully. "Go on."

"So while the Persians were storming the palace that night, Daniel wasted no time. He snatched the *tzohar* from the great hall before Cyrus or the Persians ever saw it, then ran to the home of the craftsman and had him solder the orb shut, without telling him that an unimaginable treasure was already inside."

Natalie set the damp compress down on the small table between the seats.

"So Daniel hid the *tzohar*—the pendant—the night of Balshazzar's fall. What happened to it after that?" she asked quietly.

"Daniel wrote that he buried it. But he didn't say where. Daniel himself, you know, is thought to be buried in Kirkuk."

Natalie went still. "My sister's last assignment was in Kirkuk."

No one spoke. Finally, D'Amato cleared his throat.

"Does Daniel write anything more about the *tzohar*?"

"The scroll is still being deciphered, but so far the only other thing it's revealed is a detailed description of the pendant—and of the pouch Daniel tore from his waist to bury it in." Lior shifted in his seat. "He wrote of copying the protective eye symbols on both sides of the leather pouch as well, hoping all those eyes would deter anyone from looking inside."

"And Daniel's Chaldean name inside the pouch—Belteshezzar—confirms this is the real deal." All levity had vanished from D'Amato's tone.

Lior nodded. "No doubt his name was there long before he decided to hide the pendant inside."

"So," D'Amato mused, as Yuvi headed back and handed Natalie a fresh compress full of ice, "ever since the Scroll of Daniel was deciphered—what? in 2000—2001?—the whispers about the *tzohar* leaked out, and the search for it was on."

"It became an open secret," Nuri said, his lips twisting.

The voice of their pilot came over the loudspeaker, a bit tinny, warning of more turbulence ahead.

"The United States wants it, too," Yuvi muttered, bracing his hands on the armrests. "So does the entire Arab world—not just the Guardians. Everyone for their own purpose. The Muslims? They call it 'the Eye of Dawn.' Their mullahs have predicted it will shine as a beacon signaling the triumph of Islam over the West."

Natalie closed her eyes. *Tiny treasure from the Middle East.*

Dana had been trying to make peace. She never would have guessed that her accidental discovery would trigger anything but.

45

Muslim Quarter, Jerusalem
The next day

The street where Fatima Al Mehannadi worked smelled pleasantly of cumin and mint and lemons. But it was hardly peaceful. It roared with the chatter of shopkeepers hawking their wares and customers hunting for bargains as they made their way through the narrow lanes strung with merchandise. Here they could choose among rugs, ceramics, postcards, religious items, and filmy scarves and tunics that formed a colorful canopy overhead.

Women, many with children in tow, hurried from shop to shop, past men waving people into their carpet stores or whiling away the hours smoking cigarettes or heady tobacco from their hookahs. People clustered in cafés drinking small cups of thick black coffee, talking about the very real possibility of peace, whispering about the summit that had the world's eye focused on their city.

The door of the little souvenir shop where Fatima sold brass teapots, ceramic plates, and Arabic music tapes was flung open to the dust of the cobbled street to let in whatever air could filter through the congestion. It was hot air, but without even a fan in the tiny premises, any type of breeze was welcome. Fatima fanned herself with a sheaf of paper in between waiting on customers.

And waiting for Hasan to arrive.

She felt warm in her high-necked, long-sleeved shirt and the flowered cotton skirt that fell to dust her sandaled toes. She longed to lift her black woven *hijab* just long enough to fan her neck, but Hasan might walk in at any moment, and he'd be displeased. He didn't accept the modern tendencies of the Bahraini upper classes in which she'd been raised, where a more relaxed and Western mode of dress for women was acceptable—unlike in Iran, where he'd grown up. It irked her sometimes, but Hasan was a generous husband and a great leader. And she loved him for both.

They'd been married less than a year, but she still quivered with a mixture of excitement and trepidation whenever she thought of him. Whenever she looked in the mirror and saw the scar that glistened pink and jagged across her right cheek.

Some women might have been terrified to marry Hasan, but she felt no regret. Only a twinge of sadness. She knew that there would always be a price to pay for loving a man who possessed the evil eye. His gaze was dangerous. But she felt worse for Hasan than for herself.

The day after the Sabouri and Al Mehannadi families had announced their engagement, the curse everyone whispered about had visited her father's home. Fatima had glanced up at herself in the hallway mirror as she hurried to the kitchen, and had caught Hasan's gaze following her. In that instant the mirror fell from the wall, showering glass onto her head.

But Fatima refused to be afraid. As long as their eyes never again met—while they made love, while they shared their meals, or when they greeted each other—she had to trust that no further harm would befall her. Hasan needed her. No one else would risk being close to him. Even his brother, Farshid, kept his distance, though they were brothers by blood, brothers in a shared cause.

Fatima knew the depths of her husband's isolation. Outside of the business of the Guardians, he had few dealings with others. He feigned indifference to friendship, yet she knew that the boyhood he'd spent feared and shunned had left its wounds. She wondered what kind of man he'd be if he'd been born with brown eyes. But then, she reminded herself, he wouldn't be the man destined to lead the Guardians, destined to bring them the Eye of Dawn.

She spotted Hasan through the shop window before he reached the doorway and adjusted her *hijab,* pulling it more snugly toward her cheeks. She lowered her eyes as he crossed the doorway, a smile breaking across her heart-shaped face.

"Fatima. You look well." Hasan strode toward his bride, glancing quickly at her and then away.

"I am better now that you are back," she replied, love flooding her, her gaze fixed carefully on the center of his patterned tie, daring to roam no higher than the lapels of his tailored black suit. "Sayyed was here earlier. He is eager for today."

"May Allah bless his clumsy hands." Hasan's eyes narrowed. "His success remains to be proven. He'd better not fail us on this of all days."

Seeing the worry flicker across her face, he turned the conversation.

"I brought you something to mark this day of victory. It's nearly as lovely as you."

Her sudden smile rewarded him. Reaching into his trouser pocket, he pulled out the *hamsa* charm, threaded on its delicate silver chain. He dangled it from his fingers, letting the amethysts catch the light and splay tiny transparent stars across the walls.

Fatima beamed with pleasure. It *was* lovely. Her dark eyes shone at the glimmer of the amethysts, the turquoise cloisonné eye, and, most of all, at the shimmering pearl at its center. Her parents had told her when she was a child that pearls were formed when mermaid tears fell into open oyster shells. The Bahraini legend said that certain pearls possessed supernatural powers, helping their owners to find lost objects—or love. She'd never seen a Hand of Fatima quite like this one.

"Hasan, it is extraordinary," she breathed. "Thank you!"

"It's more special than you know," he murmured, and there was an edge to his voice. Fatima wondered why, but she didn't ask. "This will protect you today. And *in sha'allah,* for many days to come."

She turned around so that he could clasp it around her neck.

46

Natalie awoke in a strange bed. She was in a small room where slatted wood blinds blocked any ray of light. For a moment she couldn't remember where she was. She felt dazed and confused, with fuzzy remnants of dreams whirling in her brain. Then where she was—and why—came flooding back in a rush. She jerked upright in the narrow bed and winced. Her body ached all over, adding to her reconnection with reality.

The Mossad. The plane taxiing down the runway in Tel Aviv. The car ride at night to this safe house somewhere in a northern neighborhood of Jerusalem. A slim young Israeli woman in cropped white cotton pants, sandals, and a black tank top meeting them at the door, leading her and D'Amato up the stairs to their bedrooms. She checked under her pillow and scooped up the pouch, reassuring herself that the pendant was still safely inside.

As she stared at it, the words of Rabbi Calo and Father Caserta came back to her. The Light of Creation was in her hand. A smidge of it, anyway.

But a smidge so powerful, the whole world wanted it.

She tried to imagine what the crystal gem encasing this primordial light looked like. Tried to picture it hanging aloft in Noah's Ark—powerful enough to illumine the darkness of the Flood. She imagined it aglow in Nebuchadnezzar's palace and

It dangled at her throat, just beneath the juncture of her *hijab* and her blouse.

"Your trip—I am sorry it did not go as well as you hoped." How she longed to gaze into his eyes, to see if he was troubled by the failure in Rome Farshid had told her about. But she couldn't risk the danger or Hasan's anger over her tempting fate.

"The game isn't over." His tone was grim now. Determined. "My quarry has come to me. If Sayyed does his part, there's no doubt we'll triumph."

Fatima's heartbeat quickened, thinking how close they were to achieving everything they'd worked for. Hasan, his brother Farshid, her own brother, herself . . .

She dropped her voice to a whisper. "The Eye of Dawn is here—now—in Al Quds?"

Satisfaction suffused his voice as he caught her hands in his. "Yes, Fatima, the Eye is here. Exactly where we need it to be."

marveled that Daniel had managed to rescue it as the Persians charged the palace gates.

She caught the scent of coffee, heard the clink of kitchen utensils from below, and suddenly her stomach hurt from more than Barnabas's kick. She was starving.

Throwing back the covers, she stumbled to the bathroom, showered gingerly, and dressed in the clothes Tali, the female Mossad agent, had left folded for her on a wicker chest near the sink.

The cropped khakis were a bit loose in the waist, a bit tight in the tush, but they were clean and fresh, as was the pale yellow T-shirt that Natalie tucked into the waistband. There was nothing she could do about the bruise purpling across her cheek, but she fluffed her damp hair, grabbed up her shoulder bag, and went down in search of that coffee.

As she reached the bottom of the stairs, she could hear the television. It was always on in Israel. Israelis hung on every word of the news as if their lives depended on it—which they often did.

"*Boker tov.*" D'Amato's tone was dry as he wished her good morning in Hebrew over the low murmur of the TV on the counter. "As you can see, I still remember some things from my stint here with the network."

"I guess you do." She managed a smile as she slipped into the chair beside him. "I don't know about you, but I slept like the dead." She nodded at Doron, scrambling eggs at the stove. He was unsmiling. He looked tense. So did Lior, his brow crinkled as he handed her a cup of coffee, then slung himself into one of the four remaining chairs crammed around a small round table.

"This'll revive you. Tali brews it so strong you could chew it."

"Where is she?" Natalie asked, spearing a slice of melon from the plate at the center of the table. "And the others?"

"They have a different assignment today," Lior replied. "Only Nuri and Yuvi are staying here with us—they'll be back soon to escort you to the IAA. Prime Minister Rachmiel sends his regrets that he won't be able to meet you there to thank you personally."

"I imagine he's a tad tied up today." Natalie smiled.

Doron portioned out the pan of stiffly scrambled eggs and joined them at the table. "You can't imagine the excitement at the IAA this morning. Two momentous events in Israel on the same day—peace and the *tzohar* come to Jerusalem."

Lior set down his coffee cup. "As we say during the Passover Seder—*dayenu*—'it would have been enough.' Well, the prime minister's office said, if only peace had come to Jerusalem today, *dayenu*. And if only the oldest biblical treasure in existence had come to us today, that would have been enough, too. But to have them both—and to know that the primordial light of the *tzohar* has the potential to illuminate the world—that's a miracle of riches."

"The IAA is extremely interested in the *tzohar,* since it's our most precious antiquity," Doron added, "but the government will be eager to explore its properties as an alternative source of fuel."

"I'd be most interested in seeing them prove that," D'Amato said wryly.

"So you, too, believe it has such power?" Natalie asked the Israelis in surprise.

"Thanks to you, we're on the verge of finding out, aren't we?" A pensive expression settled over Doron's face. "I'm sure you're familiar with *tikkun olam*—the Jewish concept that humans are here to repair the world, each person in their own way."

As Natalie nodded, he continued. "I'm not a particularly religious man, but I'd like to think that the *tzohar* surfaced now to do some *tikkun olam,* too. It seems likely that the light that helped create the world could go a long way toward helping to heal it."

The only sound in the kitchen was the low murmur of the TV newscast, until Lior stopped chewing and stared at D'Amato.

"Your injury—the explosion on bus 27," the gray-haired Mossad agent said out of the blue. "Just so you know— remember how quiet Rafi became yesterday when you told us what happened to you? His cousin died on that bus."

D'Amato went still. "Damn. For all I know, he could have been sitting right next to me."

Lior set his fork down with a clatter. "You were lucky."

"That's what I keep reminding myself. I spent four eye-opening years here with the network, Lior. I know exactly what you're up against."

Doron grunted. "Well, we're up against a lot more of it today."

"How do you mean?" Natalie folded her napkin, wondering if he was worried about getting the pendant safely to the IAA.

The two Mossad agents exchanged glances, but neither of them answered her. Instead, they turned their attention back to the television.

"It would be nice if you leveled with us," D'Amato remarked, as the newscast switched to video of President Owen Garrett's arrival in Jerusalem, a smiling First Lady at his side.

Lior slid the remote closer and pumped up the volume.

"Is it the summit?" D'Amato guessed, noting Doron was equally riveted now to the screen. He sensed the increased tension thrumming through the two agents.

Lior pushed back his chair. "As you can imagine, not everyone is in a celebratory mood."

"Are you anticipating trouble at the ceremony?" D'Amato asked.

Lior responded by stacking the plates and hauling them to the sink. He peered out the window, checking up and down the street. "Why aren't they back already?" He drummed his long fingers on the countertop.

I'm right, D'Amato thought, watching him. Watching Doron's frown deepen. He listened to what was left unsaid. *Something is brewing over the ceremony.*

"Yeah," D'Amato said aloud. "We do need to get going. Natalie won't relax until she turns the pendant over to the authorities."

"*You're* not going anywhere, D'Amato." Doron scrubbed his hands down his face. "You're expecting a visitor."

"What kind of visitor?"

"Someone from your government. They contacted us in the event we found you first."

Natalie's gaze swung to D'Amato. Their eyes met, and she

felt her stomach twist. The CIA. It had to be. Was he in trouble? Because he'd helped her?

"He needs to come with me," she said instantly. "He's a part of this. It's only right he see it through."

"Not going to happen, I'm afraid." Doron's mouth was set.

At that moment, Lior spun from the window.

"They're back."

47

Nuri was talking intently into his cell phone as he bustled through the kitchen door, both eyes blackened now, and his nose even more swollen than it had been yesterday. He was joined a beat later by a sober-faced Yuvi.

Natalie caught only a few words of Nuri's rapid-fire Hebrew. *Nitsatsot shelo nitpotsa*—he was saying something about . . .

"Ready to go?" Yuvi asked her. He jingled the keys to the Ford in his hand.

"What was that I just heard . . . about bombs?"

Yuvi's olive eyes were fixed on her face, still with that solemn, neutral expression. "We're always talking about bomb threats." He shrugged dismissively. "Are you ready to leave?"

Nuri snapped his phone shut. "Okay, we're going to escort you now to the IAA. Out of respect for what you've gone through, Natalie—your sister's death, the various attacks you've suffered, and your dedication in keeping the *tzohar* safe—you have the honor of personally handing it over to the authorities. It's time we get going."

She nodded, still troubled by what she'd overheard. "You wouldn't tell us even if there was a bomb threat, would you?" She glanced from Nuri's face to Yuvi's.

"They wouldn't, Natalie." It was D'Amato who answered when no one else did. "In their line of work, everything is on a need-to-know basis. And they don't think we need to know anything."

Doron lifted a hand, palm out. "Enough. You Americans think too much. You don't need to worry about anything but getting the *tzohar* to the authorities."

Impatiently, Yuvi hoisted her shoulder bag from the back of the chair and handed it to her. "The pendant is still inside?"

She nodded, and pushed away every other concern.

"You'll be here when I get back?" she asked D'Amato, hooking the strap of her bag securely over her shoulder.

If he was worried about the upcoming grilling by the CIA, or whoever it was who wanted to talk to him, he didn't show it. He swung from his chair and gave her his slight, lopsided smile.

"Count on it."

The Reverend Ken Mundy paced his suite at the David Citadel Hotel, his cell phone pressed to his ear. Gwen was still in the marble bathroom, completing her lengthy beautification process. He'd been trying to reach the Sentinel all morning, to no avail.

He was about to toss the phone on the bed in disgust, to give up on speaking to him before the ceremony, when suddenly he heard the familiar voice on the encrypted line.

"Where in God's name have you been? There's been no word from Barnabas, and I'm growing very concerned."

"With good reason. Barnabas is dead."

The words hit Mundy like a jolt from a taser. "How . . . ? When . . . ?"

"This isn't the time for details. I only have a minute. The Light is here with us, Ken. In Israel."

Mundy sank to the bed, trying to absorb this hopeful news along with the shock that his most promising protégé was dead. The boy who'd worked so hard for the chance to build the Third Temple with his own hands would never touch a single stone, a single trowel of mortar.

"How are we going to get the Light without Barnabas?" he asked, his tone as heavy as his heart. "Are you sending someone else—Derrek?"

"It's too late for Derrek. You'll have to depend on me—and our friends."

Yes. The Shomrei Kotel, Mundy thought dazedly. But he couldn't stop thinking about Barnabas.

"I don't understand," Mundy mumbled. "How could this have happened?"

"Ken." The Sentinel's voice was uncharacteristically sharp. "Enough. You have to pull yourself together for the ceremony." The line went dead.

He's right. It's almost time for the ceremony. Mundy drew a breath and forced himself to focus. He walked to the mirror and began adjusting his tie, concentrating on perfecting the knot. *In a very short time, I'll be standing where the Temples stood. Where Jacob slept and dreamed of the ladder. Where Jesus threw out the money changers.* His hands trembled with excitement as he tugged at the two ends of his tie until they were even. *And where soon the Sons of Babylon will dig the foundation for the Third Temple.* He held fast to the most promising news the Sentinel had told him.

The Light is here in Jerusalem.

48

Hasan read the text message as the car sped north on Route 60 and smiled to himself.

It was about time Sayyed finally delivered on his promises. He'd failed more times than he'd succeeded in the past, but Farshid had insisted he be given chance after chance because their parents had been neighbors in Tehran. Hasan had not been as patient. He'd beaten Sayyed once when he'd bungled the simplest of deliveries. Since then Sayyed had applied himself. He'd performed well in his latest endeavor. And now his efforts were finally coming to fruition.

But Hasan refused to give Sayyed all the credit. The Bahraini legend was right. It was the fortuitous pearl now gracing Fatima's neck that was going to help deliver the Eye of Dawn into his hands.

Yuvi watched the odometer as he drove down the winding two-lane road, both hands on the steering wheel. The nail he'd shoved into the left rear tire while Nuri preceded him into the house should cause it to blow any time within the next two kilometers. In the backseat, Nuri was on the phone again. Distracted. *Good*.

He glanced over at Natalie Landau in the passenger seat alongside him. She'd been holding onto the *tzohar* long enough.

There was a sudden deafening pop as the tire blew. The Ford

egan to tremble out of its lane, and an oncoming Mercedes
swerved to the shoulder, splaying dust across the road as Nata-
ie Landau gasped and Nuri swore. Yuvi wrestled the car under
control. It took all of his strength to steer it onto the narrow
houlder of the hilly road.

"A damned flat," he yelled disgustedly and threw open his
door. His hands were shielded from their view as he headed
toward the trunk. It only took him one second to key in their
ocation and send Menny the text message.

"Right on time." Menny Goldstein pushed his sunglasses
higher up on his nose and scanned the incoming text message.
The next instant he jerked the car away from the curb, his foot
stomping a little too heavily on the gas pedal, lurching them
awkwardly onto the lonely back road.

Excitement thrummed through his fingers as he tapped the
steering wheel. He was elated. "Yuvi had it figured almost exactly. They're less than five minutes from here."

"*Baruch ha Shem,* praise God's name," Shmuel said beside
him.

The tzohar *is home,* Menny thought. And he'd be a man
privileged beyond his merit when he held it in his hands. *Very
soon now.*

Then, God willing, the Shomrei Kotel would keep it hidden
and safe until Moshiach—the Messiah—came at last, and the
zohar could shine once more in the Third Temple.

He tried not to think about the gun beneath his seat, which
would be in his hands very soon also. Not that he was hesitant
in the least to use a gun—he had shot one in the army. But
never as a civilian. And never at a fellow Israeli.

He deliberately refocused his thoughts, switching instead to
how fortuitous it was to have such good Christian friends as
Reverend Mundy and the Sons of Babylon—men as equally
committed as he and the Shomrei Kotel to rebuilding the Temple.
The Sons of Babylon were trustworthy and zealous partners in
this sacred mission. More than the politicians and the diplomats, they understood the truth of the Torah's prophecies. They'd
help defend Jerusalem against any takers.

The signing today of the absurd, meaningless peace documents was designed solely to mollify an ignorant and misguided world. Many in Israel and around the globe understood that the peace would never hold. The decades-long indoctrination of Palestinian schoolchildren against Jews and Israel would see to that.

Palestinian children's television programs, video games, and textbooks had for years glorified martyrdom and *jihad*, while denouncing the establishment of Israel as an "evil crime." *It was impossible for a piece of paper to create peace,* Menny thought, *when Israel didn't even appear on maps in Palestinian textbooks, and when so many young Arabs had grown up learning hate along with math and science.*

Still, the return of the *tzohar* to Jerusalem on *this very day* gave Menny hope. He took it as a sign from God that Israel would endure.

"Think of it—the Temple will be rebuilt in our lifetimes, Shmuel," he said joyously, turning to regard his friend. "Our children will worship there—and Moshiach will soon return."

But Shmuel was all business, his gun already in his hand, his eyes trained on the road. "There they are." He pointed ahead to where two men were changing a tire and a woman stood, arms crossed, alongside a green Ford Focus.

49

Nuri had just fitted the spare tire onto the wheel when Yuvi saw the silver car approaching fast from the south. It was just distant enough ahead of them that it shimmered in the heat, like the dusty pavement that stretched toward the center of Jerusalem, an optical illusion in the broiling Israeli sun. Nothing else moved in the rocky hillside that hugged the empty road where he stood behind Nuri, tire iron in hand.

Yuvi waited, watching the front wheels of the oncoming car as they angled toward the shoulder. *Now.* He turned and lifted the tire iron just as Nuri glanced up, squinting at the silver car that had stopped in front of theirs, its motor still running.

In one brutal stroke Yuvi drove the iron against the back of Nuri's head. He flinched despite himself as the man he'd worked with for the past six months toppled onto his side. Yuvi didn't think he'd hit him hard enough to kill him, though. He hoped not. Glancing down, it was unsettling to see blood seeping from the gash behind Nuri's ear.

I'll need to leave the country either way, he thought mournfully, even as he sprang around the car toward Natalie Landau. *I'll never see the Temple rebuilt, but my sacrifice will make it possible.*

Two men spilled from the silver car.

"What are you doing?" Natalie screamed, backing away from

the disabled car, and from the Mossad agent who'd just attacked his partner. "Why did you hit Nuri?"

She whirled toward the silver car, toward the two men running toward them with guns drawn.

But it was a mistake to take her eyes off Yuvi. He was on her in a blink, snatching her shoulder bag with such force it wrenched her arm. Before she could grab it back, he flung it to the shorter of the two men, the one wearing sunglasses, the one in the lead.

"It's in there, Menny," Yuvi called. "Inside the center zippered—"

He never finished. The bullet tore through his stomach and blew out his spine. Menny froze for a heartbeat, shock on his face. "What the—" He wheeled to face Shmuel as Natalie's screams circled through the dry, dusty air.

"Shmuel—" Menny began, disbelief in his voice. It was the last word he ever uttered. Shmuel shot him in the chest at point-blank range. His body blew backward, and Natalie's shoulder bag blew with it.

"Don't move." Shmuel now had the gun trained on her. "And shut up!"

The screams clogged in her throat, winding down like an air-raid siren. Going silent.

"Who . . . are you?" she whispered, bracing herself for the next shot.

He seemed to realize what she was thinking and smiled. He was young and craggily handsome, with smooth dark skin, a short beard, and a heartless smile.

"No, you are not going to die. Not yet—and not by my hand."

He strolled around the car slowly, almost casually, and saw Nuri's eyelid twitch. Saw his stubby fingers crawling toward the weapon in his shoulder holster.

"It's his turn next."

The bullet he put in Nuri's chest thundered in Natalie's ears.

She dove for her bag and rolled frantically with it, praying to make it under the car. Her reaction was instinctive, even though she knew he could kneel down and shoot her under the car just as easily.

Or kick the jack out and let the car fall on her.

Confusion and terror fought for a foothold in her mind. Yuvi had betrayed them. With a sickening lurch in her stomach, she wondered if he had a partner in betrayal at the safe house. If D'Amato was in danger, too.

Trembling, clutching her bag, she flashed on how quickly Shmuel had turned on Yuvi. Yet they obviously had orchestrated the ambush together. Yuvi had told them where to find the *tzohar*.

But Shmuel—he hadn't only turned on Yuvi, he'd turned on the guy he came with, too. The man in the sunglasses, Menny. Who did each of them work for? Her brain was numb with confusion.

One thing she did know—she knew what they all wanted.

Breathing hard, she watched Shmuel's feet as he rounded the car. Knelt down. Smiled at her.

"Come out. *Now.*"

D'Amato wasn't surprised that Bob Hutton, his former CIA handler, had known D'Amato and Natalie were headed toward Israel even before he did. The CIA and Mossad observed certain courtesies. There were certain circumstances in which they shared information and cooperated.

A long-awaited summit meeting in Israel involving both their governments—with the ever-present possibility of terrorism looming over it—was one of those circumstances.

"Why the hell didn't you contact me on day one, when all this started going down?" Hutton pinned him with those bullet-gray eyes D'Amato had first seen in March 2003.

They were sitting outside the safe house in Hutton's car with the engine running, AC blasting, seats ratcheted back so the two of them could face each other. He'd been debriefing D'Amato for nearly a half hour now. D'Amato hadn't held back. Much.

"Last I heard from the agency was a 'don't call us, we'll call you, asshole,' message. With no callback number," D'Amato retorted, stretching out his legs.

He'd told Hutton as much as he knew about the bastards who'd been trying to kill him and Natalie. He'd gone over details, descriptions, impressions—several times over.

He couldn't get a bead on how Hutton was processing it all. Which wasn't surprising. In the years they'd worked together, he'd never been able to determine whether his handler was angry, satisfied, or impressed.

Hutton was a tall lethal machine of a man, fierce as an eagle. He had a whipcord build, an IQ in the upper 130s, and a full head of salt-and-pepper hair. And he was particular about his single-malt scotch. His grimace of disgust during one of their earliest meetings had clued D'Amato in instantly that Oban was drunk neat, and never over ice. Hutton had cut his milk teeth in the latter days of the cold war and sprouted his molars during the nineties as a top covert field operative in Central Asia and the Middle East.

D'Amato glanced at the dashboard clock, wondering how Natalie was faring. She must have the pendant safely inside the Rockefeller Museum—and into the hands of the IAA by now. *Mission accomplished. Over and out.*

With any luck, they might still get out on the last plane from Tel Aviv tonight, while half the world was waking up to the news of what had transpired on the Temple Mount today.

Still, part of him, the hard-core journalist junkie part, craved a front-row seat at the hottest news event of the decade.

Hutton wasn't finished with him yet, though. "You and the Landau woman have left an impressive trail of dead bodies behind you, D'Amato—Luther Tyrelle, Rusty Sutherland, the NSU agents, the 'Osamas' who crashed and burned in Brooklyn." He paused as a car came around the corner, waited until it had continued down the quiet suburban street of stout, white, stone houses with reddish-orange roofs. It turned left, going out of sight.

"Then there was the Rome hotel clerk, Ken Mundy's wacko hitman, Barnabas Lewis—not to mention a few more 'Osamas' who weren't exactly lighting votive candles in that Catholic church yesterday." Hutton's lip curled. "Did I leave anyone out?"

"And your point is?" D'Amato glared at him.

"Did it never occur to you that your own government might

want to get its hands on the object Ms. Landau's been carrying around with her? Did it never occur to you to come to *us*?"

"Look, you guys cut me loose six months ago when I went back into rehab. I've been persona non grata—have you forgotten?"

"Don't you forget that you're still alive because of the training we gave you. That object you've been shepherding across the globe—we've been searching for it for years. Didn't you think you owed us first dibs?"

"It wasn't mine to give you, Hutton. Are we through here?" His hand was already on the door handle. Then he turned back. "Hearing any chatter about the summit?"

"You think I'd tell you?"

D'Amato studied him. "How about a truce? I'm here, on the ground. Another pair of eyes and ears. A freelancer, if you will. Give me a hint, and if I pick up on anything, it's yours."

Hutton looked like he wanted to tell him to go to hell. Then he thought better of it.

"Hell, why not? You've managed to keep a dozen steps ahead of the NSU. It was *their* job to net the pendant. But they've been swiping at dead air every step of the way. Yeah, there's been chatter about the summit." Hutton snorted. "Those Osamas who've been trying to snare the pendant—the Guardians of the Khalifah? They appear to be pretty interested in what's going down at the Temple Mount."

"Interested how?" D'Amato asked.

"Interested enough to set off alarm bells."

50

Natalie stayed where she was, sandwiched, sweating, between the car and the road.

"Don't make me tell you again." Shmuel's lips were smiling, but his eyes weren't.

"Who are you working for?" *Buy time.* Time to think, to formulate a plan. "You know this belongs with the IAA."

He snorted. "You're going to meet the man it's going to belong to any moment now. Better for you if you come out before he gets here."

Despite the heat radiating from the ground and from the engine of the car, a chill soaked her. She could hear the engine running in the silver car—if only she could get to it, get past the murderer leering at her.

"Stay there then," he told her, his cold smile widening. And then he straightened. She heard the driver's door open, saw the shadow fall across the ground. Felt his weight lower the car as he swung onto the seat.

He's going to drive it right over me, she thought in horror, imagining the jack ripping loose as he did.

"Wait!" she screamed. And still clutching her shoulder bag, she flung its strap out onto the pavement near the driver's door, where he could see it. "Take it! Just leave me alone!"

Instantly, his left foot stepped back out of the car, stomping right into the loop of her strap to prevent her from yanking it back in. Taking a deep breath, Natalie dug her toes into the ground and waited. Waited until his weight shifted above her as he exited the car.

In the split second that he was balanced on only one leg, she yanked the strap upward and toward her with all her strength, toppling him with a crash.

Clutching her shoulder bag, she scrabbled toward the opposite side of the car, rolled out from under it, and sprang to her feet, running hell-bent for the silver car. As she tore across the road, she heard him cursing in Arabic behind her.

Arabic. Shock mingled with terror. His heavy footsteps pounded after her. Closing in. She pushed harder—the car was less than five feet away. *Please God . . .*

Then he tackled her, sending her crashing headlong into the hood, falling with her onto the blazing metal. The breath whooshed out of her and her head cracked against the hood. Dazed, she struggled, but felt him rip the shoulder bag from her arm.

Then a new sound. Another car motor. She screamed, praying it was someone who would help, but the prayers died in her throat as the car screeched to a stop and a flood of Arabic flowed between the man pinning her and whoever had just arrived.

Someone was here to help—but not to help her.

She bit back sobs as the man called Shmuel pushed himself off her and yanked her backward. Dizziness made her sway on her feet. The sun beat down as she blinked and tried to orient herself. Shmuel had her shoulder bag and was holding her arm in an unbreakable grip.

"Well done, Sayyed. For once."

That voice. She knew it like she knew the sound of dirt on a newly lowered coffin. Her sister's coffin.

"*You.*" Her eyes cleared at last and she focused on the man whose taunting voice had followed her from Brooklyn to Rome to Jerusalem.

He was younger than his voice. He couldn't have been thirty. He was sinewy, handsome, with slanting brows, thick eyelashes. And the most piercing, unnerving blue eyes she'd ever seen.

An Arabic man with blue eyes. A man traditionally feared in his own culture as one who could inflict the evil eye.

Those blue eyes locked on her as he strode forward. She refused to look away, refused to blink. *He* might believe he could curse her, but she didn't. Wouldn't.

Then, his gaze still on her face, he extended his hand and the man who held her—not Shmuel, Sayyed—tossed him her shoulder bag.

"The Eye of Dawn—inside, Hasan."

"No!" Anguish tore through her. And rage. After everything they'd done to prevent this, the *tzohar* had still fallen into his hands. She glared from Sayyed to Hasan, fighting to make sense of what had gone so terribly wrong in this past hour. To comprehend betrayal upon betrayal.

But there was no time to connect the dots. Hasan's fingers were digging through her bag, groping for the pouch, his gaze still nailed to her face. Those strangely electric blue eyes seemed to burn into her irises, hotter than the sun.

She flinched as he found what he sought, lifted it out. Carelessly, he discarded her bag, tossing it aside like garbage.

Nauseated, Natalie watched a slow smile spread across his face as he lowered his gaze at last to study the painted eyes adorning the aged leather.

Suddenly, from the ground, came the faint ring of a cell phone. Hers.

Natalie's heart lurched. *D'Amato,* she thought, staring at her bag as if she could somehow will the phone to fly into her hand.

But her captor and the man he called Hasan ignored the soft insistent ringing. Hasan turned without a glance at the shoulder bag in the road and began walking toward his black car.

"Bring her, Sayyed," he said, almost as an afterthought. "I'm not ready to kill her just yet."

51

D'Amato redialed Natalie's cell number. He frowned—still no answer.

Circling the kitchen with a restlessness that grew more intense with each unanswered ring, he fought the dread gnarling in his gut. He should have heard something from Natalie by now.

Hutton had left at least a half hour ago. Natalie, Yuvi, and Nuri should be on their way back.

He sought out Doron in the living room, but Doron was on his cell. From upstairs came the hiss of water running—Lior in the shower.

"I can't reach Natalie. Try your guys," D'Amato demanded as soon as Doron disconnected.

The Israeli dialed calmly but then started to pace, his expression darkening with concern. "Nuri's not answering. Let me try Yuvi."

But Yuvi didn't pick up either.

"Could be they're still at the IAA and can't get a clear signal inside?" D'Amato gripped the back of the couch. He didn't like the doubt he saw in Doron's eyes.

"There's one way to find out." Doron punched in another set of numbers.

By the time Lior joined them, his gray hair still damp, Doron had confirmed that Natalie and their partners had never arrived at the IAA.

Full-blown panic lit in D'Amato as Lior called headquarters while they piled into the Hyundai.

"With all the detours and roadblocks because of the summit, they probably avoided the freeway and took back roads." Doron's voice was tense as he screeched out of the drive.

D'Amato didn't answer. His gut told him what they'd find long before they spotted Yuvi's green Ford.

Still, he clamped his eyes shut for a moment to block the carnage splayed on the road beneath the broiling sun. The ambulances from the Red Magen David Adom were already there, flashers streaking.

He sprang from the Hyundai even as Doron braked, praying he wouldn't find Natalie's body among the dead.

52

The all too familiar odors of earth, stone, and minerals stung Natalie's nostrils. Her sense of smell was sharpened by the blindfold Sayyed had bound around her eyes.

Even if Hasan hadn't been dragging her down rough-hewn steps and along a downward-sloping tunnel, she'd have known she was underground.

She recognized the distinctive scents just as she recognized the way the voices bounced around the space. She'd spent enough time on excavations in tunnels and underground tombs to know that they were in a narrow, low-ceilinged space belowground.

Dazed and aching, she tried to guess how far below the surface they'd come. But it was difficult. She was disoriented and hadn't begun counting her steps until they'd been trudging downward for some time. Her face throbbed, her shoulders burned where Shmuel—no, *Sayyed*—had wrenched them. Her raw flesh stung where the road had scraped away her skin.

She was weak—and so thirsty. At least it was a few degrees cooler down here than it had been in the rear seat of the black car, when she'd been driven, bound and blindfolded, to somewhere, she guessed, in East Jerusalem.

She'd heard the sounds of a neighborhood when he'd pulled her from the car, a neighborhood devoid of Hebrew. Heard children calling in Arabic, men shouting, horns blaring, women jabbering, music.

And then Sayyed had led her, still blindfolded, down alleyways that smelled of roasted lamb and cigarette smoke, across cobbled streets and uneven pavement—before they began this endless descent underground.

How would anyone ever find her now?

When they finally stopped walking, her heart jerked violently in her chest as she wondered what Hasan was going to do to her. Then she was flung to the ground. She fell hard, sprawling, her scraped arms once again seared by hard-packed earth and loose stones.

She heard an ominous ripping sound and the blindfold was torn from her eyes. Light flooded into her dilated pupils, and she winced at the brightness of a naked lightbulb overhead, bathing them like a spotlight.

Hasan's gun was trained at her head. Sayyed towered over her, tearing off a long strip of duct tape.

"Bind her hands and feet," Hasan ordered. "Tightly."

She fought down panic and looked away as Sayyed began strapping the tough, wide, sticky fabric around her ankles. It was then that she spotted two water bottles beneath a small table in the shadows. She licked a dry tongue over her cracked lips, knowing it would be fruitless to ask for a sip.

Then fear lodged in her chest. On top of the table sat a battery-operated headlamp, a flashlight, and an array of tools—a vice, several hammers, pliers, an ice pick.

What are they planning to do to me?

She attempted to wriggle her ankles. But the duct tape was wrapped perfectly tight, just as Hasan had commanded. Despair and hopelessness closed in on her like a dark fog.

She pushed them away and tried to relegate her pain to the recesses of her brain, so she could focus on her surroundings. She needed to be ready, she told herself, ready to use any opportunity that presented itself to change the outcome.

"What's wrong, Sayyed?" Hasan sounded amused. "You look uneasy."

"How long until the C-4 goes off?" Sayyed was glancing

warily at the ceiling, even as he snapped Natalie's arms behind her back and began winding tape around her wrists.

"There's plenty of time. Why are you so nervous? There's no chance of a premature detonation. You'll be long gone by the time I give the signal and our guest here has her eardrums blown out." He circled Natalie with the gun, surveying Sayyed's handiwork. "Of course, that will be mere seconds before the whole of the Al-Haram al-Sharif comes crashing down on her. The crater charge from three hundred pounds of C-4 will see to that."

C-4. Al-Haram al-Sharif—we're under the Temple Mount. The blood drained from Natalie's face. *Oh, God, they're going to blow it up. The summit . . . all those people . . .*

"Now you're afraid." Hasan looked pleased. She looked away. He bent down swiftly and jerked her face up by the chin, forcing her to meet his strange glowing eyes.

"If you won't tell me," he spat contemptuously, "your eyes will."

"*You* should be afraid. The Mossad will stop you."

He laughed, and the sound echoed around the gloom of the tunnel, which was illuminated only by the glimmer of light-bulbs strung sporadicly along the ceiling, stretching like ghostly eyes into the shadowy distance.

"Stop me? The way they stopped me from abducting you? And from reclaiming the Eye of Dawn? The way they stopped me from drilling holes deep into this ceiling and packing them with bombs?"

Sayyed jeered, too, as he tore off more tape. "And like they stopped me from infiltrating Shomrei Kotel? I've succeeded in parading as a Jew for almost two years, keeping tabs on them, with none of them the wiser. Don't hold your breath waiting for their help."

"Enough, Sayyed!" Hasan's voice was sharp with irritation. "Her wrists are bound too loosely. More tape. Tighter."

Sayyed's words sang through her head, penetrating even her fear. It was beginning to make sense now.

Yuvi. Yuvi must have secretly belonged to Shomrei Kotel— Menny, too. They set up the flat tire, they stranded us in the middle of nowhere—to capture the pendant.

But the Guardians of the Khalifah outwitted them both. With a double agent the Shomrei Kotel knew as "Shmuel."

"Your Mossad certainly didn't stop us from planting evidence laying today's events at the door of Shomrei Kotel. So much for the brilliance of the Israeli intelligence services." Hasan loomed over her, unable to resist gloating openly. "The destruction soon to take place—all those deaths, all the outrage, all of it will come down on the heads of the Israelis. And there won't be a nation in the world who will raise a finger to help them."

"It'll never happen." Natalie stared down those chilling blue eyes. "The Mossad suspects something. You're going to fail."

"No, Natalie Landau. We're going to succeed. And you're going to die." He cocked his head, as if in thought. "Your sister had no time to contemplate her death. The fool who killed her was too hasty. Too reckless. You, on the other hand, will have the next three hours to anticipate yours." Hasan glanced at his watch. "Correction—less than that."

At his mention of Dana, Natalie sat taller on the lumpy ground. "You told me you had my sister's *hamsa*. Where is it?"

Hasan's lip curled. "And what good would it do you now? You're already a dead woman—just like her."

He turned to speak in rapid Arabic to Sayyed. With his attention shifted from her, Natalie tested the strength of her bonds, straining to force her ankles a fraction of an inch apart. The duct tape was taut, there was zero give.

Still, she had three hours . . . *almost* three hours. Before the unthinkable happened.

Her tongue felt thick in her mouth, her thirst growing by the minute. She fought the dizziness that signaled she was becoming dehydrated and continued flexing her ankles, her wrists, against the slick gray tape.

Hasan was still busy giving orders to Sayyed. She picked out a few words and realized he was telling the man to stay with her. Even without comprehending the words, she knew Sayyed's protests were being sharply rebuked.

Then Hasan drew the leather pouch from the pocket of his khaki pants. Her heart twisted as he lifted the pendant up to the bare lightbulb, smiling as he studied the jeweled eyes for which Dana had died.

Bile rose in Natalie's throat.

"It's time to free the Eye of Dawn from its golden cocoon." Excitement thrummed through his voice. "For too many centuries it has been hidden from the world. Now I have the honor of liberating it in the name of Allah."

"The pendant doesn't belong to you," Natalie said in desperation. "It belongs to Israel."

He ignored her and went to the table, followed by Sayyed. As Natalie watched, he secured the pendant in the vice, seized the hammer, and raised his fist.

"No!" Panic coursed through her. And anguish. She twisted against the duct tape with a frantic energy. "Stop—you can't—don't destroy it—"

He gave no sign that he even heard her. He slammed the hammer into the pendant with all of his strength.

53

Jammed inside the hotel elevator with seven other guests, Elliott Warrick looked away from the dandruff dusting the thousand-dollar suit coat on the secretary-general's attaché, preferring to watch the floor numbers click by on the door panel instead.

He was on his way to the presidential suite for the emergency meeting he'd called with the president, the Secret Service, and Israeli officials.

At this late moment, based on the latest intel from NSU, he planned to recommend moving the site of the summit from the Temple Mount. Though they'd yet to pinpoint anything concrete, both the NSU and Mossad strongly suspected that the location had been compromised.

The area had been sequestered weeks ago, checked and re-checked daily. Secret Service advance teams had scoured every inch and secured all rooftops and multistory buildings within a thousand yards of the platform. Bomb-sniffing dogs had patrolled not only the perimeter but the whole of the Temple Mount—nothing had triggered a reaction.

Still, the increase in chatter today was alarming. Warrick knew all hell was about to break loose in the presidential suite, and he was bracing himself for the battle royale. It wouldn't help that there'd been no update on the whereabouts of Firefly.

He knew the Secret Service would back him in changing the

locale, but he also knew Owen Garrett was married to the Temple Mount backdrop, with its unique symbolism and its importance to the world's three major religions.

Garrett had staked his presidency on this momentous peace accord, and in his mind, nowhere else in the holy city would embody its essence more than the site where Abraham was willing to sacrifice Isaac, where the Holy of Holies had stood, where Jesus had preached, and where Muhammad had ascended through the heavens.

This commander in chief wouldn't give up his vision—or this landmark—lightly.

D'Amato felt a temporary, almost blinding relief. Natalie wasn't among the dead.

Then the sight of her shoulder bag lying abandoned in the road stopped his heart.

As Lior and Doron sprang toward the bodies, he tore through Natalie's bag, looking for the *tzohar,* knowing it wouldn't be there. But he had to look, despite the fact that he knew he shouldn't be touching anything. *Screw Forensics.*

The Israelis were stunned by the sight of the two dead Mossad agents and a third man they didn't know, but whose identification bore the name Menachem Goldstein. Doron was already calling the name in to the database, trying to piece together what had gone wrong.

Lior's face was ashen as D'Amato handed over Natalie's bag with a negative shake of his head. "It's gone," he heard himself saying numbly. "They've got Natalie—and the *tzohar.*"

"This dead guy, Menachem, he's the key." Lior took a step back, giving the medics space to zip Goldstein inside the body bag. "Looks like whoever brought him here killed him."

Doron hurried over, his round face as grim as the death scene that surrounded them. "Yuvi and Nuri never had a chance. Neither of them drew their weapons, much less fired."

"No way this is random." Fear for Natalie twisted D'Amato's gut. "What are the chances they'd just *happen* to have a flat tire on a back road, then *happen* to be ambushed? Whoever did this was after the *tzohar.*"

Nobody argued with him. "I found two separate sets of tire tracks, both approaching from the south," Doron said. "Fresh tracks." He pointed toward the shoulder of the road. "Two cars stopped here recently, but not to help."

The Guardians of the Khalifah. D'Amato knew they were all thinking the same thing. The Guardians may have gotten their Eye of Dawn.

Natalie needed help. And fast. He needed a ride.

54

"Stop, damn you!" Natalie's only weapon now was her voice.

A second crash of the hammer against the gold was Hasan's response. As he lifted the hammer yet again, she strained fruitlessly at her bonds, wrists and ankles simultaneously, aghast at what she was witnessing. The most ancient treasure imaginable being bludgeoned in an underground tunnel by a lunatic.

And she was powerless to stop him.

"If you smash your Eye of Dawn, it will be worthless to you!" she shouted.

But he paid her no heed, and with all of his attention focused on the pendant pinched within the vise, he wielded the hammer again.

The gold split, cracking open like a walnut, emitting an arc of white light so sudden and brilliant in the tunnel's darkness it made her blink. Even as the lightbulbs strung through the tunnel began to flicker, the light within the pendant grew in brilliance.

Blackness swooped down on the elevator. It lurched to a halt between floors.

What in hell? Warrick gasped along with everyone else crammed into the now pitch-dark space. He held his breath as the woman closest to the panel groped for the emergency button.

"Nothing's happening," she said, frustration raising her voice an octave.

Shit.

"Help!" A man behind him started shouting in his ear. "Can anyone hear us?"

Someone else began pounding on the elevator walls.

Not that it did a damned thing. The lights weren't coming on; the elevator was still frozen.

Is this part of it? The attack? Are they striking the whole city, not just the Temple Mount? He thought of Garrett upstairs in the presidential suite. Had he been hit? Or was the Secret Service spiriting him down the stairs and the hell out of here?

Warrick wasn't accustomed to being in the dark. Frustration ate through him. *I need to get the hell out of here.*

The traffic signal over the busy East Jerusalem intersection suddenly went as dark as night. No red, no amber, no green for go. In the backseat of his cab, D'Amato was jerked forward as the driver slammed the brakes, nearly rear-ending the van in front of them.

What now? he wondered, tension vibrating through his body. The Mossad agents had gotten him as far as the Old City. Now he was on his own, only a few miles from the home of Ahmad Zayadi.

His former contact from his days as Jerusalem bureau chief was expecting him. He was praying Ahmad would know something, someone who could help him get a bead on where Natalie might have been taken—and who had done the taking.

D'Amato had been a visitor to Ahmad's home on several occasions, meeting with Palestinian sources who'd discreetly provided background information, though refusing to be seen publicly in the company of an American—much less an American journalist. If anyone had an ear to the underground currents here in East Jerusalem, it would be Ahmad. And D'Amato couldn't get there soon enough.

But he was going nowhere. The cabbie was slamming his hands on the steering wheel, cursing. Horns began blaring all around them. Traffic was now at a standstill. But not for long, it seemed. Several cars accelerated from different directions all at once and three collided in the intersection.

It was D'Amato's turn to swear. This was getting worse by the moment. He craned his neck to see up ahead as he yanked out his cell phone to call Ahmad.

No signal.

"Can I borrow your cell phone for a minute? Local call."

The cabbie flipped his cell open, then met D'Amato's eyes in the rearview mirror. "It's not working either. Who knows what they're doing with this crazy summit?"

People had begun streaming from buildings, calling to one another.

"What happened to the power?"

"My lights are out too!"

"Bin Khoury was in the middle of speaking! Boom, no TV."

Their shouts interspersed with the insistent horns and irate shouts of the trapped drivers. Grimacing, D'Amato scanned the meter, paid the fare, and shoved open his door. At this rate he'd be better off taking a camel.

Dodging the distraught residents now jamming the streets, he burst into a run.

Ben Gurion Airport
Tel Aviv

One minute the air traffic controller was sipping black coffee, his eyes pinned to his screen as he juggled communications with the five incoming pilots, tracking their planes as they blipped across his monitor. The next he was gaping at a blank screen. His headset was eerily silent.

"Down!"

"It's all down!"

"What in God's name happened?"

All the air traffic controllers were shouting at once. In an instant, all visual and verbal contact with planes flying in and out of Israel had ended inexplicably.

The supervisor grabbed the phone, desperate for help. But

the phones were down, too. Landlines and cell phones alike. Useless.

"Why aren't the backup generators kicking in? We've got no lights, no phones, no GPS, *no nothing*!"

White-knuckled, the controllers glanced fearfully at the planes circling overhead. Praying. Wondering.

Was this a temporary glitch? Or a plot? Terrorism?

But there was no way to know. They couldn't communicate with anyone outside of the control tower. And there were hundreds of lives at stake up there in the air.

Two planes were already into their descents.

Please, God, help us. What is going on?

Amman Queen Alia International Airport
Jordan

The control tower shift supervisor frantically tried to raise the silent system. He'd never before seen a situation like this one, where all the screens were blank, all the communications down.

He knew solar flares could cause these kinds of disruptions, but there'd been no warnings of any such thing. Again he tried the phone, desperate to reach his superiors or to contact the ground traffic controllers, but the phones were still not working.

Nothing was working, not the electricity, not the GPS tracking, not the cell towers. His shirt soaked now, he switched rapidly between the radio frequencies—all to no avail.

A sickening thought came to him. *Can all the satellites be down?*

Fighting the panic filling his chest, he prayed those 747s wouldn't end up slamming into each other like blinded gulls. *Insha'allah,* they would all land safely—before they ran out of fuel.

As the light surged from the damaged pendant, Natalie felt shock radiating through her body. Hasan and Sayyed fell back, instinctively throwing their arms across their faces to protect their eyes, but Natalie stared, mesmerized by the stunning clarity of the light.

A moment later, as Hasan's pupils adjusted to the slim dazzling rays, he grabbed up the pliers and bent over the cracked pendant yet again.

She watched helplessly as he wedged the tool into the opening to force Daniel's protective golden shell farther apart.

The bulbs began flickering again. She glanced at them, a new apprehension coming over her. *Oh, God, it's more than just an ancient pendant. I don't believe what I'm seeing . . .*

With an effort, she found her voice. "You don't know what you're doing," she croaked. "What you're unleashing. That light is ancient, it's . . . God's."

"Shut up!"

Yet Hasan glanced up and hesitated a moment before he dug into the pendant once again.

"Do you see what's happening? Look what it's doing to the lightbulbs!"

He ignored her, wedging the pliers deeper.

But she had a tool, too. Her knowledge. She understood more about the Middle Eastern belief system surrounding the evil eye than Hasan realized. Most Westerners would have no idea how his blue eyes would have affected him within his culture, but she knew those eyes had marked him his entire life as a man to be feared, a man who could curse another with a single glance, intentionally or not. She'd noticed how Sayyed scrupulously avoided looking at Hasan's eyes, and she knew the reason for it.

"The Eye of Dawn has far more power than your blue eyes," she burst out. "It will reflect your curses back at you. See how it's disrupting the lights? It must be doing the same thing to the energy field above us—at the Temple Mount. Your plans are going to fail."

He spun then, turning the full fury of those sparking blue eyes on her. "One more word and I'll take this pliers to your tongue."

He meant it.

Natalie fell silent. But she continued to meet those glaring eyes, refusing to look away, showing him that the curses he thought he was raining on her didn't frighten her. That his stare didn't have the power to make her tremble.

As he resumed his attack on the pendant, she watched in silent agony, unable to tear her gaze from the growing beam of light flooding in a luminous stream from the jeweled shell.

No human eyes have seen this in three thousand years. Now she was trembling from head to toe, unable to stop herself. Not from fear, but from awe. Under other circumstances, she'd have whispered the *shehechiyanu* prayer to thank God for keeping her alive to reach this day, this moment, for allowing her to witness this miraculous sight. But it hardly seemed appropriate to thank God for this travesty of an unveiling. Not when this ancient treasure from His own hands had fallen into the hands of a madman.

A madman who had almost succeeded in separating the two halves of the pendant just as the lightbulbs stopped flickering. They glowed intensely for a second, like a power surge after a brownout, and then they went completely dark.

Because of the pendant . . . the tzohar *. . .*

As Hasan pried the final bits of ancient solder free, the illumination surging from within the pendant expanded, filling the tunnel like a widening floodlight.

Natalie gasped when Hasan drew a small shimmering crystal from within the cracked orb. His fingers glowed orange as they clenched it against his palm, the light streaking in narrow rays from between his nearly luminous fingers.

It emitted a radiance far richer than full daylight. It illuminated every crevice, every crumb of earth, every dust mote floating in the dank underground chamber. Staring as if hypnotized, Natalie could well imagine how the *tzohar* had illuminated the ark against the blackness of the sky and the sea during those forty days and forty nights of apocalyptic doom.

Doom. The sense of it grew in her as the terrorist gripped God's creative light in his palm. He was staring at it in dazed triumph. Sayyed stood dumbstruck.

"Praise be to Allah, the most compassionate, the merciful one," Hasan whispered, clamping the *tzohar* against his chest.

She could barely catch his faint words. "With the weapons we can create from the ancient power of this holy stone there will be no nation on earth able to oppose us—none capable of stopping the rule of the khalifate."

He took a step toward Natalie. His indigo eyes seared into her like blue flames as he dangled the *tzohar* before her, taunting her.

"Good-bye, Natalie Landau. Take a good look. This is the last glimpse of light you'll ever see."

And on those words he scooped up the leather pouch from the table and strode off down the tunnel.

She watched him and the brilliant light until they disappeared in the distance, leaving her alone with Sayyed, the two of them trapped in darkness so absolute they could see nothing.

55

Sayyed waited until he was sure Hasan had gone before he groped his way to the table and switched on the headlamp.

"Don't you think it's strange that he wanted you down here to guard me when I obviously can't get away?" Her voice floated toward him in the dimness.

"Shut your mouth or I'll tape that, too." Sayyed whirled toward the woman on the ground, scowling. Yet something in her words prickled at him. Hasan had insisted he wait with her until only a half hour before the C-4 would be detonated. Why?

Relations between him and Hasan Sabouri had never been good. Even now, after all he'd accomplished, there hadn't been a single word of praise. At least this time, Hasan had found no excuse to beat him.

Whenever he was with the man, it was all he could do to hide his hatred. A hatred mixed with fear. The Bedouins had said it better than most. *The evil eye can send a man to his grave and a camel to the cooking pot.*

Am I in my grave now? Sayyed's armpits dampened.

Natalie noted the subtle shift of emotions twitch across her guard's face. Doubt. Anger. Fear.

"He dislikes you, doesn't he? He treats you like a dog."

Sayyed flinched at the truth. He could listen to no more. He grabbed up the tape.

But even as he ripped a length of it, her words flew faster.

"He's moving up the time of the explosion, you know that, don't you? You're going to die down here right beside me. But neither one of us has to die. You can release me, and we can both live."

Hatred poured from his eyes. *What if this bitch was right?* He threw the roll of duct tape at her head. It glanced off and rolled away.

"*You're* going to die, *sharmuta*. Make no mistake about that. *I* plan to live."

He grabbed the headlamp from the table and ran, leaving her once more in absolute darkness.

Natalie had lost all sense of time. But she knew the minute hand on her wristwatch was ticking.

Her hands were bound behind her back. Useless. They couldn't pull the fastenings from her ankles or feel how much progress she'd made in stretching the tape that bound her legs together.

She ignored the thirst cleaving her tongue to the roof of her mouth and forced herself to continue flexing and stretching. First her ankles, then her hands. Resting the one, while she worked the other. Pointing her toes forward, pulling them back. Twisting them to the sides and then straining her wrists as far apart as the tape would allow, wriggling them, one forward, one back, slowly, ever so slowly, loosening the bonds.

If she could free her hands first, she could rip the tape from her feet. If she could free her feet first, she could get to that table, grab the tools. And use them to free her wrists.

How long has it been? How much time is left?

Where's the tzohar *now?*

And how do I stop those bombs?

56

Ahmad wasn't at home when D'Amato arrived. He sat on the stoop trying to tune out the growing confusion percolating through the streets, then worked off his anxiety pacing in front of Ahmad's small house on Hagai Street—better known here, closer to the Damascus Gate, as El-Wad.

Was Ahmad at the mosque? D'Amato didn't remember the time of afternoon prayers. Then he realized just how distracted his thinking had become. El-Wad was filled with men grumbling over the loss of power. They'd all be at the mosque instead if it was time for prayer.

He was almost ready to give up and leave when he caught sight of Ahmad at last, rounding the corner, spotting him, coming forward with a smile of surprise.

"All power is down—throughout the city, it appears." Ahmad ushered D'Amato into his dim living room. The shades had been drawn against the strong afternoon sun, and the pleasant room with its high ceilings and white-washed walls was draped in semidarkness.

"It is very bad. After all this time and planning, no one will be able to see the summit live on TV," the Palestinian said, his face troubled.

"If there *is* a summit." D'Amato spoke quietly. His mind

kept turning over the possibility that the power outage was no accident, that it was part of someone's plan to disrupt the signing of the treaty. But whose?

His host stared at him, then gestured for him to take a seat on the worn striped sofa. "You think the blackout signals a problem?"

"You've got your ear to the ground, my friend. What have *you* heard?"

Ahmad's angular face grew increasingly troubled as he settled into a cane-backed chair. "I've heard some things." He shrugged. "But didn't give them much credence. Until now. We know there are some who oppose bin Khoury, oppose this accord. But most of us welcome it. It is time to coexist in peace."

"The Guardians of the Khalifah oppose it."

Ahmad snorted. "They oppose anything that smacks of democracy. Of freethinking, of choice. They would choose for you, for me, for everyone." He cleared his throat. "May I offer you some tea? My stove is gas. I can still heat water. And there are figs and grapes in the kitchen—"

"Thank you for your hospitality, but there's no time." D'Amato struggled to contain his impatience as his fear for Natalie forced him to risk offending his host. "I'm looking for a woman—an American. She's in trouble, Ahmad. She's carrying something the Guardians of the Khalifah covet. They'll kill her for it—they may already have."

"Then I'm sorry for you. I know very little of the comings and goings of the Guardians of the Khalifah."

D'Amato studied his gaunt, intelligent face. "But you know something."

From outside, the shouting seemed to have increased. The streets were still flooded with people, with confusion. Horns blared, adding to the noise and chaos and D'Amato's own agitation.

Ahmad was strangely silent.

"Tell me, Ahmad. Please. If you know anything that can lead me to the Guardians of the Khalifah, or if you've heard anything about the abduction of an American woman, I need you to tell me now."

She was almost there. She'd managed to stretch the tape enough to twist it into a figure eight.

Hunched on the floor, her muscles aching, Natalie focused solely on extracting one foot from the bindings. She nearly wept as she finally pulled her right foot free.

Scrabbling to her knees, she shuffled on them in the acrid blackness until she reached what she was looking for—the tunnel wall. Leaning against it for support, she maneuvered herself to a standing position.

The table. She tried to envision how far away it sat. Hugging the wall with her right shoulder, she hobbled along in search of it, gasping when she finally bumped into it with her hip.

She used her chin to drag the ice pick to the front edge of the table, then turned, bending her knees until she could grab it between her bound hands.

Hurry, hurry.

But it took several precious moments before she managed to wedge the pick between her palms without stabbing herself with its point. Her breath coming in ragged gulps, she scraped the pick repeatedly into the tape, pricking blindly at the woven threads, ignoring the pain whenever she overshot and scraped the sharp pick into her flesh.

It worked. As soon as her hands were free, she fumbled for the small flashlight Sayyed had left behind, and a pale stream of light pierced the blackness. Now it was easier to strip the adhesive from her wrists and ankles. She nearly sobbed with joy when she was finally free. Grabbing a water bottle from under the table, she gulped it until she choked.

How much time is left? She peered through the gloom at her watch. It was 2:30—the summit was set for 4:00. Ninety minutes to go. Unless the bombs went off before then . . .

She seized the damaged pendant and wedged it into her pocket. Then she grabbed up the flashlight and the large hammer Hasan had used on the orb. Drawing a deep breath, she allowed herself to flex her aching shoulders for a quick moment; next, her cramped legs.

Then she hobbled down the tunnel, trying to ignore the pins and needles tingling through her feet. She held the hammer ready, but met no one. Not even when the tunnel curved and dipped, widening as she climbed upward, her thighs aching. She saw no living soul, no trace of life, nor anything that might be a bomb.

The pins and needles faded away. She started to run.

She didn't know how long she raced through the winding tunnel. At some point, the bare bulbs strung along the timbers began to flicker again—on and then off. She swung the beam of the flashlight upward. Was what she'd told Hasan true?

The flickering had started the minute he'd smashed open the pendant. Could it be a coincidence that the lights became erratic then? She didn't think so. The energy of the *tzohar,* which had been contained for thousands of years within its gold shell, was now loosed in a modern world, a world far different from the days of ancient Babylon.

If solar flares could disrupt GPS and power grids, what might the *tzohar* do when its God-given energy encountered a manmade counterpart?

But even as the question surged through her mind, her attention was diverted by a huge hole gaping in the ceiling. *That's one of them—one of the holes they drilled for the bombs.*

She froze where she stood, shining the flashlight up into the hole. But all she saw was dirt.

How many other holes like this one had she passed farther back, when the beam was aimed at the floor?

She had to get out of here fast—had to warn somebody. Somebody who knew a lot more than she did about finding and disabling bombs.

Tumbling down the tunnel, she was oblivious to her cramped muscles. Adrenaline propelled her feet. Chest heaving, she finally reached the rough-hewn staircase she remembered descending— how many hours ago? Half sobbing, she tore up the steps. She was almost at the entrance.

Almost free.

57

The lights in the elevator flickered. On and off. On again. The car jerked into motion, then the light went out, and the elevator stalled with a shudder.

A groan went up as the eight occupants jostled against one another in the small space, their hope dying.

It was stifling, and someone had eaten garlic for lunch. Warrick had never been claustrophobic in his life, but as the minutes ticked past he felt the anxiety building, tightening in his neck like an invisible noose slowly choking off his air.

Suddenly the lights blazed back on again, and the car lurched upward. The doors slid open on the twentieth floor and everyone spilled out into the corridor in a rush, desperate to escape before the power died again.

An instant later it did, and darkness clamped down on the corridor. Not even the exit signs glowed. But a man hurrying out of one of the guest rooms held a miniflashlight, and Warrick reached him in three strides.

"I need this. National security." He snatched the penlight, ignoring the man's protest, and swung it upward until it showed him the exit sign. He charged up the stairs.

The presidential suite was empty. The door ajar.

Secret Service had hustled him down the stairs the moment the lights went out. Where the hell did they go?

Warrick was startled at the shrill ring of his cell phone. He was more startled by the stream of words that rushed into his ear.

He listened without saying a word. Then closed his phone.

The plan had failed. Firefly was still out there, still in play.

"I'm going out for a few minutes. Perhaps there is some information I can gather for you. It's best if you stay here."

Ahmad rose from the striped couch and headed for the door. He pocketed his house key from the table in the hall and closed the door behind him.

D'Amato bit back the questions screaming in his head. He was familiar with the various ways by which his old friend chose to gather and share information. Taking a deep breath, he leaned back in the dimness of the living room to wait.

An agonizing fifteen minutes passed, then another five. Impatience drove D'Amato out of the chair to pace the floor. He couldn't erase the image of Natalie's abandoned shoulder bag from his mind.

He wheeled at the sound of the doorknob turning. From the entry Ahmad beckoned silently for D'Amato to follow him into the teeming street. Traffic was still in gridlock, worsened by those who'd abandoned their cars.

In silence, quickly, they walked southeast on El-Wad. Away now, from the Damascus Gate. They were heading deeper into the Old City.

58

Warrick fought the crowd surging across the plaza flanking the Western Wall. Beneath a cloudless blue sky, this open area below the Temple Mount was in chaos. People were shouting, running, shoving, pressing their way back toward the narrow entrance. Panic rippled through the distraught, well-dressed crowd that a short time before had been ensconced within view of the platform where the peace accord would be signed.

Their fright was as tangible as the varied accents and languages competing in the cacophony of voices.

"There must be a bomb!"

"Has the president been shot?"

"It's Iran—they're attacking!"

"No—bin Khoury's been assassinated. The summit has been canceled!"

"Why don't the cell phones work? Everything's down."

"They've attacked the communications networks. It's only the beginning!"

With each rumor that swirled as fact, the voices rose in escalating fear. Israeli soldiers were shouting, steering, directing the invited guests and dignitaries out, away from the security checkpoints and the steps leading up to the sacred site. There would be no summit on the Temple Mount this afternoon.

Warrick scanned the frantic faces while he pressed on against the madness. As everyone else streamed toward him, he resisted the flow of bumping and shoving bodies and struggled through to the front. The afternoon was warm. Beneath his suit coat, his white shirt stuck to his back. But he had to get through. Without any means of communication, he had to know firsthand.

Were Garrett, Rachmiel, bin Khoury, and the secretary-general up there somewhere? Were the soldiers evacuating everyone else while a private, abbreviated version of the summit took place in defiance of the terrorists? If there was a bomb, it could go off at any moment. But he was still too far away to see anything, to recognize anyone in this teeming crush of bodies. There was no sign of the Secret Service, of anyone else in the official U.S. delegation.

"You must leave the area. Everyone. Now." The Israeli Defense Forces soldiers patrolling the plaza were adamant, employing the sides of their Uzis to funnel people toward the stairs. Warrick managed to avoid them, burrowing himself toward the center of the throng. He kept plunging ahead, bucking the flow of disappointed, panicked, and confused humanity.

"No farther. Go back!" A stern Israeli soldier blocked his path. She was tall, blond, sunburned, and determined.

"I'm with President Garrett. I need to get through." He flashed his Department of Defense credentials, but she was unimpressed.

"Your president is not here. The summit is canceled. Our orders are to clear the area. That means everyone."

"If they're not here, where are they? Do you know why the communications are down?"

"The only thing I know is that *everyone* has to leave this area. And that includes you."

A second soldier joined her, his thin face dark with impatience. "What's the problem here?"

"That's what I want to know." Warrick directed his attention now to the man. "What's going on? Where's the American delegation?"

"We have no authority to disclose that information, even if we knew." The second soldier glared at him. "For your own safety, leave. Now."

It was useless. Warrick turned away. He'd done his best. But he wasn't about to fight the Israeli army when chances were slim that he'd find Garrett or the others here anyway.

That left Firefly.

Time to shift his energies. He had one last chance.

Natalie staggered up the last step and cautiously shoved open the door at the top of the stairs. She found herself in a window-less storage shed stacked high with rolled lengths of carpets. Otherwise it was empty. She swung the flashlight until it gleamed across a thin metal door. It was just wide enough to permit a small car to enter.

She swiveled the light, looking for another, less conspicuous way out. But there was no other door. No windows. Only a light switch beside the door and a push button above it. *Has to be the garage door opener,* she thought. She took a deep breath as she punched it.

Nothing happened.

She tried the light switch. Nothing. The power was out.

There has to be a manual release, she thought wildly, sweep-ing the flashlight across the ceiling.

Bingo.

With a solid yank she disengaged the mechanism. Setting the flashlight and the hammer down, she grasped the crossbar and heaved the door upward. It moved slowly, reluctantly, creaking so loudly she thought everyone outside would hear.

But at last she heaved it high enough to slip beneath. She snatched up the hammer and shoved it into her waistband, then rolled under the metal door and out into sunlight.

The sudden daylight was blinding. She sprang up, shielded her eyes, and peered left, then right, trying to orient herself, trying to decide which way to run.

One look at the narrow street and the stone buildings, at the flowing robes and head scarves on most of the men and women hurrying along the street, and she knew she'd been right. She was somewhere in East Jerusalem.

She started up the street at a run, taking deep gulps of air and praying she was heading toward the Old City. She needed to warn the soldiers at the Western Wall. At the Temple Mount.

Her chest was tight with fear—how would they evacuate in time, locate the bombs . . . ?

She needed to tell them how to find the tunnel.

At last she saw the signs. She was on El Hariri Street, crossing El Akhtal.

People turned and stared as she tore past them. And no wonder, Natalie thought, her sides aching, her face throbbing. Not only was she an American, and running down the street as if fleeing for her life, she was a woman, a woman with bruises purpling her swollen face.

But no one stopped her, questioned her, and she ran on in desperation. Harun E Rashid Street. Thank God. She turned onto it, knowing it led south, toward Herod's Gate.

It seemed to take forever until she finally crossed Sultan Suleiman. But as she neared the gate, she was forced to slow. A throng of jabbering people surged toward her from the direction of the Temple Mount.

"Ari, wait for me! Don't get separated," a woman called frantically.

"We'll never have peace," a man muttered to another in despair, amid the hubbub. "The summit's off. It's over."

The summit's off? Natalie's mind spun. This crush of people, they're all leaving the area of the Wall? Of the Temple Mount?

Was it being evacuated?

At least lives will be saved, she thought, with a sudden flash of hope. But the bombs will still go off. The Temple Mount will be destroyed.

She caught snatches of Hebrew, Arabic, English, and half a dozen other languages. Amid the panic and dismay, she finally spotted a soldier at the end of the street.

She elbowed her way through the crush of bodies and began speaking to him in halting Hebrew.

"I know where the bombs are—they're planted beneath the Temple Mount. There's a shed on El Hariri—east of El Akhtal. On the left side of the street. It's stacked . . . with rolls of carpets.

The door inside leads to a tunnel—I saw the holes in the tunnel where they packed the bombs, they're in the ceiling—"

"What do you mean, you saw them?" The IDF soldier stared at her as people jostled all around. He took in her bruised face, her wild dark hair, trying, she knew, to determine if she was deranged or telling the truth.

"I was down there, I'm telling you—I saw the holes. There were two men, Hasan, Sayyed. They left me to die—"

A surge of people rocked them, and she was suddenly caught in their midst, carried backward several feet away from him.

"Four o'clock . . . there isn't much time—" she shouted, fighting to make her way back toward him, but the crowd was too strong, too panicked, and only carried her farther away.

"Go to your consulate! Nablus Road!" he ordered, trying to shove his way through the crowd, forging after her, one step, two. It was useless—she was stumbling backward, trying to keep her balance. Fighting to turn around and merge with the flow. But she could see from his expression that he was deciding whether to follow her or to alert his superiors.

Then Natalie forgot all about the soldier. Her attention was riveted on a woman not two feet from her, about to pass her in the crowd.

The woman was young, dark-haired, and beautiful, despite a scar on her cheek. She was wearing a pink head scarf. And Dana's *hamsa*.

Natalie nearly stumbled. She fought to catch up with her, struggling to keep sight of the pink head scarf bobbing through the crowd.

Her heart was thumping in her chest. She knew she was right—it was Dana's *hamsa*. It was unique—the amethysts, the turquoise cloisonné eye, their mother's pearl at its center. Her glimpse had been brief, but the image was seared in her brain.

Desperately, she wedged her way around a stout man with a beard, then cried out as she lost sight of the woman. But a moment later her frantic gaze found the pink scarf again, and by now the crowd was beginning to thin. Natalie pushed after her, ignoring the annoyed complaints of those she bumped into in her haste. She knew only one thing—she had to keep the dark-haired woman in her sights.

Then the woman rounded a corner and Natalie scurried to keep up. She spotted the pink scarf again just as it disappeared into a doorway.

Heaving to catch her breath, Natalie edged up to the souvenir shop the woman had entered and ducked to the side of the door, pretending to window shop. But she only had eyes for the woman wearing Dana's *hamsa,* standing now at the counter, lifting the landline phone from its cradle and putting it to her ear. Natalie watched her for a moment as the woman frowned, then slammed the phone down hard.

The power. It's still out.

Even as the thought took hold, the woman whirled and slipped through the beaded curtain that punctuated the back wall.

Pretending now to admire the evil eye amulets and silver crosses strung on kiosks on either side of the doorway, Natalie scanned the shop's interior. There was no one else inside.

Her stomach knotted, she slipped across the threshold and moved quietly toward the beaded curtain. Peered through. To her surprise, it led only to a steep wooden staircase.

From above came the sound of conversation, low and urgent. The words were Arabic. She could pick out the voices of several men—and of the woman.

Her knees went limp. She didn't know the identity of the woman, but she knew the voice of one of those men.

Hasan. Right upstairs. In this very same building.

She heard the door upstairs click closed, and the voices were muffled.

Half of her wanted to run. The other half of her couldn't. If she left now to find help, there was no guarantee Hasan would still be here when she returned. It might take hours to explain, to get anyone to believe her. And if he was gone, they might never find him again—or the *tzohar.*

As quietly as she could, she climbed the stairs.

59

The fourth step from the top creaked beneath her foot. Natalie froze, certain she'd given herself away. The sound had seemed to reverberate through the narrow stairwell, loud as a gunshot.

Three seconds passed, four. The low murmur of voices continued unabated from above and her breath wheezed out in a slow exhalation of relief.

Hugging the wall, she inched up onto the next step. And the next. Then cleared the landing. Before her was a stub of a hallway with two doors to her left, side by side. The first door was open, the second closed, and it was from behind the latter that the voices emanated.

But voices weren't all that emanated from the room.

A distinctive silvery glow escaped beneath the door.

The *tzohar*. Her muscles burning with tension, Natalie crept closer, easing her way through the first doorway, the open one, into a small space that looked like a storeroom. It was crammed with metal shelves stacked with various-sized cartons, some still taped shut. Stock—boxes of incense, ornate metal matchboxes, jewelry, candles, and the usual cheesy souvenirs.

Sidling between the shelves, Natalie maneuvered closer to the wall that adjoined the next room. Pressing her ear against it, she closed her eyes to block out the pain of her bruises, the fear corroding her stomach, everything but the swift flow of the

Arabic words. Her brain struggled to string them into English sentences.

"The Eye of Dawn. Finally. It is ours." Farshid Sabouri held it aloft as his brother, Hasan, and Fatima stared. Excitement and nerves hummed through all three as the lamp on the desk fluttered wildly and went out again.

"It is a sign," Fatima crowed. "A sign that today is the dawn of a new beginning."

"Yes, Fatima, but—" Hasan's brow was creased as he reached for the glowing crystal. Farshid relinquished it to him. Hasan's fist closed around it.

"Perhaps Natalie Landau is right. She insisted the Eye of Dawn would disrupt the power. We all can see what's happening to the electricity throughout the city. It seems we have much to learn about the wonders, the powers of this stone," he said. "Its energy must be causing this unexpected interference."

Farshid squeezed the edge of the desk. "Without working cell phones, how will we detonate the bombs simultaneously?"

"We must destroy the Temple Mount!" Fatima exclaimed.

"We will—but with far fewer casualties," Farshid said in disgust, "now that the Israelis are evacuating the platform."

As Hasan paced around the desk, the furrows in his forehead deepened. "Our six heroes are already circling their stations, waiting to take their positions."

Farshid leaned over the map on the table, tracing his thumb across the six locations circled in red. Each corresponded to a point on the drawing below—a schematic of the tunnel and the placement of the bombs. A vein of tension began throbbing in his neck. "If only you'd left the Eye in its case, Hasan, we wouldn't be facing this problem now."

Farshid could not resist the criticism. He folded the map and stuffed it into his pocket.

"There was no way to know—" Hasan erupted angrily, but Farshid cut him off.

"Of course not, but your impatience has complicated everything. And on a day when we cannot afford complications." He strode to the window, past the tiny corner bathroom, and back again. "When you think of how long we've dug, shovel by shovel, how much money has gone into the tunnel, the bribes, the secrecy, the deaths—" He stopped himself, scrubbing his hands over his face.

"Why don't we try to reseal the Eye of Dawn in the jeweled pendant?" Fatima interjected hopefully. But Hasan shook his head.

"That isn't possible. I left the pendant in the tunnel." He exploded at Farshid's angry indrawn breath. "It doesn't matter! Metal is metal—whether it be gold, tin, copper, lead. Let me show you!"

He whirled toward the wall safe behind the desk and spun the dial, left, then right, then left again. With a tiny click, the vault yawned open, revealing stacks of cash, gold coins, and two Glocks, along with several fifteen-round magazines.

Slipping the shimmering crystal inside its painted pouch, he hid it behind the stack of cash and relocked the vault.

The glow that had suffused the room was extinguished with the closing of the door. But still the lamp stayed dark.

"Now—your cell phone," Hasan ordered his older brother tersely. "Try it."

Farshid flicked it open and saw three bars. He nodded grudgingly. "It's reading the tower."

Fatima smiled as the lamp suddenly sputtered back to life.

"Now, my brother," Hasan said smugly, "you and I will go to witness history. The rebirth of the khalifate. And you"—he turned to Fatima and touched the pearl centered in the Hand of Fatima amulet at her throat. "You have the honor of safeguarding the Eye of Dawn."

"Hasan." She touched his arm, keeping her gaze just below his eyes. "I would dearly like to see the explosion."

"You will hear it, Fatima," he told her, his words a caress. "Close the shop and remain up here until we return."

D'Amato cursed as a teenager pushing a cart loaded with watches nearly ran over his foot. The road was narrowed now, a ribbon of mobbed confusion. Three little boys playing kickball in front of a doorway laughed as he jumped quickly aside, momentarily falling a step behind Ahmad.

"How much farther?" he asked, scarcely able to contain his impatience.

Ahmad lifted a hand as if to say *trust me*. They reached El Madana Elhamara only to be confronted by a fresh wave of pedestrians. From the snatches of excited conversation, D'Amato realized that the summit on the Temple Mount had been canceled. Everyone had been ordered to leave the area.

Ahmad and D'Amato pushed on, turning right at the corner, heading now, D'Amato realized, for the Via Dolorosa.

Jaw clenched, he wondered just where his friend was leading him. He wondered if Natalie was still alive.

They passed a huge, modern bookstore, a toy shop bright with puppets, a café buzzing with people, tourists and natives alike. Suddenly Ahmad came to a stop.

"Continue on a short distance, not much past the silversmith, and you'll find a very interesting souvenir shop. My source hinted that the people you seek meet sometimes above the store. Be careful."

He clasped D'Amato's hand. "It was good to see you again, my friend. I pray you find what you're looking for. And I pray we find peace. And may it be soon."

Then he was gone, slipping seamlessly into the throng, threading back the way they'd come.

When the door creaked open in the adjacent room, Natalie dodged behind a tall carton and crouched out of sight. She held her breath, trembling, as footsteps thundered down the stairs. Then came the soft clinking of the beaded curtain, and the woman's voice coming from below now, Natalie moved stealthily around the carton and into the hall. In two steps she was inside the second room.

It was an office, a messy one, the desk piled with papers and files, tape, markers, and scissors. Against one wall stood a metal file cabinet, along with more stacked boxes.

She spotted the safe at once. And she knew. *Metal is metal.* Isn't that what Hasan had said?

She yanked the hammer from her waistband, but she controlled the urge to smash the dial. The woman—Fatima—was sure to hear the first blow and know immediately that she wasn't alone.

First I'll have to take her by surprise. I'll make her tell me the combination. . . .

She listened as the woman's light footsteps crossed the shop floor below. Heard again the click of the beaded curtains. Fatima was coming back.

Mundy paced beneath the large archway trimmed with Jerusalem stones. He was at the entrance to the Church of the Holy Sepulchre, scouring the paved courtyard for a glimpse of the Sentinel as pilgrims and tourists flowed past him, intent on exploring the site where Jesus had been crucified, laid in his tomb, and resurrected.

He'd visited the huge church yesterday with his wife, praying in the many chapels tended by various faiths. He'd crawled beneath the altar in the Greek Orthodox chapel lit by candle and oil to stare at the bronze disk purported to mark the spot of Christ's cross. This church, raised in A.D. 326 by Empress Helena, mother of Constantine, had a history—like the Temple—of being repeatedly destroyed and rebuilt. But the cycle had ended after it was demolished the final time by Khaliph el-Hakim in 1009, and the Crusaders rebuilt it to look much the way it still stood today.

A sense of awe and excitement competed in him as he watched impatiently for his second-in-command. The Sentinel had only told him that the Light of Dawn was for sale, and Mundy was prepared to pay any price.

Finally, he spotted the tall, imposing figure, the sandy-haired man who stood head and shoulders above most others.

"Have you heard anything more? Other than that we're to meet the seller at the Church of Saint Anne?" Mundy asked quickly, softly, as the Sentinel joined him. They strode inside where it was more secluded, past the rectangular pink slab of stone—the Stone of Unction, where the faithful believe Jesus' body was prepared for burial.

"Not yet," the Sentinel said curtly. "Phone usage has been spotty, or haven't you noticed?"

"Of course I've noticed. Did you recognize the voice of the caller? Do you know who has the Light?"

"It was impossible to tell. He spoke in a whisper." The Sentinel's frown was even more sour than usual. He had no clue which of the many players had managed to steal the Light from Shomrei Kotel's grasp.

"Well, I have a damned good guess who it might be." Mundy lowered his voice. "I've just left some of our Shomrei Kotel partners. We've been betrayed—*all* of us."

His companion stopped in his tracks. "What are you talking about?"

"Menny Goldstein is dead, so is Yuvi Katzir."

"And Shmuel . . . what about Shmuel?"

"Vanished—along with Natalie Landau and the Light." Mundy's eyes sparked with anger. "You connect the dots. Shmuel was one of the few entrusted with your encrypted cell number. It looks to me like he's now in business for himself."

"And a mighty big business it is." The Sentinel's jaw was tight, his hawk eyes narrowed. "He wants the money wire transferred to a Cyprus bank account at the time of the exchange. His asking price is ten million dollars."

Sayyed stopped for nothing and no one as he wove his way along the slick limestone of the Via Dolorosa.

By now the Sabouri brothers are up on the Ramparts, eager for their birds'-eye view of the destruction. Eager for me to make the phone call and claim Shomrei Kotel responsible for the carnage.

He smiled to himself. Hasan would never anticipate what he was going to do instead. He'd had his fill of the insults Hasan had rained on him ever since Farshid had recruited him. While Hasan was in charge, he would never be anything but a lowly foot soldier. Oh, how he would relish his revenge. Soon he'd become more wealthy and more powerful than the Sabouri brothers and their esteemed council altogether. He'd no longer be subjected to Hasan's evil eye. And evil tongue. Sayyed knew of the vast sums the Shomrei Kotel had raised, and he knew there was even more in the offshore accounts of the Sons of Babylon.

He knew where Hasan would be standing by now, the precise spot. Just as he knew the combination of the shop's safe and the cash bundles it contained. Most of all, he knew how that cash would help him get to Tunisia once he'd tracked Hasan to the Ramparts, put a bullet in his accursed heart, and relieved him of the Eye of Dawn.

The tiny bathroom was as stifling as a sauna. Wedged behind the door, Natalie listened to the desk chair scraping along the floor. Fatima was scooting herself closer to the desk. Natalie heard the rustle of papers. Then Fatima began to hum.

If she's at the desk, her back is to me. It's now or never. Clutching the hammer, Natalie eased out of the bathroom, planting each foot carefully upon the floor. But just as she neared the chair, the linoleum creaked and the woman whirled in the chair. Natalie sprang forward, raising the hammer.

"Take off that *hamsa* you're wearing. Put it on the desk."

"How did you get up here?" Fatima gasped, anger flushing her delicate features. "Who are you?"

"Put it on the desk or I'll knock you out with this and remove it myself." She took a step closer. "Hurry up."

Fatima's gaze took in Natalie's determined expression, then shifted to the raised hammer.

"So you're a thief. All right. Calm down. I'll do it."

She reached behind her neck and unhooked the small silver clasp. Shrugged. Set the necklace down atop the binder.

But as Natalie reached across her to snatch the *hamsa* with her free hand, the woman moved like wildfire. One moment she was as still as a wood carving, the next she had grabbed up the scissors from the desk and was springing from her chair in one fluid motion.

Using her hip, Natalie shoved the chair, striking Fatima at the knees. But the maneuver only threw the woman off balance for a moment.

With a scream she was on full attack, slicing the scissors

upward toward Natalie's throat. Natalie jumped back, then aimed a kick, but the blow merely grazed Fatima's thigh.

Natalie kept her eyes on the point of the scissors. As Fatima drew back her arm, Natalie dove, seized her wrist, and twisted hard—but her left hand wasn't as strong as her right, and Fatima held fast to the scissors. Grunting, Natalie drove her heel down on the woman's instep, but it seemed to have no effect. Fatima was fighting in a frenzy, wild, determined, much stronger than Natalie would have guessed for a woman her size.

She slashed out again, and the scissors tore into Natalie's arm. The sudden pain brought tears to her eyes, stinging tears, but also kindled an instinctive response.

She smashed the hammer into Fatima's temple, and the woman crashed down like a toppled statue.

And like a statue, she wasn't moving. But she was still breathing, Natalie realized, as she knelt and found a pulse.

So much for forcing her to tell me the combination, she thought bleakly.

Breathing hard, she stumbled back to the desk and scooped up the *hamsa.* Despite her shaking hands, she finally secured it around her throat. And now the tears that stung her eyes sprang from the realization that only days ago, this *hamsa* had been around Dana's throat.

For a moment her emotions threatened to overwhelm her. But she turned her grief to fury and attacked the safe with the hammer, slamming it against the dial, again and again.

It dented, but didn't break.

In desperation she filled a plastic cup with cold water from the bathroom sink and was about to dump it over Fatima's face to revive her, to demand the combination, when she heard a sound from below.

She froze. Her heartbeat roared in her ears as she strained to listen. A man's heavy tread. Coming up the stairs.

She dove for the bathroom again and slid behind the door, even as his footsteps stomped across the stubby hall.

D'Amato hurried along Via Dolorosa. It was far from the first time he'd traversed this street where Jesus had trudged to his crucifixion, but this was the first time he was completely oblivious of the crosses and signage noting the Stations of the Cross.

The limestone beneath his feet was uneven and slippery. He scanned the facades of the buildings left and right, looking for the shop he sought, ignoring the welcoming calls of the merchants in the doorways.

"Ahlan wa sahlan." "Come, you are welcome."

He dodged around a group of boys kicking a soccer ball, absently kicked it back to them.

Where the hell was that damned shop?

"D'Amato!"

He spun to see who was calling his name.

60

It was Doron, racing toward him, his face nearly as red as his hair as he dashed recklessly across the path of a pushcart laden with produce. "Natalie—"

The Mossad agent skidded to a stop as D'Amato froze, fearing the worst.

"An American woman matching her description approached an IDF soldier not a half hour ago," Doron panted. "I've been trying to reach your cell, but the towers are only working sporadically—"

"Are you sure it was Natalie?" D'Amato interrupted. "What did she say?"

"She claimed there were bombs in the ceiling of a tunnel beneath the Temple Mount. Before the soldier could question her, they were separated by the crowd."

"If it's her—" D'Amato felt hope for the first time in a long time. *Natalie got away.* "Where was this?" he asked quickly.

"Near Herod's Gate." Doron's eyes were roving all along the street, darting at everyone, everything, in a constant surveillance sweep. "We've got men searching for the tunnel entrance she described right now. The soldier told her to go to the U.S. consulate—Lior's on his way there. I'm canvassing this area. Keep your eyes open for her, and if you find her, both of you get to the U.S. consulate on Nablus. And stay there!"

* * *

Sayyed stopped in his tracks. What was this? Fatima on the floor, bleeding from the ear, her pink scarf soaked in blood. The chair on its side, a pair of scissors inches from her hand.

Without touching her, he placed a finger beneath her nose and felt warm breath.

He wondered if she and Hasan had argued. But he didn't wonder long. He stepped over her, toward the safe, and it was then that he saw the dents in the metal dial.

Was she stupid enough to have tried to steal from Hasan? Almost amused, he went to work on the dial. Many times he'd stood fuming in this very office while Hasan harangued him. Many times he'd surreptitiously watched Hasan work the combination while he'd pretended to concentrate on unloading boxes of stock.

The dial was slightly damaged, but it still worked. Sayyed eagerly yanked back the metal door, then jumped back, startled, as light poured out, radiating throughout the room.

The Eye of Dawn. Right here in this safe.

He laughed out loud. *What a fool you are, Hasan Sabouri.* Eagerly he grabbed the bundles of money, stuffed them in his backpack then, his hands trembling with excitement, he lifted out the pouch with the crystal gem and drew out the Eye of Dawn.

To his surprise, the glowing jewel wasn't hot to the touch. But its light was still brilliant in the daylight. It was intense, much whiter and clearer than any light he'd ever seen or imagined. *Like the light of heaven, of Paradise,* Sayyed thought, almost giddy with the triumph of holding it.

It was then that he heard the woman.

Closed.

The hand-lettered sign mocked D'Amato as he finally reached the souvenir shop door. He jiggled the handle. The door was locked.

All around him the other shops stood open, the cafés overflowed. The street was full of chattering people, everyone buzzing about the canceled summit and speculating about why the

Israelis had cut their power and suddenly reneged on the promised peace.

Only this shop, the one Ahmad had sent him to, was closed. He stepped back, peered up at the second-story window overlooking Via Dolorosa, and wondered if anyone was up there.

He rapped on the door. Once, twice. And then a third time, louder.

Shoving his hands in his pockets, he moved away to lean against a wall near the storefront. *I'll give it five minutes, no more. If no one shows up, I'm breaking in.*

Fatima had pushed herself, moaning, to a half-sitting position. With one hand braced on the floor, she was staring at Sayyed and at the Eye of Dawn, her mouth agape. Then, from downstairs, came a sudden rapping on the door. More than once. Insistent.

Alarm in his belly, Sayyed jammed the Eye of Dawn deep into the right front pocket of his jeans. The pouch into the other. First things first. Then he slid the silencer from his backpack and, with practiced ease, screwed it onto the gun.

Fatima's eyes grew wide with terror. She shook her head in silent pleading. "Say . . . yed . . ."

He fired.

Quickly, he removed the silencer and shoved his gun back into his shoulder holster. Listened again. Silence. The tourist had given up.

Without a glance at the dead woman at his feet, he leaped over her body for the door.

Gripping the edge of the bathroom door to keep from swaying, Natalie listened to his footsteps pounding down the stairs. That bastard had the *tzohar.* She'd seen its light flood the office. And now it was gone again.

Stomach lurching, she forced her legs to move as the shop door banged shut below.

Go. Follow him, a voice screamed inside her head. Then she was running, averting her gaze from the body on the floor, nearly tumbling down the stairs in her haste.

She screamed as a figure charged through the shop door.

D'Amato.

She hurled herself at him, grabbing his arm. "Did you see that man leave the shop just now? Which way did he go? He's one of the men who kidnapped me—he has the *tzohar*!"

61

Sayyed was striding quickly down Via Dolorosa, not running. He was headed east, toward the Lion's Gate, Natalie realized. She and D'Amato were following from nearly half a block away, darting around carts and kiosks, past men in doorways playing *shesh-besh,* dodging peddlers and pilgrims, fighting to keep the tall, solid, always moving figure in sight. D'Amato had warned that if Sayyed turned and spotted her, he'd bolt.

Or shoot.

So they kept their distance but stayed as close as they dared. Discreetly, Natalie filled him in as they walked. He was stunned when she told him that the crystal inside the pendant actually did possess an incredible, ethereal light, which she believed was linked to the electrical disturbances going on around them. Still trying to absorb the magnitude of what she'd told him, D'Amato managed to bring her up-to-date on what he'd learned.

"The Mossad is looking for the tunnel right now?" she asked breathlessly, as they rushed past two wizened men sipping their Turkish coffee as if nothing else in the world mattered. "Thank God!"

D'Amato tried his cell again, hoping to reach Doron.

"Don't worry," she muttered as he cursed in frustration. "Right now, I think Sayyed is doing us a favor by exposing the *tzohar.* As long as it's in the open, they won't be able to detonate the C-4 with their cell phones."

"Where in hell is he headed?" D'Amato squinted at the tall figure dodging purposefully through the pedestrians ahead. "So you're actually convinced that the pendant really contained the *tzohar*?"

"I don't know any other way to explain what I saw," Natalie said.

They reached the juncture where Via Dolorosa ended and street signs announced its transition into Lion's Gate Road instead. They hurried to keep up as Sayyed picked up his pace.

"Are you okay?" D'Amato asked. Beside him, Natalie was drawing ragged breaths. She looked like hell. The bruises on her face were puffy and purple, and the gash in her arm didn't look too good either.

She nodded, and for the first time he noticed the necklace she was wearing. How the hell—?

"Is that Dana's *hamsa*?"

"One and the same. That son-of-a-bitch Hasan gave it to the woman in the shop, the one Sayyed killed."

Her voice sounded stronger now, as if thinking of the charm she wore had refreshed her energy. Their quarry was nearing the Lion's Gate.

"Look, he's turning left." D'Amato pointed suddenly. "He's going into that courtyard."

"That's the Church of Saint Anne."

Melting into the midst of a small tour group, they slipped into the church compound after him, entering a courtyard dotted with palms and drooping pepper trees. Waving her red flag, the tour guide sent her charges surging toward the vaulting stone entrance to the tall Crusader church. Natalie and D'Amato's eyes, however, were not focused on the impressive architecture, but on the burly, dark-haired young man veering off toward a garden that hugged the side of the building.

It was suddenly much quieter here, within the grounds, than outside on the teeming, bustling cobbled streets. A tangible serenity seemed to fill the space as they broke from the tour group just short of the door. Quickly, they crept along the wall toward the garden, breathing in the tangy clean scent of sage and mint.

Suddenly, D'Amato skidded to a stop, one hand on Natalie's arm, holding her still. From around the corner came the quiet murmur of men's voices.

"Show it to me." Ken Mundy had waited long enough. He had no desire to exchange pleasantries with this man—Shmuel or whatever his name was at the moment—who'd betrayed him and Shomrei Kotel. His contempt showed on his face, but he was far from caring. If this Judas thought he was going to continue calling all the shots, he could guess again.

"Show me the money." "Shmuel's" broad grin was cocky, triumphant. He shot a glance at the briefcase clutched in Mundy's manicured hand.

But the Sentinel wasn't having it. "You first." His tone was that of a man used to being in command. "Be quick about it. The longer we stand here, the more dangerous this becomes. For you as well as us, I'm sure."

Shmuel gestured toward the centuries-old church and the excavated Pools of Bethesda beyond. "You're worried about those nuns going in to stand on the famous star-shaped stone to sing before the altar? They frighten you?"

"Cut the crap, Shmuel, or whoever you are. Either let us see the Light or our business with you is finished." Mundy shook off the warning hand the Sentinel put on his arm. *No. I'm not going to pull any punches. Not when everything I've been working for is within my reach.*

It grated on him that his success was now dependent upon this smug, arrogant traitor. The Sentinel had risked the most of all of them, risked everything. The next moment or two would determine whether it was all for naught, whether Mundy would have to return to the Sons of Babylon and admit to them that the Light had slipped from their fingers again.

"Do you want the ten million? Or don't you?" The Sentinel's keen gray eyes bored into the man's grinning face.

* * *

D'Amato tensed, hunching closer to the corner of the building. "I know that voice," he whispered in disbelief.

"Whose is it?"

He leaned around the stone for a quick instant, needing a visual confirmation. He jerked back, incredulous. "I don't believe it. Your government at work. That's Elliott Warrick—our Assistant Undersecretary of Defense."

The burly young man snorted in contempt. "My price is now fifteen million. And this is what you'll get in return." He dug deep into his right front jeans pocket and withdrew a tin matchbox. He lifted the lid to reveal a glowing crystal. Light pulsed from it, bathing the garden in a dazzling aura as brilliant as a streak of lightning.

Mundy choked back tears. It was luminous, beautiful beyond words. He couldn't tear his eyes from the Light. He reached toward it, aching to touch it, but Shmuel jerked it back with a laugh, his fist clamping over the ancient jewel.

Warrick flashed a swift glance around, checking to see if anyone else had entered the garden. "Where's the pendant it was sealed in?" he demanded. "That's part of the bargain."

Mundy drew a breath. Yes, Daniel's pendant of carnelian, lapis, and jasper. He'd been so dazzled by the Light that he'd forgotten about the jeweled pendant that had concealed it for thirty centuries. He needed that, too.

"It's gone. You'll have to settle for this." Shmuel produced the worn leather pouch, painted on each side with eyes of protection. "Now the money. Wire it to my bank account in Cyprus, and we're finished here." He shoved a slip of paper at the Sentinel.

"Do it," Mundy ordered, still hypnotized by the magnificent light spilling from between Shmuel's chunky fingers.

But as Warrick lifted his phone, his expression darkened. "The cell towers are down again. It's impossible to transfer the funds."

"Then we have no deal." For the first time anger simmered in Shmuel's deep eyes. "You are screwing with me? Fine, I have other buyers." He dropped the tin cover back in place and shoved the matchbox, along with the pouch, back into his pocket.

Instantly, a dense cloud seemed to descend over the church grounds, yet the sun still glowed unobscured in the sky.

"No—wait!" Mundy cried.

Shmuel regarded him with insolent eyes. "I have no time to wait—not for you, not for the cell towers."

"I have five million dollars in this briefcase," Mundy bit out in a low, furious tone. "That's a down payment. You'll get ten more when the damn cell towers start working."

Shmuel laughed, kicking at a stone. "You insult me."

Warrick's face was pale, grim. "You're living on borrowed time, my friend. You're a marked man. And you're on your way out of the country. It's all over your face. Five million cash would ease your travels. Take you as far away as you want to go. If you think you'll find someone else who can wire the money to you—today—right now—then walk away."

The only sound in the courtyard was the muted echo of women's voices lifted in song, floating from within the acoustically perfect hallow of the church.

Sayyed didn't hear it though. All he heard was his own voice telling him this bastard infidel was right. The five million in cash was too handy to pass up. And the hour of the explosion was too near.

Hasan is busy right now, but as soon as the Noble Sanctuary goes up in pieces, he'll rush back to the shop and find his wife dead and his safe empty. Then all of the Guardians of the Khalifah will be hunting me down. I don't have time to haggle.

"Five million now. Ten million later."

Mundy snapped open the briefcase, lifted the false bottom without a word, and showed him the stacks of bills. The exchange was made without a handshake, and Mundy stared in awe at the eternal treasure now glowing against his palm.

"Praise be to God. The Light is home. And the Sons of Babylon will return it to the Third Temple."

He hesitated only a moment before slipping the gem back into its pouch, sighing as the Light diminished once again.

Elliot Warrick took a deep breath. "Time for us to get out of here." He spun toward the courtyard and Mundy joined him without another glance at the man now holding his briefcase.

Fools, Sayyed thought, watching the Americans scurry away beneath the grapevines.

He fired two shots, muffled to low pops by the silencer. The Americans were beside the church wall when they toppled.

He raced toward the older one. The pouch had rolled from his grasp when he'd struck the ground. Sayyed snatched it up and bolted along the north side of the building, elated as he spotted the driveway leading back out to the street.

He didn't spot Hasan Sabouri—frozen in his tracks while pacing the Ramparts overlooking the church grounds and beyond. But Hasan Sabouri had spotted him. Drawn by the unearthly glow emanating from beneath the Lion's Gate, Hasan had thought for a split second that one of the bombs had exploded.

But no bombs had gone off, though they should have by now. He had stared at the intense white aura below in a rage, his brilliant eyes nearly opaque with fury. The bombs weren't *going* to go off. The phones couldn't trigger the detonators. *Because the power of the Eye of Dawn was no longer neutralized in the safe.*

He saw exactly where the ancient stone was. Who had taken it. Who had ruined his beautiful plan.

With hatred, he watched Sayyed exchange the Eye of Dawn for a briefcase in the garden of the Church of Saint Anne. As he headed for the stairs, he watched Sayyed shoot the two men and retrieve something from the ground. It was then that Hasan spotted something equally staggering—Natalie Landau and her friend D'Amato crouching in wait.

Shock at her escape from the tunnel rocked him like a blast. Had Sayyed freed her? Was the world inside out?

But there was no time for questions. Or for lamentations.

It was time for vengeance.

Hasan scrambled down from the Ramparts, swift as a lizard. He'd watched enough.

62

Sayyed had double-crossed everyone. He outwitted us all.

And he's coming straight toward us.

Around the corner, paralyzed, Natalie felt sick.

Sick of the killing. Sick of the treachery. Sick to her stomach from running and from fear. Tension bunched every muscle in her body as she squatted with D'Amato, hardly able to breathe. She was determined that Sayyed wouldn't get away. Determined that Dana's death wouldn't be for nothing in the end.

He burst into view—a streak of royal blue shirt and dark jeans. But in a flash, D'Amato launched himself at him, bringing him down sideways and sending the briefcase skittering. D'Amato slammed a fist into Sayyed's face and heard the satisfying crunch of breaking bone. Ignoring the pain reverberating from his knuckles to his wrist, he slugged him again.

Sayyed was wriggling out of his backpack even as he swung an elbow up toward D'Amato's throat. The blow glanced off the side of D'Amato's neck, but in the instant it took him to recoil, Sayyed rolled out from under him, scrabbling for the gun in his unzipped backpack.

"No!" Natalie charged at him, but before she could land a kick, Sayyed had the pistol out and was firing at D'Amato. Missing.

"Get down!" D'Amato yelled, rolling to his knees, drawing

his own weapon. She threw herself to the ground as shots
cracked through the air, horror choking her.

And then Sayyed's body bucked on the ground, blood spray-
ing from a gaping hole in his chest. She saw D'Amato clamber
to his feet, the pistol still pointed at the wounded man.

She threw herself at her kidnapper, revolted, shaking.
Choked back bile as he shuddered, blood dribbling from his
whitened lips. She dug in his pocket for the pouch, for the *tzohar*, trembling as she snatched back the treasure her sister had
sent her from Iraq.

63

People were flooding from the church, pointing, staring.

D'Amato holstered his gun and grabbed her arm, pulling her to her feet. "Time to get to the consulate!"

He was right, she realized, as two men ventured forward, fear in their faces. Then she and D'Amato were tearing back onto Lion's Gate Road, racing through the slippery narrow street once again.

"Cut right when we get to El-Wad, and after the Damascus Gate we'll find Nablus Road," D'Amato called, as they skirted a woman in a *hijab* pushing a baby carriage.

And pray we find an IDF soldier on the way, she thought wildly. Then she nearly stumbled as she realized that the consulate might not be the ideal destination. She was confused—the U.S. government had been about to hand over $15 million to a terrorist for the *tzohar*? Yet the man with Warrick had claimed it for the Sons of Babylon. He had to be Mundy.

"Wait." She skidded to a halt, grabbing D'Amato's wrist. "Something's not right. Why were Mundy and the assistant undersecretary of Defense working together? We can't trust anybody. We can't go to the consulate—they'll take the *tzohar* from me. It has to go to the Israel Antiquities Authority. It belongs *here*."

He'd been scanning up and down the street as she spoke. "Alright, Rockefeller Museum it is."

"Then we need to go back and turn left on Qadasiya to Suleiman." Natalie could have kicked herself. They would have been at the IAA already if they'd gone straight there from Saint Anne's.

Spinning, they retraced their steps, but even as they reached Qadasiya Natalie saw something that made her throat close up.

"It's him," she gasped, stopping dead. "Hasan. He's coming straight toward us!"

From down Via Dolorosa he saw her at the exact same moment.

"Shit." D'Amato grabbed her hand, and together they dashed for the intersection, pounding north on Qadasiya. The smell of spices and roasting meats wafting onto the street roiled through her stomach.

Natalie risked a backward glance as D'Amato tugged her through the doorway of the first restaurant they reached. Hasan was closer now, less than ten yards away, darting through the congested street like a man possessed.

He'd seen them duck inside.

Hasan slowed only a fraction as he reached the front window of the restaurant, elated to glimpse the glow suddenly radiating through the glass and onto the street. Even if he hadn't seen them trying to escape him in the crowded eatery, the Eye of Dawn had shown him exactly where they'd gone.

Satisfaction burned in his veins as he barged through the door just in time to see Natalie Landau racing toward the rear of the restaurant, toward the alcove where he knew stairs led down to the toilets.

She was alone.

He pushed past the waiter offering to seat him and pelted after her down the narrow steps, fueled by equal measures of rage and adrenaline. He smiled as he heard the bathroom door thud closed.

Halting outside it, he debated whether to burst through or

wait and spring on her when she exited. Spittle gathered at the edges of his lips as he made his decision.

He shoved open the door.

Her back was to him as she bent over the sink, splashing water on her face. She jerked upright and caught sight of him in the mirror and gave a small cry.

The fear in her eyes as she whirled around was his reward. He had her.

But where was the Eye of Dawn?

It didn't matter. He'd kill her first and search her body for it after. Then he noticed the glimmer of the pearl at her throat. Fatima's necklace—around Natalie Landau's neck.

"I got it back," she said. "In this lifetime."

"Your lifetime's almost over!" he screamed, whipping out his Glock.

She didn't flinch. But he did, his body jackknifing sideways as D'Amato shot him at close range from the doorway of a toilet stall.

Blood sprayed the room. The sink, the mirror, the stalls.

And the two of them.

Natalie met D'Amato's eyes. Slowly, she touched the *hamsa* at her throat.

It was over.

64

Two days later
U.S. Consulate in Jerusalem

Patrick Dunleavy, presidential assistant for National Security Affairs, rose from the gray leather couch and extended his hand first to Natalie and then to D'Amato.

"Everything we've discussed here, as we agreed, remains privileged information," he said, in his flat West Point baritone. His deep-set hazel eyes were like thumbtacks in his fleshy face as they pinned each of them in turn. "Warrick's death will go down on record as accidental, in the line of duty. I can guarantee you, however, that our investigation into how he could have been a member of the Sons of Babylon without our knowledge will continue."

"Yeah. So will mine," D'Amato said tightly.

For a moment Natalie wondered if Dunleavy was going to revisit his displeasure—and the president's—that the *tzohar* was now out of their country's reach. She braced herself for a final politely worded reprimand, but he only glowered at them with a chilly air of dismissal as he wished them a safe journey back to the States.

Stepping out of the consulate into an unexpected light rain, Natalie felt suddenly refreshed and relieved that she was finally free to go home. The past two days had been a blur of endless interrogations, interviews, and debriefings with Israeli and U.S. officials alike.

Still, much of what had transpired remained a mystery to her. A mystery it would take time to puzzle through and eventually comprehend.

But she would never understand how Elliott Warrick, an assistant undersecretary in the Defense Department, one of the principal advisers to President Garrett on defense matters, had managed to work undetected with a clandestine fringe church group—all while feeding false leads to the NSU during their pursuit of the *tzohar*. Nor how the Mossad had never discovered the traitor in their midst.

One of the only good things to come of all this was that the Guardians of the Khalifah had been crippled for the time being. Hasan Sabouri and several of their leaders were dead, and Farshid Sabouri was in custody, along with four of the six would-be bombers.

Also, several members of Shomrei Kotel had been arrested and charged with attempted theft and kidnapping.

At least this nightmare hadn't prevented the chance for peace. Owen Garrett, Ze'ev Rachmiel, Mu'aayyad bin Khoury, and Gunther Ullmann had convened at the Knesset even as Israeli Intelligence had raced to find and dismantle the bombs. In the presence of a select group of dignitaries and members of the press corps, they'd signed the historic peace accord. And later that evening, after power had been restored, they'd all gone before the television cameras to shake hands in front of the world.

As she and D'Amato headed for the cab waiting for them on Nablus, she suddenly felt hungry for the first time in days.

"El Gaucho," she said suddenly, as D'Amato opened the cab door.

"Come again?" For a moment he looked puzzled. Then his face lit with an appreciative grin.

"On Rivlin Street—the Argentinian Grill."

"If it's still there."

They'd been sliding across the worn backseat cushions, and the driver had overheard.

"Twenty-two Rivlin Street. It's still here," he said gruffly.

"Go for it." Leaning back against the warm seat, D'Amato winced as the cabbie jerked out into traffic. For some reason, despite today's dampness and rain, he was finding it easier than usual to ignore his ever-present pain. Possibly because he was just glad—again—to be alive.

Natalie recognized the grimace that flitted across his face and was gone. If not for D'Amato's instincts from the very beginning, so much would have been different. Aunt Leonora might have had to bury two nieces within a week. She glanced at him as he stared out the rain-speckled window and was surprised by the surge of warmth she felt.

"After all you've done for me," she said lightly, "the least I can do is buy you dinner."

"I don't know about that. You look a helluva lot worse than I do."

"Thanks a lot."

D'Amato chuckled. The fact was, her purple-and-red bruises were yellowing now, and he knew he wasn't telling her anything she didn't already know. "Give it up, Landau. Dinner's on me."

She laughed. He'd never seen her laugh before. But it suddenly occurred to him that he'd like to see her laugh again.

The beat of the windshield wipers slowed as the driver bounced down an impossibly narrow street. The rain was diminishing to a fine silvery mist, casting an added sheen on the Old City of Jerusalem as it slid past their window. The holy city was jammed as always with Jews, Muslims, and Christians intermingled on the ancient pathways, most of them now buoyed with hope for a lasting peace.

Peace.

Natalie was touching her fingers to the *hamsa* at her throat. The *tzohar,* the unimaginable treasure her sister had sent her, was safely ensconced now in the IAA's National Treasures Storerooms in Bet Shemesh, halfway between here and Tel Aviv. It had been authenticated at the IAA soon after she'd handed it over to the director of the Antiquities Robbery Prevention Unit, along with the pouch and the cracked pendant.

"Dana knows," D'Amato said quietly.

Natalie met his gaze, feeling her shoulders relax for the first time in days.

"I know. I was just thinking the same thing."

65

"I thank you for welcoming my family here. It is an honor to follow in the footsteps of my father." Taleb Zayadi was a short man with a stocky body and a thick black mustache. His voice was low and somber as he addressed the director of the storerooms.

Then his gaze drifted down once more to the swath of royal blue velvet cushioning the shallow case that sat on the table between them. He peered again at the three items arrayed upon it—the cracked gold pendant adorned with the jeweled eyes, its matching leather pouch, and the shimmering crystal gem that long had been concealed within them both.

"My father, Nejeeb, was murdered on the night this was stolen from our museum," Taleb said softly, sweeping his hand through the aura of light radiating from the *tzohar*. "He never knew the nature of what our family had guarded for so many generations."

"And that they will continue to guard," the director said warmly. "Now the Zayadis are among the handful on earth who know for certain of the *tzohar*'s existence—of its power— and of the imperative need to keep it safeguarded. It's fitting that you succeed your father in protecting it, Taleb, since the Zayadi family has long served with such honor."

The director replaced the velvet-draped case inside one of

the lead-lined vaults on the wall, and sealed it. The room was suddenly much dimmer. Taleb followed him from the rectangular humidity- and temperature-controlled storeroom. It was Taleb who locked the door with the combination he'd just memorized.

They took seats around a small table in the outer office where a tray had been placed, set with glasses of steaming tea and small dishes of honey, sugar, and lemon.

Taleb bit a cube of sugar between his front teeth and sipped his tea through it as the director described the routine of the storerooms, the passwords and watchwords, and reviewed with him the list of who had clearance to access the steel-reinforced chamber they'd just left.

"We'll be studying the treasure," he explained, setting down his glass. "Analyzing its properties. Working to harness its energy in ways that will benefit mankind."

Taleb listened and nodded, approving of what he heard. But all the while his thoughts were centered on the ancient holy treasure locked securely in the next room.

Until his son was called to take his place, he would guard it—and well. With his life, if need be. As his father had.

It was what they did. They were a family of caretakers.

Read on for an excerpt from

THE BOOK OF NAMES

by Jill Gregory and Karen Tintori

Available from St. Martin's Paperbacks

PROLOGUE

January 7, 1986
Saqqara, Egypt

Two men shoveled the sand under cover of darkness. Their only light in the cave was a lantern set beside their packs. This series of caves and tombs, fifteen miles from Cairo, was a treasure trove of artifacts and antiquities. For three thousand years, Saqqara, the City of the Dead, had been the burial place of kings and commoners—archaeologists might spend several lifetimes and never discover all of its secrets. And neither would the tomb robbers.

Sir Rodney Davis, knighted for discovering the temple of Akhenaton and its dazzling treasures, felt the familiar tug of excitement. They were close. He knew it. He could almost feel the crisp papyri in his hands.

The Book of Names. Part of it. All of it. He didn't know. He only knew that it was here. It had to be here.

The same tingle of exhilaration had coursed through him on the hill of Ketef Hinnom in Israel the night he unearthed the gold scepter of King Solomon. Topped by a thumb-sized pomegranate carved of ivory and inscribed in tiny Hebrew script, it was the first artifact found intact to link the biblical king of the tenth century B.C. to the fortifications recently discovered there. But unearthing the Book of Names would dwarf that and every other discovery. It would ensure his place in history.

He trusted his instincts. They were like a divining rod pulling him toward matchless treasure. And tonight, in the sands where ancient kings had walked, Sir Rodney dug on, fueled by the lust of discovery, the thrill of uncovering what no one had seen since the days of angels and chariots.

Beside him, Raoul threw aside his shovel and reached for his water canteen. He drank deeply.

"Take a break, Raoul. You started an hour before me."

"You're the one who should rest, sir. They've been here all these millennia, they'll wait for us another three or four hours."

Sir Rodney paused and glanced over at the man who had been his loyal assistant for nearly a dozen years. How old had Raoul LaDouceur been when he'd started? Sixteen, seventeen? He was the most tireless worker Sir Rodney had ever seen. A reserved, dignified young man distinguished by his olive Mediterranean coloring and deep-set eyes—one the color of sapphires, the other the deep mahogany of Turkish coffee beans.

"I've been waiting half my life for this discovery, my friend. What is an additional hour's work at this point?" He shoveled another load of sand from the cave floor. Raoul watched in silence for a moment, then recapped his canteen and took up his own shovel.

They worked for more than an hour, the stillness broken only by the sound of their own labored breathing and the soft thud of shovel against sand. Suddenly, a chinking sound froze Sir Rodney's hand. He dropped to his knees, his weariness forgotten, and began to brush the sand aside with his long, calloused fingers. Raoul knelt beside him, shared excitement racing through his veins.

"The lantern, Raoul," Sir Rodney said softly as his hands rounded the curved sides of the clay vessel embedded in the sand. With small, careful rocking motions, he freed it.

Behind him Raoul lowered the lantern, the light revealing a roll of parchment tucked within the vessel's mouth.

"Good God, this could be it." Sir Rodney's hand actually trembled as he drew the papyri from their hiding place.

Raoul rushed to unroll the tarp and stood back while his mentor unrolled the yellowed sheaves across it. Both of them recognized the early Hebrew script and knew what they had found.

Sir Rodney bent closer, peering at the minute letters, his heart racing. The greatest find of his career was here beneath his fingertips.

"By God, Raoul, this could change the world."

"Indeed, sir. It certainly could."

Raoul set the lantern down at the edge of the canvas. He stepped back, one hand slipping into his pocket. Silently, he withdrew the coiled length of wire. His hands were steady as he snared Sir Rodney's neck in the garrote. The archaeologist couldn't even squeak.

It was over in a flash. With one movement, Raoul yanked him away from the precious parchments and snapped his neck.

The old man was right as usual, he mused as he gathered up the papyri. This find would change the world.

Raoul was too elated by his victory to notice the amber gemstone nestled at the bottom of the vessel left behind.

Carved upon it were three Hebrew letters.

ליו

January, 7, 1986
Hartford Hospital, Connecticut

Dr. Harriet Gardner was slumped on the lumpy armless couch in the hospital lounge contemplating her first bite of food in twelve hours when her beeper summoned her right back to the ER.

Chomping at the apple, she raced down the hallway. This has to be a bad one, she thought, or Ramirez would be handling it on his own. She tossed the half-eaten apple in the wastebasket as she pounded past it, wondering if this was a car crash or a fire. She burst through the white metal doors to find three trauma teams working at warp speed. There were three kids on gurneys, one of them screaming. Five minutes ago the only sounds in this wing had been the quiet murmur of monitors, the periodic whoosh of blood pressure cuffs, and the occasional whimper of the five-year-old in bay six waiting for X-ray to confirm a broken leg.

Now paramedics and police swarmed the ER, and the surgical resident, Ramirez, was shoving an endo tube down a teenage girl's throat.

"Get that kid up to CT stat," he yelled to Ozzie, as the male nurse jockeyed a boy on a blood-soaked gurney toward the elevator. The teenager lay unmoving, his leg twisted at an impossible angle. There was a gash over his right eye and blood dripped from both ears.

"What do we have?" Harriet flew to the boy in the #18 Celtics jersey, and Teresa, the intern on rotation, stepped aside. The boy's jersey had been cut apart up the center, revealing a bloody chest.

"They fell off a roof," a paramedic answered. "A three-story drop with a gable in the way."

Kids. "Get some blood gasses over here," Harriet bit out. "And a stat portable chest X-ray." Even after three years in the ER her stomach still dropped when she had to work on kids.

Get over it, she told herself, as she peered at the monitor. His pulse was 130, blood pressure 80/60.

This kid was in trouble.

"This one is Senator Shepherd's son." Doshi wheeled the oxygen tank to the head of the gurney. "And the kid Ozzie took to CT is the son of the Swiss ambassador."

"What's this boy's name?"

Doshi peered at the chart. "David. David Shepherd."

Harriet frowned at David Shepherd's battered upper body. "Looks like flail chest, broken clavicle, dropped lung."

Deftly, Doshi inserted a plastic oxygen tube into his trachea. "The others have been drifting in and out, but he hasn't regained consciousness."

The cuff whooshed again. Harriet's gaze swung to the monitor. The kid's blood pressure was dropping like a rock.

Shit.

United Nations, New York City

Thunderous applause rang through the room as Secretary-General Alberto Ortega concluded his remarks to the assembled nations. Smiling, Ortega made his way through the diplomats, shaking hands and accepting congratulations on the adoption of the Amendment of the Slavery Convention first signed in Geneva in 1926. His long-lidded gaze roamed the room and at last fell upon the familiar figure of his attaché.

Ortega's expression didn't change, not even when Ricardo slid through the throng and slipped a folded scrap of paper into his palm.

Once inside his own office, away from the noise and the press of bodies, he locked the carved oak door and unfolded the yellow square of paper. His eyes narrowed as he scanned the message.

LaDouceur bagged a prime specimen. The hunt goes on.

Hartford Hospital, Connecticut

Nothing hurts anymore. David gazed down at his body on the hospital gurney and was startled to see so much blood on his chest. *Five . . . six . . . seven . . . there were so many people leaning over him . . . so much commotion . . . why didn't they just leave him alone . . . let him sleep?*

Now Crispin was walking toward him. Strange, there was no floor under his feet either.

As he reached David's side they both looked down and noticed that the activity in the ER had reached a fever pitch.

David heard someone call his name, but at the same time Crispin pointed upward toward a brilliant light.

"Isn't that incredible?"

Yeah, David thought. *It is. Even more fantastic than the Northern Lights I saw last summer.*

Crispin started toward the light and he followed. Suddenly the dazzling brightness enveloped them. They were inside it, drifting down a long tunnel. A still more brilliant light glowed ahead and they quickened their pace.

David felt so peaceful now, so exhilarated. So safe.

Suddenly he saw movement within the lustrous aura ahead and a strange murmur began pulsing through the luminous silence. Crispin dropped back, hovering where he stopped, but David was pulled closer, as if a giant magnet was tugging him.

And then his mouth dropped open.

The murmur became a roar, filling his head. Before him he saw faces. Blurry, begging faces. Hundreds of them. Thousands. *Oh, God. Who are they?*

He heard a long scream. It seemed a millennium before he recognized it was his own voice.

"We're losing him. Code blue!" Harriet yelled.

Doshi positioned the paddles over David's chest. "All clear!" she warned. And then she zapped him.

"Again!" Harriet ordered. Bending over the dark-haired kid, Harriet felt perspiration bead along her upper lip. "David, come back here. David! Listen to me now. Come back!"

Doshi stood by with the paddles ready as Harriet frowned at the monitor. Still in V-Fib. A heartbeat away from flatlining. Damn it.

"Doshi—again!"

Three hours later Dr. Harriet Gardner finished her paperwork. Some day. It started with a thirty-five-year-old female with a heart attack and a toddler with the tines of a fork embedded in his forehead. It ended with three kids who'd risked their lives on an icy winter afternoon climbing a fucking roof.

One got off with only a bruised larynx and a broken arm.

One had shattered his right femur and was locked deep in a coma.

And one she had barely snatched back from the jaws of death. She wondered if he'd seen the light.

Sighing, Dr. Harriet Gardner shoved the files across the nurses' counter and went home to feed her dog.

1

Athens, Greece
Nineteen years later

Raoul LaDouceur hummed as he opened the trunk of his rented Jaguar. As he slid the rifle from beneath a plaid wool ski blanket, he became aware that his stomach was grumbling. Well, not for long. He'd spotted an open air taverna some ten miles back and had a sudden irresistible yen for a platter of braised lamb shanks and a glass of ouzo.

He checked his watch. There should be time. He'd already dispatched the two security guards and rolled their bodies down the hillside. He was ahead of schedule and still had five hours before he had to return the rental car and fly back to London to await his next assignment. Time enough even for two glasses of ouzo.

He walked purposefully through the olive grove, feeling vaguely uncomfortable. Despite his sunglasses, he was aware of the waning, still-hot Mediterranean sun. He preferred to do his work in darkness.

But as he'd learned to tolerate the sun on so many scorching digs during his younger years, so, too, he would tolerate it today. Ignoring the perspiration running from his armpits, he selected his position, the one that best afforded him a view of the entire rear of the house. Then he took a puff from his inhaler and settled in to wait.

The fragrance of these olive trees made his throat burn. It

brought back memories of his grandfather's farm in Tunisia, where he'd labored as a grafter from the age of six. Slicing off branches and rooting them into new olive trees, he'd spent ten hours a day at monotonous work beneath an unforgiving sun, his throat dry and raw as pipe ash.

And what did he get when he was done—a crust of bread, a scrap of cheese? And more often than not, a beating with a switch made from one of the very branches he had cut.

His grandfather was the first man he'd killed. He'd beaten him to death on the day he'd turned fifteen.

Today, too, must be someone's birthday, he thought, his gaze flitting over the balloons tied in bunches to the lounge chairs, then to the table piled high with gaily wrapped gifts.

The party was about to begin.

Beverly Panagoupolos had been baking all afternoon. It wasn't that her brother's chef was incapable of making a birthday cake, it was just that for *her* grandchildren, she liked to do it herself.

Her littlest granddaughter, Alerissa, was nine today. In an hour the birthday girl and her big brothers, Estevao, Nilo, and Takis, would all be gathered around the pool deck with their parents, their cousins, aunts, and uncles. Alerissa was so timid she would be shy throughout the party, then would talk of nothing else for days to come.

Beverly licked the cinnamon frosting from her thumb and strode outside to check that the pink and silver balloons and bright array of gifts were arranged as she intended.

She paused for a moment, gazing with pleasure at the silvery blue water of the pool, where soon all the children would be splashing before dinner.

She didn't hear a thing until the gunshots cracked through the palm trees.

She didn't feel a thing until the bullets razored across her back.

She didn't see the silvery blue water turn crimson with her blood.

She died with cinnamon frosting at the corners of her lips.

* * *

The car snaked out from the secluded hilltop and roared down the road. Flipping the radio dial in search of a classical station, Raoul caught the tail end of a news broadcast. Terrorists had blown up the Melbourne Airport's international terminal and thousands were feared dead inside the collapsed building.

He smiled to himself. He was good. The best. The proof was written across the ever-increasing chaos in the world. Soon he'd be hailed as one of the principal heroes of the new order.

The thirty-six Hidden Ones were dwindling. Beverly Panagoupolos was the fourteenth to die by his hand. No one else had ever killed so many. Now, only three of the thirty-six remained. Once they were eliminated, Raoul thought with pride, God's foul world would be finished.

Already it was deteriorating. War, earthquake, famine, fire, disease—one by one, every type of natural and man-made catastrophe was proliferating across the globe like never before. It was merely a matter of days now.

When the final three were gone—the light of the Hidden Ones extinguished—the time of the Gnoseos would dawn and the world would be no more.

Brooklyn, New York

Time was running out.

Nearly five thousand miles away, in his small office on Avenue Z, Rabbi Eliezer ben Moshe closed his rheumy eyes and prayed.

Throughout his eighty-nine years, those eyes had seen much tragedy and evil, *simcha* and goodness in the world. But of late, the evil seemed to be multiplying. He knew it wasn't a coincidence.

Desperate fear filled his heart. He'd spent his entire life in the study of Kabbalah, meditating upon God's mystical secrets, calling upon His many names. He'd murmured them, praying for protection—not for himself—for the world.

For the world was in peril, a peril greater than the Flood.

The dark souls of an ancient cult had found the Book of Names. He was convinced of it.

And all of the *Lamed Vovniks* listed in the ancient parchment were being killed, one by one. How many were left? Only God and the Gnoseos knew.

Sighing, he turned to the talismans arrayed on his desk. Some he understood. Some he did not. He picked them up, one by one, and stuffed them back inside the cracked leather satchel sitting open on his desk. His fingers ached from arthritis as he pulled the ancient volumes of the *Zohar* and the *Tanach* away from the bookshelf and spun the dial of the safe hidden behind them. Only when the lock clicked and the satchel was again secured within the fireproof metal did he pick up his worn Book of Psalms and shuffle toward the door.

His long silver beard quivered as his lips moved in prayer.

Dear God, give us the strength and the knowledge to stop the evil ones.

Beneath his desk, the tiny microphone carried his prayer.

But not to God.